# A TALE OF TWOBEARS

An Aversion Bureau novel.

S.R. Ringuette

SRR Publishing

First Edition

ISBN: 0987941453
ISBN-13: 978-0987941459

To Bear.

Other Aversion Bureau novels:

*Regicide On The 51st Floor.*

# PROLOGUE:
# AS IF FROM NO BEAR

There are many things that a bear does not concern itself with; each one is recorded, and kept for ongoing reference in a biological notepad somewhere safe inside their living brains, organs which typically, tragically, are located on or around any bear in question. As you may be able to see already, this presents a bit of a problem for anyone with aspirations to the sparsely considered but well-intentioned field of ursine psychology. We all know what bears *do* concern themselves with: berries, picnics, being falsely marketed as cuddle-ready by the likes of toy manufacturers to cull impressionable young children with lack-luster survival instincts. . . but what do bears find distasteful? What do they disapprove of so much so that it's worth remarking on? Such is a winning thesis.

For the sake of congruence it will be divulged that the going theory is bears care least of all for three things in particular: time, property rights management, and most assuredly, most absolutely, a bear does not concern itself with magic. As a rule, they distrust wizardry and all who practice it, but very soon, this will change – none know it yet – least of all, the bears.

The wet, sniffing snout of nature's direct answer to snooping, curly-haired blonde girls lead the rest of itself through a thick brush of red-berried bushes and tall grass in search of something – something that the brain hadn't quite figured out yet. Vague images and fragments of a mental language from a creature that knew no spoken one combined to form an objective. The bear's body knew it needed something in a bad way, whatever it was, so the neural door-to-door began. One slow electric tallyman  travelled ponderously from brain to bowels and back again, gathering on his trip the first rumblings of many different bodily impulses. Outermost back hairs needed goose-pimple step ladders to ward off the chilly morning air, and though there were certainly some raised hands in the colon, those could be dealt with in due time. The loudest and most restless organ, however, seemed to be the bear's stomach. It was time to eat a thing – perhaps even two things. The bear looked over its shoulder with a heavy movement and lazily regarded the bushes behind. Small, plump, densely-clustered red berries hung low and beckoned with their freshness and general inability to physically resist being eaten – always a healthy option – but today was a cheat day, and this bear was going to need a stream.

As ventured earlier, bears are not terribly concerned with the ownership of land. They consider all the natural world to be open to whoever is bold enough to enjoy it. But for the sake of doling out some descriptive justice, it should be noted just how picturesque a scene it was that this animal had indifferently come plodding towards. Ahead, wistful blue skies gave contrast to an impressive regiment of stoic pines that climbed a wide hill with wild flowers, grass and shrubbery. The hill was outlined by a modest stream bloated by mountainous ice melt, with similar accoutrements gradually and noticeably being flattened by the approach of a big, furry, lumbering vandal.

All of this was surrounding the base of a rather large and rather impressive horn of grey stone – a spire of Earth's own bone that stood well above the forest in this particular area, with a sense of great meaning. But one could only call it a 'mountain' by using their hands to misgauge its size, lying like the last time they measured out a fish for a crowd. This remarkable formation of rock looked like it could convincingly have been the tectonic appendage of something that once dwelled Down Deep, and hadn't gotten much farther than poking its finger out into the world before realizing it had quite a wicked allergy to our golden sunlight. . . a self-actualizing troll, most likely.

Beneath this rib of stone the wide, cool stream divided all that gathered around this verdant rock-crowned hill from everything so much less grand nearby – most currently our bear – in silent definition. With the help of the dense trees and treacherous mountain-like terrain in every direction the stream did not cut through, an island of sorts was formed. Lush and relatively untouched, things seemed to grow wilder and more purposefully there. It was a curation of nature so deliberately eye-catching one might be inclined to paint it, master that technique, then teach it to others through a sort of public-access television program, for example. Many of the trees on the forested 'island' could easily be referenced to as 'happy little', at the time, if one was so inclined.

The Bear of Growing Consequence reached this horned hill's border-stream with great determination, scanning the moving surface waters for signs of any edible life below. There may have been something there, but even if there was, he wasn't going to grab it just standing by the edge. Our bear made a few exploratory splashes of the stream and decided it was not so prohibitively cold as it looked. Even creatures as physically daunting as great brown bears try to avoid the sudden elemental shock of frigid water wherever possible, or, perhaps it was just playing – that sure would have been adorable.

Somehow, it knew that this was the place to be, and our bear had made a long journey to this particular stream, drawn by an internal calling that had suddenly arisen some time four sunrises and three sunsets ago. He stood there, on four great carpeted legs against a backdrop of natural wonder like most men and women go their entire lives never witnessing, ankle deep in the bank of a brisk mountain stream, waiting patiently for lunch to swim by. This wait was often long, but bears do not perceive time like we do. A bear expects to see the sun once for every time they see the moon and beyond that, they habitually maul travelling backwoods watch salesmen on sight – they simply have no great enemies, and thus no great impetus to hurry anywhere. Any animal that can sleep away an entire season at a time is capable of waiting for a salmon to come along for at least as long as the runtime of your average sitcom.

And there it was, soon enough, a nice plump salmon in the deep center of the waterway. With each traversal leap, it flaunted bright iridescent scales and the hubris by which generations of its kind combated all the sense and design that went into rivers in the first place. Should this bear have possessed a higher consciousness now, at this moment, instead of later, at another moment, he might have noticed the strange colour of this particular salmon. Specifically – its glowing greenness, or even the simple emerald ether that trailed from beneath the water through the air and back again behind it. Unfortunately, this particular moment of the bear's mental arithmetic was occupied with wordless equivalents for "Whoa there," and "Hey!"

And so The Bear of Rapidly Approaching Significance found it was slower than the Salmon of Mysterious Origin, which would come as no surprise to your advanced bear nutritionist, or even to your intermediate vet: he hadn't had breakfast yet. Regardless, a powerful snout crashed below the stream's surface and large teeth yellowed by an entirely absent dental regimen found purchase on a hard, tube-like shell. The bear struggled to retrieve his lunch, which seemed to be holding on, as fish so often do not, with great resolve to the slippery stones below. By much effort and no small amount of coincidence, the hard-shelled 'salmon' suddenly wrenched free from its silt bed and was subsequently flung thirty feet shining like a pale amethyst to the lush island's stony shore. It landed amongst a congregation of forest animals that our bear had not so much as noticed up until this very moment. There were three deer, two beavers, one owl and a chittering gaggle of lower mammals being watched with interest by a rather opportunistic snake. The group of them had been waiting at the edge of the stream for some time without moving, they wore as much hesitant fascination as sub-sentient beings can express, leering in the direction of the water. But they drew in, in unison, to inspect the object that had been retrieved. Then they drew away, in unison, because a bloody great bear was headed over.

With bear-like determination, The Bear of Imminent Relevance clomped soggy and undistracted to the hill's shore and towards its prize, aiming to inspect it, and scattering the assembled wildlife. It was a long something, whatever it was, and maybe as long as a metre stick. Which, in most cases, is about a metre, but growing ever shorter when something needs to be retrieved from underneath a couch. Still comfortable sticking with the theory that this was in fact His salmon that stretched motionless and long and pearlescent before him – like the world's most heinous earring – he eagerly gormandized the tube. Each time delivering completely un-scathing dental blows that would surely draw the bass, hidden giggles of his bear peers. After each unsuccessful rending, however, as the bear looked down upon the defiant cylinder, he noticed more and more about it. The first time it had seemed to our bear that his 'salmon' had learned an extremely convincing and perhaps even marketable impersonation of a funny-shaped stone. The second time, however, there appeared to be more to it than that. It clearly was not, nor had it ever been, a salmon. That was important. The third time, bear historians fingering hieroglyphics carved into driftwood would later recount, was likely when everything crucial started to happen all at once.

The Once and Future King of Bears had finally, slowly, started to recognize his own mind's dialogue. He found it a bit higher-pitched sounding than to his liking, but more importantly, he was suddenly able to self-doubt – a tell-tale sign of sentience. New thoughts were woven of clear images and definite words – new words, in the way that all words were new, to this previously simple, previously inconsequential, beast of the forest. And for a reason that it could not yet comprehend, with the newly granted dexterity of at *least* a clumsy gorilla, this Bear of Grand Destiny located a little calcite circle, on a little dangling cord, in the middle, and on the bottom, of the long, hard, non-salmon entity. He gave it a drawn out tug and from the shell was dispensed tightly rolled inch after inch of ancient, impossibly dry, improbably warm paper. It unfurled before these fresh eyes like a new butterfly. Entirely unknown symbols swam up from between the surface of the scroll, and some other world one would rather not want to hear about, given the choice. To this bear, the symbols were unreadable, though he began to recognize them as a language, quite like the one he was quickly evolving in his own brain at that very moment. Reading them didn't matter either way because in short time, the symbols began to read themselves – *to him* – with a silent transference of information so eldritch in design that it's honestly a little hard to describe.

There they all stood, one fateful bear emboldened by its position on the food chain neatly assembled around the scene – three deer, two beavers, one owl, one fewer of the small creatures and one satisfied snake who really didn't give a damn anyway. Each and every one surreptitiously witnessing the telltale signs of the one thing bears consider absolutely least worthy of attention: magic. And although you may have been expecting one, they don't have any particularly special reason for this view of theirs. Just that magicks are complicated, and a bear likes to keep things simple, dealing only in what it can see and eat – of which magic is neither.

Something was inside the bear now, making two of them, something that wasn't his or him, and this something had intentions as obvious as a wolf's in wool. Whatever it was, it reached deep within the bear, and pulled itself even further inside to mental storage closets that nothing had ever been through. Whatever it was, it went down towards what the good men and women who devote their lives to the commendable but disregarded field of bear philosophy know as bear kind's intrinsic notepad of things that they'd rather not have anything to do with, and pinched it tightly from both ends. Two metaphysical appendages tore this notepad into a pair of smaller, less useful ones and tossed each of those straight into the bin of creation.

Whatever it was, now it was whispering.

# 1

## A REASON TO GET DRESSED (UP)

Agent Max Martin of the Aversion Bureau sat up in bed chasing a final, disobedient marshmallow around his cereal bowl – wondering against the limits of imagination if he would ever have sex again.

"... Maybe if I stop shaving," he said optimistically, to the tiny mirror that was in actual fact a spoon.

And he would have tried it too, if there were any promise at all that a beard was actually waiting to grow there, on that smooth, barren field. Max glanced leftwards to his alarm clock, which spoke of some ungodly hour, as noonday sun broke fruitlessly against thick curtains positioned to defend against both dreaded computer monitor glare and something dubiously known as 'Vitamin D'. He then looked right and found a wall, exactly where he had left it. After carefully storing the empty cereal bowl beneath his bed where it was sure to be remembered later, Max got out from underneath the wrinkled, burgundy (once solely red) covers of his corner-hugging single bed and began building confidence in regards to opening those curtains. Against much mental fortification, his nagging personal desire to occasionally see other humans in the flesh coerced him to do just that. Hot beams of God's own solar campfire illuminated places on Max's body that were very unfamiliar with this kind of light. A gentle reminder that he needed to get dressed.

You see, ever since, oh say, six months ago, Max Martin had been living alone – nude and free as often as not – and contrary to the opinions you may already be forming about him, this *was* an unusual situation. It was unusual because ever since the age of twenty and up until just now, as he crept across the unremarkable mire of his twenty-*something*'s, Max had been living with a woman. She was a friendly, platonic kind of woman: a woman who is strictly a roommate and nothing more, especially as that might relate to coitus – he would often have to explain, to expertly lay out his situation to male friends already in the process of typing lewd insinuations. This would always deflate them – the lewd friends – for now the world would never get to hear the especially sharp and illuminating original comedy they had been poised to deliver. Comedy about 'banging', and how much of it their friend Max should be prepared to engage in shortly. Comedy about the frequency and location of all kinds of sex and sex-like acts, because that is what One Who Lives With Women should expect at all times, right? They would be legitimately asking by now. This would be their only way of knowing.

The typical living space of a twenty-something is something of a twenty, on a ten-point scale where a ten is all of the wroth and ruin man can possibly exact on an ecosystem. Where a great hall may bear tapestries and ancient portraits, a twenty-something's room will be shot with ragged taped-up posters depicting the five(ish) greatest movies and television shows ever made only coincidentally coinciding with a similar list of movies and shows whose posters are commonly available at mall outlets. Occasionally there will be proper art, though purchased from the internet of course, framed in something *rhombussey* that was on clearance at the time. Where teens and tweens may merely dream of chaos, a twenty-something has the resources and raw command of time to achieve the kinds of nightmares that interior designers wake up screaming about.

"Shit," Max swore softly, to himself, as he realized his dark dress pants had been donned with their stitching on the outside, interrupting the narration.

Anyway, this room was a bit of a mess – all the way from bed-end flat screen television on small Swedish stand to Brobdingnagian jet-dust computer table seven feet away. A table larger and more intricate than anything else in the apartment by a good margin, fully adorned with all the assorted knick-knacks and doo-dads one extended family could potentially purchase for their relative with the hobbies and interests nobody shared, across a lifetime of birthdays and Christmases. But aside from any dangerous overuse of poetic description a person might attempt to impose on you, Max's bedroom was really just like any bedroom in a small apartment. Lots of clothes and tossed-aside papers covered up whatever personal clues might be lying around underneath, and despite his outrageous, mountainous black hair, he was a fairly unremarkable human being – but perhaps that was what made him *truly* special. At least, that was what his last girlfriend had told him, shortly before she found someone truly special in an obvious way.

Max Martin of the previously referred to but not yet described Aversion Bureau stood in front of a smudgy and toothpaste-speckled bathroom mirror now, flexing his ever-more-refined left bicep and trying to ignore the fact that his right one still looked like a short girl trying to see anything at a concert. It bobbed, sub-dermally, and tried to pretend it was still having a good time. Ever since breaking his left arm in a work – but also genetically altered livestock – related incident a couple of months ago, it had been healing remarkably well. Somehow it was now the stronger of the two limbs, despite his initial right-handedness, and he was now favouring it. Max really didn't know how to account for this but the doctor-ordered physiotherapy must have been the cause, as he had never voluntarily lifted anything heavier than he had to, across his whole life before now. The left arm's improvements sure looked impressive, but still were not quite inspiring enough to get him to try and do something with the rest of the pale, pinkish, five-foot-nine somehow secret agent still alive by way of pure dumb luck who was grinning stupidly back at him in the mirror.

Max was paying special attention to his body today, in a way that most respectable people try to do always. This unusual level of personal detail was due to one very specific reason: a lunch date.

"Yeah, that's looking nice," Max cooed at himself once the regular forward-hanging and shelf-like properties of his classic hairdo came to form.

He always found that skipping a shower here and there kept his jungle of licorice scalp grass easier to manage. *She's going to love that one strip that keeps falling in my eye, it's got a bit of danger in it,* Max thought, as he blinked again, slyly turning it into a wink.

In order to sharply dress two dead birds with one stone cold suit, or something along those lines, this factory-defected model of manliness had organized a long overdue lunch date with a wonderfully patient woman on the same day that he would later be going to work, at a bistro located conveniently on the ground floor of the same building. A woman who unfathomably still sought his company long after learning many of the kinds of things that we've just discussed, about one Max Martin.

Somewhere else, but not so far away as to make the happy conclusion of this situation impossible, a sensibly green-dressed woman sat patiently in a factory-made vintage wooden chair. She thought long and hard about all the good reasons in the world that the other, empty, robotically artisanal seat directly across from her could be unoccupied so close to the commencement of their date. Nothing came to mind.

The diner's tables were small and circular with a speckled turquoise laminate and rippled chrome ringed around the sides. They carried wire baskets filled with ketchup, brown sauce and tiny spreads, shoulder to shoulder with a bamboo incense holder and five of about seven completely different menus. She was currently looking through the one titled 'Breakfast: North America'. A variety of fried eggs, potatoes, front *and* back bacons as well as differently arranged variations of those solitary three things assaulted her with pure volume of choice. When the waitress, a kimono-clad blonde woman with dreadlocks, traditional Maori tattoo sleeves and the roller skates of a fifty's era drive-thru burger maiden, approached the table sketchpad in hand – a decision had to be made right away. Politeness aside, the waitress was not born with eight tiny rubber wheels under her feet and was expectedly not going to be able to stay upright forever like this. Whether her particular style of clothing was her own or that of a dress code as structurally insane as the rest of this diner, the woman didn't know, and likely, neither did the waitress.

The woman at the table, whose name was Rose, made a snap decision and ordered something called 'Sushi-Hashi' from the third menu, the one designated 'Breakfast: Japanese fusion: Please just try it'. Luckily for one Max Martin, Rose had the time today to see this through, and she was going to. Least of all just to hear what the excuse was this time.

Somehow between the three minutes of dressing, five minutes of hair-prep and forty five minutes of sitting in front of the computer checking up on nothing in particular, fifty three minutes had passed. Upon realizing how exceptionally close to being late he was,

Max burst from his room in a mad flight to collect all of his work things and get the hell going. He found his wallet in the middle of the living room floor which, now that his old roommate had left, held no furniture whatsoever. He found his keys in the sink for some reason that surely must have seemed good at the time and finally he located his jacket, stuffed into the towel rack in the bathroom. There he had lost some time checking the coat hangers by the door, believing for a fanciful moment that it was possible someone had hung it up for him – a tell-tale sign of haunting by fastidious ghosts.

And that would have been it – that would have been all there was to do before barreling out the door and arriving only slightly behind schedule – were this not a date. It occurred to Max, right as he was about to leave, that he wasn't wearing any cologne: the one thing that was what four-out-of-five – the fifth voice ever advocating for the devil – online advice columnists regarded instrumental in the weaving of dates. The problem was, though, that cologne was really expensive. It was the kind of expensive that one could be tempted to steal if they felt athletic enough.

He *was* desperate though, and began to scan the small, empty living room with attached kitchen for signs of scented oils and/or musky balms. There was nothing, of course. Dish soap had long since been replaced with hot water and pure, animal, brush-driving muscle coupled with low standards. There was a can of air freshener, but the scent of a 'mountain stream' would almost certainly disagree with him as he had all the rugged visage of a smooth cube of plasticine.

All hope had nearly evaporated, like a spritz of air freshener fifteen seconds after being sprayed, until Max noticed something down by the door frame. It was plugged somewhat ajar into an outlet hidden by his only other pair of shoes. This something was a small white plastic machine attached to an empty glass canister stained magenta. There was no way he had been the one to install this. So much had changed since Jackie moved out with her fiancé and left him here to fend tooth and nail against life. . . perhaps this was her small way of sending him a message, a way to let him know that she still cared, or perhaps a spent mechanical room freshener was literally just garbage in every single situation besides this one right now.

Max's consistently average powers of deduction whirred into action as he began to devise a plan. Although whatever little spritz of artificial flower scents remained now would never do the job, the fluorescent gunk that accumulated in a few years of spraying finely-scented ethers from the same tiny nozzle was surely some kind of concentrated pheromone. He grew bold in the same way a mad scientist might, having discovered a shortcut through what we all accept to be the structured rules and regulations of day-to-day life, as he bent down and scraped a finger's worth of the crusty violet ejaculate from the top of the plug-in dispenser. He dabbed a little behind each ear, swabbed some under his neck, then patted the rest into his sparsely-haired chest. Max was immediately engulfed in uncharacteristically strong lavender humours, and the pure chemical shock of it nearly knocked him right out like an escaped zoo animal.

He smiled, internally, knowing that despite being more than twenty full minutes late for his one o'clock lunch date, his on-point personal presentation was certainly going to be worth it. He strode out into the apartment hallway sporting red tie and white shirt, forgetting to lock his door for the second time this week, reeking of a faraway lavender patch that died some time before you or I were even born.

# 2

## NO FINER DINER

Rose did not have much trouble finding the place, and said as much to the sweaty, guilty looking big-haired man who moments prior had leapt into the seat opposite her, putting on admittedly the greatest impersonation she had ever seen of somebody who'd always been sitting there. He had asked her if she had trouble finding the place because that was perhaps the most casual possible question he could have asked – and casual was the name of the game when pretending that this one o'clock lunch date wasn't starting now, at *one thirty-five*.

She did not honestly believe that anybody could possibly have trouble finding this place. 'This place' being the ground floor diner inside of a building that stood fifty-one floors high on the outskirts of their city surrounded by nothing even remotely as tall. She knew it well enough, as the infamous RGI building. The 'Really Good Insurance' insurance company, they called it. She would have to remember to see about the validity of that titular claim another day because it had stood out quite obviously to her when she saw it, that this particular office building only had windows for the first twenty floors and once again on the fifty-first. Whatever went on in those thirty windowless floors between probably wasn't related to any kind of insurance, 'Really Good' or otherwise.

Rose had asked a few people about those oddly blank storeys on the way in, and most seemed pre-programmed with the answer that they were 'Japanese Luck Floors', a high-concept architectural ideal from the Far East. Though somehow, she wasn't entirely convinced. The employees sure seemed to believe it though, and of course, secrets on that scale don't stay secret for long without a great number of idiots willing to stand around under the open sky on a clear day discussing how lovely and green it has always been.

"So. . ." Max offered the promise of an actual sentence non-chalantly over the top of his selection of menu.

Unsurprisingly, he held the North American breakfast offering. Max liked to play things safe.

"Sorry, I was just hoping that you might start by telling me what happened to make you so late. It's not crazy to think that I might worry about—

Whatever words of kindness or understanding had been on their way out of her mouth retreated, dying quietly back into her lungs as the haunted souls of a thousand dead lavender sprigs cleansed the air around them with an almost religious zeal. Like pure alcohol poured over pro-biotic yoghurt, all that had once existed between them: laughter, hope, assorted micro-organisms and perhaps the coy beginnings of a love to one day come – were at that moment erased from time by the flowery reek that could surely, if left unchecked, end the Earth.

Rose gave her date a look that sat uneasily between abhorrence and perhaps a feeling of betrayal, in the way you would, had your friend ever brought a singly-loaded revolver to game night. Max only coughed innocently.

"Oh God, did you smell that too?" he began, sniffing the air suspiciously and searching over his shoulder almost convincingly.

"It's that waitress again, I bet," Max leaned in to imply that this information was both important and secret, while not at all made up.

The brutish emanation of his flowery odour managed to physically knock over two of the four remaining menus on the small table: 'Mexican Food Et Al' and 'Candy, For Breakfast?!' respectively.

Max must have seen Rose's pupils dilating madly as her brain tried to process this phenomenon that transcended the mere human sense of smell.

"Some people are just really desperate for attention," he continued, on conversational eggshells, looking around at different patrons in the diner accusationally.

Rose had begun to regain control of her senses, but decided not to bother asking if that hypothetical story she had just heard was really as fake as it sounded. She held fast, and directed the flow of conversation back to where it was supposed to be going. Max received a dish he had probably ordered sometime whilst her brain scrambled to repair itself.

"Almost a year ago, we met at a club," she

addressed him through a slowly retreating mental haze, "you bumped into me on the dance floor because you were wearing those ridiculous sun glasses your friend gave you. . . *indoors*."

Max nodded along with the truth insofar as he remembered it.

"We talked for a long time, and I decided that you were the kind of guy that I wanted to see more of. To speak to more often." Rose had a serious tone as she spoke, trying to command his attention.

"You called me a week later, we kept in contact, and we finally went out for a real date," she said.

". . . And on that date, we were attacked by dog-men." Max finished her thought, remembering the night well.

"Yes. Despite your utter refusal to explain the situation to me in any way, I did notice that they had the faces of dogs and the bodies of people," she added, "that was definitely the easiest part to remember."

Max looked guiltier still. He must have felt like this conversation was headed to an unfavourable conclusion and swung for the fences with a childishly hopeful:

"It was fun before that though, right?" To which Rose sat silently, weighing her thrashing curiosity against the small garden of red flags that bloomed around this man, eventually allowing the former to win out.

"It was," she forced a smile, though she was still deeply annoyed by the memory of the whole situation.

This Max Martin, who claimed to be an every-day accountant despite having a long-standing abusive relationship with math, had done a competent job dealing with at least one of those dog-faced thugs. This was her first hint that perhaps the man sitting before her knew more than he ought to about things more important than himself. Well, maybe it was her second hint, if she counted the talking cat named Mister Whiskers who had crashed through the window moments earlier that night, declaring himself a coworker of Max's, shortly before the sisters sense and reason leapt hand in hand back out that same window. Rose focused.

"But seriously Max, is there anything else you could tell me about that night, maybe why those. . ." she hesitated, ". . . *guys* were after you? And your friend?"

Max frowned into the napkin he was using to wipe his mouth, and the napkin wondered what it had done wrong. He gave it a moment, pretended to chew something, and spoke:

"No. I mean, not really. Agent – er – *claims agent* Whiskers gets himself into a ton of really wacky situations. It comes with all of his out of town work."

"Yes but, men with dog faces?" Rose asked as patiently as possible.

Max took a moment and then offered "Masks!" with a simultaneous and improvisational snap of his fingers.

"Because, well, you know. . . crime," he added.

"And your 'coworker'? He was a cat who spoke English?"

Rose also noticed that night that Mr. Whiskers had spoken with a bit of an accent. She had thought it

23

strange, but this was also the first talking cat she'd ever encountered. She felt no need to point it out.

"Yes."

Max seemed to have completely run out of smart answers, so he only ate a forkful of hash browns and stared her down throughout the process, hoping to win out through sheer force of wishful thinking. Rose began to get a sense that she would have to play along with the story in order to see the end of it. Much like taking a dog to the vet, it is always wise to speak loudly of the park whilst doing so. She didn't want Max running headlong into the closed door in an attempt to escape.

"I like cats," she declared blankly.

Max seemed pleased with that, and happily went back to his dish. They both smiled.

Something of a secret agent she had almost thought him, that was, until Rose herself had to save Max by putting down the second assailant with an improvised trash can hammer-shield. She had enjoyed that, honestly, and maybe that was why she was sitting here today.

Rose still felt *something*, unclear to him or her, for the naïve young soul that dwelt within this skinny, neurotic mess sitting across from her – but the allure of the secrets he represented was, in all honesty, the primary reason that she had contacted him to make this second try at all. And now she was here, in the place that Max worked as an 'accountant', in the insurance building with the thirty windowless floors, thinking about the day when she would eventually be driving her car through all of the holes in his story. She sipped at her coffee and found, through her own insufficiently careful reading of the drink menu in this bemusing establishment, that it contained watermelon seeds. It wasn't terrible.

Somewhere else, but not so far as last time, there sat a very large man, and not large in the way that people often refer to morbidly obese folk to avoid being offensive – just large. Large enough that he had to sit all the way in the far corner of the diner to avoid being immediately recognized. When God, or Whoever Else, put this bronze-skinned goliath together they ran all the masculinity sliders to the end of their bars and then, on the track that referenced the build of his chin, they snapped off the end and added more room. He sat and ate his bagged lunch of cellophane-wrapped peanut butter and protein powder sandwiches, shooing away several serving staff insistent that he would have to order from one of the menus soon if he was going to be allowed to continue using the tables.

The relatively short distance between this man and the two diners he was watching was no match for the high-powered binoculars he was currently looking through. The massive and individual nut-brown strands of hair, tastefully bobbed upon the head of the woman on which he was focusing, belied her secrets. His overly intimate view of her face would surely allow him to read the success of this date, and later pass that information along to a certain younger agent always eager for help with 'the ladies'.

Stationed expertly to the side of the designated

smoking yurt in the center of this diner that had clearly been designed with all possible culinary futures and pasts in mind at once, Max Martin's fellow agent watched the proceedings with extreme vigilance. He was making brief entries here and there in a small black notebook, and only occasionally stopping to doodle cute little dogs holding badass guns.

"Great job bro," the man chuckled to himself, "I can see her crackin' already. Get ready to go to smooch town."

The man made little kissing noises that a passing roller-bladed waiter in a sombrero mistook to be directed at him, causing the poor young man to career into a waist-high jade carving of Buddha set stubbornly in the middle of a vital walkway. The dish he had been carrying, whatever it was, went spelunking into the diner's prominent koi pond, thriving in the low-competition environment and killing several of them over the next five days. It would later have to be removed with a fishnet and a revolver.

Rose sat with her newly arrived order of 'Sushi-Hashi,' pecking over it with her fork and listening to Max weave rambling and poorly-directed lies about how he came to work at this particular place of business. Something about a "burning passion" for managing the kinds of accounts that needed to be accounted for. Something about how all these damn numbers, one day, would have to be held accountable, and that he might as well be the one to do it. . . something about meeting a large man on a beach flying a helicopter, and how that somehow lead to him being here. None of it was true, so she continued to try and identify all the different components of this thing on her plate – small shreds of sea weed were curled around clusters of imitation crab with bits of cucumber and avocado doused in soy sauce, all nestled on fried sticky rice, somewhat like an open-faced sushi roll writ large. She tried a bit, and was taken aback by the fact that it was actually quite delicious. Rose may even be brave enough to try something from the final menu next time, the somehow iridescent black one covered in question marks from a hundred different fonts.

"Well I'm glad to hear that you're happy here," Rose finally said, half hoping she hadn't timed that wrong.

Max nodded through a mouthful of back bacon.

"I don't think we've ever talked about what you do, actually," Max returned with his mouth still half-full.

"Well it's nothing so exciting as all this number stuff," she said, "but I do work at a desk most of the time."

"I'm glad we did this," Max admitted, smiling. "I'm sorry that I'm so bad at initiating these things."

"It's really not a problem," said Rose.

She moved the rest of her almost overly-creative lunch to the side and placed some cash on the table. It had actually been nice just to see Max again, with all of his bumbling charms, but this was all the useful info that she was going to get out of him today. The only course of action she saw going forward was to fast-track this relationship if there was going to be any hope of finding out what he truly knew about the strange events of their last date. And while she was at it, maybe even get an idea of just what the hell went on around here anyway.

"Listen Max, I have to get going for work as well, but I'm going to call you tomorrow and we're going to go out again this weekend, alright?" Max smiled and nodded while she spoke.

Ever since that night with the dog men, Rose hadn't been able to close her eyes without thinking about them. She was no stranger to a midnight shake down, but usually the criminals were fully human. And the nonchalant way that Max – and his friend the *talking cat* – had regarded them showed her there was something much more to know. Curiosity consumed her, so much so that she didn't notice the shadow of a giant falling across her and her. . . boyfriend? They were going to have to work that one out.

"Bro," said the giant man, he was extending his hand towards her in a very hand-shake sort of way.

Rose finished standing up, and found that her eyes did not even come as high off of the ground as his nipples, which she could almost make out, through the flesh-tight suit he had somehow buttoned across the fertile farmland of muscles that was his chest – pectorals so expertly formed that they looked like geometric shapes. Rose generally found that she did not get along with men like this, and she saw a lot of them at work. To that end, she did not give him the satisfaction of a commensurable 'Bro!' in return. She simply stared up, silently pressuring him to try that greeting again.

"Muh. . . *am*," he said.

Then, after hearing himself out loud:

"Ma'am."

The very large man winced through this second attempt, apparently employing great mental resolve in his search to find the correct social terminology for this situation.

Rose smiled and shook his hand firmly. She turned to Max, who was still looking angry and surprised at the appearance of whoever this was.

"I'm here to uh. . . here to pick up my best seller," offered the man, gesturing towards Max.

Max delivered what he probably thought was a well hidden "No" to his colleague by scrunching up his neck and turning his head briskly back and forth while keeping perfect eye contact. The large man looked confused, silently mouthing his interpretation of the mummery back at the smaller man, when suddenly and with an audible mental *click* he jumped back to face her, eyes wide with sudden comprehension.

"Best *accountant*," the man stated matter-of-factly.

"Are you sure we haven't met before?" Rose asked him.

She remembered a fellow who was about this size and social caste causing trouble at the club where she and Max had first met. Quite sarcastically, she couldn't imagine why.

"*I'm* the best seller," he continued without hearing her, pointing to his name tag hard with a big thumb.

The name tag read, supportively, 'Dick Davison – Sales'. Although a mysterious third party had clearly attempted to write 'Best at' in the margin above the word 'Sales', in letters too small to impress anybody.

Rose began to walk out of the diner, spinning around to wave at the two of them, smile and tell Dick Davison that it was nice to meet him, even if that was an exaggeration. She walked briskly back out into the main lobby of RGI Insurance, heading for the doors at the front of the building. On the way she passed by multiple small conference rooms, a reception desk, and two elevators, of which one was spidered with caution tape. Even out of the corner of her vision and on her way out of the building, the receptionist caught her eye. For some reason that an unquestioning person could surely only chalk up to coincidence, RGI Insurance employed the most beautiful woman who has ever walked the Earth as their main floor general secretary. Rose had to look away so as not to be distracted and lose time, even though she was almost one-hundred percent sure she was straight. Eventually, inevitability reared its head and she snuck a peek towards the desk, for just a second. *Maybe eighty-five percent sure.*

Once out in the parking lot, Rose made a final glance up and backwards towards the towering building. It was grey and bland and completely inconspicuous in its design. It looked just like a tall rectangle of unadorned clay some stubborn man reluctantly enrolled in a mandatory psychiatric art therapy class would *call* a building in order to be allowed to go home. He would have impatiently punched little 'windows' only two-fifths of the way up the structure, just like this one – with a toothpick – and when told that there was no such building in the world that looked this way, shortly before flinging his creation at the nearest window where

30

it would squash anti-climactically, he would drop down to fetal position and begin screaming into his knees.

As Rose made her way to her cruiser, she reflected on the chain of events that lead her from being dragged out to go clubbing on a Friday night months ago by her friends to briefly dating the one small, silly man who would eventually lead her here, unpredictably, to the biggest mystery of her career.

She changed out of her green dress and into spangled navy pants-and-jacket combo expertly in her backseat. She removed and tossed her assortment of earrings into a cup holder, all the while planning the next move. Her mother had always told her that it wasn't healthy to think of relationships in terms of 'moves' and 'endgame', but this one had gone far beyond the dinner and a movie stage already – albeit in different way than she was expecting.

Rose cinched up her black leather belt, the one with the holster and badge, fired up dispatch, and drove to work.

# 3

## BUSINESS AT THE BUREAU

Agents Max Martin and Dick Davison of the Aversion Bureau – who were not in any way capable of performing any duties at all related to the management or distribution of insurance of any kind – watched a woman in a green dress walk out of a diner for a long time.

Max, still high on success, watched her a little too intently. He couldn't help it, drunk on the rose-coloured wine his eyes were pouring into his brain. The woman had a tanned, round face and a stout frame. Some might have thought her a little on the heavy side, but Max found himself consistently intoxicated. Her short heels clicked the seconds away on a little clock as she made her way out of the building, then Dick Davison gave Max a hard shove that jerked him back to reality, as well as a look that informed him he was not being very cool. Max had seen this look many times and recognized it immediately.

"That went well!" Max yelped a statement that sounded suspiciously like a question as they took a few steps out of the eatery and into the lobby.

On their way out of the insurance building's infamous "Allplate Diner" a woman from the cook line burst out of the back and careened headfirst into the restaurant's sliding doors with a wet *THUMP* as they closed, trying desperately to dislodged a disgruntled blue and purple octopus that had made good friends with her face. She fell to the floor, cephalopod-free, enjoying oxygen like never before as the dazed creature slunk away. Dick Davison gave her an "Oh, you!" smile and caught up to his friend.

"So are you ready for the meeting, bro?" Dick asked, smiling about something else now.

He smiled a lot, Max always noticed.

"Yeah I guess so. I mean I really don't have to say much at these things, just nod and pretend I've been doing whatever we talked about at the last one," he admitted, trying to remember what exactly that had been, while they walked.

Usually what would be discussed at the hepta-annual general meetings run by the true employer of these two men was of little consequence. As a pair of outside eyes peering in may astutely notice, the Aversion Bureau is an operation that flies very much in the face of traditional logic, and very much by the seat of its pants. Both Mr. Martin and Mr. Davison were what you would call 'secret agents' in that they were agents, who completed missions and objectives known only to the Bureau itself and sometimes the government – certain governments relative to the mission parameters, and only when strictly necessary to avoid getting in trouble.

They were not secret agents in the same way that James Bond, Jason Bourne, or anyone socially adept at the same time as legally owning a gun license and a suit, can often be.

The Aversion Bureau optimistically stakes its claim to being the world's 'foremost apocalypse prevention agency' – and it does just that, on occasion, through sheer well-meaning, despite being woefully underfunded and often dangerously mismanaged. Money to fuel the exploits of this world-saving collective of bargain bad-asses comes directly from its eccentric billionaire owner and the reasonable profit margins of the actual RGI insurance company. While every one of the handful of agents who work for the Bureau has a cover job under the RGI umbrella, the company itself is an entirely legitimate operation. It helps just so much that, in combination with the founder's impressive but fluctuating bank roll, and by bringing their lunches from home, the Aversion Bureau strives ever forward, directly responsible for saving literally dozens of lives each calendar year. They are also responsible for the questionable deaths of a great deal more upstart, crowd-funded, do-it-yourself supervillains than you were likely even aware of. These are preventative measures, they assure you.

The mismatched pair made their way to the lobby's elevators carefully staying behind the receptionist's desk whilst doing so, or at least trying to. Dick noticed his partner's eyes starting to wander over to the right.

"No! Stop that," he cuffed his friend on the back of

the head, "we don't have time to talk to her today."

Max searched his pockets for a keycard as they arrived not in front of the perfectly good polished steel elevator placed into the wall across from the front door, but rather in front of the one right beside, with 'OUT OF ORDER' signs nearly hiding it entirely.

"I can't find my swiping badge-thing for the elevator," Max shrugged, "should we take the stairs?"

"Are you crazy? Remember what happened the last time the elevator broke? The building's only got stairs for the first twenty floors, then you hit the Bureau and it's like, *Chutes and Ladders*."

Dick found his own access card and tried to fit it into a reader set right beside the theatrically broken machine while gradually losing focus for something that was back the way they came.

"Besides, our meeting's on the thirty-fifth or uh. . . something. . ."

Agent Davison trailed off completely and Max realized he was staring towards the secretary, falling in love with the back of her head, where only a tight black bun sat, held by a jeweled elastic. It seemed an odd thing to get so in to.

"Why do we even have her here, anyway? She's just so. . . *distracting*." Max pronounced the last word with a dreamy quality that undermined his opposition.

Dick snapped out of the apparent trance and stopped clacking his card ineffectively – horizontally – into the vertical slot.

"Better here than out there makin' sailors crash into rocks," he said, finally getting it right.

The elevator that was so broken you couldn't believe it gave a happy little *ding* and opened. The two agents took a cursory glance at the lobby for any uninitiated who might be watching and stepped inside carefully, moving aside the hanging caution tape gently, so as not to ruin the illusion.

Once inside, Dick Davison punched in numbers for the thirty-fifth floor: first a three and then a five, turning to his little friend.

"Now that we've got a few minutes," he smiled and cracked his knuckles, "let's talk about that date."

"Yeah? How do you think it went? I think it went pretty—"

Max stopped talking as Dick pulled a small black notebook out of his pocket and flipped through to the appropriate page.

"Glad you asked, bro, I've got some notes."

Max ran a hand through his thick asphalt locks and took a deep breath, frowning. While his cohort's advice was certainly professional, there was always a bit of hard love involved – but that was likely only because Dick 'Hard Love' Davison occasionally liked to pretend people actually called him that. The elevator, and Max's stomach, lurched into motion.

She arranged papers on a long, egg-shaped table, the dissymmetry of which she had to continually focus on ignoring to stop from becoming distracted by obsessive compulsive rage. A fresh pot of coffee steamed in the center of the table and half of that pot steamed in her steel thermos across the room. Aside from that, there weren't going to be any snacks today, or croissants, or anything of the like. If her fellow agents weren't capable of feeding themselves lunch she wouldn't be sympathetic, or surprised.

Agent Natalie Stone of the Aversion Bureau exhaled onto the side of her thermos and rubbed it with the sleeve of her long, jet-black pea jacket until it had at least the reflective properties of a dirty piece of glass. She inspected her mirror-self for any deviation from the norm. Her light blonde ponytail was pulled tight as always, not a single hair out of place, and a minimal application of eye makeup was again present. Stone could already crush a man's resolve simply with the set of her brow, and this only made it easier. No lipstick, though. If Agent Stone ever ended up in the unlikely situation of reciprocal kissing, she wouldn't dare allow there to be any evidence of the act.

There was a lot of important information to talk about today, and with all the current, full-time agents of the Aversion Bureau assembled, Stone hoped sincerely to be able to get through at least half of it. Director Bilge had warned of a 'quite pleasant' surprise earlier, however, and that was sure to take more time than it should. The stern agent took a seat at the tip of the egg-shaped table and waited for the others, who would surely arrive any moment, trying not to think too hard about how the end of the table she was looking towards was so much wider than the one she was sitting at. Worse still, the wideness of the wide half of the table was insistently attempting to remind her of the one fellow agent for whom she reluctantly possessed a configuration of emotions strongly resembling, as far as she could tell, all-consuming love. A non-reciprocal state of affairs that nothing short of plagued her every waking moment spent at the Bureau. Natalie lowered her gaze, tapping her pen against the desk to the beat of something an old person would surely hate. She re-read the last meeting's minutes, sighing sharply upon being reminded that last weeks' attempt at a meeting had been interrupted by an emergency expeditionary mission to the nearest gas station for slush drinks. It was summer, after all.

"Of course I didn't! IT IS NOT OKAY TO TAKE YOUR CLOTHES OFF IN A RESTAURANT." Max yelled his awfully reasonable declaration right at Dick Davison, who responded by coming out of the elevator and starting to take his shirt off, instructionally.

"Bro it's not about what the rules are! It's about how easy it is to do, and how much ladies like it!" the last part of his sentence was muffled by a yellow undershirt that had become stuck on Agent Davison's Velcro-like dark brown close-shaven hair.

Max started desperately attempting to pull his friend's shirt back over his body, but was nearly lifted off the ground along with it.

"Dick, damn it, I don't look like you do without a shirt on!" Max used his increasingly capable left arm to win the torso covering tug-of-war, releasing Davison's massive chin, somehow, through the tight V-neck of his shirt.

"And whose fault is *that?*" Dick shot back at him,

he who still hadn't let go of the shirt due to some kind of completely unfair trust issues he obviously had.

"God's!" Max barked the name so hard he spat a bit, unearthing only a little evidence of a lifetime of self-consciousness.

There was a long moment while the two men seethed, yelling at each other like a couple of guys with their jaws wired shut.

"Bro. . ." Dick Davison's curious expression broke the silence, "that super gross flower smell. . . is that you?"

"That could be anyone!" Max lied, unskillfully, launching himself away and starting down the completely empty hallway again.

"Now come on, we're going to be late," he added.

Dick buttoned his jacket back on, recovered his name tag from the floor and carried on down the thirty-fifth floor hallway which was lined with secret conference rooms of all shapes and descriptions, painted dark grey-blue and unassuming. Complete with off-white tiled floors, it was one of the most boring areas in the entire Bureau, with nothing to distract one from an important meeting – an often discounted but nevertheless important design decision. As well, paint in boring colours is easier to steal off the back of a loading dock, as it doesn't tend to stand out.

The agents attempted to find the conference room where their meeting was being held by looking inside each one until they recognized human shapes. Most were empty, except for the one room that was always filled to capacity – but it was only for delegates from the

Bureau's sloth consultancy installed at the request of one Agent Dick Davison who was himself, mostly South American. Nobody really knows what they get up to in there, but a fading itinerary taped to the door states that their summit began five or six years ago and they've just now finished with attendance. The anticipation is said to be gradual.

Dick Davison and Max Martin finally headed inside meeting room seventy-one, the one with the oak door and the bright sticky note meant to make their search easier. Inside they found only Agent Stone, who, even through her granite, unsmiling demeanour looked momentarily excited before she realized that it was them.

"Take a seat," she said to the pair.

The two men took chairs on either side of the weird table across from each other, enjoying an uncomfortable silence with their colleague.

Max had always held an immense respect for Agent Stone. She was a strong leader, intelligent, capable, prettier than most if she would ever smile, ruthless, a hard-ass, condescending. . . *oh crap she's looking right at me did she hear that? She couldn't have. Nobody can read minds, she—*

Stone was staring at his face, his mouth, his un-meeting eyes. She was studying the pale worms that wriggled under his brow to make those damning lines. *She's reading it right now! She's a witch! It's all over, I'm done. I'm meat. I'm never going to see my computer again—*

"You're sweaty," she asked him, with a statement.

She turned to Agent Davison.

"Why is Max sweating?"

Dick laughed a whole body kind of laugh that jiggled his elastic pecs. Max was suddenly comfortable enough to remember that she wasn't psychic and relaxed, but only a little.

"Hah hah hah! Max had a date!" Dick spoke with a sing-song tone that implied this was less a matter of pride and more like when a seal gives his trainer a successful high-five – it implies sentience, but not enough to ignite an intrinsic fear in the human of being overthrown.

Natalie gave her larger partner a crooked frown that seemed to wonder how that would lead to such profuse perspiration. She was not one for dates, or dating, for that matter. Dick shrugged at her to avoid what would surely be a lengthy explanation.

"Well that's neither here nor there!" Max laughed nervously and smacked a clammy hand down on the meeting itinerary in front of him, where it stuck, and as he was shaking it free someone much more put-together arrived at the door. Two someones, actually – both of them more put-together.

A tall, very pale man with the bushiest and most majestic twin-peaked all-white mustache ever grown strode merrily into the meeting, whistling something straight off of The Queen's own mixtape. He smiled at the table over his small reading glasses and slapped Dick Davison, who was only slightly larger, right on the back with enough force to make him cough.

"Good morning, friends and agents!" the rotund

and beaming square-jawed man addressed the whole of the world in this one small room.

The energy that came with the dancing walk and smiling, laughing blue-grey eyes of Director Thomas Bilge was second to none. Imagine that you've just met Santa Claus in person for the first time, and as it turns out, he is also your dad – your dad who would break the neck of a whale if it meant protecting you. A man who made you feel safe, happy and loved all at once without even lifting a finger. All of that and more was what went through Max Martin's mind every single time he saw his boss. While he was sober, anyway. The director so often was not, but that is a story for a different time. The problems of the day were already meaningless by the time Bilge took his seat on the wide end of the egg table.

"Afternoon," Stone corrected him, without so much as looking up.

"Yes my dear, quite right," Bilge twiddled his thumbs and waited while the last primary member of the Aversion Bureau's mighty team assembled.

Veteran agent and head of research, development and science operations at the Bureau: Wade Andersen, strode through the closing door like a specter. So silent, the floorboards would strain to hear him, despite his considerable weight. As everyone present expected, he said nothing, acknowledging every other member only with simple eye contact as he made his way to an open seat right next to Max. He was the most monotone, emotionally absent human being that Max had ever met, but not in a hurtful way, he just appeared uninterested by his own existence. They got along pretty well, Max always thought, but he felt he got along with statues really well too because none of the ones he knew had yet come alive and tried to strangle him.

Max looked back towards Agent Stone, his trusty supervisor and all-around physical superior, waiting for her to make a throat-clearing noise, or any kind of noise – something that might initiate the meeting. She looked distracted, specifically, in the direction of the latest arrival. When Max met her glassy stare she gave a little "ahem" with waning vocalization and restacked her papers.

"Is everyone ready?" she asked.

"Whenever you are, ladybro," Dick responded.

Everyone else nodded.

"Very well, let us begin."

Agent Stone pulled a small remote out of her pocket and thumbed one of the little buttons triumphantly, pointing it at what appeared to be a clean whiteboard behind her. The board flickered and began to display flashing images accompanied by buzzwords and nine second snippets of music, just enough to subvert copyright law. The screen showed the agents everything from a gaming console controller, a weight bench, an expertly soldered motherboard to a formidable and foamy mug of Old Speckled Hen. Each image flashed only for a fraction of a second, long enough for the brain to recognize it, but not long enough for anyone to be sure of what they saw. By the end of the light show every set of eyes besides her own would be glued to the screen, for reasons they couldn't have explained to you at the time. No one was going to lose focus today, through no application of hypnosis or hypnosis-style techniques, she would insist, if you asked her.

Abruptly, the music and images stopped, being replaced by the bulletin '1. Wear your God-damn badges' in a rather large and rather imperial looking font. Max was still thinking about video games, bacon, women, and for some reason pigeons, when Agent Stone turned first to him and asked why he wasn't wearing his badge.

"I have definitely been doing exactly what you said I should be doing the last time we had a meeting," responded Max without even needing to think – not that he could have at the moment. There were a lot of disjointed thoughts bumping around up there right then.

Agent Stone decided to test his follow-up:

"And what was it that I asked you to do last time we met, Agent?"

"It was something about pigeons. But I don't know why. Learn their language?" Max suggested.

He was still focusing intently on the board behind Agent Stone. Whatever she had done was working maybe *too* well. He may have been influenced in that memory by something that came up on the flashing screen, but decided to stick with it on a hopeful fifty-fifty spread that it could be correct. Stone gave a sarcastic once-over to the sheet of paper that held the previous meeting's minutes and said:

"Nothing about pigeons on there Agent Martin, sorry."

"Well I know a lot about pigeons and it couldn't have all just come from me," said Max.

Right now, for reasons that a neurobiologist would probably have to explain, he felt confident he could 'coo' his way into a decent hotel should he ever wind up alone in an all pigeon neighbourhood.

Agent Stone had lasted only this long with her attempt at a welcoming attitude and switched tracks back to the cruel and condescending arbiter the rest of the team was far more comfortable with just due to familiarity. She jabbed her finger at every man present as she spoke, Davison, Bilge, Martin, stopping short of Andersen, to Max's complete lack of surprise.

"Since the dawn of the damn Bureau I have been the only one who actually wears their badge at work. The badge is important, because it symbolizes our team. It embodies our commitment to representing the shared vision of this organization."

Stone was of the highest possible rank, along with Director Bilge. She wore her badge over her heart every single day atop her long black jacket, and of course she did, hers was one of the cool looking ones.

"It's also important because it gets you into a few drink-serving establishments around the city for free, heh-heh" Dick added, sharing a knowing wink with the director.

Thomas Bilge sat up straight and pulled the chest of his warm-looking knit sweater tight.

"Got it covered today, I do believe," Bilge beamed and directed attention to the pattern on his clothing.

Director Thomas Bilge was quite famous for his

comfortable wool sweaters. Every single day of the year regardless of the forecast he wore a new one, each with an adorable or stylish or even occasionally prophetic design. Today's was a depiction of the Aversion Bureau's badge itself, done in a tasteful gunmetal grey with accents in gunmetal *gold*. Sometimes, when blood diamond trade is enjoying an especially good season, like around Valentine's day, a warlord or two will commission himself a golden AK-47 to oppress freedoms with style – and this was that colour.

Yes, Bilge's sweater accurately depicted the badge that he would be wearing if he were actually doing so. As with all Aversion Bureau badges, the design was a simple symbol consisting of a 'T' an 'A' and a "B" arranged into a single arrow-like, right-angled shape. The differentiation between the ranks depicted by the badges came with the shapes cut into the third arm of the symbol. Circles, squares, diamonds and then stars referenced the four ranks of the Bureau in ascending order. The two little shapes would create the holes that a 'B' normally has, in the respective part of the design. It was such a difficult concept to explain that apparently when Agent Stone had initially gotten the badges commissioned, years and years ago, most people seemed to agree that the design came out looking a hell of a lot like a seventy-one. Max agreed on that, but it was too late to change anything.

"Yes, I suppose so. But wearing the actual badge might set more of an example," Stone told him.

"What about you two? I'd love to hear the excuses."

Dick and Max both noticed at the same time that

they were the two in question. Dick spoke first:

"I don't want little holes in my workout shirt, bro," he sounded adamant.

"I guess I don't wear it just because everyone else is a higher rank than me?" Max was a master of stating facts about himself like he was asking for permission from a higher power – such is the way of someone not looking to start a lot of fights in life.

And it was completely true. Max was a 'rank four' as it was called, which was the lowest rank possible. Low, but still technically a secret agent, he would often remind himself, in the mirror, right before bed.

"That's quite true, lad, even the cat ranks more highly than you," Bilge interjected in a tone that was so much friendlier than its subject matter.

Max was choked but not terribly surprised. He had always assumed that he was, in fact, the lowest ranking agent. It was to be expected of course, because he was only nearing the end of his third year with the Bureau. As far as Max knew, everyone else around here had been working for at least eight, and Stone herself had been around from the very beginning. Back then it was only her and Bilge, and although he wasn't quite sure where old Bilge found her, or even how old she was, he figured that the Bureau would not have lasted even a single year without her de facto leadership. Her jerkish, over-bearing demeanour that often brought him to the edge of. . . nothing, never mind. He wouldn't even think it. Secret agents don't cry. Well, not in the middle of the afternoon at least.

"Think about wearing it, it's a matter of pride,"

Stone said to Max.

She probably felt she was being positive, then looked up and addressed the room again:

"So, speaking of the cat brings us to our next point."

Max interrupted her with a raised hand and spoke, pointing to Agent Andersen beside him, who was also badge-less:

"Wade never wears his and you didn't bug him," Max said, knowing she would never reprimand him, looking to taste a small drop of petty revenge.

Agent Stone always seemed to have a weird thing going on with Wade, for as long as Max had known them. She, who was staunch as her namesake, appeared to lose all composure around this man, Wade Andersen. Wade was an un-athletic two-hundred and some pound platinum blonde, utterly expressionless, winning contestant in a robot act-a-like competition. He did his jobs extremely well and with calculated efficiency. He never smiled, or frowned, or seemed to interact with anyone beyond the simple trading of information through curt and undecorated sentences of as few words as possible. Max may have been vain to feel this way, but he just couldn't see what Stone saw in that guy that made her act so unlike herself around him – despite the fact that Wade had saved his life once before, in a situation involving robots that Max didn't feel up to thinking about right now. It's not that he was jealous, either. The ship that held the hope that Stone's chiseled beauty could overcome her suffocating and sympathetically desolate personality had long ago followed a kraken to the bottom of the sea. Max just wasn't interested, and neither was she.

Stone looked at Wade for a little while, and he stared silently and expressionless back at her.

"No, he's perfect," Stone said quickly, looking down to her papers.

"*Good*. He's *good*." She corrected herself even more quickly, without letting on for a moment that she recognized any personal fault – a well-honed skill of hers.

Stone clicked the little remote she held nonchalantly and the screen behind her swapped to a new heading, which read '2. What happened to Agent Whiskers?'.

". . . Well?" She asked, after everyone had finished reading it.

Dick Davison shrugged.

Wade Andersen stared.

Director Bilge opened his mouth to answer.

Max Martin tensed. Max Martin tensed because he knew exactly what had happened to Agent Whiskers but didn't want to say anything because it might jeopardize a deal they had made immediately after the thing that had happened. . . *happened*.

"Haven't seen the little bugger since the day I threw that ripping good party with all the small folk downstairs," offered Bilge with a smile brought on by good memories.

Good memories for him, at least. The day had been hell for everyone else.

That night, the last night that anyone had seen

Agent Whiskers, was indeed the night of a party. To make a short story even shorter, that was the night that Whiskers had taken it up on himself, the devious little bastard he was, to use the RGI Insurance staff party Bilge was throwing as an excuse to get the Director liquored up to a point which everyone was familiar with as 'a really bad idea'. Thomas Bilge, despite being a scholar, gentleman and a generally kind-hearted soul, has a Jekyll and Hyde relationship with too much good drink. He becomes tyrannical and possessed by whatever thoughts take him at the time. He loses all his usual ability to restrain himself from unleashing a lifetime spent battling live human opponents for the British Special Air Service and other, similar organizations, on every day people. And on that particular bender he became obsessed with the notion that the Aversion Bureau itself hemorrhaged money in the pursuit of a goal that could never be achieved. He was convinced that the resources put to use here would be more directly beneficial to the people of the world if they were sold or donated directly to children in need, instead of used to buy grappling hooks and sniper rifles for less than a dozen agents looking to stop small time megalomaniacs. Max and co. ended up stopping him and injecting some liquid sense back into the old man before too much damage had been done, although Max had broken his left arm in the process, and someone he didn't personally know had died and been consumed by an out-of-control bird monster. So no lasting damage, really.

"He's not currently assigned to any of his usual

long-term undercover operations. Any idea what he might be getting up to, Agent Martin?" Stone addressed Max, who was clearly lost in thought.

The problem with admitting that he knew where the missing feline agent was last seen lay in that, as it turned out, Agent Whiskers had been *behind* the whole mess. The cat had been turning Bilge towards charitable acts during his inebriated reign and siphoning some of that money towards his own ends with a whisper here and there. Whiskers had only revealed himself to a broken and half passed-out Agent Martin after everyone else had believed the situation resolved with the dethroning of Bilge. Max might have ousted Whiskers to the rest of the team that very day had he not been in desperate need of a roommate at the time. Whiskers had agreed to move in with Max and help him pay rent as well as keep him from becoming too lonely and insane, whenever it was that the silver-tongued tom returned from a personal foray departed on after that day. Something told Max he could trust the cat, and that whatever possessed him to manipulate Bilge and abscond with company resources was quite possibly entirely legitimate. Max found himself agreeing with a lot of things that Bilge was going on about that day, especially about how the Bureau's resources could more directly benefit people than they currently did – the existence of a sloth consultancy being an excellent argument for that case. However, Max still appreciated being employed. That, and he really desperately wanted to have a roommate again.

"No, I have no idea what he's up to. I'm really more

of a dog guy," responded Max.

The other agents had no idea of Whiskers' involvement in the all the craziness from nearly two months ago and Max didn't feel that it was quite important enough to share right at the moment. The cat was a great agent, when his psychoses aligned, and Max may have missed him a little, again, despite his orchestra of chaos that resulted in at least one death – that they knew of.

"Well, alright then. I expect he's off walking on somebody else's keyboard right now, or licking himself on somebody else's coffee table," Stone spoke with an echo of personal experience.

Agent Stone clicked her remote yet again to reveal the next point of discussion, '3. Paper work – it exists.'

"Alright? I'm not kidding. Get some done tonight." She glared at Davison and Agent Martin specifically, then clicked her remote once more.

'4. Report from Agent Fisher – activity to our North' appeared on the screen. This one was a little more interesting, as Max had no idea who 'Agent Fisher' was.

In a tree of very standard age, in a very non-particular part of the forest that few have ever bothered to visit purely out of lacking a good reason, stood the treehouse storefront of a craft-loving and entirely inept businessman and "wizard". In this treehouse sat a woman named Kayle Fisher, who swung her two-foot shiny black braid over one shoulder and set about rolling herself another cigarette on a small corner of a large oaken coffee table cluttered with small pieces of everything. Kayle carefully moved aside a 'Sea Salter,' an invention finely crafted by her current roommate and current lover, the aforementioned self-titled wizard. It was made from three distinct objects: a funnel-shaped seashell, a length of securely-wrapped twine, and a salt shaker. Once her small, tightly rolled smoke was finished, she excused herself from the kitchen, living room, workshop and bedroom simultaneously, and made her way outside. She sat down on the porch of the Treehouse where she could dangle her long jack-booted legs over the edge, forty feet of branchy free fall to the ground below. Kayle lit up her homemade cigarette with a homemade lighter she had been given, crafted out of a piece of flint, a small aluminum cog and a poorly-sealed squeeze bottle of liquid butane.

This forest she sat above was of the Northern, mountainous persuasion. The trees were primarily coniferous, solemn, grey-green and timeless. They stood stoic and dense as they marched on for miles in every direction, rustling of Old Things that the fleeting lifecycles of the deciduous could never comprehend. Below her, supporting her, was the wizard's treehouse. This 'treehome' – so called – was built around, on top, but in no way as part of the large oak below it. In the style of its conceptualizer, it consisted of three major components: a tree, a home, and a large amount of lumber inexpertly nailed and bolted together to create a manner of fifty-foot house stilts. The man who built this place trusted not in the reliability of anything that hadn't come from his own two hands – an attitude which would come back to bite him much farther into the future than he probably deserved if he were to a learn a lesson by it. So in the end, the actual *tree* component of the treehome was really just for aesthetics, and provided nothing but a small amount of ambience to the otherwise simple abode. It consisted of a single large room that was combination kitchen, workshop, living room, bed room and bathroom (if nobody was home at the time). It was cozy, and it had almost certainly sounded like a better idea back before it was built, back before you could hear the treacherous groans whispering out of the floorboards with each step – but hey, at least if the house's stilts gave out, you would fall right into a tree. There are worse fates.

Agent Fisher glanced around the forest, and squinted towards a skinny grey mountain – a stone finger, really – that poked up out of the forest distant and North of her, through a haze of hot white smoke that poured from her mouth. That thing had always looked out of place. She noticed it the first day she came to live here and had never once gotten used to it. With its un-mountainous girth and slight bend near the top it reminded her of, well, no matter what it reminded her of – but it didn't look natural.

She had seen some strange things lately, and not the fun kind of strange that a girl usually comes out to the middle of a quiet forest to see after ingesting fun things. The kind of strange that harshly reminds one to do the job that one is part-time hired to do. It had been a couple of years since Kayle's travels had produced anything report worthy, and she kind of wondered if she still technically worked there, at the Bureau. But regardless of what the drones who milled their lives away missing out on all this "majestic shit", as she would put it, thought, it was probably a good thing she had made that report. Whatever was making the trees, the plants, the. . . *everything*, suddenly grow the way they were growing now? That was the kind of stuff you called the Bureau for, or even just emailed 'em for.

The wind changed; it was cold and yet somehow humid, despite the swollen midday sun above her. Kayle shivered a little, and went back inside.


"Agent Fisher is one of the Bureau's handful of 'part time' agents. One of the oldest," Stone answered, to the question on Agent Martin's face.

"What the heck is a *part time* agent?" asked Max, "how is that a thing?"

Agent Stone gave an annoyed shrug and motioned towards Director Bilge, who stopped examining the screen of his smart phone in that way that people over sixty do: the way that anyone else might discern the very tiny text of a contract that held the weight of human lives.

"Yes. . . well," he coughed, sniffed and straightened his tiny glasses, "there are men and women in our line or work whose abilities are astounding, but whose personalities forbid long term employment in an office space. So we hire them, part-time, and reach out to them in times of crisis, for. . . commission work." Bilge looked hopefully towards his employee with the chiseled composure, she nodded in approval.

"Agent Fisher is one of the ones we haven't called upon in years, yet she's always close by. She performs. . . adequately," Stone informed them.

"I think she's a total badass," Dick raised his hand, and quickly put it back down when Stone shot him a look.

"Yes, quite a tough old bird," Bilge agreed, "But it's been so long since we've heard from her, what could be the matter?"

Agent Stone leafed through her papers and then put them aside, she reached into her pocket and retrieved her phone. It was all black, with a black case and an ugly-but-functional additional battery pack, in black. She read from an open email:

"Yo guys! Long time no see. Been staying up North lately – *then she's got the address of some craft store* – and there's some weird stuff going on! I've seen like, a lot of bears around! This is not a normal amount of bears. Everything just feels off. Recommend investigating, cause this is definitely some bad magic or something. I should know, because I'm seeing this wizard guy right now. TTYL."

Stone shivered when she arrived at the final abbreviation, but worse so when she silently read the postscript where Agent Fisher had delved into great detail on the specificities of what the term 'seeing' referred to. Max thought about bears and began to sweat.

"Ttyl?" Asked Dick Davison, who was closer to thirty than his vocabulary would generally lead one to believe.

Director Thomas Bilge of the Aversion Bureau suddenly had a very faraway look in his eye, and spoke to himself, out loud.

"Tiger Tanks Yaw," Bilge then finished, after a long pause, "Lazily. . ."

Everyone was looking at him now, with varying levels of confusion. He noticed.

"A-hah-hah! Old joke from the war!" Bilge blinked a few times and shook it off.

"Here before Kilroy, nearly" he added quietly.

Max raised his hand again and looked at Agent Stone.

"So who's going on this mission? The one with the bears?" He held his breath the entire time.

When she informed him that it would only be herself, he inhaled as deep as the ocean, as deep as the cup you can get for only fifty cents more at the theatre.

"I'm going to be heading up North on foot this afternoon. It's a four hour hike to her coordinates. I can make it in three," Agent Stone told the room.

Everyone seemed to be alright with that except for Max, who was still thinking about bears.

"Fisher is not an agent whose ability to calculate mission. . . *criticalness*. . . I hold very highly. If I find that she's honestly caught on to something, I'll send for the rest of you to join me."

"Join you? You mean hike into the forest? But she mentioned bears. . . and a lot of them!" Max had trouble hiding the warbling nervousness in his voice – trouble in that he couldn't do it at all.

"I could punch a bear," said Dick Davison calmly.

He probably could, too, Max thought, *but how many?*

"I could definitely punch two bears non-lethally, or one bear, like, super-lethally," Dick said, in coincidental answer to Max's thoughts.

With the potentially life-threatening nature of a bear encounter reduced to a simple equation of Dick Davison Over Time, Max had to think of another reason he might be able get out of this one. It was worrisome enough that they were simply heading into the woods at all, as was mentioned before, Max was rugged like one of those smooth pebbles in an aquarium. And beyond the simple, ever-present forest-themed dangers of wolves, coyotes and literally any kind of moose, there was all of this mention of bears. More bears than were to be expected – apparently – and he already lost composure at the relatively low expectation of one.

"Well, what if we get lost!?" Max fired the last, desperate arrow in his quiver without looking, with his luck it was likely whistling towards the crowd already.

"That's not—

Agent Stone began to reassure him with her condescending bedside manner, but never got the chance.

Max Martin stood up from his seat at the table attempting to simultaneously push his rolling leather chair back and away, but it snagged on the carpet and fell over loudly, muffling his first few words and rudely awakening the Director.

"What if we get lost in the woods, get hungry and have to eat our hands?!" Max waved *his* hands around the room, simultaneously demonstrating their utility and majesty.

"Why on Earth would you eat your hands, you silly idiot?" came a new voice that Max wouldn't recognize as new until a moment later, when he calmed down.

He demonstrated with nature's own efficiency, how one could use one's arms to move one's hands to one's face, without so much as a small effort.

"Because they're so easy to get to your face!" he explained.

"So's everything else, when you *have hands!*" argued the new voice.

Max sat down, exasperated, and looked for the source. Someone new was there, by the door, standing behind Dick Davison and only coming to eye level with him despite the fact that he was sitting in a low chair. Curly sable locks and massive, ironic glasses exploded from the small girl's face with fashionable gusto rarely seen in these humble offices. The sight of her was very distracting, but Max's astoundingly average brain was still giving off too much heat to let this argument die. He narrowed his brown eyes to two small slivers of chocolate like the piece of cake you pretend you're okay with when you've invited too many people to your birthday.

"Yeah? And what would you eat first to survive? What body part of *yours* is the absolutely least valuable to you, that you would eat it?"

"Appendix," said Wade, with his first and last word of the meeting – perhaps even the day.

The new girl laughed and pointed towards Agent

Andersen, nodding:

"Bright one, this bloke."

Max finally conceded.

Agent Stone rose out of her seat, clicked her little remote one final time and crossed the room to give a warm embrace to the short girl in the outrageously fashionable attire. As '5. Bilge has a surprise' registered on the screen behind them all, the new girl made a high-pitched sound and jumped at Agent Stone, reciprocating the hug with an infectious energy. This was almost certainly the first time that Max had seen Stone deign to hug a single living human other than those few times he had dreamt it three years ago when he first got his badge. As they finished their excited greeting, in which Max could have sworn he caught something even more rare from his colleague: a simple smile, Stone whispered a few things to the new arrival and stood back, resetting into her standard, uninviting pose. *Very strange indeed*, he thought.

Now Bilge stood up to address them. Dick Davison looked as confused as Max did, clearly not recognizing the girl either. Wade looked like somebody forgot to plug him in to charge overnight.

"Agents, friends, employees," the Director began, "I'd love for you all to meet one of the brightest stars in the constellation that powers me throughout this weary world, my illuminating and wonderful niece: Guinevere."

Guinevere skipped a couple of steps to hug her uncle Bilge and stood beside him. When she gave the assembled agents a mocking salute she spilled her coiled notebook and handful of colourful pens all over the table.

"Piss it," she muttered loudly whilst bending to pick them up.

She beamed on them again as she got herself sorted, and spoke:

"I should prefer if you'd call me Gwen, or perhaps, if you've got time, my full name and title, Guinevere Quilway: Dream Journalist."

Gwen adopted a deep tone more like her uncle's as she spoke the title that may or may not have been entirely invented. Max wasn't sure what a 'Dream Journalist' was, but if it was something that actually existed, it's not like he would have been invited to the meetings anyway.

"Guinevere has just completed Year Thirteen back home and before she has her way with higher education I figured it might be good for her to come across the pond and work with us for a while. She's quite brilliant, I assure you," Bilge declared, with a smile.

"I look very much forward to working with you all, and perhaps even preventing a few cataclysms," smirked Gwen, unseriously.

Max decided that he really didn't have a problem with this, as long as Gwen didn't join the cat in outranking him anytime soon. He looked between them however, and noticed a few distinct differences for two people apparently related by blood. Director Thomas Bilge was a tall, bald, very strongly built man with a large sweatered belly and a strictly casual dress code perpetually in effect on his person. He had a thick, pure-white mustache and the very pale, pinkish skin of one who is truly descended from English ruling stock. Guinevere, despite possessing a very similarly infectious positivity, was quite a bit different physically. Gwen was a bit shorter than either Max or Agent Stone, the previous low-end record holders, and grew quite a lot of hair on her head by contrast to her uncle. It bloomed out and away from her scalp in a trapezoidal fashion that run-of-the-mill elastics could barely restrain. She wore bangles and dangles and bracelets enough to style an army. Though first you'd have to find an army that wanted them – and perhaps you'd start looking in Thailand. She wore one or more shawls over other styles of flowing clothing and a long paisley skirt, very much the depiction of a nineteen-year-old gypsy girl. Her makeup was colourful and eye-catching, but perhaps what stood out the most of all was her beautiful, flawless, dark-brown complexion. Max only thought about it because her uncle, standing right beside her, had all the colour of a flash-bang grenade gone off.

Up until about two minutes ago, Max was not even aware that his boss had any living family whatsoever, especially at his age, seeing as how he had never breathed a word about children. But suddenly, now, a niece had appeared, one that Agent Stone clearly had a close personal relationship with – the only relationship of that kind she held in the whole world for all he knew. Max vowed at that moment to make it a personal goal of his to find out more about Bilge's family one day. He figured it would end up being quite the adventure.

Guinevere made her way around the room talking

everyone's ears off, especially Wade's; Gwen enjoyed a good listener.

# 4

## IF YOU GO OUT
## IN THE WOODS TODAY

To a silent chorus of zero surprise from anyone, Natalie Stone immediately departed the meeting that day and headed straight down to her office with the intention of an even more immediate departure for the forest. It was a relatively simple kit to prepare, no need for disguise, for every bear that there ever was couldn't scare her. She still packed a canister of bear spray however, not out of fear, but rather, relentless practicality. Otherwise she took her commonplace survival kit with tinder and flint, compass and watch, rations, bandages and the like. She carried a flare gun as well, because it's a handy thing to have when you're far from home, and a very difficult thing to ignore. Stone briefly entertained the morbid thought that she hadn't ever had the chance to use one of these on a 'bad guy', or even a henchperson before. It wasn't likely to be as effective as a round from one of her rifles though. In fact, for it to have any kind of effect they'd probably have to be a bit of a straw man.

The only thing that stood out amongst her

equipment was the slender, twenty-five inch black-sheathed hand-forged katana strapped to her back. This didn't really have the make of a mission that required guns, and even if it did she was likely to take the sword anyway. It had always been her weapon of choice, from an unsettlingly young age.

Even with a light frame and athleticism on her side, Stone wanted to ensure she would arrive at the rendezvous before the sun got tired of waiting for her and went to bed, so she very quickly said goodbye to Bilge, Gwen, Davison and not Max, because he was making himself scarce out of fear of being brought along. Wade had taken off right after the meeting too, but that was always just her luck. Wade was the kind of man, should he ever open his mouth for more than six words at time, that you could have a *real* conversation with. . . at least, in theory. Something interesting about politics or technology could be discussed, discussed in-depth and without the threat of any uncomfortable romantic subtext.

Stone hiked ever onwards through the day lit forest, treading quickly and carefully over fallen trunks halfway returned to the Earth and large half-buried stones specifically placed by nature to have a laugh at clumsy travelers. Old Bilge had once told her that the whole of Mother Earth was constantly looking for a kiss, and desired you more and more the higher you tried to go – the further you endeavoured to be away from her – but giving in only made your mouth taste of dirt. It was probably meant to be a life lesson, but Natalie couldn't quite see the message. Well, dirt's bad, that much was clear.

The trees in this forest were very tall and old, growing thicker and more resolutely as she headed further away from the Bureau. Every once in a while she would stop and admire one, imagining with glee the kind of siege equipment that could be constructed from these bad boys back in the day – way back, in the medieval day. Besides in the context of war time capabilities, Stone didn't care much for nature's creations. A babbling brook is a lovely thing, but a high-powered jet of water cutting through a slab of steel? Much more worthy of praise, she liked to think.

The RGI Insurance building which houses and hides the greatest misdirection of our age, the Aversion Bureau, has been previously described as out-of-place. Well this is primarily because for a fifty-one storey office building it has a very unique location, being on the far outskirts of a city, very far away indeed from other buildings it might have something in common with. It is also surrounded by the beginnings of a vast pine forest that stretches all the way from civilization to some kind of national park, surely. A forest veined with cool rivers and bordered on the West with relatively nearby mountains, very frozen and very intimidating mountains. From the base of the building, it is only a rough one hundred metres of open grass before the trees start, and Stone had appeared a tiny, stubborn speck from Bilge's office on the fifty-first floor as he watched her go. He silently wished her all the luck in the world that was within his ability to command. A small, but nevertheless helpful amount. That was an hour ago.

Stone was still headed true North, same as she had been since leaving. None of it had occurred to her at the time, but on her hike she was coming across a complete absence of forest animals where there should have been at least a smattering of friendly deer, maybe even a squirrel. They had all been away, gone from this part of the woods for quite a long time for reasons that weren't entirely theirs. What she *had* noticed, however, was that as far as the forest itself went, with its towering trees and weathered stones and bubbling creeks, nothing appeared to be wrong anywhere. What little credibility Agent Fisher's evaluations already held in her mind was eroding with every step.

Stone and Kayle had never really gotten along, and this was likely a big part of the reason that Agent Fisher chose to work away from the Bureau. Stone considered her lazy, directionless, and too much of a party animal to be regarded as a respectable agent. For crying out loud – Stone's thoughts would often begin – Kayle was technically homeless. She was a professional couch-surfer following the 'will of nature', or whichever sodden-haired flax-weaving hippy friend of hers was most likely to roll their van to a festival the soonest. Very likely, a friend named 'Will, of nature'. Fisher was a child of the Earth who enjoyed smoking, partying and the consumption of illicit drugs more than. . . well, Natalie didn't know very many people in that kind of scene. She was sure though, that there was a man out there somewhere whose entire social media presence hinged on his ability to appear constantly in the multi-coloured epileptic spotlight of whichever Western God handled the organization of EDM raves and willed glow sticks into existence in the first place. She was sure that Agent Kayle Fisher could put that man to shame.

Lost in thought, the blonde blur of pure purpose, whilst hopping slimy boulders to cross a small stream, kicked a large pebble into the running water. That pebble would just so happen to soon end up lodged directly in the eye socket of something that marched determinedly along the stream bed at that very moment unknowingly making her an enemy for life, whatever it was.

As the black shoes, white jeans and long black coat of Agent Stone pattered through the underbrush towards a faraway destination bathed in fading yellow light, she felt characteristically confident. She was more than halfway to meeting with her fellow agent, and right now, everything was going according to plan. An opinion that was not shared in any way by the bright green eyes that watched her progress several hundred yards up the same path, crouched low behind a thicket of wild flowers finned with extra leaves. Leaves enough to make a botanist take a cold shower.

Forty-some floors up in the relatively nearby feat of engineering and imagination where the Aversion Bureau conducts business, things were happening – boring, terrible things known as paperwork. This was the part of the day where each and every agent of the Bureau was coldly reminded that even the job of a secret agent isn't all kicking ass and taking names, isn't all challenging the power of a sentient seagull super-warrior race or breaking down the bone-wall dungeon door of an ambitious but behind-the-times necromancer. Sometimes, you've got to fill out expense reports. Sometimes, you've got to read and sign the kinds of endless documents that make you wish paper was toxic, and not just in the way that anything can be when you eat enough to make plaster in your bowels. Closer to something that facilitates a quick and painless death through some kind of neurological shockwave that can't be survived – like poison from the future, or a seminar on creationism.

There was an insistent knock at the door.

"Just a sec!" Max shouted at the knocker.

He had perfected this maneuver years ago, the expert and loaded stance of One Who Is Working. He assumed the position, arbitrarily leafing through a stack of papers with his left hand and writing frantic notes comprised of literally anything that popped into his head at the time during the process with his right. A low "*Hmm*" emanated from his pursed lips, the sound of a brain running on fumes. He would turn his head sometimes, switching focus from operation to operation, with an ever-deepening frown.

"Alright, come in!" he said.

The door opened and a little shuffle of thinly soled shoes barely audible over the noise of flipping paper, scratching graphite and "*Hmm*" made its way to Max's desk. His office was very modest, lit fluorescently like most, all beige and off-white, with only a standard issue drawered desk, an old computer and a clutter of knick-knacks brought from home. Nothing remarkable. There was a little more silence in which Max tried to appear even busier, now with an audience.

"What are you working on? Is it important?" said Gwen, who was in fact the knocker.

Max put on his best theatre face, developed over the course of an intense three years of junior high drama classes. He poured rocks into his brow, sand into his chin, and sculpted the face of a man more put-upon than God.

"I'm afraid so. Working here, well, it isn't all just hunting down bad guys and," he paused, releasing a multifaceted sigh to make time for some additional improvisation, "killing. . . *robots*."

"Mhmm. I see. That's why you've written 'come on, just keep writing, she's not going to read this, you can make stuff up, bad guys, killing, robots' on this sheet of paper?"

Gwen asked innocently enough, but with that insolent kind of tone that makes everyone hate teenagers.

Max finished his notes off by writing something mean and quickly crumpling the whole sheet, tossing it lazily towards the three foot high monument constructed of crumpled paper that used to be a small mesh waste basket by the door – now a shrine to the god of 'eventually'. With only one chair in sight, Gwen looked around the room for somewhere else to sit. Finding nothing so much as a tall box, she tried to move a huge stack of unfiled paperwork to make space on Max's desk. She managed to knock the whole thing over and it cascaded across the dusty floor, experiencing the only attention it was likely to ever receive, in a few short seconds. She froze up with a 'whoops' motion, but upon slowly turning to look at him, teeth clenched apologetically, she found Max mid-shrug and carried on.

Gwen hopped up onto the messy desk in front of Max, facing him. She had her notebook open and an array of pens slotted into a large bracelet on her right arm.

"Got a minute?"smiled Gwen, nudging Max a little with one dangling leg.

He was a tad uncomfortable with how close she was sitting. If a lifetime of being himself had taught him anything, it was that when a pretty girl sat really close to him, it was only because the bus was nearly full. And she was quite pretty, he noticed, but something about the way she held herself and seemed to constantly vibrate with youthful energy made him feel a little old. Max was only twenty-something himself, but he was old enough to know better than to enjoy the simple act of being alive, damn it. Besides, things with Rose were finally starting to work out, and he wasn't willing to throw that all away for—

She was kicking him in the chest now with her pointed, faux leather shoes. It was really annoying.

"Come on you lazy sod," she teased, "I know you aren't working. I highly doubt you're important enough to be busy right now," she said with another damn smirk.

With that, all the small promise of romance, cute smiles or no, evaporated. If there had been any windows on these secret floors, it would have floated out of one of those to disperse through the air and find someone more willing. For now, however, it hung around the ceiling, inspiring amorous behaviour in passing flies.

"I want to interview you for my column," she informed him.

"Column? What, for a newspaper?" Max asked.

Guinevere shook her head and showed him a page of her notebook, one with many roughly sketched boxes and wide headers in various arrangements. She said:

"I'm going to start a little newsletter for the office. Even including the silly ones downstairs who don't know any better. Like I told you, I'm a 'Dream Journalist' and I like interpreting people's dreams. With your permission, of course, I'd like to publish our interview. I'm going to ask you some questions about your dreams, do some deciphering, and hopefully help you figure yourself out."

Max held up a finger to show he was thinking about it. It sounded like a neat idea, and it would definitely be putting him in Bilge's good books to help out his niece with her newsletter. But there was always the trouble of having to lie a great deal about the actual content of his dreams. There were a lot of good reasons to lie, too, because his dreams were either very disturbing nightmares, or sloppily pornographic. . . nightmares. Was it even legal to describe that kind of dream to a – what was she – nineteen year old?

"Look I'm pretty much down here on vacation," Gwen told him, "working for uncle Bilge in the office really doesn't mean anything. I'm not a field agent like you lot are. I don't get a gun or anything, but I do get a horrendous amount of free time, and I'm pretty sure I can pull rank you, Agent Martin."

She pointed at him with her current choice of pen, then dropped it and swore the whole time until she had it back in hand.

"So gimme something to work with or if I keep staring I'm pretty sure I'm going to have a nightmare about your massive hair coming to life and crushing me like a snake, or suffocating me like a living pillow held by an impatient loved one or—"

"Alright! Alright I'll share something, Jesus," Max started talking just to make her stop.

"Give me a minute to recall the one I had this morning, and I'll tell you about that."

"Mint," she said, "I'll be corresponding with my peers until you're ready."

Gwen took out her phone, the same one as Max had, only newer, and began to peck at it thumb and forefinger with all the speed of a hen testing focus-enhancing drugs for the military. Occasionally she would dispel more air from her nose than was normal, this is how you would know she was Rolling On The Floor Laughing Out Loud.

Max began to think of two things: first, the details of the actual dreams he had been having, and secondly of something less incriminating to deploy later with his conversational legerdemain. He leaned back in the frayed fabric office chair and put his feet up on the desk, knocking aside whatever he had been pretending to work on a few minutes ago. He stroked his chin thoughtfully and listened to the soft, whispering finger-pats created by one extremely social youth.

Lately, come to think of it now, Max had been feeling much more tired than usual in the mornings, but his sleep schedule was always so erratic that he didn't ever take notice. It had started sometime within the last month or so, he managed to deduce. Sometimes when he woke up feeling particularly unrested, he would find that things were knocked over around the bed. Always things that weren't close enough for him to get at in his sleep. Maybe there was some kind of sleep walking going on, and since he lived alone now, there was nobody to really confirm with. Two nights ago he had even woken up to find the window slightly ajar. Usually, Max *never* opened the window, even when it was hot, due to a mostly unfounded yet very gripping fear that valuable objects could go flying out of open windows entirely of their own volition. It just wasn't worth the risk. Max clicked and unclicked a red pen with his bored left hand, in time with Gwen's incessant typing. Suddenly, the cap on the writing end popped off and the guts of the pen shot across the room, powered by a modest spring that provided the mechanism for sheathing and unsheathing the nib.

Nearby, a witnessing mouse who would one day make bloody purchase on the annals of mouse kind – after narrowly avoiding a skewered death at ballpoint – got his lightning and kite notion for a them-sized arbalest and began meticulously collecting a large amount of discarded pens.

Max held the shelled writing utensil, turning it over and over, looking at the spring as it hung limp and mangled from where the ink used to come out. It reminded him of something that was so familiar, something that banged at the back of his memory, falling on a deaf frontal lobe. He grabbed the clicking part – that had only fallen on his lap – and stuck it back on top of the spring unskillfully. It sat there like a head connected to a skinny red body by a roughly improvised metal. . . *spine.*

Max was thinking very loudly now, frantically, almost loudly enough to hear, were that possible. A little electric flight director waved two little electric batons as freighter after freighter of hard-packed memories in long shipping crates encrusted with the dust of suppression slammed up front and center in his conscious mind. Max opened each one carefully, and knew now what he was being reminded of. They were only called 'Scoria'.

Dense pine needles and leafy summer canopies broke and scattered the resolve of the sunlight that would dare to try and enter this glade – this glade that the small blonde woman with the very big sword was barreling through at that very moment. The area had a dream-like quality, with thin shafts of stubborn sun individually lighting small and probably holistically significant areas of flower growth. There were so many flowers in this one particular stretch of forest, you'd almost believe that somebody put them there on purpose. Natalie didn't notice any of them, but she did notice the heavy sound of a branch breaking, and the heavier still sound, of breath. She froze, still as stone.

Max was remembering a lot of things right now. Things that he was so certain were long gone and far from capable of hurting him, that he tried very hard to stop thinking about them entirely. Max remembered at this time, the very real feelings he experienced the first day he ever came to the Bureau. It was an unseasonably warm spring day, a day that he had chosen to spend at the rocky beach of a nearby lake. It was that particular day that Max encountered a force utterly disconnected from nature, a force that would alter the course of his life forever. Almost forty people died on the beach that day, only moments before he headed down there himself. Traumatizing enough as that may have been, the true problem had lain in their complete and utter refusal to remain that way.

The agent in the forest moved in utter slow motion, simultaneously turning her head towards the sound, and moving her right hand up and towards the hilt of her sword. Another earthen creak met her. As she looked now, she saw a bright shadow beginning to raise up to its full height, back along her route, from a very wide and dense thicket of flowers too small to ever hide such a thing. Pink petalled flowers, beautiful, and wholly unlike what was coming up from behind them.

The jagged hump of its back came first, rising into view, its shard-like fur shining emerald and bright as a jeweled carapace. As one of two massive, shovel-blade ears came up, the thing began to emit a low roar – that resonating bellow which is so uniquely characteristic of bears. The kind of sound that first seems out of place, in nature, until you see the sort of creature that makes it and immediately understand. Agent Stone shifted her stance defensively, knowing she'd never live if she ran.

Agent Martin had barely survived the afternoon he was currently reliving in his mind. From the sky that day had come a machine which struck itself deep within the beach, sprayed a fine, shimmering mist into the air, and then had promptly detonated – maiming and scattering the bodies of all assembled. Max, emboldened by adrenaline, had run down to the beach when it was over to see if he could help, cellphone in hand. He winced, remembering what they looked like. Each person affected by the transformation came out like a pig that had gone under a wheat thresher, thereafter brought to a mad machinist who was told on pain of his life, to rebuild them using the contents of a small town scrapyard. These meat and mechanical drones lurched after him with a combination of engineered, and intrinsic murder behind what crude reconstructions they had meant for eyes.

He was rescued that day by agents Natalie Stone and Dick Davison, and would later be recruited to their order for his own brave actions – which tasted so ironic now – by Director Thomas Bilge. Attempting to discover the true cause and origin of that mysterious robotic plague defined his first year at the Aversion Bureau, during which time Max suffered from constant lucid nightmares. He was now gripped around the chest by a clammy vice, his breathing was shallow. What if the nightmares were back, and that's why he couldn't sleep? What if—

The great green bear slammed one pile driver paw into the soft earth and roared its disapproval. Stone was not afraid, but she was not confident either. This was clearly a powerful brand of magic, and her sword, to the best of her memory, was not at all magical. She had killed some other magical beings with it before, here and there, but was pretty sure that kind of thing didn't build up through osmosis. She could barely believe what she was looking at, it was a truly massive grizzly bear standing at least thirteen feet tall on four tree trunk legs. Its fur looked hard, more like scales than hair, and it shimmered with a green light that glowed softly. The bear stamped again, and shook its head angrily. Agent Stone did not move a muscle, she simply waited.

The bear turned its head, in that animal way people often equate with a question. It *huffed* heavily, sending a few flower petals spiraling away. More sun broke now, as wind rearranged the branches overhead and a thick bright beam shone right through the bear's massive head, bright green, lending no heat at all to the cold air that was all around them. This light made the beast appear transparent, but she didn't find that any more comforting, because solid or not, the forest still swayed under its weight. It dug into the dirt with powerful hind legs and lumbered forward, hammering the ground with each paw rhythmically as it closed the gap between them. It gave a final baritone howl and swung its massive glowing forearm directly at the unmoving agent. She was ready for this, and hopped back, avoiding the swipe, reflexively thrusting her sword straight upwards as the ursine monstrosity's mountainous momentum carried it within striking distance. The silver katana held by the small warrior plunged under the bear's chin and through its neck, mouth and skull, presenting two final inches of itself between the massive ears on top. An expertly timed riposte, she allowed herself a smile. However, Stone had seen enough monsters in movies, and enough monsters in real life, to know that this probably wasn't entirely going to do it. She gripped the handle of her sword tightly with both hands and prepared to wrench it free, causing as much damage as possible on the way out – but it couldn't be moved.

Its eyes focused on her, sublimely lit with the eminence of an alien star. It focused on her and her defiance through two small points of bright jade set in a fur-covered mask of angry muscle. The bear opened its jaws, revealing the blade inside, and revealing the jaws themselves. Jaws that your friends stand inside while you take a picture for them. Jaws that hang on the wall at whatever cabin-based bed and breakfast can acquire them, justifying the exorbitant price of food there.

Then, still skewered on her sword, teeth bared, it turned to smoke – rematerializing behind the agent and striking her down with a massive blow while she scrambled to process the maneuver. Four dinosaur teeth disguised as bear claws raked her back and tore open her jacket, it knocked her sheath away, and drew the first blood. There would be more.

Max was slowly calming himself down, because all things taken into account, the Scoria were gone. That same year, they had launched two separate assaults on the Bureau, and both times the brave agents repelled them. Back then it seemed as though they were coming specifically for him, for simply having the audacity to survive one of their infection sites. When they came to the Bureau the second time, they had found Max operating a remote sentry turret deep inside the building. There, one of them brought him down. If not for the brilliant science and quick-thinking of Agent Wade Andersen, Max would probably be one of them now. They never found out where the Scoria had come from, or where they ended up, but it had been almost two years now and no major defense organization had reported a single sighting. Max was glad for that, for being cured of the robot-zombie virus, and for not being dead. He squeezed his hands together, hurting himself a little bit. *Why does bad stuff only ever happen to me?* he wondered.

Natalie didn't feel the wounds, not yet anyway, and she rolled aside to avoid a second attack. She struck at the bear and cleaved two claws from its right hand, sending them spinning into the air before they turned suddenly to nothing. The bear didn't flinch, and bull rushed her as she rose, knocking her eight feet away into a small shrub with sharp fingers. It came for her again, and she hacked at it, she sliced its face, and stabbed at its eyes. It backed away and allowed her to stand, just so it could knock her over again.

Natalie fought with the wild strength of a dying animal but it made no difference. She finally missed a parry, was struck hard on the leg by one of the beast's paws, and fell on her back. Blood soaked all the way down her waist to her toes, she could no longer stand.

*Just once more,* she thought, *just come and stick your neck out you son of a bitch.* The broken woman held her sword against the length of her arm, waiting to make a final, desperate slash at the beast's throat as she knew it would come and disembowel her soon – then they could die together. She waited, coiled like the spring in a pen, for what felt like minutes. Stone loosened her trap, and looked up to see an empty glade. Beautiful and verdant, lousy with wildflowers. She slowly propped herself up and leant on her sword. There was no bear. It had left, but why?

"Coward. . ." she spat, under her breath.

A cold wind blew through the trees as the sun began its slow descent to the cool side of the pillow. Light peeked through the leaves at her hair, and everything was deathly calm again. Two hours from both where she started and where she was going, the choice was still obvious. She had to get home, she had to get to Bilge, and she had to do so immediately. Her phone was not in her pocket anymore.

"Go on then," pressure Guinevere, pen and pad in hand.

*Go on with what?* Max wondered, as he hadn't started speaking yet. She was clearly ready for something, however, so he had to finally give it a shot.

"Well, last night," he began to spin his cover story so expertly it would attract the attention of a fairytale king with a tower full of straw, "I dreamt that I was making bread."

"Right," she said.

"But the dough. . . had my father's face. He was speaking to me, with his little flowery dough lips there, about responsibility, and being a man."

Guinevere took some notes and looked back up at him through her huge owl-like glasses, waiting. Max began to really act out the story as he painted this increasingly worrisome scene.

"Well then my childhood dog Racer jumps up on the table and starts chewing on my dad's face! I totally just kind of. . . let it happen. Then I take him to the park," described Max.

Gwen nodded, looking right at him and holding back what was surely *constructive* criticism by miming a stitch across her lips with a fabric of pure will.

"I take Racer to the park, not my dad," Max clarified, continuing, "it's a beautiful day out, too, the birds are friendly and the ice cream man's declaring chapter eleven so everyone has a free cone."

Totally lost in this made-up dream, which was actually more psychologically telling than he could dare to realize, Max continued to a darker part, his face reflecting the change.

"Then uh, well, I see my mother at the park, so I go and say hello but she's with this guy. . . and the guy, I can see his face, he's got this huge chin, he's. . . oh my God Dick Davison is dating my mom. *That bastard!*"

The little lady sitting on Max's desk was scribbling very quickly now, enjoying herself immensely. The pure shock of where that bit of improv had ended up took Max out of the lie right away and returned him to reality. In order to maintain the illusion, however, he had to come up with an ending for the 'dream'. Max waited for Gwen to stop writing and looked her right in the eyes to convey his seriousness.

"I take out my sidearm, the one Davison trained me to use himself, and I shoot him seven times in the chest just to watch him die."

Max took his feet down from the desk afterwards, and sat silently, hoping he had managed to convince her, trying hard not to think about his mother and Dick at the same time.

"Well, *that*, I can definitely work with," Gwen declared triumphantly, snapping her notebook shut and hopping down off the table.

"Thanks Max, it was a pleasure."

He extended his hand to shake hers, but she stepped in a gave him a hug instead.

"I think that you're a lot more brave than you think you are," she smiled at him, "now, Bilge has invited us up to his office to do paperwork there instead, which, as you probably know, means no more work for today."

Max was happy to hear that, and tossed the broken and poorly re-assembled pen he had been holding tightly for the duration of the conversation down on the ground. It rolled away, forgotten for a time. Not long afterwards, however, an expeditionary team of scavenger mice who now eke out a living by collecting scraps of coiled metal would retrieve it, another cog in the furry little war machine now churning between the Bureau's thin walls. Max put all thoughts of robots out of his mind.

Two ridiculous hairdos bobbed side-by-side down the long plain hallway to the elevator, one tall and black and arched forward, one wide and bouncing and deep brown. Gwen spent the entire walk to the elevator and subsequent ride up to the fifty-first floor excitedly talking to Max about all her ideas for post-secondary education. With her marks, and the pedigree of the schools her parents – who must have been exactly as rich as her uncle Bilge – sent her to, she could *easily* grow up to be anything. But at this point, Max had long since fallen back into the mental well of imaging his mother with his Adonis-like coworker, and was currently waiting for
Lassie to get Grandpa.

"I'd like to take a real stab at legitimizing study of the occult. The kind of stuff you guys run into all the time. Ancient magicks, science fiction kinds of things, all that. Especially as those old practices can be applied to modern situations. I'm sure we've yet to see something really crazy like that," Gwen explained.

Max nodded, hearing without hearing anything, seeing all too much without seeing what was right in front of him. As the elevator got close to its fifty-first ding, Guinevere spun and touched Max on the arm, prompting him to look at her, confused. She wasn't going to touch his mom, was she?

"Listen, about the dream interview, I'm not going

to publish any of that stuff about the robots, okay?" Gwen told him.

Max's eyes widened, he tried to speak but it all got caught in this throat like it was Black Friday in his mouth and his lungs were full of shoppers with no regard for human life whatsoever. Gwen patted his shoulder and smiled:

"That was some heavy stuff, and I'd like to talk to you about it some more, another day. But it's not for everyone else to hear just yet, I understand that." She gave him an understanding look.

"But I never told you *anything* about robots!" Max protested, throwing his hands around, "there's nothing to say! I don't. . . I don't even know what you're talking about!"

The elevator arrived at the top of the building, so it was time to put a presentable face on. She had timed this well.

"Lots of people say that, they never want to tell me anything at first but they always do. You were talking a lot back there, but don't worry about it. It happens to everyone," she winked at him as the elevator doors opened, and they stepped out into the Director's office.

Max smiled and nodded, but he really hadn't told her anything. He had only *thought* about it. . . hadn't he? Today was consistently vying for the title of 'Longest Possible Day' and even though it wasn't quite over, the polls were a massacre.

Up in the Director's office, there at the top of the fifty-first floor, Dick Davison, Max Martin, Thomas Bilge and

Guinevere Quilway spent a few hours getting to know each other as the yellow light of afternoon became the orange light of evening. Although the Bureau operated mainly out of the building's thirty very cleverly disguised windowless floors in between the twentieth and the fifty-first, Director Bilge has chosen to put his office here, at the absolute top. Such was the right of any crazy-rich old man who would build this kind of place. Though in truth, the building had existed prior to Bilge even coming to Northern North America, as he had won the deed in a duel back home from an international business man who, each morning, must have taken a bath in liquid hubris – and rye – to believe he could have defeated Bilge in gentleman's single combat. Back then the RGI building had been only twenty floors tall, or something like that anyway. It hadn't lasted for long.

Bilge's office had a very warm and welcoming decorum, much like the man himself. The walls were hung with old wooden frames depicting great men and women in the Bilge blood line, and there were ornate dressers and shelves holding several lifetime's worth of trophies and military accolades. His desk, which stood at the end of a long blue rug leading straight out of the elevator doors, was solid mahogany and quite expensive looking. On the desk sat a name plate, a few books and a small, stuffed, goat and polar bear hybrid-looking thing. Behind the desk was a large portrait of the symbol of the Bureau, set between decorative sconces that would later come to life with a warm glow as the sun sunk lower and lower. Agent Stone had been gone for almost three hours now, but nobody had heard a word from her yet.

Bilge worried quietly in his head, and didn't concern himself with whether anyone else was going to.

Max, Gwen and Davison were treated to coffee and board games by the doting director, who was very pleased indeed to have his niece visiting. He had set up a folding table and chairs near the wall-to-ceiling windows so they could enjoy the view East out of the building while they played. Everyone seemed to get along marvelously, until a slogging game of Monopoly had nearly torn the world asunder. Dick Davison could not, for the life of him, comprehend the value of a long-term property investment and insisted on saving his money, raking in cash while endlessly circling the board looking for a nice rental. Later, he nearly flew off the handle after winning only second prize in a beauty contest, so Max slyly reshuffled the deck of chance to make sure that didn't happen again. Further problems arose, beyond simply that Monopoly is history's most emotionally draining game, when Bilge, bloated by immense wealth, became so torpid on his turns that Max had time during each one to play a full game of Scrabble on his phone with Guinevere, who ground him into ash and blew him away like a chimney sweep every single time. This didn't help their relationship's current strain in that Max still wasn't sure if he had mistakenly thought all of his secret nightmares out loud earlier, or if she had stolen them directly from his brain. She *did* seem smart enough to accomplish that, so honestly he wasn't going to think about anything vitally private whilst in the same room as she was, for a little while. Not even that one weird growth – *damn it.*

At some point, finally, when Davison was especially bored, it occurred to him all of a sudden how shockingly similar the little Monopoly man looked to a certain Thomas Bilge, mustache and all. After this point, his niece could not so much as look at him without bursting into hysterical conniptions. After a few instances of this, Gwen had to excuse herself to the washroom. It was at this point that the game of Monopoly ended as they all do eventually – somebody flipped the board. In this peculiar case, however, Agent Davison and Bilge had the exact same thought at the exact same time, and seeing how they were seated across from one another, the table was all at once snapped in half, clapping together like an alligator's jaws, crushing the game inside it. The room shared nervous laughter after that and Gwen moved to leave.

"Well Uncle it's been a riot, but I've got to get out there and meet a couple of my friends. See the city a little bit," she said.

"But my dear you've only just arrived in the country this morning, how do you know anyone here yet?" Bilge asked, with a little worry in his tone.

Gwen held up and shook her phone, with the little penguins and other adorable ephemera dangling from the case, chiming happily.

"Internet, Uncle," she said, "I've got loads of friends, and I intend to keep it that way."

"Alright but just be aware! I don't think I need to warn you about the dangers of the world anymore but please just—

Gwen reached up and stroked his bald head

affectionately.

"I still carry the taser you gave me, and if anyone tries to put something in my drink. . ." she spoke lower now, only to Bilge, "I've got a little sachet of potassium cyanide to return the favour, and *very* plausibly deniable instructions for my mates."

Bilge smiled at that.

The young girl made her way to the elevator and rode it down, waving with an armful of jingling bracelets until she was out of sight.

"Cheerio!" said Max, who immediately regretted it when everyone looked at him.

Bilge kicked the broken table to the corner of the office. He motioned for the two men to join him in the ornate wooden chairs that looked across his desk. They did so. The mood of the room took a heavy turn as the last lights of the evening were lost against the Western side of the building. Bilge slowly made his way to a seven-foot cabinet in the corner of the room behind his desk, it was sealed with a heavy iron chain that ran in four directions all centered on one lock that seemed to politely insist that nobody was supposed to get in here. He turned like molasses, looking very seriously at the two of them.

"I assume she gave it to one of you chaps," spoke Bilge, incredibly deliberately, "you know better than to test my assumptions."

Max wasn't sure what Bilge was talking about, but Dick coughed and reached under his bright, tight yellow work-out shirt, beneath the strap of what Max could only hope was a tank top, producing an ornate silver key. Davison lobbed it at Bilge, who caught it expertly. Bilge gave a lazy smile and unlocked the massive chain, opening the liquor cabinet and removing a rectangular amber bottle and three crystal tumblers. He sat down at the desk across from the agents heavily. He sat down as an elephant off his shift at the factory sits down, when he expects to be nothing more than bones before anyone finds him.

Thomas Andrew Bilge, Director of the well-meaning and yet so often woefully ineffective Aversion Bureau, uncapped a fresh bottle of 'Old Thirsty Bastard' and held it above each of their glasses, awaiting some sort of sign. Max noticed that the little man depicted on the label of 'Old Thirsty Bastard' looked extremely similar to the Director himself. So much so it probably wouldn't have surprised him to learn that it was in fact the Bilge family label, started by his late great-great grandfather, Tiberius Augustine Bilge. Dick held up two fingers, and received as much scotch. Max held up one finger to ask a question, and received as much scotch, along with a little chuckle from his boss.

"Child's portion, eh, you always find ways to tickle me, boy." Bilge had a warm laugh, even when we was making fun of you.

"I don't think that there should really be a child's size when it comes to whiskey," said Max sarcastically into his first sip, which he winced through expectedly.

This stuff could boil a lobster in its shell.

Bilge then poured the third glass nearly an inch full, and set it to the far end of the table before tucking in on the bottle himself. Dim orange light from the wall lamps and the black shadows they produced gave the director a look like Max had never seen. One of a man, and nothing else. An old man in a chair, who could have been anywhere, or anyone. It occurred to Max that for all of his usually flamboyant attitudes, the agents of the Bureau were Bilge's responsibility – one that he did not bear lightly. The old man looked across the tips of a thousand dark trees toward a vast expanse of uncertainty.

"Kids," he muttered.

It would be another forty minutes before anything else was said.

Deep into their cups, the three men now slumped within the magnificent chairs of the fifty-first floor office here at the top of the world. Max was not much of a drinker, and two small glasses of scotch had nearly done him in already. He was about to drift off, now, at what was it? Ten-thirty? Well it was dark anyway. He wanted to, at least, but there was this annoying red light outside, and it grew and grew until Max had to shut his right eye to block it out, then it shrunk gradually until it was gone again. It returned, twice more, brighter each time. It wasn't going away on its own, so he finally turned to look in the direction of the annoyance, out of the window and into the utter blackness.

*THUMP* went the tiny red dwarf star that slammed straight up against the massive window of the office like a tragic, but evolutionarily necessary bird. Max fell backwards out of his chair at the surprise of it, and everyone else was finally paying attention.

"What the hell was that?!" yelped a sleepy Agent Davison, reaching reflexively under a pillow that wasn't there, for a shotgun that wasn't either.

"The sun! It was the friggin' sun trying to get in through the window!" Max informed them, rather hysterically.

"Probably wants the rest of my whiskey! *No!*" Director Bilge screamed his refusal at the now long-gone sun lazily, throwing his entirely empty bottle at the window, where it shattered, slightly cracking the glass.

"There we go. Scared it off." Bilge swatted at the window with his empty hand.

Max tried to get comfortable in the chair again, but the sun apparently had other plans, as the floor-to-ceiling glass window pane suddenly exploded inwards with a shower of burning phosphorous and very sharp silicon.

*FWOOSH*

Erupting through what used to be the window came a tear from Ra himself, an angry hissing emissary from somewhere in the vast, mad world that cursed them with existence. The flare, not a sun at all, buried itself into the carpet in the center of the office and roared deafeningly as little baby flares tore off from its cherry-red actinic mane and rocketed around the room, trying to set the whole place alight at once. As long as he lived, Max would never forget the image of Thomas Bilge and Dick Davison's horrified expressions as they realized what was happening, burned into his mind red and blurry by the Devil's own nightlight.

Many things then happened all at once: Dick

Davison hid his eyes from the dying flare and stripped naked in record-breaking time in order to smother the flames and maybe even show off just a little. Max Martin crawled to the edge of the world and looked down, where he saw, in the parking lot, the tiny collapsing figure of a very familiar woman. Thomas Bilge, unfortunately unaware of what Max had seen, up-ended the third glass of scotch that he had poured an hour ago, all over the empty chair that Agent Davison had been using. He lit it with a match struck across his forearm and held the flaming chair aloft, bellowing:

"We have to fight the fire with a stronger fire! One that we can control!"

Bilge lumbered towards the small hell mouth that a currently naked Dick was trying to stomp out using his own pants, winding up the meaty gears of his broad chest to smash the burning chair straight into the sputtering indoor bonfire and all it represented.

"Wait! Bilge, bro! Don't do that!" pleaded Davison.

Bilge froze in mid-toss, reluctantly.

"The fire came from outside, you gotta deal with the source, bro! Throw that shit outside!"

Bilge saw the sense in this immediately, turning on his heel and launching the flaming office furniture right back out through the missing window into the night, roaring obscenities.

"Curse you, flames!" hollered the drunken old man, who tossed the chair with utter ease.

Max did not have time between recognizing the lifeless form fifty-one storeys below and realizing what Bilge was about to do, to warn him. Max only covered his eyes.

From another angle, it must have been quite the spectacle. Screaming from the heights of the topmost floor of the 'Really Good Insurance' insurance company – the one that held no other purpose on this Earth besides the fair and measured distribution of protective financial policies – came arcing through the night, a large mahogany office chair wreathed in flame. It crackled and glowed majestically like a shard of sinking sunset enjoying a graceful final moment before reconciling with gravity – much like the passing of Denethor II, Steward of Gondor, from the high walls of Minas Tirith.

On any other night, it would have landed harmlessly in an empty parking lot. Not tonight, though. Tonight found it crushing a modest sedan that a hard-working accountant staying late on the thirteenth floor would later be reimbursed for in full, only, without a word of explanation. He would take those questions quietly to his grave, forty years hence.

A bewildered and not entirely sober agent with very big hair un-hid his eyes and looked way far down upon the broken form of his friend and superior Agent Natalie Stone – who lay unmoving on the concrete, just fifteen feet clear of a singularly unlucky car with a burning chair fused into its flattened roof. Director Bilge looked down, utterly mortified as he realized what had happened. He rushed to the elevator, punching the panel so hard that the other agents would later have to hotwire it to get it to work at all. In the cool air of the night, Dick Davison: Champion Of Fire sat with Max, naked and sooty and sweating like a pig. He gave his little buddy a worried look, and Max tried very hard to keep his eyes straight ahead.

In the world of ants below, the tiny director picked up the tiny agent, and rushed her inside.

# 5

## THE LONG NIGHT

The woman in the bed, the bed in the infirmary, the infirmary deep within the misleading walls of the Bureau, had been staring at the ceiling for what felt like hours. The ceiling here was one of those tiled with drywall squares, the ones with dozens of small holes cut into them just in a sad attempt to keep things interesting in the workplace. She would count the dots well into the hundreds, never missing a single one, then she would count them again. Every single time the number of dots was the same. That was how it was supposed to be. That was how everything was supposed to be. Things that are real, and things that had spent the last two hours feeling like the most real sensations one may ever have experienced, did not suddenly disappear without a trace. They did not disappear without a single scrap of evidence to explain to one's fellow agents why one had stumbled back the way they had come, from exactly half-way there, bandaged up to the nines and whispering about magic.

Stone rolled onto her thigh, she put weight on her back, she lifted herself slightly from the bed, and flopped down heavily, trying very deliberately to make herself uncomfortable. She couldn't, however, because her thigh, her back and the whole rest of her body – besides being tired from long hours spent hiking – was all in one piece. Her back showed *no* signs of being raked by four tremendous bone claw hammers, her leg was *not* missing a chunk of flesh and the blood that had nearly frozen her clothing to her skin as she limped back through the chilling night wood's wind on two legs of pure resolution, was nowhere to be seen. She had awoken in the little white cot of the infirmary to discover this, and was currently balancing confusion and anger, trying to decide which emotion she would act upon first.

Back there, in the flowered glade within the woods where a manifestation of all the evil nature could conjure was set upon her – Natalie had bandaged herself tightly with what supplies from her torn and missing backpack were still in useable condition, scattered amongst the grass. She looked for her phone, or any way she could have contacted the Bureau, and found nothing in one piece, so she set to walking. Back along the cool creeks and back amongst the old trees she limped and struggled for almost two hours to make it home, entirely convinced that if she even thought for even a second about the amount of blood she was losing, it would surely bleed out even faster.

Once within a few hundred metres, Stone had begun to send great fiery exclamations from her flare gun straight into the sky. These are the kinds of signals that she imagined were almost impossible to miss.

Routine dictated that Bilge would likely be in his office at the time, and likelier still, be looking out across the forest waiting to hear from her – he was just like that. Routine did not dictate, however, that Agent Davison would so easily relinquish the key to the liquor cabinet and that the whole team would be completely piss-faced. On top of that, wherever Gwen was she could only guess at. *That kid could surely spot a God-damn flare falling the God-damn sky*, Stone thought to herself, bitterly.

She had been visited on that late night over the next hour, one-by-one, by every other agent of the Bureau that she possessed no patience for whatsoever, and ignored each of them until they left. Max had arrived first, nervously spewing apologies and rationalizations as to how, when he was a boy, he had looked at an eclipse briefly, rendering all solar-similar sources of light – as he put it – so dull by comparison that they were hard to notice. Stone spent the time that she did not spend listening to him, imagining the logistics of starting up a bullshitting department within the organization, and allowing Agent Martin to head it.

Immediately after the sooty white shirt and red tie combo retreated from her clandestine recovery room, an even bigger mess walked in. Agent Davison didn't say much when he came, head bowed, and just held out his fist awaiting a consolatory knuckle-bump – though it was probably more for his sake than hers. Stone snubbed him, as she planned to, but did take a quick peek his way as he walked defeated from the room, because out of her peripheral he had appeared to be wearing something quite odd. Dick Davison had come in to greet her, dressed only in one of Bilge's older sweaters, and nothing else. The front and back depicted a big red lobster on a green field, a sweater Bilge used to wear during his brief courtship of eating contests. He had become incredibly sick on shellfish during that time, and swore to kill the next he saw, in defence of his digestion. The sweater looked like an elephant's raincoat on Davison, but because of his height it still left a little bit of ashen buttock exposed – an image that Stone would spend the next while scrubbing desperately from her mind's eye.

The last of her guilty visitors was old Bilge himself, who poked his great bald head around the door frame and waited for her to meet his gaze. She never did, and he slumped away. Natalie returned to counting the dots on the ceiling. Those things didn't just disappear. Nothing should ever just disappear.

Max sat in a semi-circle of waiting chairs near the entrance to the building as his giant, half-naked friend joined him. It was calm and silent in the lobby, except for the faint tapping of glass. A sixty gallon fish tank stood along one of the walls, giving bored people something to stare at for a while – inside that tank a tiny fiddler crab had taken to aspirations of escape, knocking the little decorative diving bell man against the glass, perhaps accidentally, perhaps not.

The disastrous action and excitement of the evening had sobered the two men significantly, though you wouldn't believe you were looking at sober people should you happen across them: one disheveled man that had narrowly survived a close encounter with a fiery orb of desperate communication, and another one in the same boat, except wearing only a lobster sweater that barely covered his own fiery orbs.

"I'm gonna go home and change," said Dick quietly, rising to leave.

"Yeah good idea, me too," added Max, when suddenly his phone rang, and it wasn't his mother for once – it was Rose.

"Hey, Max?" she said through the line.

"Oh, hi! Uh, what's up?" Max put on his coolest voice. Davison deduced the nature of the call and leaned in to listen while Max batted him away silently.

"Well I've gotten off work early, and I thought it might be fun to go out. Can you meet me at the club, the one we met at? I think it might be fun."

"Da Club?" Max confirmed, as that was the fine establishment's storied name.

"Da Club, yeah. See you there at midnight? Drive safe!" Rose chimed.

Max hung up. Dick was staring at him with two very excited brown-yoked eggs.

"Ooh-ho-ho-ho my *man!* Hell *yes* we're going to the club!" Dick was bobbing his head rhythmically as he spoke, smiling a smile made even whiter by the black ash on his face.

"No way! No way you're coming to this thing!" Max protested.

"I was there the last time! I gave you all the confidence you needed to meet that super rad lady." Dick looked legitimately heart broken, his sweater sagged empathetically.

Max shook his head and left the wheel to Jesus, assuming, irresponsibly, that a man literally as old as time would know how to drive. Dick took it as a yes. The two of them made their way out to the parking lot to retrieve their cars, yelling across at each other as they went to either end.

"Last time you got us both kicked out because you thought some girl wanted to fist fight you!" Max reminded his friend, who was his friend for some strange reason he currently couldn't recall.

"She did! She totally wanted to go! Man, and I'm not sexist, if a girl wants to fight me, I'll fight her!" Dick held up his fists over the roof of his low, bright yellow sports car, ready to box an invisible woman, no doubt.

"Ladies can kick ass too, man."

Max, who had had his ass thoroughly kicked by various women multiple times before, saw the logic in this, and appreciated it, but still worried about bringing Dick along. Dick Davison held clubs in as high regard as children hold playgrounds that are attached to fast food restaurants – with a kind of revelry one can only experience when all of their favourite things in the whole wide world have been brought together in one small location with never-before-seen ease of access. Max himself was still waiting on the founding of a strip club LAN café with energy drink fountains set into the walls. That, or just like a place where you could pay nice women to hug you for a while without it being weird.

He found his rusty, trusty Volvo and got inside stiffly, as Davison tore out of the lot and onto the highway, his totally sweet car growling the sexual thunder of a tiger made with bones of lightning and striped with roiling plasma. Max putted along behind him until the yellow rocket was out of sight.

At their individual paces, the pair headed home to shower and change, and then, both possessed by a deep desire to unwind in a room that was only metaphorically on fire, headed to 'Da Club'.

A wide, pale moon that was actually Wade Andersen's expressionless face, passed over her back and arms, examining beneath now-embarrassing useless bandages with a cotton swab, a tongue depressor, anything to prevent any unnecessary skin-to-skin contact. Stone patiently awaited his diagnosis. She had already explained the entire event to him, and to Bilge, and was really beginning to lose hope that Wade would find any kind of evidence to support it. Not that they didn't believe her, as Agent Stone was never the kind of person to fabricate a mission report, but regardless, it was a very difficult story to believe.

"Psychosomatic," said Wade, definitively.

"What? You think I imagined my wounds? I've been wounded before you know, I know what it feels like." Stone was on the defence immediately, impatiently.

"Precisely why it was effective," suggested Wade.

She was listening again, trying not to become distracted by his platinum curls, his eyes that were bluer than arctic ice and the best Kool-Aid. She coughed soberly.

"Magic," said Wade, turning his empty hand into a closed fist in front of her, "subsists entirely," he then opened his fist to reveal a small, red, pill-shaped candy, "on our willingness to perceive it."

*Son of a bitch's a wizard*, thought Stone, quite impressed. He offered her the candy by way of not taking it immediately away, so she picked it up and ate it. She was not usually a candy eating kind of girl, but this seemed like an important candy. It tasted of cherries and a small step towards closeness – but that could have just been her imagination.

"Mental supplement," he informed her, about the sweet, "potentiates clarity."

"Pleasing cherry flavour," he advertised.

She nodded, trying not to come across in that way people kept frustratingly informing her was "needy".

"Magic is artifice," Wade said this whilst collecting his modest notes and medical utensils.

"Therefore," he looked to her, "surmountable."

*Yes*, she thought, *it is a matter of strength then, not physical strength but still. . . strength*. Natalie enjoyed problems that could be solved with clever applications of overwhelming force.

Wade went lightly and quietly from the room, just as young Guinevere was entering it, dipping into a smiling mock courtesy as she passed him, and Wade Andersen returned a nod so slight and unprovable that cryptozoologists would clamour to believe in it. Stone watched him go, just emanating respect for his practicality and intelligence. Those were the kind of traits that a woman could really wrap her arms around.

Gwen must have seen the look on her face.

"I think he's great and all, but it's bloody hilarious how much you like him," the teen snorted out a laugh.

Stone would have struck out and given a good wallop to anyone who would have suggested such a thing had it not been her, Gwen, one of the only people in the world the agent had met so far, who didn't deserve a professionally executed kick to the head.

"I wanted to talk. Bilge told me you were hurt so I rushed back here, then I heard you explain it all to him, so I think I'm caught up." She sat down on the bed beside Stone.

"That quiet fellow, he's got a good head on his shoulders, but he doesn't know anything about *feel*, you know?" Gwen was making a wincing, splay-fingered grasping motion to help illustrate the alien concept of "feel" to a fellow adult human.

The agent sat quietly with her friend and listened, willing to hear anything enlightening, especially about magic.

"I've been effortlessly blowing through bloody awful course work my entire academic career, and where does all of that extra time lead, you may ask?" Gwen began.

Natalie did not ask, nor play along, she just waited for the information to come out.

"To the occult, Nat! To the intellectual pursuit of things that Cannot Be Explained."

Gwen swapped phone hands and threw her left arm up in the air, it was covered from wrist to elbow in bracelets and charms of gold, silver and woven hemp, to name a few of the more common materials. Some of these trinkets had symbols and icons dangling from them, some had the glyphs carved in, but each and every piece she was wearing was the representation of some certain belief or ideology. Stone only recognized a few of the obviously religious ones. Perhaps it had been ignorant of the only somewhat older agent, and probably everyone else as well, to assume that what Gwen wore on her fingers, wrists, and ears were exactly what they appeared to be and nothing more – just. . . *jewelry*.

Save for a single black stud in each ear, Agent Stone did not fuss around with any of that sort of thing. She wasn't concerned with looking 'pretty' or attracting anyone's attention – with one specific exception – beyond what she herself was initiating, and as it appeared, neither was Gwen. Agent Stone felt a selfish kind of respect for the girl. She enjoyed imagining someone else doing exactly what she thought was correct.

"From the dawn of time, throughout all that we have ever been," Guinevere began, somewhat theatrically, painting a wide canvas with her bedazzled limbs in the air ahead of them, somewhere for all the words to land.

"We have believed in *things*. We *love* to believe in things. Whether they be mythological beasts, faraway lands of impossible design, or divine purpose for our mistakes. . . anything to keep from settling on the truth that most of us are secretly just twats."

This was speaking directly to the bitter agent.

"While so much of it is, in fact, trickery and a way to keep people under control by pain of *divine retribution*," she warbled those last syllables and threw her hands to play patty-cake with Zeus, "you might come to realize that over time, as we have been inundated with notions that certain things are impossible. . . we have lost our ability to perceive beyond the mundane!" Gwen was standing now, in front of the seated woman, swaying with her shawls and aggrandizing her sentences with ecclesiastic physical motion.

"Quite contrary to what you've just heard, is what I submit to you: Magic is real. Very real, and it plays upon the world in ways that even many of those who have experienced it firsthand can never fully comprehend."

Stone wasn't quite sure how much of this was really landing with her, but was at least enjoying the effort the young woman was expending. She wasn't able to think much about her various frustrations at the moment, which was nice.

"Magic, so simply called, is the energy that scientists seek with their mile-long particle slamming Ouroboros, something that cannot be quantified because all quantities are born of it. An energy that governs all things from within the things themselves – such a force seeking to explain itself can only end up with its own tail in its mouth." Guinevere Quilway relaxed a little, coming out of the brief trance she had achieved during that last sentence.

"Sorry," she said, "I had a drink before coming here. The age is eighteen where I come from."

"Here too," offered Stone.

"Ah, brilliant then," Gwen relaxed, but stayed standing. "All I'm really saying is while some hold to the belief that we must ignore, and perceive beyond magic, I say we must perceive within it! Follow its own rules, and subvert it from the inside! For without a very specific environment for it to exist within, it simply cannot."

"I expect that even those who claim to wield it are only one stop on the journey that particular energy was headed along anyway," Gwen finished, a little winded and worked up.

"We can know it, we can change it, but we cannot ignore it."

Stone smiled mildly and thanked the woman she once knew as a similarly excited little girl, then got up to leave, removing her useless bandages calmly, much to Gwen's surprise. Gwen brushed the dark hair from her eyes, fixing the elastic that held it all back, and spoke:

"If I know you well enough, and I feel that I do, you'll be heading back there soon. I plan on doing a little research as soon as I can, and with the uh, green energy, and the bear as a starting point, I know I can dig up something." She caught Stone by the arm, before she could leave.

"It was real, I believe you, whatever it was used magic to convince you something was true when it really wasn't. The only question is why a being with influence like that wouldn't just kill you dead." Gwen squeezed her friend's hand.

The solemn agent nearly, reflexively, pulled away, but suppressed the urge.

Agent Stone walked out of the infirmary and towards the elevator in the center of the beige hallway. Everything she had just been pitched sure had sounded well thought-out, but nearly a decade of dealing more than occasionally with this kind of threat taught one to act abruptly and lethally wherever possible. When something came at you, even something alien and magical in nature, you killed it before it could kill you – if that required you to steel your thinking to prevent the threat from altering your perception and tricking you, then so be it. See beyond the plumage, keep a level head, submit to nothing. This idea of following magic's own rules, and perceiving within it? Those were the wishful thoughts of scholars. Thoughts for the kind of people who read scrolls.

"You didn't really lose!" the little girl offered kindly from far away.

"I know," said the agent, as the elevator doors closed.    And she did know, but that didn't make it any less the last time she would.


The long, slow elevator climbed each floor in turn, skipping not a one, while it took its passenger closer and closer to the sky. She reached the fiftieth floor and departed there, into an entirely empty room with nothing but old taped-up boxes from another lifetime. Musty things with banged-up corners, the contents of a normal person's basement. Their only hope of being opened walking right on by, it wasn't the kind of night for them. A short, wrought-iron emergency staircase accessible through his floor only offered a quick route to the rooftop, what would technically be the fifty-second floor, she supposed. Gravel crunched under Stone as she walked across the roof to sit on the Northern tip of the helicopter pad that once had held an actually pretty decent helicopter, before it was destroyed by zombie robots and their flying mechanical whale emissary – a long story from a long time ago.

The moon was huge tonight, though battling against gathering clouds, and the air was cold in that awful damp way that they didn't get too often on this side of the mountains. Luckily, she always kept a small pair of knit gloves in the pocket of her work jacket and she put those on. They were black as well. Agent Stone didn't like to stand out, she didn't like to afford potential prey the benefit that bright clothing provides a hunter. Natalie, on the other hand, just didn't like standing out.

She dangled two small feet over the edge of her fortress, staring into the vast woods whose sameness generated a light visual static in the dimness of the night. Perhaps she expected to see a face – or even a funny sailboat – she wasn't really good at this kind of thing. Not really good at the whole practice of introspection. Stone enjoyed her matters black and white, like her clothing. Good and evil were best when separated cleanly by the width of a blade – preferably hers.

Why would a spectral demonic animal such as what she saw, capable of forcing her to see and feel herself being ripped apart flesh and bone, not simply crush her into the grass like the ant she clearly was? That is not how she would wield such power, nor was it how most others would. Her eyes became lost in the blue-green, eerily lit peaks of the trees that marched away to the edge of sight. They were like a beveled piece of soft metal, where the play of light makes it look both indented and raised at the same time. The bend of the forest now made the trees all appear to be walking Northwards – back up to whatever waited there under dark leaves.

*BZZZ* went her phone, the crappy old backup one she always left at work – not the one that had been crushed under a spectral bear's paw. It was old enough she had to flip it open, and instantly felt five years younger.

"Hello—

"STONE HEY. HEY? STONE?" A voice that sounded somewhat similar to a coworker of hers forced its way against her ear, vying to be heard amongst a din of 'oontzes' and 'wubs'.

"Agent Martin this is ridiculous—

"LOOK DICK AND I ARE AT A. . . THING TONIGHT AND TOMORROW'S FRIDAY AND WE'RE BOTH TIRED AND YOU'RE DEFINITELY TIRED AND," Max Martin's dreadfully unmanly yelling voice dipped away again, allowing even more onomatopoeic representations of 'boots' and 'cats' to stumble out of the small grey phone's unimpressive audio rigging. She was already holding the phone two full feet from her head and still making everything out just fine.

"YEAH ALL OF US ARE TIRED, FOR SURE, SO WE'RE NOT GONNA BE IN TOMORROW SORRY I HOPE YOU FEEL BETTER TAKE IT EASY, EAT A. . ."

Agent Stone, feeling back to her old self when faced with this particular, familiar brand of insubordination was ready to interrupt him and issue a full and scathing reprimand to the two agents apparently trapped inside of a malevolent living subwoofer – the only reasonable excuse for missing work she would accept in this situation – when something caught her eye from way down below.

The something was bright green and was actually two somethings. *Eyes.* Those were the same eyes from not too long ago, she just knew it. They were gone as soon as they were seen. She dropped her phone, and held onto the railings around the side of the building, hanging over the edge to see as well as any human eyes could – trying to find where the hell the green had gone, or where it was going.

". . . PPLE OR SOMETHING, 'KAY WE'RE GONNA GO SEE YA MON—

The phone snapped shut and created a wonderful silence in doing so.

Natalie hung there, over the edge of the fifty-second floor, daring gravity to stop her from seeing what she wanted to see. If only she had the presence of mind to bring a rifle to the roof with her like she usually did. The little green spots were nowhere to be found now, and there was no sign of movement in the forest anywhere, especially no sign of the behemoth that possessed them. Stone settled back and waited, more patient than time. Magic was artifice, someone once told her – it was a trick played on the natural order of the world. Whatever the eyes belonged to when she had seen them yesterday was not real, and whatever they *really* belonged to, she would see it for what it was, and would defeat it.

In one of the few buildings of our world that, presented with the specific situation of a burning roof, would not require water and simply be allowed to burn, human bodies *writhed*. They bumped up against each other in a crude mockery of the beautiful act of procreation high on the ichor that repetitive rhythms played loudly blasted beneath their skin. Some of the affected use this mass hypnosis to slither with strangers that would otherwise spurn them, while some only gyrate on familiar armatures, even here, where morality was a mere book report on the desk of a leather-clad teacher directing an orgy via complicated whipping.

Yet a few of the people in this sinful construction offered their bodies in no such way, because some of them were currently on their phones. Max Martin, faced with the realization that his hospitalized friend and colleague may have taken his news a little harder than excepted, to not reply at all before hanging up, felt a little bad – and not at all appropriately lecherous for his current location.

Max left what was laughably considered the 'quiet' section of the club and tried to find Rose and Dick Davison, who had shown up after all, to perform some aforementioned faux-copulating under pulsing lasers and lights. Max made his way around the tabled section, not daring enter the labyrinthine dance floor, for fear of being lost forever and subsequently ground upon by a lusty minotaur.

A club, any club, and especially 'Da Club,' was never a place that Max felt comfortable, or very much like he belonged. And it wasn't as though he were raised dotingly in a pearlescent castle and constantly set upon by Disney movies either – his browser history would dispel any such illusions – the only valuable education he felt as though he missed out on by avoiding that kind of programming was that he held no predilections that would lead him to marry the first man he slept with, prince or otherwise. But as he figured most decent people felt, this sweaty meat grinder was only suitable for a very particular offshoot of humans.

Max was only here once before in a desperate attempt to be placed in the same focus group as women, for a change, and when he had ended up meeting Rose, perhaps the loveliest and most level-headed of them all, he had pretty much thrown the idea of further clubbing away forever. He had no clue why she wanted to return here, and was wondering about it as a tall, polo-shirted man carrying two drinks and roughly fifteen pounds of gold bullion walked through him as if he were an illusion – a sad illusion of someone else's life.

Rose was by the bar and waved him over when he returned.

"That wasn't a very long call," she said to him.

"Yeah, well, a good accountant deserves a day off here and there," Max reasoned, feeling guilty.

"You said your supervisor, she was in the hospital? What happened to her?"

"Ran into a bear," he replied without thinking, a well-honed skill of his.

Rose sat in her stool, taken slightly aback.

"A bear?" she clarified.

The world's greatest accountant brought his foot up to his mouth, metaphorically, a bit too slow.

"It's uh, an insurance term which refers. . . to. . ." Max trailed off.

"Our ladybro ran into a tough case, and she's in the hospital getting her brain looked at," a familiarly large man butted in, smoothly saving the situation.

Davison was holding two martinis, he handed one to Rose and kept one for himself – Max felt left out.

"Psychiatric stuff, eh?" Rose asked from behind a little olive.

"Bit of a workaholic, that's all," Davison smiled.

"Don't downplay yourself, buddy," Max allowed a plastic chuckle and went to continue the story, "Dick here got taken by a bear at work once!"

"Carried me right off to his lair! Didn't see my friends for days!" The two agents shared a well-timed artificial laugh and secret smile, successfully having buried the lead, as far as they could tell.

The big agent smoothly clinked martinis with Rose and made his way to the dance floor, sensing babes in the water – as he put it – the water, in this case, surely being human perspiration. Max watched his pal dip away into the press, at least a head above all of them, little pink polo shirt collar up to his ears like insect antennae. *All the better to woo them with,* Max could hear the thought in Davison's voice. He turned to his date.

"You're wearing the same dress as lunch I see," he

applied a sultry tone to what was perhaps the worst icebreaker on record.

"Haven't been home yet, but I must say I really like how *you* wear the same plain white button-up every time I've ever seen you," she threw back, playfully.

"Touché. Would you care to try and dance in. . ." he looked over at the floor, Davison's gleeful expression bobbing over it all like a giddy shark, "all of that?"

Rose hopped down from her seat extending her wrist gingerly, and still with a hint of mockery, saying:

"Oh heavens, may we?"

On their way there, she grabbed his hand. Max felt his balls slam hard into his lungs in that special way that new love can rearrange your vital organs. He took a sharp breath and tried not to blush like an idiot.

"So how was work today? Anything interesting happen up there, in that big building?" she squeezed a little.

Max took a moment while they walked in time with the rhythm of whatever passed for music in these godless halls. He looked over at her, more seriousness in his eyes than he intended:

"Felt a bit like everything was on fire."

"Fair enough," agreed Rose and hurried him away to start getting down.

The two of them danced for a long while, moving slowly before the beat dropped, and repeatedly feigning surprise when it continually refused to do so, simply to please the DJ, who clearly considered himself quite clever despite entering the profession only a week ago in a desperate attempt to keep the lights on. Rose swam her body in the practiced, erotic way that One Who Is Graceful can often manage, while Max desperately cobbled together bits of what he saw other people doing around him, and must have done so well enough, because she was getting ever closer.

Occasionally they would see, off in the distance, a tall guy they both knew, lifting two scantily-clad women atop each massive shoulder, briefly becoming a human battlement of gyrating funk. In defence of all things rhythmic he would hold them aloft, until the age of his brain compromised with the age of his back and he had to put them down again.

Rose danced even closer now, brushing against Max in what could only have been very carefully calculated movements. Each time their hot skin touched, all the blood in the area would run away, straight to the safety of the brain where it immediately set to work on carefully deciphering the very meaning of touch itself.

Max was vaguely aware of his own seduction, but for all the time he spent in his head, he could not find a single worthy reason to refuse it. Rose was right against him now, coyly avoiding eye contact while doing the exact opposite with every other kind of contact. She leaned up a little, slipping a warm hand against the back of his neck and pulling him in.

"I'm really glad you wanted to see me tonight," she whispered with hot pink breath that made Max immediately reposition his crotch to avoid any awkwardness.

*So close*, Max would later think, about the time he nearly kissed a beautiful woman he had begun to really care about, on the dubiously weathered danced floor of 'Da Club'. So close, and yet so rudely interrupted. Just as the thin, tangy wall of Rose's personal bubble was breaking against the tilt of his lips, Max was knocked right over, right onto the floor, right into a lost and upturned high heel soaked in vodka. He looked up to see a man almost as large as the infamous Dick himself all decked out in dress shorts and a pristine white-collared shirt bursting with black chest hair, wearing a crown of wax and putty with just a little bit of spikey human hair in there somewhere. The bro looked down and shrugged confrontationally. What *was* Max gonna do about it?

Well, first things first, he stood up. This guy's problem, whatever it was, was no clearer up close, where eye-level for Max met collarbone for bro. This aggressive creature was even more offensively dressed from three inches away. He sported a thin strap of beard hair that ran from one singly diamond-studded ear to the other and he had the artificially tanned skin of a man who fetishizes carrots. There was even a rather expansive tattoo of a kraken on this very man, it spread from his exposed V-area down his left arm and up around his neck. Angry looking tentacles, the mark of a man who either very much loves sea food or one who has never seen even a second of Japan's darker animations – likely both. The caricature of testosterone shrugged impatiently again, his sea-beast glaring at Max as well, clearly not a fan.

Perhaps it was the grinding music, and perhaps it was a primordial male response, perhaps it was even the small amount of whiskey ingested what seemed like forever ago – but like the first human to ever protect his pride from a douchey saber-toothed tiger – Max did something impulsive he never knew he'd ever be capable of, and took a swing. With the moderate amount of hand-to-hand training he had received through the Bureau, this was a relatively clean punch with his dominant right fist. However, the man he swung upon was exactly the kind of guy who got this reaction everywhere. The bro caught Max's arm in a practiced way around the elbow, holding it with the vice grip of a professional arm-wrestling crab. Luckily for Max, this was not the end of the fight already.

Something about that near-kiss with the lovely Miss Rose had replaced his blood with sexually frustrated magma, and with one of Agent Martin's volcanic outlets clamped off, all the heat and power had to run somewhere.

*CRACK* went the jaw of the bro, as Max drove his underdog left fist up and erupting into the man's face – knocking his smug expression literally into next week, where it found another man with similarly bad luck, and so continued a cycle of violence as old as time.

Max exhaled, shocked at his own combat prowess and slowly entertaining the kinds of thoughts that it is good to have before making a move like this one. Such as thoughts of consequence, and at least rough calculations as to how many similarly dispositioned friends this one jackass probably arrived with. He selfishly expected to turn and see a look of damsel-like amazement in Rose's eyes, but what he saw instead was a joyless look of condemnation and the turn of her head as it went "Nope".

Max deflated, seeing that. Rose hurried over and pushed him out of the watching crowd – some people cheering, some booing, some who had just lost five bucks. The bro spat out some teeth, adding even more texture to the disgusting floor.

"Max that was definitely assault!" Rose denigrated his actions with every step and breath.

She was extremely unpleased, for some reason.

"I've never. . . I have no idea what happened!" He wasn't fighting her now, they both made their way out of the club with haste. Dick noticed them and caught up quickly on long legs made for dancing.

"BRO, that was so friggin' cool!" Dick hooted, "where'd you learn that? Not from me!"

"I should hope not, *because it's a crime!*" Rose insisted.

The three of them bolted through the front doors after quickly grabbing her purse from the bar stool and did so just before security had enough time to realize what had happened. They do their best, those guys, it's not their fault that some people are just naturally punchable and choose to go about anyway.

Once in the parking lot, trying to decide whose car to take out of this mess, it became clear that Max was the only one amongst them who hadn't had a drink recently, and despite Dick's insistence that he did that kind of thing all the time, Rose wouldn't allow it. Unfortunately, Agent Martin's trusty junker was too old to be located via space-age beeping remotes like his upper-class compatriots. So they worked in tandem, trying to find his car in a hurry so they could escape and return for theirs at a later, more sober time – but they hadn't so much as spotted a similar tailgate before the hounding footsteps of a frat pack were upon them.

They were eight, all so freakishly similar in appearance, with only miniscule variation in height, weight and hair colour, that Max could have been fooled into thinking *he* was the one who had been struck about the head. Their leader, the one with the bloody mouth, hollered something unintelligible and spray little red drops that fell brightly on his shirt. The hounds advanced, breath visible in the damp, chilly air.

Dick Davison loved this part – he hopped forward and took two of the quicker and smaller bros around the neck, holding them aloft with ease. A tall, skinny bro tackled him in a roughhousing brotherly way, or at least it seemed like that, while he unsuccessfully wrestled the unmoving Dick. Soon, the split of the revenge party was two and six, in order to be considered fair, and the bloody leader, backed by a very squat and muscular bro advanced on the two absconding lovers. Max didn't think he'd be able to repeat his earlier luck, but got into fighting position anyway, adjusting it slightly after realizing it was wrong. Rose was reluctant to move, it seemed. She was eyeing the advancing crowd, Max, Davison, the whole situation – calculating the timing of a very specific action in her head.

"FREEZE," she roared, in a husky kind of commanding voice that Max could really get behind – some time when his guts un-shriveled from the shock of it.

They did so, on command, because Rose had raised in her hand, a bright and shiny silver police badge. She also exposed the handle of her service issue revolver ever so slightly from the mouth of her purse.

"Time to go home, gentlemen!" she suggested, not unkindly.

Dick Davison dropped one bro from his grasp, and released another from a head lock, laughing at them. They all backed away as instructed, except for the leader. That swollen mouthed, tight-shirted trope reeking of leather left to rot in bull musk for decades, pointed angrily at his broken face, then to Max, then back to 'Da Club'. Rose understood him.

"I don't know what I saw in there, it was loud, it was crowded. I do know what I'm seeing right now, and I think it's going to stop," she warned.

The human embodiment of unpleasantness stared daggers at the both of them and walked back inside, bros in tow, swearing something fat mouthed and hard to understand.

Max looked at the woman he had come here tonight to meet, and saw her in a wonderful new light. She was a warrior to him, bathed in the bronze glow of an aging streetlamp above. She had never been sexier.

"And I really thought your buddy here was going to be the trouble maker," she said, relaxing, putting away her gun.

Dick gasped in an obviously hurt way, clutching gingerly at his massive chin and still smiling.

As things calmed down, these two children forever trapped in the bodies of men whiled away a couple of late hours in the parking lot being regaled with cop stories and, at the expense of having to cab back here in the morning for their cars, Rose agreed to drive them both home in hers, which was significantly cooler than even Davison's expensive sports vehicle. Apparently neither of them had ever been friends with a cop before, or perhaps even met one, from the way they were acting.

Although he never received the punch-related praise from her he was hoping for, Max counted himself incredibly lucky to be seeing this woman, and really wasn't sure how on Earth he had managed it at all. Perhaps he hadn't – perhaps *she* had, and he was okay with that.


Gargoyle of the Bureau's peaks, ever-vigilant watcher of the deep and mysterious forest, professional ass-kicker and deadly swordswoman Natalie Stone, awoke to the beginnings of cloudy sunrise under a wooly blue blanket that quite successfully warded off the chill of this high-altitude morning. No birds were chirping, for they were hundreds of feet below, if they were there at all. The wind was nevertheless quite vocal, whipping loudly against the building and travelling downwards where a person might be the rare victim of errant pocket change if they weren't careful. The blonde one rubbed her eyes and looked at the big weight that was holding this blanket down against the wind, the big weight was wearing blue mittens and a toque with a fuzzy pompom on top. The big weight was not from around here, and didn't handle the cold quite as well as she did. The big weight sipped at a tremendous cobalt tea thermos and spoke to itself:

"I have always said to myself that if I ever had a child, *however* that might come about, and it was always a daughter I pictured. . ." came the voice of Thomas Bilge, an old man with a lot to say, "always a daughter, yes, that I wanted her to be brave."

Bilge braced against the cold morning wind and sipped more from his thermos.

"I wanted her to be of such strength: mentally, physically and emotionally, that she could never come to harm, but would always know when to balance strength and compassion," he continued with a toothy grin now.

"She would certainly have to know great compassion, for there is no better way to understand the time and place to act, than to know a little about who you are acting upon."

Natalie watched him, laying on her arm quietly.

"Finally, and perhaps a bit selfishly, I always imagined that my daughter would be beautiful. Beautiful in that true way that inspires leadership. The real beauty of a person who knows themselves, and never hesitates to express that." Bilge looked at her.

"You, Miss Stone, are all of those things, and in my head I thank your fine parents every day, for showing me what that could have looked like. I—

"I forgive you," she said flatly, "it's alright."

He smiled. They watched the sun rise from the top of their unusual edifice, high above the day's many problems soon to greet them, immune to fear or worry, basking in silence.

Stone motioned for him to pass the thermos.

"No, my dear, that won't be to your liking," he said.
She looked at him sideways.
"One-hundred percent hooch, I'm afraid."
She sighed, not unhappily.

# 6

## THE LONG TOMORROW

His dreams were vague. The kinds of dreams that were dark, cloudy, absent and as hard to recall as the exact plot of a novel read in childhood. As he woke, the images floated away from him, retreating to the back of his mind until they could reemerge when most unwanted. They were the shapes of people he didn't know. That, or the shapes of things that wished to look more like people than what they were.

Max opened his eyes that morning feeling cold and rigid. He reached up to his alarm clock, the servos of his shoulder whirring tiredly. Yet, for once, the alarm wasn't already buzzing, and he still had three minutes of carefree life to enjoy. As the dream world faded further, in that time when what was so real that it could cause sweat and movement, suddenly and blisteringly separated from what was obviously real, only a hollow feeling remained with him.

The brain does a strange thing when waking up from deep sleep. It takes its manuscript, thirty thousand intricate words that it has written over the course of one six hour night, a work that it showed to the unconscious mind moments ago, proudly declaring the existence of no truer truths than what it held – and discards it suddenly. It is now saying that what the eyes see, what the light illuminates, what the hands touch – that these are real, that this is what real is. It occurred in this time, to Max, that the physical brain and the conscious mind work independently from each other, taking turns convincing one another of what is most correct. It also occurred to Max that neither could be trusted above the other, that it might just be that anything was as real as it told you it was. He flexed the pistons of his shivering left arm, there was a bright green paper bracelet wrapped around it. A fresh memory came to him, a happier one, and just like that the day had a different face.

Max climbed out of bed, still wearing half of his "goin' out" clothes – the half he had been too tired to fully remove after getting in very late last night. He thought about his friend, his friend who was a girl, his friend who was a girl with whom he had very nearly seen a late night dance floor kiss all the way to completion. It had really been some kind of night, what with the excitement of a grimy, bustling music pit and the raw animal heat of holding hands – not to mention it being the very first time that Max had ever successfully physically defended himself from a bully. Max had been in lots of fights as an agent of the Bureau, but there generally wasn't any one-on-one animosity there – just regular old impersonal gun shots and death threats directed at whole populations instead of just himself.

That night, Rose had been so into him, right up against him, just more enthralled with him than any other woman he had met to date, and in the way that it was *finally* reciprocal. Max wasn't sure if it was something he was doing or just accumulated life experience finally making up for his lack of facial hair and natural musk. Regardless, a beautiful woman was interested, and he wasn't going to muck that up with too much thought. He finished in the shower, cleaned up after himself, and started to get dressed for work.

Max had apparently left the bedroom window open again, that must have been why he'd woken up so cold. He went to correct this, noticing how once again this week it was getting unseasonably chilly, and today the heavens were sampling paint swatches that ranged unimaginatively from 'Dreary Bedrock' to 'Grumpy Neutral'. Even for a biome that trudged through snow six out of twelve months of the year at a minimum, the dead of summer was usually nicer than this. It wasn't just wet, it was cold too, and cold in a way that was out to make you miserable. Like a rainforest under the influence of great evil – or Ireland.

In a rough facsimile of breakfast, Max hurriedly put two slices of bread in the hot silver box that meant to cook them. He retrieved those same pieces not forty five seconds later. Max enjoyed the taste of warm bread, yet he often wondered if he would ever possess the patience to one day experience toast.

On the way out of apartment 404 – remembering to lock it this time – he decided to check the mail. Inside was a cheque made out to one Max Martin. The payment was coming from a Mr. Whiskers and a private institution, the amount was exactly half of one month's rent. This was a little surprising, as the last time Max had seen him, despite making arrangements for this exact situation to occur, Agent Whiskers had not disclosed where he would be going for the seven-ish weeks that had preceded this moment – and his mission, anything that it could be, was certainly not official Bureau business.

Well, anyway, his money was here, and that meant he was sure to follow suit. Max decided to keep this development to himself, and carefully placed his spare key – as well as a great deal of trust in human decency – under the thick rubber mat on the outside of the apartment building, heading off to work. Well, first to 'Da Club' to retrieve his car, *then* off to work. It was still a worthy price for being driven home in a police cruiser last night. In the front seat of course, much to Dick's chagrin.

Somewhere halfway from where he was going and where he was coming, he thought about the phone call made last night, a surprisingly ballsy attempt to take today – Friday – off, for no other reason that he didn't think Stone would be up for finishing the week after her ordeal, and he had planned to get a fair bit more drunk last night than ended up happening. The fact that his ever-unyielding superior had done not so much as scoff at his request and had simply hung up the phone, had stuck with him. He'd never felt quite so guilty over the thought of missing work, and because of it decided to go in anyway. Perhaps he was just worried the incident had actually left a crack in her hard ass.

Max swerved to narrowly avoid a drowned squirrel

floating face down in a backed-up storm drain – it was already dead, yes, but still, *eww*. The clouds loomed.

Inside the ground floor lobby of RGI Insurance on a dreary Friday morning, the shapes of things that on any other day of the week may have appeared human, shambled to and fro propelled only by their fear of the rotary nature of existence. Accountants, interns, people dealing with smashed cars and pubs set alight mysteriously on the eve of bankruptcy all moved in disorganized ranks silently promising commensurable understanding that between them all – between all of their collective energy – no more than a single paper would be pushed this day.

Max headed straight for the receptionist's desk which sat in the dead center of the lobby, prefacing the wall with the two elevators – one normal, one rather secret agency – and surrounded on all sides by clusters of cushioned benches that by their very nature insisted upon patience. There were a lot of people around today, though none of them stood out. He stepped in something wet.

"Sorry about that one, Max!" came the jolly yet somehow discordant tones of someone that Max had never seen before, but looked a lot like a janitor.

"Just cleanin' up, sorry again!" the friendly man smiled and nodded towards a shattered fish tank off in the corner that some of the benches were pointed at.

Water had spilled all over the floor and some of it had made its way to the door, probably only because the janitor pushed it there. He smashed the dirty mop up against Max's feet, depositing as much water as he was trying to remove – a bit like a child who had seen his parents sweeping but a single time and immediately started a business, broom in hand. Luckily, Max was wearing shoes that looked a little newer when soaked through.

"I'm sorry, I don't think we've met," Max admitted, as he was still having trouble processing this man who patted his shoulder apologetically upon seeing the mess he had made.

The janitor was very wide, and they were about the same height, so this made him look enormous. He had a very meaty face, and bore a smile that did nothing to gentrify it. Something about the man just hit Max. . . *incorrectly*. This fellow had the glassy eyes and waxy smile of something straight out of the uncanny valley of human likeness, like a video game character from eight years ago made to speak up close to the camera for an in-engine cut scene – all of that, or just like a mannequin. The big janitor held out his big left hand, still smiling. Max reciprocated with his left arm as well. They shook.

"Oh, that's quite a grip you've got, son! It is a pleasure to meet you, and I'm so sorry about your shoes. My name is Smith, by the way, and yours?"

"Yeah I'm uh. . . I'm Max. You already said it," Max pointed out, the janitor shook his head apologetically and looked ashamed.

Smith made his way, mop snaking behind him, back to the broken glass of the aquarium, humming softly.

"Oh brother, such a forgetful old head I have," he apologized again, running calloused fingers through antisocial tufts of grey hair that refused to stay very close to one another.

"Whatever it was broke this thing must have done it real early, just before everyone arrived. Watch your step young mister Martin! You don't want to slip up now, not with your whole life ahead of you," Smith chuckled at his own cleverness, looking away now.

Max took a moment to get moving again. It may have been the shock of unwanted early morning small-talk or it could have been the overly friendly attitude of the weird janitor, but that conversation had left him with an uncomfortable feeling. He noticed a presence now, by his side.

"You ever look at someone with very tiny features and a huge round face?" then there was a little pause, "does it remind you of a baby trying to climb out of a pie?" asked young Guinevere, more curious than sardonic.

Max choked on a laugh and returned the high-five she had prepared for him. That went a long way to getting things back on track.

"Come on, we're going to the front desk to see if Stone left a message on where to meet her," he instructed.

Gwen followed behind.

If all the radiant beauty possessed by every living person were measured in luxes, the woman before them now would have certainly registered as statistically significant. Pecking away distractedly at a Sudoku puzzle on her tablet, the main floor receptionist of RGI Insurance was unknowingly doing Max and Gwen a big favour, for when this woman gazed upon you it was like being caught in a tractor beam fired from the sun – you could not escape its pull, even when every cell in your body knew that getting any closer would only lead to total evaporation. Such was the beauty of this woman with the laughing amber eyes and golden brown complexion of one who bears proud heritage in sunny, sandy places. Woman or man, it did not matter, her unique combination of objective physical perfection and complete obliviousness to her own powers created an utterly intractable gravitational pull. Also my God, she was so nice. Like, *so nice*.

"Uh. . . good morning!" ventured Agent Martin.

The receptionist looked up and smiled at them in a perfect, not-too-toothy, not-too-eager way that bolted her job security firmly to the foundation of the building itself. Max froze, double, triple, even quadruple-checking his every thought before attempting it. It took him an agonizing fourteen seconds just to complete an entirely unnecessary nod after she greeted them back. Gwen took a shot instead, not unaffected.

"Blimey it sure is morning isn't it? Yep, well. . . we're looking for any messages from an age- I mean, uh, Miss Stone," she managed, barely, trying not to make eye contact with the two flawless topaz that tried to do so with her.

The receptionist, who was also the entire building's general secretary anyway due to everyone bringing everything to her regardless of her requiring the information or not, looked at some notes she had made earlier.

"Hmm, that's odd. . ." she mused, in the voice of singing angels finding money on the ground, "Miss Stone told me to tell anyone asking after to head up to the twenty-third floor to meet her. That must be a mistake."

Sally – so said her nametag – looked up again and smiled, sending another wave of blindingly good looks to break against them, they who were dealing with all the chemicals their brains could possibly produce being released at the same time.

"That's all the way up on the Japanese Luck Floors! Why, there's nothing up there but power cables and dust bunnies, I reckon."

"Hah, yeah," chuckled Max, looking towards a nearby ficus that was apparently completely engrossing, "but you've definitely got enough room for like, a whole world-saving secret agent organization up there don't you."

Gwen stomped on his foot and prepared to deliver something defusing to the conversation but was surprised to see that the secretary only paused, wrinkled up her mouth a little, and laughed. She laughed, and in doing so was about to create a noise that could only be describe through the extreme application of metaphor and hyperbole, but please understand that extreme measures are sometimes perfectly necessary.

Now, this was some kind of laugh. It started slowly, with tiny little whistles and small squealing peals on the edge of hearing. . . and as though the primordial way that certain mammals know how to laugh at all had been genetically inversed in this woman, the secretary began to sharply swallow air, instead of expelling it, to create what could only be called a laugh due to its familiar position in the conversation – to create what any other mortal on this Earth would know to be the language of reality itself tearing apart. This woman, whose beauty was inconceivable, had a laugh that could be described exactly the same way, only with the exact opposite meaning. It was an inhuman wail born deep within the black sea of infinity come here to taste our ears, and know us from the inside. Somewhere, miles Westward past the reach of the mountains and at that very moment, a lone coyote would begin to sprint for no perceivable reason, and would make it about twelve yards before its brain burst within its own skull.

The spell was broken then and there for the young Max Martin and Guinevere Quilway, who proceeded to awkwardly make their way to the Aversion Bureau's secret elevator hiding in plain sight right behind her. They made sure that everyone around was looking elsewhere, and climbed past entirely decorative warning signs and bumble-bee coloured tape meant to keep muggles away. As the doors were closing and as the final small, wailing spirits escaped from the once-deafeningly beautiful receptionist's cursed lungs – as if to *add* to the feeling of corporeal dread that Max was currently experiencing, he got a good look at the janitor again. Smith had this funny way of walking, he now noticed; the man waddled mechanically and childishly, like a robot that just wasn't quite there yet. *Just like a robot,*

Max thought, coldly. He shook that notion away and finished the elevator ride reevaluating his idea of the limits of Earthly sound.

Gwen and her older compatriot arrived on the twenty-third floor of this building with all the secrets, making their way straight for the boot room, which was the only room of note here. Floor twenty-three was especially unremarkable and in that way it was actually *more* like most of the other floors of the Aversion Bureau than the interesting ones were. On average, most of the floors here experienced an overpopulation of rooms and hallways leading to empty places that waited for expensive equipment that lived only near the bottom of long lists. Bilge had invested most of the money spent building the building, on building the building, and there was such an abundance of space here that even the man who created it tended to forget exactly what was on what floor and when – everyone else was very supportive of that fact and did what they could to pretend things weren't actually moving around every other week.

The boot room really was the only thing on this floor worth seeing. That, and a rather comprehensive collection of garbage bins from back when Bilge was still balancing the cost and style of such a decision. It had taken him two weeks to settle on something cylindrical and made of mesh.

Max had a fairly good idea of why they were meeting here, and wasn't overly fond of it. There was only one purpose for a boot room, and that was going outside.

"Agent Martin! Gwen! Good morning," greeted a sharp-looking and clearly-much-better-feeling Agent Stone.

Stone came up and patted Max on the shoulder, while also sincerely delivering the other half of a hug that Gwen was attempting to give her. None of this seemed right at all. *She must be buttering me up,* Max imagined bitterly.

"Glad you changed your mind from what you said over the phone last night, Agent." Stone addressed him somewhat mockingly.

"Yeah," said Max, "well I imagined you lying there in the infirmary and I just couldn't miss work after you hung up without saying anything," he finished.

"Yes, well, that wasn't on purpose I was just busy. . . preparing," Stone said.

"Preparing for?" Max asked.

"To leave, bro! We're goin' to the woods!" Dick Davison finished putting his shirt back on, over a stab-proof vest and above his trusty fanny pack, both sensible *and* stylish – the kind of fanny pack that one does not insult without finding a fight inside. Davison tightened a shoulder-slung holster on top of all that.

A beautifully ornate silver breech-loaded shotgun swung in the holster. It bore enameled roses and the wear of frequent use. Max gave his partner a questioning look of betrayal, realizing that he too had chosen not to skip work like they had planned last night at the club. Dick silently offered his hands towards Agent Stone in answer. He had apparently worried about her too, also for nothing. Stone didn't look any more shaken up than the diet pop that made his sleeve wet over lunch two days ago. *Is she on something?* he wondered.

The stern and small blonde agent was wearing a holster filled with her favourite Uzi and a sheath filled with her favourite sword. She had a backpack loaded with supplies as well, so did Davison. She handed Max his own holster with a familiar looking Glock 19 inside, obviously taken from his lockup in preparation. This was definitely happening. Max buckled up his holster and found a jacket that fit him on the wall that was lined with ones to his taste. It was dark brown and warm, much like a bear, he couldn't help but think.

"Oh, yeah, almost forgot bro, I need one more thing before we're ready to go," Dick said to him.

Max waited, annoyed.

"Hand me your phone, man," the big agent asked.

"No. Why?"

"Well I'm looking for a picture, 'cause apparently your mom and I are a thing and I kind of want to know what I'm getting into!" Dick Davison lost his wavering stone face at that, and howled with laughter, taking a small square of folded pink paper out of his pocket and waving it around whilst keeping well ahead of the very angry smaller agent who had begun chasing him to retrieve it.

"What is that? What are you talking about!" barked Max as he chased Dick around the room lined with boots and coats and scarves of various thicknesses. Gwen piped up from the doorway:

"Oh! I forgot to tell you Max, the first issue of my office-wide Dream Journalism newsletter is out! You're the feature, as we discussed."

Max stopped dead, little cogs in his mind whirring to remember what he told her. His heart sank.

"Oh, right, that dream I. . . told you about," said Max quietly.

"I don't really like the part where you shoot me dead, but I also understand how it fits into the narrative," Dick admitted, stifling another laugh.

Max pointed sternly at Davison, about to say something, but realized he really didn't have any ammunition to defend himself without admitting what his actual dreams were like. Seeing as how they dealt with a problem that used to plague the whole of the Bureau, it seemed best to keep quiet until those were sorted out.

"You're next, remember, Davison," warned Gwen, as she dipped out of the room.

Dick stopped short of launching another volley of mother jokes when he heard that. Max didn't smile though, as all of Davison's dreams for the next little while were likely to be about his mom too, just to spite him.

"If you're all finished talking about Agent Martin's mother's sexual conquests," Stone said it plainly, but Max just knew she was taking a crack at him, "then I think we should talk about the plan."

She got in front of them.

"We'll be doing exactly what I was doing yesterday, hiking to the rendezvous with Agent Fisher and investigating her report of strange activity to our North, except that no illusionary spectral bear is going to stand in our way this time." Stone delivered the plan triumphantly, standing up to her full height, which wasn't much.

"Not against all of us, and certainly not against me," she added, fixing her sleeve.

"So you're not worried about running into that thing again?" Max really wished she was.

"What I came across yesterday was simple trickery. I can see beyond that now, and it will not happen again. Whatever it was that really found me there in the woods, well. . . I still carry a sword," she finished her packing and headed into the hall.

Davison walked up and put a hand on his friend's shoulder.

"We'll be fine, buddy, between the three of us and whatever cool crap Andersen is gonna give us, there's nothing we can't beat."

Dick spoke very reassuringly, and Max almost believed him, but couldn't help thinking about the fact that they still really didn't know what they were looking for out there, and the fact that he probably could have stayed home today. He headed out of the door and Max just hung around, mentally preparing himself for the journey ahead. He did not feel even half as confident as Stone had looked.

During a brief and largely improvised deep breathing exercise, out of the corner of his eye, Max noticed small movement. He inspected it further and saw that it came from a mouse. There was a small grey mouse in the corner of the room, flat on its back amongst a pile of fallen coats, impaled and bleeding a sickly purple made from blue ink and red, red blood. Sticking out of the chest of the little mouse who scarcely drew breath was the bottom three fifths of the ink canister from a pen. It could have come from any pen in the world – or in the Bureau. It had been crudely feathered on the back end with what appeared to be shredded sticky note paper, and the whole scene was the perfect picture of a non-accident. Max took pity on the dying creature and moved to pull the shaft of the ballpoint bolt out of him, but the little mouse raised a tiny pink paw to stay his hand. The mouse had made its peace. The mouse knew the price of wearing the colours it did – which took the form of an itty-bitty red scarf – on this floor. Max covered the fading warrior loosely with an old tissue from his pocket and walked away.

Dick Davison had poked his head back into the room to check for Max, and saw the despondent look upon his face. Looking past him, Dick saw what caused it.

"Way back around when I first got hired, Wade had a section of his lab *full* of mice. He taught them a lot of things, but they learned even more after escaping," Dick looked faraway, "they lead extremely complicated lives now. It's best not to get involved," he waxed sagely for a moment, and motioned for Max to forget about it and join him.

In the hall the three agents ran into three more. Bilge was waiting for them by the elevator, flanked by the large Scandinavian scientist Wade Andersen and the stylish little Guinevere who was also the newly resident Dream Journalist slash Occult Studies expert –

apparently. Each of them held an object. Bilge ate his object, as his object was a biscuit.

"Oh boy, gadgets!" giggled the giant Agent Davison, looking at Wade, "What is it?"

"Rope," informed Wade Andersen, who held a twenty-or-so foot coil of thoroughly ordinary rope.

Dick grabbed for it and examined it closely, cooing along the length of it, registering no disappointment perhaps out of a personal inability to comprehend things he possessed as less than extraordinary, perhaps out of a heretofore unannounced, deep and actualizing appreciation for rope.

"Multi-purpose. Budget conscious," Wade told them, in as few words as possible.

"Here," said Gwen, handing Agent Stone a soup can sized rough-hewed pewter statue of a standing bear.

"Look, I did *not* have enough time to research this bear magic thing fully, but I do have this small idol. It was found in the Himalayans, if that helps."

"Does it do anything?" asked Stone.

"If it does I haven't discovered it yet, but if it's significant to anyone at all, they're probably a bear. Or at least bear-like," Gwen explained, nodding her head towards Davison, now bored with the rope and beat-boxing loudly.

Stone looked at him too.

"Throw me the rope, I'll give you the idol?" she offered.

Davison happily agreed, immediately stowing it in his trusty belted sack next to a plastic bag of trusty emergency snacks, and zipping up the trusty zipper.

"Even if it just turns your fingers black, it's more magical than a naff bit of rope!" Gwen teased, looking towards the horizontally substantial Agent Andersen, nudging him. He only looked at her blankly and emotionlessly, the same way he looked at everything – not in a serial killer kind of way at all – then he looked back at the team.

"Frustrating," he said.

"Yeah, he's right, we really don't have much for you lot, we're going to have to continue our research while you're out in the field and call if we find any magical advice to help you with," Gwen assured them.

"Scientific advice," Wade corrected.

"What's that?" she said, to everyone, "I do believe this man-shaped appliance is achieving sentience! Heavens above, unplug him before he enslaves us!"

Wade's response was again unclubbable silence. Then it was:

"Frustrating."

Max looked around, then, to his empty hands.

"Anything for me?" he asked.

Bilge wiped at his mouth with the sleeve of a deep blue sweater featuring an orange fox and walrus chasing each other in an endless loop that Max looked at, hoping it was not as augural as Bilge's clothing often was – as he couldn't imagine a single version of that scenario in which one of his two favourite animals wouldn't end up dead.

"Well, I had a biscuit a minute ago but. . . time changes everything, I'm afraid," Bilge told him.

Max did remember something he meant to ask

though, perhaps the answer could be as good as a gadget:

"Bilge, I met a guy downstairs doing some mopping just now. He was really kind of weird, and he knew my name somehow. Do you know who that is?"

"Ah, yes! Smith, I do believe. Poor old bugger was away for a long time due to a work-related injury," Bilge pulled a little on his collar at that, "He fills the vending machines, waters the plants, mops the floors. . . and not just for the insurance downstairs either."

Max was slightly taken aback at that, the Bureau was an extremely well-kept secret. He knew that somebody had to clean the place but really, did it have to be that guy?

"I see that look, boy, but don't worry. Smith's a very simple man, and very good at keeping allegiances. He's only been back to work recently, so you should get to knowing him."

"Well alright I suppose, if you trust him. But how did he know my name?"

"Perhaps through reading about your mother's illicit relationship with Agent Davison! It's a ripping good yarn, that, and gaining popularity every hour as it works through the departments," Bilge laughed.

Max fumed, and Gwen looked slightly ashamed. Not terribly ashamed though, as the first issue of her Dream Journalism newsletter was being taken off of stacks for free – like hotcakes. Like *free* hotcakes. Can you imagine? Delicious.

"Good luck," wished Director Bilge.

"Luck will not become a factor," retorted Stone,

already pressing the elevator buttons, not looking up.

Outside where the bland sky hovered low, the three agents walked in a rake towards the start of the forest that surrounded the Bureau. There were no birds chirping, there were no rabbits rustling and there were no squirrels squirreling. The party had only just made their first steps beyond the outermost roots of the outermost trees when Agent Dick Davison, almost purely out of boredom, just to see what would happen, turned to the group and said flatly:

"Max is dating a cop."

Stone's ponytail ripped around behind her turning head as she locked eyes with a frantically *shushing* Agent Martin. Everything was in her face, and everything was clearly not okay with this development.

It was going to be a very long hike.

# 7

## BEAR IN MIND

*I know that he is coming. He will be here very soon, and there is nothing that I can do. If he does not come himself then I will surely be seeing the faces that we have made together, and by their loyal hands I will be retrieved.*

Brush and berry, root and stem made way for the large animal that came lumbering through them now, two-legged and hurrying awkwardly.

*I once imagined no two souls more cursed than ours, until there was time, until there was time to let the others feel what we had heard. I can remember what the spark felt like as it took hold in every different mind. Their first thoughts will never leave me.*

The powerful clawed feet of forest life's best attempt at an armoured-up horse pounded back the way it had come, accidentally yet thoroughly destroying a cluster of clover which grew back over itself almost immediately, wilder and thicker than before sprouting ever leafier stalks – seriously devaluing the overall luck of the plants, sending the clover market spiraling into a deep and abiding recession.

*I have grown weary of wishing that events that once transpired had not. . . and my attempts to become separate from his enormity have only taken me from one insurmountable stone wall to another.*

A pair of solemn green eyes peeked up through the gaps in the coniferous canopy above, looking for the hundredth time now, upon the absolute top of the human mountain ahead, looking at where the girl once sat. There were foreign symbols, likely letters, on the mountain, and it was very uniform, like so little you can find in nature. It had thought about passing the mountain before, about going out into the open, but the mountain had too many eyes. Yes, this mountain had eyes around the bottom and again at the peak, ones that shone bright in the sun and looked out in every direction all at once. The humans seemed very skilled at mountain crafting.

*I could never fool so many watchers, and without the cover of my trees I would be found so easily, for I am not small.*

The bear looked down at its two front paws which, in its current bipedal configuration, acted as very big, un-opposable hands. A butterfly happened upon them at that very moment, landing impossibly softly on the tip of one great claw. The bear's huge round face watched it settle.

*Fluttering flowers. They are so peaceful and unknown to grand designs. In that I envy them. This tiny creature could never be taught what we were taught, it could never be told what we were told. Nobody would have even asked it to listen.*

The bear's thoughts turned to that of colour, and small things. It would think of petals and the play of dim blue light upon flowers under the moon. It would think of the slow way that green things crept. As it thought of these things, its concentration would waver, and the bear would lose its handle on the strict and vital focus so important for maintaining the radiant power that came from within it, unbidden and searching. The air around them began to vibrate in a small way, as if beaten by the wings of humming birds.

In time, the delicate butterfly with cream coloured wings veined in gold would begin to shudder and lurch, in the small way that it only could. As its thorax swelled and its wings became ragged and wide and like that of a terrible pike, extra legs would worm their way from beneath a thin carapace, caring little for their avenue of escape. One misshapen and wholly uncomprehending eye would meet the bear's two worried ones briefly before the entire wretched creature, now doubled in size, would burst into greenish smoke and pus.

Defeated and now indirectly responsible for the death of yet another beautiful thing, the large brown bear sat down heavily on the long forest grass, leaning against a sturdy tree whose bark gnarled and thickened in response to the touch.

*There must be no more lapse in my composure. I have to contain what is seeking every second to subvert me and have its way upon the world. It flows from me because of what I am. I am a conduit to something greater that is also responsible for me. I cannot afford to forget this.*

It thought of where it came from, and of the other bear who once was only an arm's reach away at all times, the one who found the scroll in the river. The bear who knew nothing before he knew everything. There is no mortal mind that can remain un-maddened by such learning.

*We cannot not see eye to eye, and our god has not seen fit to bless us with guidance for too long. He grows restless in His absence but I am so very tired of gods. I do not miss the voice.*

The tall grass and taller trees blew North in a freezing gale that was wet and heavy with an advancing ocean too small to see. The great brown beast laid down and placed two soft paws under its massive chin in meditation. Small flowers and blades of grass slowed their constant growing and winding around his legs as his breathing relaxed.

*Can I blame him for being what he is? Or he blame me for the choice I now make? He will find a way, sure as the voice is waiting to speak from inside of us again. Why did he share this with me? My old mind did not ever wish that it could worry and weep, or care for doomed things. It changed us, and now we are no longer the same.*

Two heavy eyelids began to close against a bracing chill. Clouds of condensation rose from a large black nose. Time passed.

*We had found His scroll, we had built His shrine in the earth. We had done exactly as He told us, and then He left our minds with no further instruction. . . just to wait. Within our first thirty moons voiceless under the shadow, we were visited by many of our own kind and many more from every branch of life with fur, feather, beak, and a mind to hear Him. Though His voice was gone from us, His call was irresistible as it spread under the leaves and over the streams, under the hills and over the trees. They could all hear it, and follow it, but until I laid my will upon them they could not understand it, and once they understood it they could think like we do, and know some of His power. That is what we decided was our purpose when the voice of our god left us, telling us only to wait. Though it was not a kind magic we worked upon them, time showed me this.*

*Now despite the absence of His voice from our minds, His power is still apparent. Where the other one sits, in the shadow of the mountain, at the mouth of the cave it had us dig, all of nature grows unnaturally wild. And in turn, all nature's greater creatures have been drawn, in ones and twos and more they have come. Birds, bears, and mammals of all sizes have made their pilgrimage to our mountain, wishing to know the source of the call they hear. It was from them that we built our family, we begot the clan of Twobears, and began to leave our mark on time. However, elevating them became less and less successful with every friend we found, and I will not attempt it again.*

A single blue blossom brushed against the mass of brown fur, and stayed there to hide from the wind.

*The influence of Him has grown almost to the feet of the humans, and they will surely be involving themselves soon. How could they not have noticed already? All but a few of the creatures of this Southern wood have long since travelled North to know the Call. Our god forsakes us yet still draws our brethren and smaller allies to the mountain, and I wonder why.*

*When the girl came I tried to stop her, but the girl was not deterred even when I showed him to her, even though I was sure she would be. She has an unusual resolve, and her green eyes reminded me of someone else's, but she does not realize what is waiting. I tried to show her.*

Faraway sounds perked up two big trowel-sized ears on the top of a furry head. Pounding footsteps from heavy bodies running on four legs. *Of course,* the bear thought, *send the new ones just in the event I defend myself.* The bear stood up to its full height, and made ready.

*But I will not harm a single other animal, not any more than I already have by sharing the Gift. These beasts are only slightly more than they ever were, and it only causes them anguish. I will not be returning to that mountain, not as long as I wield an outwards power that can convince and change.*

Just then new, lighter, and all around faster footsteps were heard, patting and rushing towards the quiet bear with ever more urgency. He stopped and waited to see what they belonged to. Not his bear cousins, that was for certain.

A small, scared, and thin white rabbit in desperate allegorical need of a timepiece burst from the underbrush and stopped before the bear, breathing the sharp breaths that adrenaline loves. It paused and looked sideways at all the possible routes of escape.

There was something different about it, the bear noticed.

*Its ears are that of a fish's arms. They are flat and wide and scaled. This small cursed thing can no longer hear, I can see that much.*

The bear reached out and plucked the rabbit from where it sat. Oddly calm in its arms, it did not try to escape. The concerned bear inspected this rabbit that was so different from how it should have been.

*What foul source could have caused this? I know of only one magick in this forest and there is no reason why a rabbit should grow so un-rabbit-like through Him. Otherwise, I do not know.*

There were yet more footsteps, a third source now closer than the others. The pounding kind, not thundering, and not the pattering of rabbit feet either. The deaf, fin-eared rabbit did not hear him approach, but the bear did.

A large, bronze skinned human in a tight yellow workout shirt carrying gun and backpack, ducking low through the high bushes with his arms outstretched – plowed his way through a tangled shrub and grabbed at his best guess of the rabbit's current location triumphantly and with a big, quickly fading smile. He then noticed that the space he hoped to find occupied by one small rabbit, was instead occupied by two large, claw-toed, hairy feet. The man raised up to his full height and jumped back in surprise. There was a significant disparity between the topmost reaches of their two heads. The man tried to yell, but found himself silent and unable to move. His hand frozen inches from the handle of his ornate silver shotgun.

*This man carries a weapon, and he pursues my smallest friends. I can see that he must be a hunter. I believe that he should be dealt with.*

Beads of terrified sweat broke on the brow of the frozen man. He would have appeared to a coincidental onlooker to be playing the part of a human statue being restrained in no other way than by his own volition, or perhaps, one that had been forced upon him.

*This small creature has not yet been called to the mountain, and that is of no consequence, but this rather large one. . . he might go.*

Crashing and stomping footsteps coming down from the North-East generated by eight padded, tree trunk legs were getting louder and louder, less and less far away. They would have found his scent by now.

*Those young guards are going to need something to bring back to my brother, and it cannot be me. I cannot return to that mountain and become a tool for the changes that run opposite to all that I am.*

"I am so sorry," said the great brown bear to the frightened mind behind the scared eyes of the tall human.

# 8

## THE WHO AND WHERE

"I cannot *believe* that friggin' idiot," barked Stone, rushing off of their intend path to find what should have been quite easy to spot – a six and a half foot rabbit-chasing buffoon in a bright yellow shirt.

The group of stalwart adventurers had only made it roughly thirty-five minutes into their four hour hike before they had lost him. Someone back at the Bureau was poised to make a little money.

"Well I definitely don't blame him for wanting to get away from you! You're just this unending fountain of. . . of. . ." Max called back at her, whilst digging through especially tall tufts of weeds that could not possibly have hidden the infamous Dick Davison, all the while hoping against hope – and spatial reasoning.

The only thing he had spotted, almost unnoticeable on a low leaf, were two rather un-ladylike bugs doing that thing you're never actually sure if insects do or not, that procreatory mamba, specifically.

Stone stopped up ahead and spun on him.

"Grief?" she offered impatiently to complete his trailing sentence, pulling a twig from her collar.

"Yeah, grief! Grief and bring-downs and. . ." he stopped again, searching for a word on this particularly non-literary day he was having.

The grief-causer grumbled and ran down the same mildly worn path she had taken yesterday. Around here somewhere *had* to be evidence of where Davison flashed away from them going after that stupid rabbit and into the dense brush ahead. This was not the first time Dick had run off like this – he was well known to chase fast moving things simply for sport and exercise. It was never a matter of hunting them, he just enjoyed the challenge. Today's departure from the plan was not also a departure from the norm. Perhaps she could have avoided this situation by simply killing the rabbit, or Davison, whichever would have delayed them less. Unfortunately for her, Max had this infernal insistence to keep arguing against her position on a matter that had been brought up not too long ago, the matter of his thoughtless decision to fraternize with law enforcement in his personal time. He finally caught up to her, panting like a very ordinary man dipping his foot into an extraordinary situation.

"You didn't," he caught a little breath, "wait," a little more, "for my word!"

"For the love of—

"SCORN. Good woman," Max gestured with a flourish as proud as he was himself, over his vocabulary.

"You have such *scorn* for me. Always. Never letting me enjoy even a moment of pride without reminding me how small I am next to you," Max was firing his battery dry this time, before she ran off again.

She was still searching, only half-listening to him.

"Eh? You know it's true, so what's your problem?"

The last of his missiles puffed out its chamber and fell a little short of the others, outing its French manufacturing. Stone took a breath and summoned a little energy into her chakras, or some equivocally dumb hippy garbage like whatever Bilge had taught her that one time. It didn't work, she had to bite.

"First problem: right now, you aren't looking for Dick! You're too busy defending yourself in a conversation that ended as soon as it began! Shut up and just help me find Dick," she said.

"Second problem: You can't date a cop! Are you insane?" Stone tore off again after noticing a trail of Dick-shaped footprints near a cluster of purplish flowers somewhat muted by the grey light of the sky.

Max trotted along behind her, adamantly blasting life-giving volts into the corpse of this conversation. It twitched.

"What, only because we're secret agents? I'm not suddenly going to just start sharing confidential things with her! She's never going to figure it out!" he promised.

"Can you just—

"I am the Fort Knox of secrets except that one time—

"Please just focus—

"I mean she was like a succubus or something I—

"CAN YOU PLEASE JUST FOCUS ON DICK?"

Stone was forced to interrupt him by way of shouting, something she did not like to do. Max was quiet for a few moments, just letting the sentence sink in.

"Sometimes," he said blankly, "I think we should probably just call him Richard."

However, they couldn't, because Dick Davison's full name was, unfortunately, Dickson Davison, with no reference to a Richard of any kind – also featuring a middle name so dreadfully embarrassing that it could be, and was, often weaponized. There had been talks of sending Davison to the courthouse one day with fifty dollars and a mission to change his first name to something that wouldn't make roll call so uncomfortable, but he seemed so proud of it, they couldn't take it away from him. Sometimes they wouldn't even have to say the name out loud whilst talking about him, and their minds would automatically insert it, making everyone sick of hearing about Dick before they even had.

"There," said Stone, pointing to a hedge-like line of bushes that stood back South a little, where they had come from, just to the side of the trail.

Max followed her, not wanting to shake the natural order of things up too much.

Past the bush, under a low tree and past another bush taller than both of them, they found a very small clearing. It was large enough a space to lawn bowl, but small enough to inconvenience the only six people in the world who might be interested. This little clearing was covered in patches of wanton flower growth: small, indistinct wildflowers ranging all the way to some tufts of striking poppies. A very random assortment to be sure, were it not so damned familiar to one of them.

When Max arrived behind her he saw the paw prints first, dozens of scattered and random marks in the ground made by very big feet. It looked to him like a struggle had occurred, except there wasn't blood, there wasn't a weapon, there wasn't even a scrap of clothing – there really wasn't dick all.

A chilly breeze whistled past them, blowing the carpets of growth and light strands of Stone's loosening ponytail away from her eyes. Now she could see.

"This is not a normal amount of bears," Max recited coldly.

He walked over and touched the old gnarled bark of a young tree absent mindedly. Stone watched the wind play with small life while he spoke some more:

"Well they took him. I guess that's a good sign, because it means he isn't dead. But I suppose that this also means whatever we're about to get tangled up in involves bears smart enough to take prisoners instead of just. . . mauling people."

Agent Stone made several more very careful steps into the open grass of the clearing. She was crouching on top of the paw prints now, focusing only on the plants, the weeds, the clover and the patches of flowers. They were so dully familiar and it was eating at the back of her mind like a hungry drill, trying to get up front.

"Now, I'm no. . ." Max began a quiet mental search, high and far, across fields of reaching thought and through psychological swamps entirely unknown to the profession of gardening – he returned with

"*Bearologist.*"

". . . But I definitely think that while it's fantastic that Dick didn't get mauled to death *yet*. . . that it's still not totally off the table. Don't you agree?" he looked at her.

She remained focused.

"He was here. The one I saw before," she explained to Max without looking at him.

Max reached immediately for his gun, remembering the story of the massive spectral bear well and not quite trusting Stone implicitly if that fight were to happen again.

"He's here still," she said.

"Dick?" asked Max.

"Bear," answered Stone, somewhat reminiscent of a coworker of theirs.

Max's throat tightened and his skin grew clammy with fear's hearty and particular brand of sweat. It was going to be a bad start to their adventure if that thing decided to pop up out of nowhere and tear them both to pieces. Even if it apparently wasn't real, Max didn't feel up to being *convinced* he was dying either.

The seemingly fearless though more likely crazed Natalie Stone walked out into the center of the clearing, to a certain spot that wasn't particularly clear. She knelt down beside a roughly seven-foot long and half as wide patch of flowers that raised in the middle like they had grown over a large bump in the earth. These were wide-faced, fat-petalled, bright pink flowers with large yellow centers, and not being a botanist as well as not being a bearologist, Max did not recognize them. They were the kinds of flowers a child might draw. Especially if he was in a rush to drink some apple juice or throw a ball – whatever it is kids do.

Agent Martin trained his nine-millimeter on the flower patch's center of mass, trusting nothing less in the world than this situation right here and now. Both surprising and unsurprising by comparison with the rest of his job at the Bureau, was what his co-agent decided to do next. She stroked the end of the flower patch near her, moving gradually upwards and over the hump, then resetting and making the same motion. Her hand, Max could see, was clearly not touching even the tips of the tallest flowers, and yet it still moved definitively over a shape that wasn't there. Beyond being physically impossible, the action of petting a thing of any description was not exactly in line with the other kinds of things he had ever seen her do. If Stone thought there was something there, in the invisible space between the petals and her hand, it seemed odd that she wouldn't simply run it through. She did this for a long time though, never even stopping to see if the flowers were enjoying it or not.

"*How?*" A soft sound, faintly echoing as it impressed itself on the inside of their minds, in the place where their own thoughts normally went.

Max shook his head and closed his eyes, but the voice was still in there, he could hear the faintest possible sound, implying that it might speak again, like when you see someone's open mouth and imagine the words they are about to say. It wasn't his own voice, it wasn't even his own thought, but it was in his mind anyway, and it was not inimical.

When Max opened his eyes again, the mound of earth that had grown so many flowers. . . hadn't, and, was not. Instead of petals and stems there was a coat of wiry brown hair and the distinct shape of a head near the ground. Two big bear paws hid the head, covering the eyes as well. The bear was a little boy preparing for hide-and-seek. Stone continued to stroke the head of the bear and what could have been its voice, spoke again:

"How could you see me?"

It wasn't his own thoughts that Max was hearing, but his own were very similar at the exact moment. The bear uncovered its eyes, likely having reached one-hundred, and immediately won the game. Stone stopped petting it, and Max relaxed his gun arm, because everything about the creature besides its size and rather bear-like appearance said that it was not the kind of thing that needed shooting.

"I saw your flowers," said Stone, "just like when you found me last time, that glade had a lot flowers just like these. They were familiar."

"The others could never see through that. What are you that is immune?" softly the voice came again, un-asking.

Max was already starting to get used to the bear speaking directly into his mind, as it was oddly calming. He felt like you could probably get away with selling CDs of this to yoga studios.

The little blonde agent stood up, towering in a small way over the laying bear.

"Now that I know what you did to me was all

imagined, I can see through your tricks. I know that nothing you weave is real," she said it with a hint of smile too, quite proud of herself.

Max was not confident about this. Stone was very metaphorically poking a very literal bear. He wasn't about to put his gun away just yet. The bear rose slowly, heavily, and looked quite odd standing on two legs. As it turns out, this particular bi-pedal bear was the perfect image of a healthy pear shape, as all the bulk and fur of it pooled near its stout legs and made the top half look almost comedically small, despite its impressive natural musculature.

The bear was nine feet tall at a minimum, and looked down at Agent Stone with now unhidden, entirely un-animal-like, piercing green eyes. It was an imposing physical form, yet there was still no air of violence around it, no contention in its expression – no anger whatsoever.

"You are dangerously sure," the bear said, mouth unmoving.

Stone stared up at him adamantly.

"What happened to our friend?" Max asked, finally lowering his weapon.

The bear looked over and Max lost his nerve slightly. It was a kind face, with light brown fur around its nose, and the projection of a mild demeanour, but it was still a bear. It was still a hill of muscle with teeth near the top, and for the love of all that was holy, this one was a legitimate sorcerer.

"Your friend. Was he the hunter?" the bear asked.

"He wasn't a hunter, he was just an idiot chasing a

rabbit," Stone corrected him, as the bear's voice entered their minds again – as many minds as were around to hear it – all at once.

"The cursed rabbit," said the bear.

"Sure whatever, I didn't really get a chance to talk to it." Max put away his pistol, back into his holster. He took a cautious step towards the bear and his partner.

"My cousins took him to the mountain."

"What? What mountain, and why?" asked Max, feeling renewed urgency.

Agents Martin and Stone both looked West instinctively. There, more than a day of walking away or a short drive instead, sat a massive and well-known mountain range heading both North and South for countless miles. It was surrounded at its base on this side by farmland and plains, not a dense forest at all, so that couldn't be true. It couldn't be those ones.

"No," spoke the bear, to their minds, "North of here, we have our own mountain, much like yours," the bear raised a big claw, pointing back to the general direction of the Bureau.

"It has no snow, and it has a shape like a wide, curved bear's tooth. It is where I was born."

"But *why* would they take him there?" pleaded Max.

"They thought I were flowers, and that your friend were I. They thought that because I made it appear that way to them. He will likely be killed when the glamour wears away, but there is little sorrow in my heart for hunters. I found him only because he pursued my small friend, and he had done so bearing weapons." the bear told them this and pointed a few feet from theirs, where a small white rabbit slept against a ticket of clover, its ears were scaly and tattered, they flicked and fanned as the little critter ran frantically through a world of dreams.

"No, you've got it wrong! He's just a man who loves animals so much that he would chase a rabbit through the woods just to try and pet it! That's who he is," explained Max, as he went to get a good look at the "cursed" rabbit.

"Yet he reached for his weapon when he saw me," mused the bear.

Max looked more closely at the odd texture of the rabbit's long ears, and when he saw that they were covered in protruding scales, and that they were twitching – twitching with a kind of endless, shifting growth – he shuddered at the mutant. Stone didn't seem to notice, but she held her arms behind her back in that way she often did when she needed to be stern, and got immediately to the confrontation.

"Davison was not a hunter! No more than myself or my partner here. We were prepared to defend ourselves against *you!*" She literally poked the bear now, her small finger disappearing into a huge furry belly, but it did not cause a reaction.

"Against me? Whatever for?"

Max turned back and made the perfect mummery of a menacing bear, arms held high and fingers splayed like daggers, baring his teeth and performing that hunching maneuver so reminiscent of bears and also Frenchmen who live in bell towers. Max growled with his largest inflection. The bear was taken aback and reflexively brought one large hand up to its mouth, looking worried. Perhaps Max should have pursued a career in acting, or perhaps this bear was actually a shrimp.

"Bigger though, and green," Stone added, in reference to the one-act play.

"Ah yes, I remember now. That was not me," the bear corrected their implications.

It began to walk, or rather, began to waddle, as it took slow steps past them and found a clear spot where it could watch the Bureau again, through the leaves above.

"I'm sorry, what was that?" asked Agent Stone.

The bear stood impossibly still in a constantly blowing wind, a serene effigy in strange skin. It kept staring upwards.

"That was my brother. He sits under the shadow and sends his hands to find me. I showed him to you in hopes that you would know what you will find, and be discouraged."

"Quite the opposite," she said stubbornly.

"Will you let me past your mountain?" asked the bear silently, ignoring her.

Agent Martin shared a look with his partner. Max made a silent, drawn out suggestion of refusal with his lips. Stone looked like she had an idea. Max looked like he didn't like that look, but it didn't look like it mattered.

"Why are you running?" Stone asked, while walking up to the massive bear and feigning a sincere interest.

"I will tell you more when you allow me to go unharmed, please—

"But we need your help *now*. The forest. . . it needs you too," Stone offered.

Hearing that sickly line of dialogue come out of her mouth made Max gag a little, but he caught her backwards look that suggested she needed help so he pointed suggestively at the sleeping rabbit with the disturbing fish ears, stomaching a strong shiver while he was at it. She nodded.

"What about the poor disgusting bunny?" Stone said, rather tactlessly, putting a hand up on the bear's shoulder and finding it was soft and oddly warm.

The bear looked around at it, it was resting fitfully and twitching severely now, appearing worse by the minute. The scales were encroaching around its eyes and those were changing too, becoming wet and bulging, very gradually. The bear waddle-stomped back towards it, shaking a large paw at the deepening grey sky and projecting his thoughts very loudly:

"This was not my work! We only brought the beasts like us to a level of greater understanding. I shared His magic with them so they may only benefit!"

Max saw an innocence in the bear, for more than the first time, and began to decide for himself that this problem of great mysterious evil was going to require his help. Especially if they were going to fix it, instead of just shoot at it until it went away – like was usually done. Nobody else would have even known where to start, and yet this brown furry behemoth knew exactly where to go. Stone was clearly submitting to the same notion and gave him a subversive wheeling arm motion, so he continued.

"Well then maybe. . . your brother has done something," said Max, who, despite currently trying to convince the bear to join them, was starting to get into the story himself.

If there was any one particular source currently responsible for a weird dark magic taking over the forest – and it likely *wasn't* this very kind and gentle seeming bear right here – then it was *very* likely his brother, whatever that guy looked like. It seemed that regardless of Stone's resistance to believe part-time agent Kayle Fisher's earlier communique, she had been bang-on about what was happening. Dark magic. Forest corrupted. Lots of bears. Come quickly. It couldn't have been said better. Well, maybe.

The tall, wide animal turned and walked back to Max, aiming himself towards the suffering rabbit.

"I fear, rather, he has failed to prevent something," came a thought.

The bear placed one heavy paw on the chest of the little animal who was now gasping frantically for air, its mouth, once possessing of a 'tiny-widdle' pink nose – as Dick Davison might have babbled – now had only slits for nostrils and moist, prolapsed lips that sucked in oxygen ineffectually. It shuddered violently as it suffocated there, under the shadow of a great bear.

Agent Stone, again acting rather more assertively than tactfully, stood ahead of the bear and spoke to him:

"Will you help us stop all this?"

The bear sighed, all within his shared thoughts, and

the recipients found that an entirely mental sigh is a strange thing indeed. A sigh impressed upon your mind is the air let out of an idea, it is the potential energy of a concept evaporating – it creates a moment of serene absence in the conscious. Max hoped that this bear knew what a pun was, and wasn't a very big fan, as he would have liked to hear more sighs.

"I will help you stop Him, if that is what you wish to do," they heard, in thoughts that were not theirs.

The bear stood up again, and put a hand on each of them, thinking at them rather sincerely.

"It is honourable that you would help me do this, I only want you to understand that it may mean all of our lives."

"Sure," said Agent Stone.

"We get that a lot, don't worry about it." Max buttoned his jacket against the gathering cold – they did, and he shouldn't.

"I have left my brother alone under the mountain and our god is surely punishing me for it. Ruining what I love. I will have to return to see this ended."

The bear began to dig a shallow grave below the tree where the rabbit's corpse lay. With three large scoops his massive paws had done it – the wretched scaly hare was placed inside, and covered again. Max heaved a little when he got a final look at its mutilated face.

The rabbit was horrifying, being part rabbit and part *anything else*, seemingly assembled at random with bits from the Creator's scrap drawer. It invoked the look of a cosmetic surgery disaster so grand in scope and malice that the entire profession would be wiped from the Earth in a compensatory purge. Stone looked disgusted, but didn't otherwise react.

"Alright so we're going after Dick then, let's do it." Max started off towards the hole that four-or-so capturing bears had previously made in the foliage across the clearing.

Stone coughed a little for his attention before he had even made it half way.

"Actually, we're going to meet with Agent Fisher, and continue with the plan," she said commandingly.

"But the bear thought it himself! When they realize that Dick isn't," Max pointed descriptively to the bear who then snapped out of a personal thought, "Him, they're going to eat Davison like oatmeal!"

"Oat. . . meal? That doesn't sound just right," thought the bear.

"As much as I disagree with her personality and general attitude, Agent Fisher is vital to our ability to strike the enemy effectively, especially in the absence of Agent Davison. The bears that captured him are still bears, regardless of magical capabilities." Stone did not budge.

"Besides, they think they've got their quarry, so now they won't be out in the forest searching. We can approach them where they sleep, unseen."

Max fumed, he couldn't believe she was letting Davison act as a distraction! The guy could handle himself, sure as the sun ruins posters, but this was a coven of *wizard bears* they were talking about, and that's a little too much for any one man. Even He-Man would probably bring a friend to that fight. Actually, He-Man had a lot of friends, a lot more than Max did, and he was also in way better shape. Actually, screw He-Man.

"I agree with the warrior," thought the bear, standing beside her, making her look small and rather un-warrior like in a painting of irony.

Max did not enjoy being immediately recognized as *not* the warrior of the pair. He understood it, but he did not like it.

"My cousins will never know his true face, only my brother will see through the magic I have placed on him. I believe he will be locked away, and Bill will only come to see 'me' when the god calls us again, so we will have time to catch them unaware," the bear explained, "which will be soon, I am sure, but it is also not *now*."

"Bill?" asked Max, characteristically focusing on the mundane, "you have human names? What for?"

Bill was not a very powerful sounding name for a magical king of bears, he figured, and yet he was about to hear one even less regal. He wondered if it might be 'Ted'.

"To tell each other apart. I am Leslie," said Leslie.

As usual, this didn't mean much to Agent Stone but Max found himself squinting through a sudden and wild desire to laugh. This was a laugh that tickled his lungs with a campfire lit in his gut, the kind of laugh that just comes upon you, completely ignorant to your otherwise well-polished and frequently maintained sense of self-preservation. He didn't get the chance to concede to the chuckle demons however, as Leslie finished his story:

"We took those names from the first men that ever

found our home, quite enjoying the sound of them."

"And the fate of those men?" asked Stone, belying a hunch.

"Bill consumed them. It is a tendency of his." Leslie said that with a kind of mental smile, remembering it like a child remembers make believe wars.

"Ah," replied the agent, who smirked at Max's colourless mug.

Agent Stone motioned for them to follow her, and the trio made their way back to the trail, regaining their North-Western bearing with a cold damp cloying at their backs, pushing them forward. The two agents walked briskly, wanting to spend as little time travelling as possible, as the great brown bear took wide, waddling strides beside them, completely unaware that the weather might be considered averse. Max was not pleased about the plan to let Dick hang out in bear prison while they got help from only one additional agent he had never met before, and he was not pleased about being ridden down in conversation like a fleeing conqueree, yet again.

However, if there was one positive thing for Max to focus on, he felt a little better with a member of the abnormal amount of bears they were supposed to find, working on *their* side. Having Leslie agree to join them was kind of like showing up to your first recess at a new school and immediately making friends with the freakishly large, quiet child who first terrified you, yet showed a genuine interest in your Gameboy as soon as you brought it out. Leslie was a silly name for such a large animal, but the perfect animal for such a silly situation.

"May I ask one thing of you, small. . ." began Leslie.

"Stone," said Stone.

"Stone. I enjoy that. It is an Earthen name," Leslie smiled.

You could tell when he was smiling, it was an energy that rode along with his thoughts as they found their way to yours. More thoughts came, as they walked together.

"You are not wroth with me for the battle that I set on you, and when you saw me hiding in the flowers, you knew it was me, yet you stroked my fur with your hand and not your blade. You possess an admiral focus," Leslie rested a massive paw awkwardly on her shoulder, "and forgiveness."

They continued their travelling, and Stone seemed to be giving her response some thought.

"It's none of that," she said, "it's that I no longer have any fear of you. Once I learned to perceive beyond your magic, you were nothing but a rug on the forest floor."

Stone reached her right arm over her shoulder and patted the bear's paw. She spoke in a comforting tone, though perhaps it was only comforting to her:

"Today, to save my partner, and to protect the world from harm. . . well, I happen to *need* a rug."

Leslie withdrew his olive branch, and his next thought was not a smiling one.

Winding, winding, and unsurprisingly still in a winding way went the hempen string around the tip of the roughly five-foot-five black ash recurving bow that belonged to the roughly six-foot-five warrior woman who kind of just wanted to go sit and have a smoke right now. She couldn't though, because it wasn't settling well with her that it had now been more than a full day since her old friends from the Bureau were supposed to arrive and check in with her about her email. The email about the bears. Not the email that should have been sent to her doctor instead. The satellite internet connection had been broken via superfluous home-brewed modifications since then, so there was really no way to correct that right now. Hopefully Wade was still licensed to write prescriptions.

In the time since she had first sent them that message, a few days back, the weird stuff hadn't stopped getting any weirder. A good example of this had been earlier the same day, roughly two hours ago, when someone had stolen Levi's laundry again. Nobody else lived in this forest for many hours in any direction – that they were aware of – nobody human and certainly nobody more in need of burgundy wizard's robes. . . yet it was probably the guy's own fault for hanging his wet clothing out around ground level instead of up from the branches of the tree home. He *insisted* that his way made them dry faster because the water didn't have as far to go when dripping down.

Kayle finished stringing her bow and decided she was going to have a smoke anyway. When rolling your own it's not like you can count it by packs, so she had inhaled somewhere between 'some' and 'enough' throughout the day, while she waited.

Outside, tearing silently away from their expansive grey carriers, errant and occasional pellets of rain were finding their way to the open crack of the old window in front of her – so she shut and latched it. She didn't pay to heat this place, yet as far as she could tell, neither did the 'wizard' who owned it. He was currently in the quadrant of the hut to the left of the door, designated the living room by virtue of its characteristic couch and the pre-deceased status of its occupants. Where normal homes have all of their living room furniture pointed towards an electric pane of glass capable of presenting all the information ever known across human history at the click of a button – though normally busy showing footage of naked people jumping fences to avoid the police with narcotics all the while dislodging from their most secret places – the tree home had no such electrical accoutrements.

The couch here was instead pointed squarely at something of the wizard's own invention. The "Literati Lounger" was a stout music stand attached to a six foot scissor extension arm with a very specifically focused old person's dish-sized magnifying glass on the end. This allowed a number of people equal to the number you were capable of tricking into coming over, to sit on the couch and take turns reading passages from a book placed on the stand. An ingenious invention and certainly one of the wizard's more altruistically intentioned crafts, it unfortunately still suffered from a similar affliction as the first generation of televisions in that the short straw and/or first born child would still have to get up and flip the page every so often. Levi the 'wizard' craftsman was an inventor ahead of the times that he mentally inhabited, which were almost seventy years behind the times that everyone else did.

Agent Kayle Fisher was nearing the end of her ability to stay – even for free – at a place where every object was actually an invention, always made from an amateurish combination of three distinct things, one of which was the object that you required at the time, taped or nailed or screwed into two other items that benefitted you not at all.

Kayle adjusted her worn CADPAT tank top and made her way across the small hut to retrieve her quiver of arrows that had the Aversion Bureau badge pinned into the side like a band sticker on a guitar case. She needed the arrows, but her tobacco pouch was also inside. Whilst digging around the deep quiver for that sweet, smoky brown stuff, something touched her hand, and unfortunately it wasn't something cool like a spider or a beetle, but a shred of paper.

Agent Fisher drew one of her long, dark, exquisitely hand-made arrows out of the twenty or so that occupied her quiver to find each and every one now had a neon-bright sticky note attached three-quarters of the way up the shaft, away from the fine goose feather fletching, with a miniscule golf pencil taped beside each one. She immediately knew exactly who had done this, and turned to the back of the man on the couch.

"This is gonna change how they fly," the tall woman chuckled.

"Yes," responded the middle-aged, prematurely silver-haired man on the couch, "but imagine the

174

messages you could send! Messages like. . . "

Levi the craftsman, the inventor, the 'wizard', struggled to come up with an example off the top of his head, which currently played host to an utterly cliché conical wizard's hat done in burgundy with crude white depictions of astrological symbols such as stars and crescent moons.

"BANG," he suggested.

Kayle Fisher laughed and began to roll another cigarette on the windowsill. She looked out, this window facing southwards, towards the general direction of the Bureau. The spitting skies transitioned to a light rain, and she saw that the trees to the South were beginning to darken and slump now, too.

"C'mon Stone, we haven't got all summer."

"What?" asked the wizard.

"Not you."


Fallen needles and rotting branches crunched beneath four shoes and two large paws. It was a rather silent walk, for a time.

"How far now?" asked Agent Martin.

"Around two hours," responded Agent Stone.

The ragtag group began to pass through another pristine clearing in the trees, somewhere where the acidic coniferous needles were only very light and allowed the grass to grow. In the gathering rain, however, and the lack of bright summer rays that had penetrated these same trees a mere day ago, it was not immediately recognized, and it wouldn't have been if Leslie hadn't stopped walking.

"Do you recall this place?" he asked.

Agent Stone reluctantly stopped her march and looked around, seeing nothing but grass and bushes becoming gradually more damp from the sky, fallen branches and patches of. . . flowers.

"Well? What of it?" she said accusationally, "it looks like the rest of the forest."

"This is where I found you yesterday," said Leslie, motioning around the glade.

Stone hopped-to immediately with a realization that slapped her like a salmon with a tendency to do that kind of thing. She began to rummage in the brush around the clearing, looking into the bushes heavy with small orange fruit and kicking over logs where she found them.

Max looked at Leslie, who looked at Max.

"Watch this," he thought.

Leslie the Bear crouched down beside a patch of bright pink flowers, very similar to those that Max had seen him hiding amongst when they found him. Leslie plucked one of them and tucked it behind his humongous left ear, it stuck there perfectly, pink and yellow-eyed and beaming, somehow immune to the biting wind. Leslie then smiled and pulled a small black bag from the dense bundle of flowers, holding it aloft.

When Stone noticed, she ceased her search and came stomping over, snatching the bag away angrily. She rooted through it and listed the contents:

"Satellite phone, bandages, empty trail mix and water. I thought these things had all been lost."

"I needed you to leave then, but I kept them for

you, just in the event that you were as stubborn as you seemed," said Leslie.

"Stole it, you mean," reprimanded Stone, who immediately emptied the items into her current bag and went back to the trail.

Max stood beside the bear with the flower behind his ear and gave a consolatory pat.

"I really believed that might cheer her up," thought the bear.

The two of them walked together out of the glade, back amongst the tall pines that grew darker in the mild rain. Max hadn't thought to bring a rain-particular jacket, or even a dollar store poncho, or anything really, in the rush that they had been in to depart this morning and so hoped out loud, in the jinxing kind of way, that it wouldn't get any worse than this.

"You know," Max said to Leslie, to while the time away, "maybe the only time I've ever seen her really and actually smile, was a couple months ago back at our, uh, *mountain*."

"What was the cause? I might like to try and recreate it."

"Well you see, our boss, this old guy named Bilge, he'd gone crazy and was holed up in his office—

Leslie looked confused.

". . . Holed up in his *lair*, at the top of the, uh, *mountain*. Well when we got up there and everything deteriorated into fighting. . . him and her, they were going at it with swords! It was kind of insane. They were really evenly matched though and nobody actually died which was nice, but she had this big smile on the whole time."

"Evenly matched with an old man?"

"Well he's a pretty strong guy. You'd be surprised."

"Perhaps he taught her," suggested the bear.

Max really hadn't thought about that, ever. He assumed Natalie was brought on simply because she kicked more ass than anybody, even Dick Davison – who could very well be kicking magical bear ass right now.

"Well, either way, I think she just enjoys violence."

"She did smile when she killed my brother."

The two of them watched her, way up ahead and coming upon a small wooden bridge with handrails and a severely swollen creek below it. Water rushed inches deep over the planks, and the undeterred Stone leapt onto one wide wooden handrail and tight-roped her way across with ease.

"I believe she simply enjoys success," mused Leslie.

Upon reaching the bridge, the bear simply waded through the current, hardly noticing it, and Max decided he wasn't agile enough to take any other approach. He mentally prepared himself for the miserable sensation of having wet feet and clomped across the bridge holding the railing, which came up to his waist, as tightly as an old woman holds the arm of a good Samaritan in order to be fully prepared to unexpectedly toss him in front of oncoming traffic if need be. Leslie's continuing thoughts could be heard from up ahead:

"Failure is kind, in that it teaches us much. Success only borrows from us."

Max was fairly sure that if failure was a teacher,

he'd easily experienced enough shitty circumstance to receive his doctorate by now. Perhaps, after seeing how this whole forest adventure went, he'd finally have enough field research to piece together his thesis: 'Near-death experiences build character'. He was the third and final party member to cross the yet-unchallenging causeway, which firmly cemented his position as the most likely to see it go wrong.

Now comfortably half way across the flooded wooden bridge that spanned the small bloated creek, dramatic irony's vainglorious conductor raised her baleful baton in a familiar flourish – that battered little creature whose withered scalp barely came above the podium of happenstance wielded timing as mean as its sinister design. Max Martin only saw what was about to strike him with enough moments in-between to form the shape of a favourite expletive before his lungs were knocked wall-to-wall with massive fish.

Max *slammed* against the opposite railing and leaned, sucking in air desperately, socks now completely soaked. A grotesquely large salmon collapsed against the planks of the bridge and looked up at the man that had been the victim of its errant leaping. With a single, ugly, unblinking eye it seemed to say "I'm not even sorry" as it wriggled its disgusting fleshy body under the railing and back to the icy waters it travelled. Max saw that Leslie had witnessed the entire thing, and was currently having some kind of reaction to it, though Max had no idea what it was through the blind spots in his vision. His lungs unpeeled like a reusable zipper bag that used to hold fruit, and begin to do that thing they're supposed to do, once again.

"That! That was marvelous! Did you see that?" Leslie's thoughts were insultingly excited considering the winded agent's open mouth being only able to produce rasping whispers at the moment.

Agent Stone had already made her way back, after hearing the squealing bark Max had woofed out upon impact with whatever it was. She stepped onto the soggy bank and held out a hand to the agent, who silently accepted it and stumbled back to his feet on their side of the small river. Leslie was still marveling at what he had seen.

"That salmon! It was the largest salmon I have ever seen. This is surely a sign from our god that I have made the right decision in returning to the mountain. Perhaps my cousins and I will feast upon that very fish," the bear's excited thoughts were difficult to ignore.

Max stood up.

"A fish, eh?" asked the agent.

"It. . . almost. . . broke my ribs," panted Max, "you. . . didn't see it. . . massive."

And it *had* been a truly record-breaking salmon, travelling then down-stream, which seemed a little funny considering what they were known for. It had been heading North, in the same direction as the travelers.

"Can we just take like, a minute?" asked Max, resting all his weight on his drenched knees.

Stone removed her pack, found a length of gauze and held it up, awaiting instruction.

"Alright agent, where did the bad fish touch you?"

she asked.

Max pointed to the left half of his chest, over his heart, with a very specific finger. His long time co-agent and sometimes friend held the gauze against the space he indicated, then removed her hand. It fell flaccidly to the ground and became immediately filthy.

"Wow looks like you're good to go!" came her sardonic tones.

Agent Stone replaced her backpack and took off again, through the forest grey and cold and looming. Old thick trees and dense shrubbery lined the way.

"It was a fish, Agent Martin! Try to keep it together."

Max stretched out his back, regained his senses and started walking after her again. Leslie brought up the rear, thinking loudly of classic salmon recipes his kind passed down from generation to generation, such as 'Raw' and 'Splattered over a rock'.

He was beginning to run out of patience for Miss Stone already, and their trip had only just begun. It wasn't like any of this was new to him, she was always a hard ass, and always playing the tough love card with him, but ever since surviving the imaginary though vivid scenario of her own death and subsequently being told by Wade Andersen that she could harness her particular brand of stubborn bull-headedness to become immune to the illusions of magic – she been insufferable. He knew exactly why Wade had done this, and given her that candy he told her was a 'mental supplement', because a person like Stone operated as a storm of pure will and determination, and everyone at the Bureau knew what the notion of a legitimate defeat creeping into her subconscious could do. And coming from Andersen, one of the only people in the world she actually respected, she might just believe it. Max didn't buy that it was a necessarily sane approach, because they had all encountered magic-wielding opponents in the field before, and even if what this particular one could summon was only illusory, she seemed to be ignoring the fact that magic can often still be quite real. That salmon, for instance, Max did *not* believe to be naturally occurring. It had to have been at *least* eighty pounds and he had felt his ribs were in very legitimate danger of breaking under the force of that magic-borne professional kick boxing truck in the shape of a fish.

Stone, when drunk on her own confidence, did not stop to think about anyone else for any reason. She occupied her thoughts focusing only on her own performance, and therein becoming so spectacular that it would bring the rest of them along in a draught. She could be an excellent leader, on the days she turned down the intensity dial from eleven – however this did not look to end up a low-intensity situation, and so this was Spinal Tap. Max had great respect for the woman, but sometimes she could just, she could just be such. . . *such a. . .* he didn't want to say it.

"Biiiiiiiiiiiiiiiiiiiiiitch."

Everyone heard it. Stone stopped and looked at Max with a disdainful glare that had a lot of pent-up kicking behind it. Max looked around, wondering who was reading his mind out loud – he stared at his giant furry friend, but didn't find the answer he was looking for. All the colour in Leslie's face had sunk down to the salmon processing plant in his torso.

"Wusssss," hissed the new voice, which they had now all realized was a thought being projected at them from afar, and it seemed to have a direction somehow – a presence.

All three heads managed to catch a glimpse of the creature before it bolted off deep into the woods again.

"What the hell? I think I just saw a deer. Was that deer swearing at us?" Max looked to Leslie.

"You'd better hope so," added Stone, who adjusted her holster and sheath for optimal readiness.

"Come, come now, we'd better keep moving. In what *exact* direction must we go to reach your friend? Show me." Leslie's thoughts had a distinctly worried tone, warbling a little like a ghost sounds always.

Agent Stone looked a small bit concerned along with the bear, but no more than a little.

"Down the trail another five kilometres then we have to go North-West into the bush for another four, why?"

Leslie quickly waddle-walked to the head of the party and motioned for them to hurry, which they did.

"I'll tell you everything but we must continue."

"Wusss. Wusssssssss." Very small and faraway voices like taunting teenagers hit them again, but they couldn't see the source.

The party quickened their pace.

"When Bill and I were first left by our god, we began to share our gift with the other creatures that found us. Bears primarily, but there were times when we would. . . *experiment*," explained the hurrying hairy one.

Max felt a little bit of unease bubbling up under the salmon bruise.

"There were three deer amongst us, Bill wanted to devour them, but I wished them unharmed, so I sent them away. A great deal of time passed, wherein I gave the gift to many of the animals that came to see us."

"That seems wildly irresponsible!" said Stone.

"We were building our clan, our family, I should wonder if yours would be naught but a pile of knives, little warrior."

"So what, like cougars and wolves?" asked Max nervously, who liked the thought of an evil, magical cougar even less than a bear. Max couldn't even get along with housecats, let alone something so fearsome you name a sports team after it.

"No, never. We never raised a single other large predator, as it seemed like it would cause contention," said Leslie, "yet every time I gave the beasts my magic their enlightening became less and less successful. The process outright killed anything smaller than a beaver, and by the final time Bill forced my hand, those new bears could hardly remember their own names. They would cast spells at random and explode with small magical potential they couldn't control. Their speech was slow and unintelligent. They seemed worse than when they were simple beasts, and then, save me, those poor deer returned. . ."

"Whoa, whoa, whoa," Stone halted, "these are just *deer?*"

"Simply deer. I could only desire such a fate for

them. They returned to the mountain after I sent them away, for the call of our God is strong. I raised each of them with the Gift just so they would be intelligent enough to know to leave. When I saw what they became, I myself fled before you found me. They are wretched things now, they are capable of no learning, or understanding, they only squawk their evil thoughts at you and your mind interprets them as it will." Leslie recalled it all for them, still trying to hurry through the forest, crushing old roots and weeds along the path.

"Weak!"

"Small!"

"Churlish!" came the sharp thoughts of the two bucks and one doe, all from three distinct places in the dim woods now, all around them, all slightly different sounding.

Max knew those ones were for Stone, and yet, despite her relatively thick skin, it was more about the delivery than the message and she looked appropriately annoyed. The deer, of which it appeared there were at least three, sounded like how you'd imagine bird thoughts to sound: quick and chirping and always trying to crap on you and things you love.

"They are dread. They are woe taken form!" preached the frightened bear with warbling thoughts.

"So they're not just deer? What are they?" Max asked, getting more and more nervous with all the pageantry.

Just then a bounding blur came bursting from the grey-green shrubbery surrounding their trail. It landed behind Agent Martin almost silently and leaned in so close he could feel the breath on his neck, it felt like laughing breath.

"Dumb haiiirrrr," it thought in a whisper, and leapt cleanly into the woods again.

Max jumped out of his skin and spun around to face his accuser, hand on his sidearm, dumb hair whipping in the wind, dumb strands getting in his mouth. But the jerk had already fled.

"They're *bullies*," an entirely comfortless bear's voice arrive in their minds, next to the echoes of the juvenile insults.

"Fly! Fly like summer wind!" Leslie took off down the trail in the direction Stone had shown him, running on all thunderous fours now in an attempt to break free of the limitations his bi-pedal waddling imposed on him, and away from the penetrating jeers.

"Don't let them upset you!" came his far thoughts.

It seemed a bit like an over-reaction. Being insulted by a deer – of all things – was certainly annoying, but not exactly life threatening. Max looked at Stone, who looked at Max, and they both shrugged – but not at the same time, in order to prevent anyone owing anyone a can of pop. There was no reason *not* to run, really, as they had places to be. The pair took off after their tremendously hairy trailblazer, having a hard time keeping up, and having a hard time hearing their own dumb asses.

*Thoughts*. Hearing their own thoughts.

A self-conscious eternity passed and the insults came on ceaselessly with little flashes of movement to their sides all the while, little bits of deer that they could see bounding along with them between the trees and tirelessly flinging lewd appraisals of the way they were running. They were sprinting in waves, taking only short periods of walking to recuperate, but the insults were constant, and it was driving them all completely loony.

"Friendless tryhaaaard," went the forest.

"Flooower loooving sisssssyyy," rang the wind.

"Likely viiiirgin," said the third jackass deer.

It was endless.

Another tantara of slurs and indignities announced the party's arrival in the deep woods as they turned from the trail and moved amongst the trees. There, a while longer, after one final bought of jeers, Agent Stone couldn't take it anymore.

"Daddy's girrrrlll," wound one final mocking call, weaseling its way through the wet leaves – softly on the wind with the cold rain it came, just for her.

Natalie stopped dead, *ripped* the loaded Uzi from her hip holster, and tore into the forest all around with the deafening buzz of a million steel hornets all clamouring to escape its barrel. Max and Leslie hit the wet ground hard and stayed there. Max looked happier to have this eardrums bashed in by Stone's automatic than listen to another lazy insult from the trio of psychotic sub-sentient four-legged troglodytes that had hounded them for the last hour and a half – and smiled serenely. Leslie rolled over and played dead, in what was apparently a universal response to danger.

Agent Stone expended her entire magazine and ripped it out when it was empty, throwing it hard into the forest, hoping to bludgeon whatever she didn't gelatinize with copper hail. Everything, save for the treacherous creaks of a few thin trees collapsing, was perfectly silent. They could be dead, they could be dying, they could just be gone – any of those would be fine.

In the insanity of it all, someone had even called her a fizzle and gotten away with it. It was the first time, and would be the last.

The group stood up again, once someone had shaken Leslie out of his excellent acting and kept moving North-West. They were nearly at the coordinates Agent Fisher had provided her with in the original message. Something about a 'treehome'. Whether that was just like a treehouse or not, it didn't matter, both would have been fairly stupid, Natalie thought to herself.

Back to walking awkwardly on two legs now, Leslie the Bear apologized:

"The worst mistake I have ever made, those bullies."

Max gave the bear a pat, likely overcoming his own currently disabling feelings of self-doubt to do so. Stone didn't think his arms looked that skinny from here. Well, they did a little, but not like how the deer had put it.

"You couldn't have known that those deer would make such terrible people," said Max, he who would likely never shed another tear over Bambi's mother.

"The point was never to become as people, but only to become greater," emitted Leslie.

Max nodded and put his crazy skinny arms down.

Down below his dumb hair.

"I have been meaning to ask, why do you walk that way? It seems inefficient," asked Agent Stone.

She was curious, and desperate to fill the silence with anything other than the sensation of waiting for insults.

"Oh, well, it is sometimes uncomfortable," said Leslie as he stopped and took a long, large step to overcome a root that looped out of the ground like a super sweet track for toy cars, "but to me, it symbolizes how far we have come. None of the others do this, I have just spent a long time practising."

Leslie then tripped on a rock and fell face-first into the accumulating mud. It was like watching the statue of a dictator being pulled down by ropes, except that the statue was flailing its absurdly proportioned arms and mentally shouting "No" again and again, all the while.

When he finally righted himself, like a capsized ship with hands, he scraped mud from his fur with the utmost possible dignity. His pink ear-slotted flower was undisturbed though, that was the only thing Leslie seemed to worry over.

They all carried on whilst Natalie consulted the GPS device she had cleverly thought to bring this time, trying not to catch herself in the reflection of the screen because someone had recently told her she had baggy eyes and she was battling not to have to reconcile that with reality.

"Can you believe one of them called me salmon-bait? I mean, what, is that like a sexual thing?" said Max.

"Utter ghouls," declared Leslie, thinking loudly of

salmon again.

Upon getting the coordinates punched in, and allowing the 'You Are Here' to update, the agent noticed through possibly, kind-of baggy eyes, that they were right on top of it. The treehome, so-called, should be right ahead and inside of it, should be the agent they had come to see.

Without looking up, Stone spoke:

"Alright gentlemen we're looking for a 'treehome' which, I can only assume, is exactly like a treehouse only with a different name for no good God-damn reason."

"Could it kind of look like a house with stilts, sitting above a tree, instead of on top of it?" asked Max, coming across awfully specific.

"Sure, why the hell not," she responded.

She looked up.

"Found it," said Max.

There it was, too, just as he had described it. The trio came out of the dense trees, deciduous as well as pine, entering a modest clearing about the size of a lawn bowling game you could invite at least *twelve* people to before they all arrived, realized what was happening and went home to do literally anything else. In this clearing was a large oak tree around forty or even fifty feet high – quite impressive – with a rather do-it-yourself and unimpressive shack sitting above it, on absurdly tall stilts that seemed to have very carefully been built to support themselves only, with no help from the tree. It was a very libertarian kind of construct.

"Well, I guess that rickety looking shack is it?" asked Max.

Stone was looking at the long rope ladder coiled near the top, the thing they were going to have to climb, surely. It would have reached all the way down to the ground where there was a little wooden sign reading—

Leslie let out a physically silent, mental wail of horror, and Stone immediately noticed why. There, at the base of the tree was the carcass of one of the two bucks that made up the team of deer with the really bad attitudes. It made sense that this upset Leslie, seeing that these were his children, so to speak, seeing as how he was responsible for what little sentience they possessed in the first place. Sentience that they misused so grossly that it had almost made Agent Martin cry. He would never admit it, but Stone had seen his tears running away under cover of rain. She had heard them, taunting his close connection with salmon.

"Whoa, hey, Stone. . ." began Max.

"I see them," she said.

Surrounding the corpse, worrying at the flesh, were four of the ugliest dogs she had ever seen. Not dogs though, wolves. Yet. . . not wolves either, more like. . .

"*Squidwolves*," uttered Agent Martin, darkly.

"Don't say that as if it's a thing, Max."

Though even off in the distance, it was quite clear that they weren't simply wolves. One of them looked up from its meal, red jaws dripping, red jaw-based tentacles also dripping. The wolf's entire skull, save for its still distinctly wolf-like muzzle, had grown fleshy and porous and white, sporting the characteristic diamond crown of that very particular creature. One thick, dangling tentacle hung down from each side of its mouth and the eyes were bulging, glassy ovals. Ripples of soft, hairless flesh extended all down the back of the creature, and triangular cartilage fins struck out from its hind legs. It was a monster – but probably also a delicacy.

Stone turned to the horrorstruck bear:

"I thought you said that you never gave magic to other predators."

"This is an abomination. This is nothing that I have ever done." A deep worry rode along with Leslie's thoughts.

"I do not understand what is happening. The beasts that I gave the understanding of magic to. . . they have been immune to any such changes, just like the deer. I saw my cousins when they took your friend, they were also unchanged. Now though, with the rabbit and these wolves. . . I could not tell you."

"Well," said Agent Stone, who drew her katana and took a step forward to meet the soggy creature that motioned the same, still with a great distance between them, "let's start making guesses."

Max grabbed his pistol and flicked off the safety. He stood by Stone's side, in the middle of the clearing, waiting to see how close the squidwolf would dare to come. It was likely the alpha wolf – or perhaps alpha squid – who was menacing towards them, taking careful steps with its big paws on the wet grass, red tentacles swinging side to side, opal eyes glistening – because as soon as it had broken away from the meal, all three of the lesser wolves had fallen in formation in the style of a much worse kind of bully.

"The call of our god, His call, it seemed to cause the

trees and grass and small plants to grow wildly when we first discovered it. It called the mammals and they came. Perhaps the call has grown too strong and nature is becoming affected. We have to reach the mountain as soon as possible. My brother has let things become dire indeed."

The gathering rain ran down from Leslie's face and was lost in his soaking fur. He was just a simple creature, trying to fully understand how much wrong he had truly committed. Just a boy trying to understand what was so offensive about the prominent concentric circles he had drawn as part of his depiction of a woman – which were assuredly her eyes.

"If you do not mind, I don't much care for conflict so I'm going to keep to myself and look away. It helps calm me down," Leslie warned.

"Go ahead," said Max, who didn't realize that also entailed Leslie would begin to hum incredibly loudly like a child with fingers in their ears.

They were now beset on all sides by rain, squidwolves and a tragically tuneless arrangement of mental humming sounds that could have actually been dead-on recreations of classic ursine anthems – they would not have known the difference.

Stone readied her blade for the first enemy's pounce as rainwater made its tracks down the steel, soon to become red. One leap, that was the only moment she would need to end this foul thing. It was difficult to look at with its grotesque skin and eyes, it even had the outlines of further wriggling arms – likely the other eight a normal squid would have – running under the fur of its neck and chest, ready to burst out at any moment, it seemed. She had a long time to look while it edged left and right, baring its dripping fangs, looking for an opening.

The rabbit from earlier had come across rather reptilian to her, with the scales on its ears, or even fish-like maybe, and this horrible thing was clearly trying to become a squid of some variety. Whatever consequence Leslie didn't seem to be able predict about this magic that found him, was that it was causing all the life he hadn't shared his 'gift' with, to mutate horribly. The effects were so mismatched and haphazard that amongst the four wolves, none of them looked exactly the same, only squid-esque.

The source of this magic, whatever it was, seemed to just be taking every living thing around and smashing it together with something else randomly. It all seemed in line with a magic based within nature, she supposed, though the consequences were so horrific it made one wonder.

The alpha squidwolf emitted a low warning growl that sounded distractingly similar to gargling, and lunged for Agent Stone, who had her blade low and prepared for the perfect cut, when suddenly there was a new sound. Not rain, not discordant mental humming, not Max's weapon clattering as he shook nervously – none of those at all.

*THWAP*, it was.

A thin line blurred by motion *popped* through the top of the leaping squidwolf's skull, blowing through open jaws and burying itself halfway into the wet earth, inches from where the agents were standing. The dangerously artistic interpretation of Surf N' Turf fell out of the air whimper-less with a heavy thud, and slid up to Leslie's feet, creating a very loud divergence in the pattern of continued humming as the big bear frantically kicked at the disgusting corpse to make it go away – eyes still closed.

Simultaneously the three remaining squidwolves jumped back and, upon registering the death of their leader, began to violently vomit what could only have been ink and run backwards reflexively, heading for the safety of the woods. They moved no faster for their expulsions, despite what they may have personally believed – and the dark black trails they left certainly would make them easy to track. Not a great adaptation for land, all factors considered.

Agent Stone knelt down to inspect the arrow that had nearly clipped her toes – it had a small green note dyed in neon hues taped just below the feathers on the shaft:

'BANG', it read.

She looked up.

At the top of the treehome, standing on the tip of its modest porch, was a very lithe, smiley, tall woman holding an impressive bow with a quiver belted to her hip. She waved with both hands when they saw her, excitedly, and kicked down the rope ladder for them. It stopped just before the ground, and swayed in position.

*Show-off*, thought Natalie, a little bitterly.

# 9

# PAY NO ATTENTION
# TO THE MAN
# WEARING CURTAINS

It was a weird house. Well, it was really just one large room with loosely designated quadrants based on the house-borne *concept* of rooms, but then in that case it was *just* a weird room, which didn't quite do the weirdness justice. Max had a look around, and was finished within eight seconds.

The treehome had, in one corner, a double bed and a nightstand covered in an assortment of doodads and other small pieces of random things – there was also an area where a three-seated couch eroded by both asses and time faced what appeared to be a book on a music stand equipped with an extending magnifying glass for some reason. The low coffee table in that quarter was similarly covered in tiny bits of broken objects, only they were sorted into three piles this time. The back right-hand corner of the home contained a work bench and book shelf, both utterly enveloped in bric-a-brac, enough to get somebody placed on a reality television program against their will. Finally, in the far left corner, there was a sink that ran with collected rainwater and a modest stove that ran with burning logs and patience. Those appliances shared this small portion of the abode beside a man-sized stack of empty pizza boxes and enough take-out containers to destabilize the cardboard production industry for a full fiscal year. Also, in the very center of everything, there was a round dining room table known only to the observer for its telltale four legs, as it too, was otherwise hoodwinked by suffocating piles of crap. There were two windows on the North and South walls of the East facing home, currently closed against the pattering rain. There was a man sitting at the work bench, who turned to face them as they entered:

"Hello!" he said, "I'm so glad I thought to tidy up before you came!"

Kayle gave him a sarcastic tilt of her head, motioning towards every surface in the house at once, as none at all were clear of bits and/or bobs.

"Yes? Those are not garbage milady, you know this! They are vital components in the alchemy of design," said the man, who was dressed like a dime store wizard – not that true wizards were so common as to provide a frame of reference, but this one's robes had absolutely once been curtains, in another lifetime.

The agents Martin and Stone took seats around the dining table, facing the rest of the rooms all at once, simply because they were small enough to accommodate this. Kayle sat down on the bed, the bed that was so low she could now rest her chin on her knees if she felt like a nap. They all looked at each other, waiting for somebody else to take the lead.

"Well my name is Levi," said Levi, "and I'm a wizard."

Somehow, Max didn't quite believe that. His face must have said as much.

"It's more of an. . . *interpretive wizardry*," informed the woman who looked like a giant on the small bed, noticing his expression.

"I am a craftsman, and an inventor! I can create anything out of only three components. My magic is rooted in the practical world, because, well, obviously no true magic has ever existed. . . It's only ever been card tricks and magician's poetry," he said.

Stone nodded and gave him a thumbs-up for that. Max sighed.

"For instance, young man, your chair. It is made of three components as anything else. A back, a seat and some legs. This is all there needs to be," Levi instructed.

The 'wizard' was not extremely old, perhaps only in his forties, yet he possessed ghostly silver hair that hung down over his face and obscured his eyes, giving him at least a modicum of wizarding clout. It may have been dyed, as he seemed like the kind of person to do that. There was no beard on this man, however, and that was either just his signature look or a cruel genetic prank. He seemed nice, though.

"Alright. Agent Fisher would you be so kind as to join me in the kitchen while I wring my jacket out over the sink?" Agent Stone asked, getting up and walking to the other side of the dining table's tall stack of random parts that almost hid her completely. She left her backpack by the table.

Fisher slyly rolled her eyes at Max and got up, walking the whole ten feet to where Stone now was, in about two strides. This shack was so small that they really hadn't *gone* anywhere, but as they began to speak to one another in slightly lowered voices, Max felt like the quintessential husband left to socialize awkwardly in the company of a man that neither of them knew very well at all. There wasn't even a bottle of cheap beer to hide inside of. It was going to be quite a long couple of minutes indeed.

There was silence between them whilst the wizard fiddled with an eraser and the bowl of a pipe in his dry looking hands, but he eventually perked up and spoke:

"So would you like a drink, mister. . ."

"Max."

"Alright Max, are you at all interested in a pop?" asked Levi, with a strangely excited smile, as though he had been waiting his whole life for a moment when somebody might be sitting in his house, possessing of a dire thirst.

Max nodded hesitantly, and the wizard pointed behind him to the surface of the table, or at least to the extreme edge, where but a little surface still survived. There were two room temperature cans of lemon-lime soda sitting there, two cans with inch-long nails balanced point-down in the grooves of the tab, held in place by thick elastic bands that wound all the way around the cans vertically in the manner of a miniature pile driver. Max retrieved one just to marvel for a moment at the imagined logic that would lead such a thing to exist at all. With a wildly successful method of opening themselves already prebuilt into each and every can of pop ever produced, this invention Max held in his hand was the Manhattan Project of irrelevance.

"My personal creation, very handy for people who chew their nails off," said Levi, showing his own carven pink fingertips.

Max tossed the can to Dr. Oppenheimer's intellectual polar opposite across the room, who reached out to catch it, though perhaps with too much enthusiasm, and ended up only slapping it hard into the ground where a waiting nail plunged deep within the aluminum shell – as designed. The little can took off arced and hissing, soaring out of the open front door and into the woods never to be seen again, trailing a dazzling mist of aerosolized lymon.

"I'm good with water, actually," decided Max.

The wizard put the junk in his hands away on the work bench and pulled his chair a little closer, much to Max's growing uncomfortableness.

"Always hate to see a can go to waste. My grandmother used to say I liked sugar so much because of my 'insectuous' nature," he spoke conversationally.

Max nodded, trying not to make prolonged eye-contact.

"She always told me I was a product of insects."

"Ah," replied Max, finding something fascinating to look at in the watch-less region between his hand and the arm of his coat. When he looked up he realized that the wizard had scooted all the way across the floor and was sitting beside him now, bouncing his knee and leaning his smooth chin on his fist like someone who had only ever read an author's description of socialization, and perhaps read it from faraway sitting on a couch.

"Yeah I thought she was crazy too, but I think I actually might have inherited a bit of exoskeleton!" Levi lifted the arm of his robe, displaying to Max a patch of distinctly recognizable psoriasis.

"So. . ." Max leaned away a little, away from the diseased forearm, "what exactly do you do for a job, anyway, how did you afford this place?"

"Well, sometimes I invent things and sometimes I just make crafts. I sell this stuff online," he pointed to a laptop on the work bench, "but I don't have any electricity out here so I just occasionally hike into the city and use the library's computers."

"Ah," said Max, who had read the sign outside, at the base of the tree, which now made slightly more sense – though only slightly.

The modest wooden sign outside at ground level read, in big red letters – no word of a lie: THE WIZ PALACE. Without any other information at all, Max knew that there had to have been an 'H' in there somewhere, at some point.

"Found it in an establishment downtown once, and took it. I mean, it just *spoke* to me," said the wiz, gesturing with splayed fingers.

"Well uh, what did you do *before* this?" Max desperately probed for something normal to discuss with the man who was so far from normal that he would reach it faster if he just continued to walk away from it.

"I used to own a corner store."

"Yeah? What'd you sell?" Max asked.

The wizard looked at Max as one looks into the face of a fully-grown adult who's just asked them the speed at which the Earth rotates around the moon.

". . . *Corners*," he stated, factually.

Max opened his mouth to allow a little wheezing exasperation to escape, but said nothing. The wizard continued:

"Corners. Soft corners for protecting baby's heads, rubber corners to prevent the escape of cylindrical objects or the unwanted closing of doors." The wizard paused again.

Max inclined his head wishing to see the end of this particular rabbit hole in earnest.

"And paper corners, for when you cut the original ones off of an important piece of paper thinking it will look cooler but it really doesn't."

Max marveled at the fact that he never met such an honestly insane human being in his entire life before now. But when he thought about it, a *lot* more things possessed corners than your average person might actually realize in a standardized testing situation. If a thinking man were to tunnel his way out of the proverbial 'box' and tragically find his situation no better illuminated, who would be there to repair his corners? Perhaps this wizard was actually a genius.

"Corners. Of course," Max conceded to what he now saw was a reasonable, if niche, business model, "I'm going to go talk to the ladies now, just about confidential secret agent stuff, you know."

Levi nodded gravely and with possibly legitimate understanding, scooting his chair back to the work bench all the while seated, in an agonizingly slow process that assaulted the ears.

Kayle watched her little, blonde, former supervisor briskly drying her thick black jacket with a roll of paper towel that had a crude telescope built inside of it. You know, for when you need to see something far away but the lens keeps getting wet. It also had a stopwatch welded to the holding end because honestly Levi had just been having a really uncreative day and was too stubborn to break the arbitrary universal constant of three components that he had come up with long ago.

Stone stood there, talking about something important in the tight, white, efficient-looking exercise clothing that she always wore under the jacket that disguised her well-crafted figure. Miss Fisher was honestly a little too distracted by it for news about magic, bears, insults from deer, whatever it was she was talking about.

"So that's the situation," Stone finished, "we're travelling with a magical bear whose brother is likely causing or allowing all of this strange power to turn dark and affect the forest. After seeing what I've seen I believe it's our duty as agents of the Bureau to stop the rallying of a magically-imbued army of forest creatures from sweeping over everything."

"So I was right, eh?" confirmed Kayle, snapping back into things.

Stone grumbled and began to put her still-damp jacket back on.

"At a base level, yes. You correctly assessed the presence of a threat, congratulations."

"It's nice to see you again, too, kid," laughed the tall woman.

The little man with the big black hairdo walked over to them quietly with a look of desperation in his eyes. She didn't know this guy, but he looked new. She held out a strong hand to shake his.

"Hey man, nice to meet you. I'm Kayle," said the woman who could quite possibly knock even Dick Davison on his ass.

"Max Martin," said Max Martin, who tried to squeeze a little while shaking her hand to look strong, and ended up hurting himself against her rock-hard grip.

"You a new agent?" Kayle asked.

Max looked slightly offended. Kayle felt a little bad.

"I'm sorry it's just. . . *well*. . ." she gestured up and down at him with a morphing expression, ". . . I like your hair dude!"

Max smiled – that was probably enough. He looked back towards the wizard, shaking his head, and then back at her and asked, somewhat surreptitiously, but louder than he thought:

"You're not married to that guy are you?"

Kayle froze and began to swipe at her neck with her hands frantically. The wizard heard him, and spoke up:

"Hah! Why on Earth would they allow us to get married? We're a mixed-gender couple, and that kind of stuff flies *right* in the face of society's obsession with order and sameness, my friend! Can you imagine the backlash? A man *and* a woman? If only. . ."

Stone was opening her mouth to correct him when Agent Fisher placed her large hand over it. She gave them both a look that asked for utter silence, they gave it to her, and Kayle changed the subject immediately.

"So! We're headin' out to the mountain, huh? That's where all the messed up animals are coming from?" she said very loudly and soberly.

"Uh. . . well, yeah. One of the two bears that started it all wants to help us shut everything down, he's going to bring us there," Max offered.

Kayle didn't really take the part about a magical bear alliance seriously when Stone was talking – for some reason – but she now realized that they weren't kidding. She didn't want to let anything on, however, she who was never once distracted in her whole life, as far as they should know.

"Actually I know the place. Damn, I knew it didn't belong. When the weather isn't so bad you can see it from here, and it always seemed weird."

Kayle turned to pick up her pre-packed gear when a small, fluttering object bounced straight off of her forehead and took off in another direction. It was an invention of the wizard's that she had seen before, a hinged door bracket with an eyedropper full of water fixed along the center, continually pinched and dripping by the upwards motion of its 'wings'. It trailed a barely visible green ether as it awkwardly flapped its way around the room making everything slightly damp, extremely gradually. It had never flown before though, because such a thing was not only impossible, but extremely impossible – hilariously impossible – for Levi.

At the open door to the treehome, the wizard stood next to a bear, a bear who had to crouch to fit under the roof, pink petals of a decorative flower he wore brushing the ceiling.

"Leslie, how did you get in here? I thought you were outside burying the deer and that tentacle hound. The rope ladder could not have supported your weight," insisted Agent Stone.

The bear whose name was apparently, for some reason, Leslie, merely projected a mental smile and twinkled his upheld claws in answer – they sparked with a faint green energy. Kayle cleverly deduced that *this* was the magical bear. He was gargantuan, yet he was not at all imposing or distressing. Somehow you could feel that he was kind, and perhaps it was his freakishly bright green eyes that convinced you. Perhaps this was why she didn't shoot him immediately when she saw them all down there on the grass.

Agent Stone was still awaiting an answer, clearly not satisfied with 'magic'.

"I can climb trees," admitted the bear, dejectedly, knee-deep in crumbled veneer and little specks of bark.

The wizard joyously pranced around his cluttered shack chasing, and eventually catching his flying creation with tears in his aging eyes.

"I never thought I would ever see true magic. This is it. . . this is true magic my friend, thank you so much."

Leslie put a great paw against the wizard's back and

patted a little too hard, shown as he buckled slightly and let the 'hingerfly' go again. It swam through the air on holey brass paddles to the very top of the bear, resting for a moment to deliver its tiny life-giving payload to the bright pink flower that was tucked there. Levi the Wizard gasped with joy.

"That is exactly it! Exactly what it was meant to do! I invented the thing to water my garden without scaring away the pretty butterflies, but I could never make it fly," he sang, "this was exactly my intention!"

"It knew," thought the bear, "and I quite enjoy these flying petals myself. The softer, brighter ones, however."

Everyone enjoyed it for a while, thinking their own thoughts, watching it until it had run out of water and needed to be caught and refilled.

Kayle found their interaction, the two of them looking like a couple of kids, quite touching, and decided immediately that she was alright with the bear. She could follow this bear to a battle and stand proudly next to him, and not just simply use him as mobile cover.

The floorboards groaned. They groaned in that way that the growl of an animal or the nightmarishly subsequent movement of a spider's legs unnerves you, intrinsically, because your ancestors evolved to avoid those very ends. She had to ruin the moment:

"Alright we're a little overloaded here guys, let's get out now before the whole thing falls over."

So Max and Kayle made their way down the rope ladder together while Leslie began his uncomfortable-looking four-armed shuffle-hug down the bark of the big tree. He had lowered himself over the porch with the reluctance of getting into a cold pool, probably wishing his powers involved flight to any extent. Stone had remained momentarily with the wizard in order to make a call on the satellite phone up where she told everyone that the connection would be much clearer – just so she could be left alone. Levi tried to offer her three different teas simultaneously but she declined, even after hearing the brew's specific designation as the favourite blend of one 'Earl Grey of Cinnamint'.

By the time they reached the ground, Kayle first, she decided that this young agent Martin actually had a pretty cute butt, smoking away the thought while they waited for Stone and the bear. She took another drag and Max must have noticed her staring, the way he stayed a little stiff and always looked somewhere else, fiddling with his pockets. Kayle loved making men feel uncomfortable. It was almost always hilarious, and it made them really easy to get into bed. She exhaled slowly into the cold wind.

On a windowless floor way up high, protected from the cold wind and colder rain on this dreary day that battered on under portentous skies, the laptop of one Guinevere Quilway blipped to life with a sudden call. It was around three in the afternoon.

Gwen jerked alive suddenly as well, from underneath a heavy quilt of neglected sleep that had come upon her in the wee hours. The Sandman is an unrelenting agent who invariably lands his quarry, so thank goodness that – as far as we know – his euphoriant motivator has only ever been to see folks well-rested. She brushed the curly dark brown hair from her eyes and found her giant lensed, thick-rimmed glasses to look at the screen with. Wade was still working away at the desk across from her, seemingly immune to sleep, but it wouldn't surprise her to discover that he had learned to sleep with his eyes open in regenerative twenty minute intervals every four hours a very long time ago. She was happy to see that he was there, actually, as it meant he hadn't opted to return to his own office overnight. It was the small things that reminded you Wade Andersen was still human, extremely small things, imperceptible to non-machines in most cases.

Gwen really woke up when she realized who it was that was calling: Agent Stone was coming in over the satellite link.

"Nat, can you hear me!?" asked Guinevere, frantically pushing up an armful of bracelets to stop them from clacking noisily on the keyboard and drowning out the response.

"Go ahead Gwen," came Natalie Stone's voice, crackling slightly, but otherwise alright.

She had put the call on speaker for Wade's benefit, though he characteristically remained seated and silent.

"Well Wade's here, he's doing whatever it is he does, and uh. . . Uncle Bilge took off at some point to get some sleep I think, the useless old todger."

Guinevere straightened her shawl and untangled her necklaces, checking herself in a pocket mirror, despite this call being audio-only.

"Did you learn of anything we can use to fight this?"

"Well, look Nat," she rubbed sleep from her eyes, "the problem is that there just isn't a cure-all for magic, alright?"

"Munitions," Wade suggested from across the girl's small temporary office, in his traditional monotones.

Gwen ignored him.

". . . It all depends on context," she continued, "now I've looked up everything I can from what you've already given me to work with, but now I need you to tell me what you've *seen*."

And so she did. Agent Stone quickly ran through every eventful moment of the mission so far, leaving nothing out, and doing so in a very efficient amount of time. During the story, Thomas Bilge emerged from the hallway and peeked into the room. Hearing his agent's voice he ran to listen in over Gwen's shoulder – the right one, as the left one was already occupied at this point by the impossibly silent, looming Agent Andersen. They all wore different faces. Bilge was looking heavily concerned, Gwen was wracking her considerable mental capacity against the shape of what she was hearing and Wade, well, Wade was as blank as the first page of an essay you'd rather not have to bother with. The only sounds were the jangling notes of Gwen's left arm charm and holy symbol menagerie as she nervously tapped the rim of her glasses.

When Agent Stone was finished – right up to the door-hinge butterfly – Gwen gave her appraisal.

"Well I've got some good news and some bad news and some bloody awful news," she began, "good news is that I have figured a link between bears and magic. I found it definitively in some old druidic writings, except that nothing ever spoke of the *bears* actually having the power. Druidic magic, as it is most often described, actually sits in line with what you've been experiencing. Druids wield a kind of supernatural empathy within their chosen environment. The projection of one's self and the ability to express outwardly like with that one-way telepathy you said that. . . *Leslie*. . . has, seems to make sense there. The green colouration of magic is often representative of life, which also works."

Gwen furrowed her brow and glanced at some notes.

"Even the transformation he showed you, should that really be his brother, that's still good. Druidic magic can be used to transform, with loose interpretation, though often people are doing the transforming. . . *into* bears."

"This is good so far, what are you worried about?" asked Stone, crackling through the receiver.

"Yes dear, please tell me that you're just fond of hyperbole," said Bilge, pleadingly.

"I am, however not so much in this case, I'm afraid," responded Gwen, pulling up a file on her laptop to the side of the call that she quickly scrolled through.

"Every other part of your story like 'the Call', so-called, and the invasive nature of the god this bear keeps describing, not to mention the barbarous mutations, seem rather. . . well, *warlocky*."

". . . Meaning?" said the laptop.

"Warlock magic is for those who wish to empower themselves only. Warlock magic is often based around making deals with daemons or deities of great power in order to gain strength for one's self alone. It literally means 'oath liar' in old English, it was a name given to those who would infiltrate covens, pretending to be witches in order to betray them during the burning times."

"Well how do you recommend proceeding?"

"The bad news is that I believe the power that these bears possess is coming from another source entirely, that it is only being, let's say, *loaned* to them. I need you to pay attention for any clues of what could really be behind the magic they wield. I believe that it has manifested in Leslie in this 'nature-flavoured' way that it has because something *told* him it was bear magic. You need to figure out what the true source of their power is, find out how it works, and destroy it that way. You need to play along with the method of the magic."

Stone began to reply and was swiftly cut off.

"I know you think you can just slice right through this, but because we have no idea what is actually giving the bears their power it is impossible to prepare for, and so you must be ready for literally anything. Do you understand?"

"Have you no magical artifacts we could use to dispel the magic?" Stone repeated.

"You saw my luggage! Do I *look* like I carry around powerful magical weapons? Where do you think this stuff comes from?!" Guinevere was beginning to entirely lose her patience, channeling a frustration that was entirely her mother's.

"Look," she continued, calming down, "you're going in blind to face an unknown power, but, I believe you'll be fine if you just open your eyes."

Bilge put a hand on her.

"Figure out what's giving them their powers, figure out how it does that, then throw a stick in the sodding spokes, please," she finished in a huff.

"Before I go, the 'bloody awful' news?" Stone inquired, unshaken by her outburst.

"The last bit! It was the bit I just said, obviously! Take me seriously, damn you! You can't ignore this!"

"I'll keep an eye out, thank you Gwen."

"This is NOT bear magic! I am calling it, *right now!*" Gwen threw her final words into the small microphone just before the connection was closed.

Wade immediately went back to his chair and sat down, typing fast yet methodically. Bilge gave his niece an entirely distraught look and stormed out of the room.

Gwen collected her pile of books, her pile of notes, and stacked them neatly, feeling frustrated and at a loss – specifically at a loss for some kind of arcanic Rosetta Stone. Wade was still working silently though, perhaps he'd come up with something. Even if he had solved the problem right then and there he likely wouldn't have said anything unless specifically asked, so she got up and walked around the dim blue room to the other desk set up to face hers.

"You know, when you told her all of that shit about 'perceiving beyond magic', I think she really took it to heart. She's foregoing all of her experience to take this bullheaded approach to something so complicated it can almost not at all be comprehended!"

"Confidence crucial," he said.

"And yet when she runs into the *actual* glowing green, monolithic transforming bear that illusion was based on? When she cannot simply will it away with a stern thought?"

"Still good with sword," rebuked the big man.

"I've heard as much, yes," she said, reluctantly conceding.

Gwen peered over his wide shoulders:

"What's all this then?"

"Work," described Wade, infuriatingly vague as always.

He was currently looking at schematics seemingly of his own design for some kind of large armour-piercing ammunition far too big for a conventional firearm at all. It seemed irrelevant, but not nearly as irrelevant as the only other open window on his unadorned silver laptop at that very moment – a menu for the building's Allplate Diner. Specifically, it was their popular seafood menu: 'Can't You Sea We're Doing Our Best?'.

"Well what the hell about that, then?" she demanded.

"Needed to know what was for lunch," explained Wade without looking up, only incensing her further.

Gwen was about to lay into this man, made of marble or not, she was going to show him a thing or two about actually helping out when one's friends were in danger – except that was when Director Bilge returned. He was now wearing a pair of extremely worn brown leather gloves, and he was pointing directly at Agent Andersen with the body language of one who would not be denied.

"Mister Andersen—

"Ahead of you," interrupted the curt scientist, closing his laptop and following Bilge out of the door.

Gwen didn't watch them go, she was currently testing her frustration against a particularly unbreakable Gaelic twine bracelet she knew she wouldn't ruin.

"Don't worry."

It was Wade's voice, but he wasn't there when she looked up. She went back to her desk, worrying.

Bilge and Andersen often seemed to have a special understanding between them, one that made sense to nobody at all. There was some level that they connected on, common to no one else, and it made it even more difficult to work with them than you might already expect. Gwen was constantly feeling like the third wheel on a two-wheeled vehicle – not like the coveted position of third wheel on an East-Asian auto rickshaw, which was strictly necessary and positioned in front.

She was the only one actually trying to figure anything out about magic. Wade could design all the bullets he wanted and Bilge could wear all the fancy gloves in the world, looking quite mad while he did it, but without her research, Natalie was never going to figure out what to do – or even try. Gwen couldn't let anything happen to that stubborn woman, it just wasn't going to be allowed.

"Tossers!" Young Guinevere slung insults at targets too far away to hear, and too distracted to care.

She angrily leaned back in her chair and went right over, falling out over the floor, sundress bundling at her knees.

"*Bugger it.*"

Guinevere pulled out her smartphone, and played some games on the floor for a while.

Informative, but not definitive, was the impression Agent Natalie Stone was left with after hanging up. She would not be sharing much of that talk with the bear, and perhaps only Max at the most, because it had now apparently become her mission to find out exactly what was making the enemy strong, and destroy it. Gwen did have a point in that, and killing the brother bear was likely not going to be the simple end of it. Whether that meant losing Leslie in the process, it didn't much matter. She doubted he even really knew how his powers worked at all, and she was tired of Gwen trying to tell her how to handle the situation. That girl had not faced the things that she had, and couldn't ever know what strength of action needed to be taken when lives were on the line. No time for 'playing along', that was for damn sure.

"Excuse me? Are you about to be leaving?" asked the gentle, happy tones of the man who called himself a wizard, "I have something for you and your team."

Stone half expected to be handed a barbeque fork tied to a lighter glued to an eyelash curler, or a shoehorn double-ended with a lint brush and a laser pointer, or a cheese grater combo bass pick combo—

"Here," he said with hesitation, clearly hoping she'd like it.

What was placed in her hands was a familiar coil of rope tied to a wide-mouthed binder clip that held a thick permanent marker tightly in its grasp. Stone saw the look in the inventor's eyes and knew that she'd be needlessly cruel to throw this on the distant ground like she wanted to. She managed a crooked smirk and a wide-eyed nod that seemed to satisfy him.

"It's called the 'Far-Writer', and I made it out of a coil of rope that was attached to the front of your bag, a binder clip I found in Mister Martin's pocket when he wasn't looking, and a marker that belonged to Kayle." He listed the components with a great excitement.

"You can use it to write nicely on things up close, or ruin things that are far away," Levi recommended, "you will know when to use it. When the time comes, you will know."

Natalie looked at the piece of garbage in her hands thoughtfully.

"Chekhov's doohickey, is it then?"

"I don't know, I never watched much Star Trek."

The wizard shrugged and went to shut the door:

"Tell your friends!" he suggested, "wizpalace.net!"

*Dot net?* she choked back a laugh and started down the ladder, packing the 'Far-Writer' into her bag, forgetting to dismantle it.

Halfway down the rope ladder, whatever semblance of the sun there was at all behind the grey sky dipped even further away, and the rain began in earnest. Loud enough to cover the sound of their travel, at least. Wet enough to make Agent Martin whine the entire time, she was sure.

*Not bear magic*, Stone thought, spitting out some water, *doesn't really matter does it.*

# 10

## FOOL ME TWICE

One part bear, one part Dick, two parts mad, one more parts wrongful imprisonment, add them all together and you realize that you might be Dick Davison, longtime unwitting opponent of coming up with good one-liners.

"Let me out of here you hairy jackasses!" screamed Leslie the Bear, currently appearing before his captors as such, instead of as the mighty Dick Davison who they wouldn't have recognized anyway and probably would have eaten.

From the two grizzly-looking Kodiak bears carrying a sturdy pine litter between their gargantuan shoulders, to the very large one in back with the singed fur, or the small black bear up front wearing burgundy wizard robes stretched to their utter limit – not a single one of them had even seen that episode of Fringe that Dick had been in Vancouver at the time to be an extra on – let alone faced him in mortal combat. Actually, most of Dick's opponents – especially the ones who faced him in mortal combat specifically – never came back for round two.

To them he appeared only as Leslie the Bear,

someone Davison wasn't even familiar with, which made it aggravating when they continually referred to him by what he thought to be distinctly a girl's name, and, as he figured, simply to insult him.

"Give. . . rest. . . to it. . . Leslie," grumbled the huge grizzly bear in back, the one with the scorched fur from earlier when a loud, passing bird had squawked at him and he had lit himself with magic fire in startled response.

A bit of panicking and rolling around did the trick, however.

It was so strange when they spoke, Dick noticed, in the times when he wasn't raging against the somehow entirely unyielding splintery pinewood bars of his cage – bars that looked to be wrought by mere animal teeth – because it sounded like speech, like rough, guttural speech and yet their mouths never moved. They only looked in his direction and convulsed the muscles of their faces slightly as he heard what they were saying in his mind. It looked strenuous, like telling someone you love that you've lied to them, or taking a tough poop.

Dick would be lying if he said that he wasn't just a little disappointed his co-agents hadn't yet burst from the forest and totally beat the crap out of these jerk bears. He had the requisite tactical understanding to prevent his feelings from being hurt, however, because he knew that by the time they found out what had happened, it would be wiser to join with Agent Fisher and instead beat the enemy on their way to. . . *wherever*. Wherever they were going. Come to think of it, those guys wouldn't have *any* clue where the bear convoy was headed. *How could they?* The best course of action would have just been to follow the obvious tracks and break him out! Well, unless they captured whoever that Leslie chick was, the one holding the rabbit who cast a spell on him, maybe, and learned how to *speak bear*. He was starting to feel mad again.

Dick Davison had learned their language, he reckoned, simply through exposure and from travelling with these idiots for an entire day. Though whatever it was about them, they were terrible magicians. Constantly they would cast spells at random, never what they seemed to mean to, and you could just *watch* their dumb brains winding up for minutes at a time like rusty leaf blowers before even one sentence could tumble out as the chain snapped.

Listening to them talk was agonizing, like watching molasses communicate in winter, but it was still better than listening to Agents Whiny and Tightass go after each other over a simple misunderstanding he had caused. Rose was actually pretty badass, and Dick couldn't see a scenario where Max's dating her would lead to the unfurling of all the Bureau's secrets like Stone was convinced would happen. She should have cut him some slack, and he should have, well, been less of a weenie as soon as he was told he couldn't have something.

"Almost. . . there. . . Leslie. . . hah. . . hah" went the crude thoughts of the lead bear, the smaller black one wearing space curtains that didn't fit, for some reason.

Dick couldn't see much that was above him for the roof of his small cage, but he could see straight ahead, and they were coming out of the deep woods now, a hundred yards of open grass to the edge of a very full-looking stream only becoming more so with the hard rain. That was another thing he appreciated – always taking inventory of the silver lining, he was – the roof of this makeshift cage kept him relatively nice and dry against the watery onslaught, where the travelling bears looked utterly miserable, as miserable as their grades would be if you had to test them on anything, the dummies. The wind was still brutally cold, however, and that was picking up with every hour.

Dick Davison may have looked like a bear, but he sure as hell didn't feel like one. A sleeveless black and yellow workout shirt, which was his attire every single other day of the year, was not a wise decision at all on a day where it had threatened rain so obviously. Dick Davison often battled on, uncomplaining, through unwise circumstances that so often were born of his own unwise decisions – such was the measure of a man, his father would say – and in truth it was, only in telling ways more numerous than intended. Dick Davison—

*THWUMP*

The pinewood litter went front-end first into muddy grass and he could hear pounding footsteps becoming farther and farther away.

"No Carl. . . stream is sacred. . . never to enter!" one of the bears was speaking, it didn't really matter who, because this was a very particular opportunity.

Leslie the Bear pressed his back against the base of his prison, and used two powerful human legs – whose owner never skipped their namesake day – to push the roof of the cage off of its bars. It budged and shuddered only gradually, but it was moving – suddenly weaker than ever before – and eventually burst free, landing nowhere in particular.

Dick hit the ground running and headed straight for the waterline ahead, trying not to slip on the soaking grass. He must have been quite the vision of athleticism, appearing to all onlookers as a ten-foot tall brown bear sprinting expertly on two legs not made for such a thing at all, and making excellent time doing so. If an Olympic talent scout had been there watching at that very moment, an all-bear track team would surely have to have been formed around him, if only just to legitimize this one moment's relevance to history. While the un-burdened Kodiak and blackened grizzly took chase behind him, Dick finally noticed what had caused the initial commotion.

The leader of their convoy, the black bear in soaking robes, was currently attempting to hold back the previous lead cage-carrier from diving into the 'sacred stream' to catch what was probably the largest salmon that Davison, or this effigy of Leslie, had ever seen. It was a shiny, obese, pink-bellied shark bobbing along near the surface of the water. It even looked pretty tasty to the sprinting Davison, yet not enough to put him in a hungry frenzy quite like that other guy who, frankly, was making a scene and embarrassing everyone.

"No! Not... the... sacred water!"

The Bear That Was Not splashed hard into the Stream Of Grand Importance as it ran by, and with huge, high, heretical steps he had crossed it in no time –

making crunchy purchase into the uneven, surprisingly close to the surface stream bed. The water was not as ice-cold as expected, but perhaps he was just too rain soaked to notice. As the man in the magical bear suit reached the other side – his human heart pounding as he ran up the gradient of the wet, grassy hill bordered by the apparently very special stream – he looked up and around to see that the route of escape he had decided on was not a wise one at all. Quite the opposite, actually. But in this unwise circumstance, Dick saw an opportunity to measure himself.

As he looked up, he saw that the hill was very wide, and this was just one hemisphere of its entire conical self – dotted with six or more large fire-lit huts that looked quite like land-borne beaver damns. He steeled, barreling up the slippery hill as best he could like the quintessential horror movie victim always moving to higher ground regardless of the intense unlikelihood of there ever being a viable escape up there – and only vaguely aware of more shapes coming towards him from new directions. He stumbled into a divot filled with rain and grown over by grass, his neck snapped up and that was when he first glimpsed it. The 'it' that the world was flocking to – some kind of mountain.

Some kind of mountain indeed towered above him towards the dull, draining skies – grey, snowless and Neolithic – it was something that caught your attention as it scraped the pressing clouds. Perhaps it was not quite a mountain though, maybe just two hills standing on each other's shoulders planning to hide under an epic trench coat to purchase some mountain-only pornography. Some really tectonic, beaded-curtain stuff – magma covered peaks right there on the back cover – something that could get you arrested in a religious nation but still be entirely worth it.

Whatever it was, it had a wide-base carpeted in mighty pines, a base that then travelled upwards at least a thousand-some feet before drooping slightly to a point at the top. A rib of the Earth, a beak for the god of birds, or the largest bear's claw ever seen.

Something large and hairy and three guesses where the first two don't count away from a pissed-off, soaking wet grizzly bear caught up and slapped Dick Davison into the mud with a shovel-sized paw. He didn't even notice, still transfixed by the leviathan rock above him. Dragged through the sloppy ground all the way to a small lumber hut at the bottom of the great hill and thrown into yet another cell seemingly chewed into shape, Davison the Bear could not think of anything except for the doubt that worried at his conscious mind – the doubt that anyone he'd ever met would have even a slim chance against that mountain, or anything that stood with it.

"Sleep it. . . off. . . traitor," said the black bear slowly, from across the very small prison, drying his ill-gotten raiment over a warming fire.

"So I totally don't get it, what were you doing with that guy anyway?" Max smirked through a mouthful of his own wet hair that was hugging his forehead now, the once-impressive shelf brought low by cloying moisture.

"He was all small and weird and out of shape, and

you're all, well you're like a. . ." Max admired Agent Fisher while she walked, trying to come up with a word that was the perfect amount of aggrandizing, without being too. . . *pervy*.

"Like an enormous cougar walking upright," suggested Leslie in a helpful and entirely non-sexual way.

"Yeah something like that," agreed Max, nodding.

And she was something of a cougar, perhaps even a panther, or a puma – if he was thinking of the right animal. Kayle was exquisitely muscled and very tall, as tall as Dick Davison, though much more lean. Bulky in the shoulders and biceps and straight in the hips, but not at all lacking obvious feminine features. Her hair was jet black and always worked into some kind of braid, multiple feet long, a stark framing for her strong jaw and pronounced features that stood out from her olive skin. Kayle had the kind of face that was pretty but wasn't distracting – that is, until it was smiling, at that point it became quite grand, and she very rarely stopped smiling.   The striding agent wore black knee-high hiking boots with a camouflage-patterned jacket and toque. She was always in some kind of hat, a habit picked up whilst serving in the military. Now that they were travelling, Max was able to take her all in, every intimidating, battle-ready inch of her. He felt small.

Fisher chuckled at the remark, she had a mildly husky voice and a hearty laugh to go with it.

"Well I don't really know. . . I'd been staying with him just since summer started, and we met at a big outdoor concert earlier in the year. Nice guy, very unique and never not down to make the floorboards creak," she smiled.

Max was taken slightly aback by the thought of Agent Fisher and Levi the Wizard both... *fitting*... into that small bed at the same time. The tall agent laughed.

"But if you wanna hear about a lay that'll really break your cheap Swedish bedframe, dude I gotta tell you about the secretary back at the RGI building. The one thing I miss most about the whole job, probably."

Max's blood immediately ran hotter, and to very specific parts of his body. He listened intently, watched her speak, stiffly. As they travelled, Agent Fisher launched into perhaps the most complex and sweeping description of arousal Max was likely to ever hear, and he was hearing it from a person who held sex as high as breathing, on a list of things you can't go three minutes without and not suffer brain damage.

"Have you ever seen another human's face and it was
so beautiful that you just wanted to reach out and touch it, like, get all up in it with your hands just so you could be sure it was for real?" She laughed at the ridiculousness of her own speech as the ball got rolling.

Max nodded entirely somatically.

"I mean not at first, no, but after the initial shock you
saw something even more, and you just knew you needed to get your body involved somehow. There was something in their eyes that just dove right into your heart and squeezed, sending all the blood in your body *downstairs?*"

Leslie began to quietly hum to himself, which was also to everybody.

"A perfect human face, without even getting so animalistic as to imagine it all mashed up against your wanting genitals. . . that's some powerful, reality-altering stuff, man. I mean, have you ever seen a face that sent your mind to the red-light district with cash-lined pockets in the middle of the day? To the back-alleys of thought that you didn't even know existed up there? A face that burned itself into your eye's own flesh, making your retina only fit to become a locket insert?"

Kayle was lost in it now, Stone was trying to become lost.

"*Well I did*. Once, in a dream," she concluded, "and I promised I would grind my pelvis to dust trying to find it in our world. . . "

There were no sounds but rain and wind, for a time, and the pumping of red blood.

"The secretary has that face, man. The one you saw and probably felt the same about, only, in fewer words. . . and that kind of face? It don't get asked out very often, thanks to each and every one of us having our crushing mortal fear of failure. Well I don't have that, so I hit that, and it was utterly transcendent."

Max could only cough and nod. He was drained after hearing such a redolent description, and fully ready to go to sleep without reciprocating – thinking only about how he'd have to tell this story to Dick Davison *immediately* upon seeing him alive again, before even asking if he was okay. The RGI lobby secretary was a legendary kind of beauty, mind-blending laugh or no, and that story could burn the ears off Aphrodite.

"I uh, wow. . ." he gathered himself, and steered for cooler waters, "well since you're only part time at the Bureau, what do you do now?"

"Oh I basically couch surf a lot, go to music festivals, travel with friends, try to see as much as I can of the world while I'm still young, eh?"

"She's thirty and homeless, is what she's saying," said Agent Stone from the far right of their formation.

"Whoa there, little fox, I don't think that's fair! I choose to live this way. I have a family, man, and they *have* a home, we just don't see eye to eye anymore."

The smaller agent did not respond.

Max didn't know what Stone had talked with the Bureau about over the phone as they left the wizard's place but whatever it was had put her in a foul mood again – or maybe it was the sexy story, but he couldn't see why.

"Alright, well, that's cool. I expect the wizard was pretty bummed when you told him you were leaving?" asked Max.

"Oh yeah, no, I didn't tell him. It's better this way," said Kayle, "my entire life fits into this bag and nocks on this bowstring." She patted the small traveler's pack she wore and the bow stretched across her broad back.

A quiver was strapped at her hip, bristling with arrows.

"Little enough to easily misplace on a nightstand," commented Agent Stone.

Max winced at that.

"Hah, don't tucker yourself out kid, you can try to

piss me off if you want, but you gotta be able to take what you dish, and I can throw stones, man," Kayle was effortlessly unscathed.

"We just don't need to be regaled with your sordid pinballing in the middle of an important mission, agent," Stone reprimanded, thinly keeping her cool.

Leslie hummed more loudly now – miserably talentless music it was.

"Oh, no? Should we just listen to you tell us all how useless we are compared to you? How undisciplined and friggin' uncouth we are?" Kayle was raising her voice as well.

Max sensed a critical moment to interject, he moved closer to his friend in the long black jacket-and-sword outfit.

"Stone are you just. . . not comfortable with, I guess, *differently sexual people?*" he whispered, and she shoved him away impatiently.

"Not at all. I'm uncomfortable around *overly* sexual people!" she barked, "I mean really, is there anything else you can talk about? Do you have any other pastimes besides humping?"

"I could name six hobbies before you could name one, you judgmental little prude!" Fisher had her insults out of the quiver already, teasing on the edge of her taught string.

"I could name six *jobs* I've had before you could name one!" responded Stone with equal parts competition and plain old loathing.

Kayle shook her head and backed away from them, towards the cover of trees and away from the mountain-bound path that Leslie had shown them.

"Well you know what job I used to have? Reconnaissance, from when I was in the army, and I'm damn good at it too. So I think I'm gonna carry on by myself for a little while and if I see anything important, anything up to your exact specifi-freakin'-cations then I'll be sure to head right back and let you know," Kayle was already on her way and Stone said nothing to stop her.

"To think!" she yelled, over her shoulder, "I actually thought I missed this bullshit!"

"No! No, we should probably stick together," Max warned, his worrying being lost in the howl of the hard weather.

"Haaaaarlot!"

Max, Stone, Leslie – they all immediately recognized the familiar whining tones of this particular brand of bring-down and perked up right away, fearing another ninety-minute onslaught could be on the horizon. Expectedly, it had come from one of the two remaining bullies, the insipid deer-shaped lifeforms that Leslie was directly responsible for. Sure, one had been killed and eaten by squidwolves, but there were still two left, and it was so unfortunate they would remain living with yet so many wheat threshers in the world so in want of something to thresh.

Worst of all, Agent Fisher's yet un-familiarized psyche couldn't tell *exactly* where the sharp, intrusive, psychic insult had come from, or even what it was, pinning it instead, specifically, to the source she personally thought most likely. Kayle loosed two massive birds at Agent Stone and jogged off into the forest, likely not planning on a delivering an intelligence report for quite some time.

"Wait! Kayle, wait! That was just some magical, psychic, asshole deer, it wasn't Stone! *Wait!*" Sadly, it was no use, as Max did not have the pipes to reach her now.

She was gone.

He looked behind them to see the hazy outline of a very particular animal and it caused him a great deal of painful mental replay – some kind of Post Traumatic Insult Disorder most likely. Max now truly knew what is was to hate something. He planned to later buy a very large truck and go long-distance driving in the mountains at night, to eliminate as many of these putrid stick-legged forest rats as possible. The two agents and one bear carried on into the woods, heading North with the winds.

"I did not enjoy that," thought Leslie, who finally had stopped humming.

"I can't really believe what just happened," said Max, "Stone, can we talk about that?"

The small woman with the tight, uncompromising hairdo and subsequent personality silenced him with her raised hand, and addressed the bear instead, just like nothing had ever happened. Max could never decide if she was more a woman of focus or simple cruelty, he figured that when it came to the world-saving hero type, you really needed to find someone who selfish in exactly the right way. Stone sure fit the bill.

"I have been speaking to the head of magical

research back at our 'mountain' and I wanted to ask you a few more questions about your god," she asked.

"Anything you would like to know, I suppose," Leslie's thoughts were troubled it seemed.

"I want to know as much as you know about where your god came from. Where your magic originated, or how it works."

"I can tell you some things," thought Leslie.

The agent agreed.

"It all began when we found a scroll in the sacred river that runs at the base of our mountain, it had been waiting beneath a glorious swimming salmon. It spoke to Bill, and later I would hear it as well. It treated us both as its children, and it asked very little. It told us what we were, and we were grateful."

Max gave up on the notion that the normally jovial Agent Fisher might burst back out of the woods with a "just kidding" and everything would stop feeling distinctly like a mistake. She and Stone *really* didn't get along, to an extent he couldn't have even predicted.

"Do you think the scroll is the source of your god's power?" questioned Stone.

"No. I believe it was only how our god spoke to us, or rather how it first explained to us what it was. The scroll is only a conduit, I believe."

"Well what did it tell you to do after it told you what you were?" asked Max, seeing no point in missing out on this thread.

Stone looked approving of that question. Max didn't really care whether she approved or not. Not right now.

"We dug a deep cave at the base of our mountain, using our powers, and we left the scroll inside on a driftwood pedestal. That was all. After that day the voice left us, only telling us to wait. It has been something of fifty moons or more since then. Bill and I began to build our family, our clan of Twobears, until my gift no longer—

"Right. Cave with a scroll. Thank you for your cooperation," interrupted Stone.

The agent turned from them and quickened her pace slightly.

"You're unbelievable," Max muttered at her.

At Leslie's direction, the trio turned to follow a North-bound creek for a time, another creek slopping over its natural shape like the last, reaching for the trees that had once considered themselves safe, surely. Here in the deep North of the woods, the pines were massive. Their old bark stood dark and wet on the trunks. Their boughs hung soaking, and they too, were rather dark looking.

If Agent Max Martin were less annoyed now, at this moment, instead of later, at another moment, he may have noticed how strange the trees were becoming – something Agent Fisher could have spotted for them with ease – had she still been there, and also less annoyed.

The trees were shedding needles, slumping and deepening, and unfortunately the two agents were doing the same. Not the needles thing, the slumping thing. It was some truly despicable weather they were heading into, for reasons of a truly despicable nature.

Dick Davison was finally glad to be a bear, because being a bear was the only thing keeping him alive now, after being recaptured from his nearly-successful escape. Dick was very lucky, he thought, to have been made to look like a political-prisoner kind of magic bear, and not a drawn-and-quartered by four stout elk kind of magic bear. There were probably plenty of in-between bears to be, but still, none seemed better at the moment.

Whoever this Leslie character was, she must have done something really bad to be treated like this by her fellow bears, or perhaps what she was doing was actually good, as a lot of what was occupying this hill at the moment had the distinct tint of 'bad' to it.

It was a small lean-to that constituted their jail, with one wooden cage, one small fire, and an entrance on either side, howling with wind and rain. The sun was setting and it was growing dark out, especially in the gloom of the weather. This might be another good time to try escaping, and this time, running *down* the hill instead of up it – an amateur mistake.

In time, Dick was forced to consume the rations in his magically concealed and yet still oh so sensible – and oh so trusty – fanny pack. He chose beef jerky and banana chips happily, when he had been brought dinner in the form of a handful of bright orange, unappetizing berries he didn't recognize. It must have looked quite strange to the jailor, as the fully-grown Leslie sat staring blankly ahead, leaning back against the wall of his cage and eating nothing out of his paw as it made small trips from waist to mouth again and again – berries sitting undisturbed.

In fact, the black bear in stolen wizard's robes who guarded this particular cell came to consider himself as being outwardly mocked after a time and began to pretend he too was enjoying something invisible. Something *far* more delicious, in direct contention with his charge and against the prisoner's complete lack of recognition. Dick sat silently and plotted his escape from the inside of someone else, as the jailor continued defiantly with his acting, gorging himself on imaginary game until he became so engrossed in the pretend meal that he over-ate, became sleepy, and promptly passed out on the floor – victim of the grim, creeping poison that is make-believe tryptophan.

Dick Davison had now wheeled around to the original flaw with the plan he'd been working on over dinner – that he didn't have access to a jetpack at the moment – and decided to abandon it for something quite a bit more simple: kicking the bars in and knocking the warden out cold. *And look at that,* he thought, *the idiot's already asleep.*

Davison wound up his human legs and kicked hard against the pinewood bars of his cage, which reacted not at all. Frustrated and a little insulted, he kicked again, with much greater force. Still nothing happened, but at least this time, a little bit of very hard to notice greenish ether had shaken free of them – it wafted into nothingness, outing the construction as magical while it went.

"God damn it," swore Leslie.

Dick *hated* magic because, as he always maintained,

contrary to the beliefs of some of his colleagues: it was so much harder to shoot than technology. But he didn't get a chance to try anyway, as somebody new was coming to visit.

The snout appeared first, coming out of the rain and into the little jailhouse on four tremendous legs. Its muzzle was stout and wide, strutting out of a large round face and preceding the shape of a disturbingly large brown bear who appeared inconceivably dry. The beast barely fit inside with everything else – like walls – in the way. It shortly noticed the sleeping guard and knocked him about the head with a snow shovel paw, waking him immediately.

"Awaken, churl! My brother has been knocking on his bars to get our attention and it would be rude not to—

The mountain turned its gaze on Dick, and saw human eyes staring back. His eyes, the bear's eyes, were a brilliant green, and they burned through the back of your own with the ease of a laser commissioned to destroy the moon.

"My brother is not my brother," said the bear, mentally, and with a chilling husky tone that sounded utterly nothing like the smaller, yet otherwise extremely similar bear that Dick had first encountered in these cursed woods.

"Leslie, however, is a clever foe."

"What. . . talking of? This. . . Leslie," managed the small black bear from the other side of the fire, looking at Davison with that painfully concentrated face they all seemed to get when speaking – all except for this big one that was unnervingly put together.

Suddenly, after being told, the jailor must finally have seen through the illusion and immediately fell over against the wall in surprise.

"Not! Not. . . him. How?" it said.

Dick Davison moved up to the bars and tried to look menacing:

"I'm Dick Davison, ya fish-loving bastard. Who the hell are you?"

Bill did not concern himself with responding.

"I think I will have you over a fire before my ceremony tomorrow. You may thank Leslie for your fate," said the large one, projecting a kind of sinister smile along with his words.

"Wait!" called out the agent as the monster turned to leave, desperate for a way to delay him.

"I have something to offer," he attempted.

It turned slowly back to face him, leaning close to the wooden cage.

"Do you wish to barter, human? I have little need for anything but precious metals, those that shine brightly are best. I will wear them in my new form."

His green eyes darted over the shape of the man, noticing a glimmer of silver. The terrible bear nearly had his snout against the wood now, such was his greed.

"Yeah, actually, a bit of *lead!*" An internally very proud Dick Davison finally delivered a one-liner worth recording in his journal and with a single, smooth motion, unsheathed the artisan silver shotgun from his back and brought it right against the nose of death itself, cranking the trigger with perfect timing.

*BA-KOOM* bellowed the shining cannon, throwing deafening reverberations that shattered the senses. Along with the flash of hot light that erupted from its muzzle, a tight cluster of tiny lead soldiers marched barely even a single hair's breadth before they deformed against the impenetrable arcane surface of this bear's secret carapace – rippling bright and emerald – hovering slightly over the beast's shape and fading away quickly.

Davison was thrown back hard against the wall of his cage, while molten pellets scattered randomly around the room, punching small exits into the roof, the floor, the black bear's burgundy wizard robe – making a hole in a tiny sun specifically – as it cowered.

The great beast's fur shimmered, and he laughed a dark laugh, turning to leave.

"See you tomorrow," spoke the king of bears, mockingly, as its visage was lost amongst the water.

Bruised and deafened, cold and tired, miraculously un-hit, Davison got somewhat comfortable on the floor of his cage and began to recall, one by one, every single encounter he had ever had with a magical being. One of them would provide the answer, surely, he thought to himself loudly to beat the ringing in his ears. There *was* always punching. Punching never failed him.

The small jailhouse guardsbear got comfortable too, putting the fire between himself and everything else, looking nervously from Davison to the flames, and to everything unseen that lurked in the shallow, murky evening. Dick couldn't tell what the bear was more afraid of, and even sitting there alone, one-on-one with a still-loaded shotgun – he wasn't sure he shouldn't save his shots.

# 11

## MERCY FOR THE DAMMED

As the rain beat down on them and the wind constantly tapped them wetly on the shoulders asking if they were tired yet, they carried on.

Again a three-person team, they were currently following the path of a once-lazy stream now turned high-powered watery executive. Its outermost edges flowed through grass and roots, instead of the silty sides it must have once had. They moved out in the open fearing no ursine search parties and moved silently, frankly quite sick of speaking with each other.

Since exacerbating an already puerile argument and causing a potent fighting arm of the team to stomp off alone into the woods, the bullying deer had made a handful of strafing runs at their dumb butts and ugly, fat hands – so called – though it hadn't quite been the same cacophonous assault as earlier in the day. With a member of their insidious trio now dead by the ink-wet mouths of squidwolves, the remaining deer just didn't seem to have the same bite behind their volleys. It was almost sad to see them now, so listless in their abuse.

A *little* sad, but only up until the point where one of

them popped briefly out of the brush simply to inform you that yours was a "practice face" possessing of "accident features".

Recently they had disappeared, and this time had stayed gone for a while, after clearly running low on original insults. For a short and peaceful time not the bear, nor the woman nor the man had seen another soul. That was until up ahead, what had appeared to Max's imagination to simply be two chipmunks fighting over a mutual love interest had clarified in the heavy rain to become something else entirely. Actually it was fairly close to that, only without any messy triangular love involved.

". . . Beavers?" Max was really just asking God at this point.

They could be heard now, thinking clumsily out loud like every other animal in this forest that wasn't trying to be two animals at once.

"Give'r Terry, show it the tail!"

"Take off Sam, it bit me already! You get it!"

The beavers hadn't noticed their approach, and didn't look likely to hear them either. Leslie suddenly disappeared from the agent's side, saying:

"These two are with Bill. They cannot know that I am uncaptured. You must be very careful, as I have shown them magick!"

Max turned and saw not Leslie but a fat clump of flowers peeking out from behind a sapling evergreen, doubled over in the heavy weather. Agent Stone was still walking towards the animals while they argued, looking unconcerned. They were only beavers, after all.

"Wish me luck, Agent Martin," said Stone sarcastically, hand by her hip.

"You aren't going to need luck. Even magical or whatever, they're just beavers," said Max, unenthused, to his cocky co-agent.

"Do not discount luck! Luck is never to be taken lightly as it governs all that has ever happened, or will," said the flowers.

"Whoa there, bud, not another step!"

Max heard the cocking of a slide, and turned from the sagely growth to catch up with Stone.

Agent Stone was solidly aiming her Uzi at one of the two beavers, who was aiming what looked like a little wand, right back at her, supported by the other beaver also brandishing a stick that looked magical only because of how it was being pointed. A stick could look like a thousand things with only simple intention behind it, and these ones were being held like very straight guns, in the tiny black hands of two bipedal beavers.

When Max approached, the closer animal turned his wand on him, and Max threw his arms in the air immediately as the soaked river rat menaced him with a piece of wood – a memory that would deflate his ego for years to come.

"Hey bud you too. We don't want to have to blast anybody with these things," thought one of the beavers, and it came across nervously.

They were out-gunned for only a moment, as Stone sidled two quick steps and reached around Max, simultaneously drawing his handgun and cocking it in an expert motion. She now trained a weapon on each of them.

"Same here," she said coolly.

Terry and Sam looked at each other, clearly a little impressed.

"That was pretty neat," said one of the beavers, to which the other one nodded toothily.

"Hey but don't get any funny ideas, eh?"

The one closest to Max shook its wand at him in a threatening way, while the other one pointed his at Stone. Agent Stone pointed her two guns at both of them, and Max pointed his hands at the sky to prevent being mistaken for a participant in this interspecies game of murder chicken.

"Why are we aiming things are each other!?" lamented Max, "how did you three get all the way to *this* while I was over there?"

"She pointed *her* thing at me!" argued the second beaver.

"He had his little wand drawn before I ever took aim," clarified Stone.

"Sam was only trying to magick us up some dinner!" said the first beaver, gesturing with his free hand.

The one known as Sam corroborated with a nod.

"So wait, those *are* wands? You think so too?" he said to Stone, surprised she wouldn't just call them sticks, "well what are you two anyway, witches?"

"We don't really know, we just kind of made these sticks and it helps to focus the spells."

"Yeah, eh, so they don't just go like, everywhere," said the beaver aiming at Stone, sweeping with his free hand.

"It helps a lot. Magicks is dangerous. We have a buddy that keeps settin' himself on fire."

"Yeah, what's that about?"

Stone was laughing now, which was a rare thing indeed – but this wasn't a nice laugh, and it wasn't a shareable kind of laugh directed at the situation, it was more so targeting the people, well, the beavers, themselves.

"If these two possess any kind of harmful magic whatsoever I would be very surprised," she mocked.

"Not true bud, look!"

"Terry *don't*—

The beaver known as Sam moved his wand away from the woman and pointed it at a nearby shrub bending under the weight of falling water. With naught but a little kick, a blinding bolt of energy slung from its makeshift tip and sublimed the unfortunate foliage. Every branch above the ground itself atomized immediately, the subsequent mist reconstituting into shattered wood and leaf mulch across the stream, splatter-wise. In the cloudy, dimming evening, the spell had burst with light, standing out against the cold trees like a flaming chair falling out of a building.

Quite pleased and smiling in a beaver-like way, Sam looked back at the other one, who was still scolding him with the set of his tiny animal eyes. Sam realized why, quietly to himself, and pointed his wand arm back at Stone with slightly less gusto than before. Max noticed none of this, still thinking about being evaporated by rodent wizards, and how terrible that would look on a tombstone. Actually, he supposed that chiseling cause of death onto tombstones was entirely optional, practiced only by the likes of humans who'd died via rampant self-organized orgies gone awry, or in combat against disadvantageous numbers of lions, taking a few down with them in the process.

"So watch out, eh," warned one of the oddly accented beavers.

Stone smirked a little:

"Adorable."

Max was looking between the two beavers and the one psychopath.

"Stone for the love of God can you put away the guns? They're going to blow me to pieces!"

"Yeah I'm gonna do that, what he said," menaced Terry.

"Can you hear, like, humming?" asked Sam.

Max, Stone and the two beavers, who were both apparently witch-like magicians, stood in a square-looking circle, all pointing their weapons at each other. If Max remembered correctly, this was a 'Mexican stand-off', or, perhaps, a 'Spanish shoot-around'. He had just been to a workplace sensitivity seminar last week and really wasn't sure anymore.

"Listen fellas, this Portuguese gun-circle is going to end badly for everyone," Stone warned them.

*That was it*, Max thought.

"Just lay down your wands and we can pass on by."

The beavers looked between each other.

"If we don't stop them we're going to get in trouble with the big guy," said one, wide tail patting the ground nervously.

"Yeah but I don't think, I don't think I *can*. . ." trailed the other.

The rest of their conversation was entirely the frustrated sign-language of two people that knew each other overly well, at this point.

"Do it again," Stone goaded, "show me another spell."

"What? No!" yelped Max, covering his face, then this heart, then his crotch, not sure which was most important.

"I will! Don't think I won't, eh! I'll *roast his twigs* if he moves!" Terry stood on the tips of his tiny toes and flourished with his threat.

"I don't want my twigs roasted!" Max pleaded.

He really didn't know if that was a sloppy metaphor for his Southron regions or not, especially because it referenced multiple twigs, but he also didn't know exactly what beavers were packing that gave them their frame of reference. Perhaps it was just a standard beaver phrase? They often dealt in twigs. To avoid nervous thoughts of an entirely possible, forthcoming arcane incineration, Max spent a little while trying to remember all that he had ever learned of beaver penises.

"Do it," prompted Agent Stone, "blow him away with your. . . *magic*."

"I really regret coming out here with you!" Max snapped at her, "you suck, you just suck so freakin' much."

The little beavers looked at each other, one shook his head and lowered his wand. The other sighed and followed suit.

"I can't," admitted the one apparently named Terry.

"And why is that?" teased Stone, not putting her weapons away.

Terry grumbled and kicked some mud.

"Use your words bud," consoled the other beaver.

"Because I used up all my magick shooting at birds this morning," he said, in the way that a kid reluctantly recounts the exact circumstances under which juice has been spilled.

Max relaxed his hands and brought them back to his sides. She called their bluff and it worked, but if she had been even a little wrong, he could be painting the creek right now like spaghetti in a microwave. That was *not cool.*

"Yeah," added Sam, "and that was my last casting for the day too, eh."

"Sometimes," bragged Terry, "if I save up, I can cast three times in one day."

"Take off bud, that's garbage."

"You wanna go, bud?"

"Bud—

"Excuse me, but we're going to be passing through now," interrupted Stone.

Max held out his hand to get his gun back, he snatched it away from her angrily but she hardly noticed.

"Wait, you can't! If you go to the mountain he's gonna know we didn't stop you!" Terry ran up to them as they were beginning to walk, waving little beaver fingers.

"We're on guard duty," nodded Sam proudly.

"You're a little far from your home for that, aren't you?" Stone pointed out, knowing they still had a couple hours walk from where Kayle and the bear had described.

The beavers looked ashamed. Their big tails patted away behind them.

"Well we needed to eat, and it's forbidden to go into the stream around the mountain, Bill says," informed Terry.

"You don't mess with Bill, eh," agreed Sam.

"There was a crayfish in the creek over there, but when I went for it the hoser took a swing at me!" said one.

"Rude," said the other.

Stone holstered her sidearm, turning to continue their trek, which would next take them away from the stream and up a small wooded incline. Max had more questions for the animals, who really didn't seem like bad guys at all.

"Don't worry about your leader, he won't be around for too much longer, " Stone told them, as she got moving again.

Max knelt down and spoke to the two of them kindly:

"Hey. I'm sorry about her, but can you guys just maybe tell me a little about what we can expect when we get there? To your mountain?"

"Ton of bears, man," said Terry.

"Ton of 'em," agreed Sam.

Max's heart sank, knowing they wouldn't all be as

kind as the flower patch that was back the way they'd come.

"Bill's prepping for something big, eh. Had us building day in and day out for the last two months, but now he says he's ready. Gave us somethin' else to do."

"Somethin' big and magical is happenin'. Good luck bud, it's all way too heavy for us."

"Well, thanks anyway. You guys find somewhere else to be tonight, okay? I promise that we'll uh, try and handle it," said Max.

They looked unsure, but nodded anyway and bounded off together, Southwards.

"Oh, hey, look out for squidwolves!" Max attempted, but they were already out of sight thanks to the poor visibility.

He hoped they would be okay, and caught up with Stone. Leslie appeared on their flank, out of the trees.

"That went well. I am grateful you did not end them," he said.

"Would have been a waste of bullets," decided Stone, as they walked.

Max found that rather impudent. Even in the short interaction they had, he found the pair of magically-sentient beavers were honestly, truly, better people than countless others he had met with years behind him in the service industry. As they climbed the hill ahead gradually, what little remained of the daylight was finally leaving. It was almost too dark to see the trees in front of them now. No moonlight would pierce the clouds and show them their path this night. Only the wind, freezing them with a Northwards direction, really ensured they were on track at all.

"Yeah right, and letting one of them *erase* me with magic wouldn't be a waste?"

"They had no power Agent Martin, you're just worrying."

"Screw you, Stone! One of them *blew up* a *bush!*"

"Are you a bush, or a man?"

"Seriously? That's your response?"

"Well did you watch them after that? They knew that was everything they had. It was only a matter of time then, until they cracked."

"You put down my life on a hunch," reiterated Max.

"They were nervous from the get-go, Agent Martin, you need to watch your enemy extremely closely. We were never in any danger."

Max dropped it at that point, as walking arm to arm with her and the bear pressed on by wet, leaning tree trunks was claustrophobic enough, without having everything he might think to say refuted immediately and shoved back down his throat.

The trio arrived at the top of the incline and Leslie motioned for them to stop. Max noticed that they were standing quite high up at the moment, on this hill that immediately turned down again before raising to the location that Leslie was pointing at in the distance. He directed their eyes straight ahead, and in the foggy faraway, tiny firelights glowed – they were little windows set in small, impossible to define, dark shapes on this wide hill of Earth that climbed higher than their own elevation, and seemingly, straight into the sky.

"You cannot see it for the blackness, but at the crest of that hill begins our mountain. Below it, my brother and our family sleep."

Max could not see anything except the little lights climbing the distant ground, but he took Leslie's word for it, finding shelter under a massive tree that stood at the tip of their small hill. Some kind of ash or maple or something, he really wasn't a woodsman.

The rain was getting through the leaves, the way it blasted them like soldiers dropping out of orbit, but it was a little dryer, and a little less damp, than anywhere else. The tree was so big around that you could really lose somebody on the other side. Leslie joined him for a rest against the bark. Stone was looking thoughtfully across the tips of the trees that were now lower than them, all bent towards the mountain and glistening with moisture. Max could barely make her out even ten feet away. They weren't going to be able to travel any further tonight, not in this black ocean they walked through.

As if in answer to his thoughts, Stone retrieved a chemical light from her bag and cracked it, nestling it in a knot of the tree above them so that it illuminated them all with a sickly green glow. Faintly lit and surrounded by water they looked as if they were sitting in a submarine waiting to battle the deepest depths of the ocean.

"Alright are you two ready? I don't want to bring flashlights, it's going to give us away."

Max looked to Leslie, then down at his own wet bones, and then back to the person he had spent most of the day really not getting along with.

"You can't be serious. You want to finish the, what, two hours it's gonna take to get over there in this crap, then fight them in the *dark?*"

"They won't expect it, and those that are awake will be fire blind, despite their good sight" offered Stone.

"Not the owl," said Leslie, "her job, unfortunately, is specifically to watch for invaders at night."

"I think we need to wait for Agent Fisher to find us and let us know what's ahead," argued Max, "we should take a rest, we've been walking all day."

"She's made her choice, and I believe she's far more likely to just meet us there, if she hasn't already run back to the treehome for a *booty call*," Stone did not sound kind.

"Look, I just don't agree that we should attack the magic bear mountain when we can't even see three feet in front of our faces!"

"Are you afraid of the dark Agent Martin?"

"No! I'm not!" he lied, "but I'm being practical and you're being insane!"

Max was finally standing up for himself, literally, and staring her down – both of them under the cover of the high branches, only occasionally being pelted with fat rain drops that were more like gobs of sap than what they should have been. Leslie sat quietly, twiddling his claws and trying not to get caught in their crossfire.

"All day long you have walked all over me, all over Leslie, all over Kayle, and I'm *sure* you said something shitty to the poor old wizard at some point, but who can keep track?" he laid into her, like a mad knife through stern butter.

"I will not apologize for being the only agent attached to this entire organization that does not take the job of world-saving, monster-slaying, or magical-despot-dethroning to be some kind of ridiculous comic adventure," the stubborn woman rebuked him in the practiced way she always did.

Stone invariably had an answer for every single complaint – every single issue somebody might have with her – but Max had a lot, and he was going to test her now, under the green light of a military-grade glow stick, and see just how much she could defend herself before simply turning into a turtle with shells on both sides and nowhere for a human face to go.

"I don't believe that for a damn second and neither should you. Davison, Fisher, Wade, Bilge, hell even Gwen and I and the freakin' cat. . . we *all* do the same job as you do, and solve just as many problems without pissing everybody else off."

"It doesn't matter to me whether you like me or not, just that you do what you're supposed to do, and don't screw up."

"No, I'm not taking that answer either. You can't just disassociate your message from your attitude and pretend it doesn't affect the way people see you! You're supposed to be a leader, and if all you ever use is your strength, you literally will just come across as a giant. . . *well*,"

"A stone," offered Leslie, who was humming a little already – he was getting better, at least, it didn't sound quite so much like a kazoo lost in a hurricane anymore.

"You're both very clever," the woman placated

them.

"My word was not as nice," said Max.

She grimaced.

"I imagine you wouldn't concede that your constant whining and complaining affects morale as well?" she asked.

"That could be. . . *argued*, but it definitely wasn't the biggest problem today."

"And the problem you're having with me, what is it specifically? Don't try and pretend you'd like to become my psychologist here and now, Agent Martin."

"Well you let Dick wander off because you were too busy telling me who I should and shouldn't be dating, you didn't bat an eye when a giant freakin' fish almost crushed my lungs, you picked on Kayle and forced her out of the group because you personally disagree with her lifestyle, and then you wantonly goaded a magic beaver to try and blow my head off simply because you are so Goddamn stubborn as to think you knew exactly what it was capable of. The same beaver with the unstable magic we were already warned about!"

"I have handled these situations with nothing but the requisite efficiency. Agent Fisher is not conducive to focus in a group setting, she'll be a stronger asset on her own, and Davison is not a child, nor are you I like to imagine, and can handle yourselves in tense situations. You've worked with the Bureau for three years and it's like you haven't learned a single thing."

That one dug a little deep, but Max had found his foothold. The rain pounded around them, even stronger than before, to the tuneless mental humming of an uncomfortable bear.

"You *have* to accept it Stone, what happened to you in that clearing *was* real, even if it didn't leave any scars that we can see, and what we are walking towards is real too. If you march us all in front of a train and tell us that it isn't made of steel and steam, even if you believe it with every fibre of your being, you are going to get us powdered across the tracks." Max was on a rampage.

"So now you've decided that you can't be beaten, and we've all patted you on the back and given you praise and told you that you are exactly what you feel like you are. Yet now, for some reason, instead of just becoming more strong and confident, you have also become careless and insufferably arrogant, making your partners feel like buoys pulled along in your wake." He slid back his massive, soaking hair from his face and spat out water.

Stone just stared straight into him, looking incensed, offended, maybe even hurt? That wasn't likely, but it was easier to see when the dim green light cast blackness on her face, showing in garish detail there was an actual, if subtle, expression on her practiced granite blankness. She did not respond. At least, not before Max had more to say, scared he would lose the advantage he seemed to have, simply in that she was actually listening to him for once.

"If you were so sure that those beavers with their stick wands didn't possess *any* dangerous capabilities, why did you point your guns at them?"

Stone cracked, just a little.

"Agent Martin if I told you that I was afraid would

that make your job easier? Would it make you more confident, to know that your strongest weapon could not differentiate the smell of her own blood from a dream?"

Max started to respond, but she cut him off.

"Would you follow me if you knew how much I didn't know? Would you face a demon with me, if you thought that I didn't have the exact play-by-play in my mind already that would keep us both safe?"

"I—

"*Do you want to pity me? Is that what you want?*"

Max was drowning in the struck oil that he had so much wanted to taste, but it was bitter now, exactly as a sober mind would have known it would be. He began to dig upwards.

"Well. . . I mean, I don't think you actually realize how much we care about you. We all do, the whole team cares, because that's the kind of bond you need with people to survive in a world where monsters are real. And the only person whose opinion seemingly matters to you, is the only one who hardly recognizes that you exist. Is that just safer for you Natalie?"

Stone did not look pleased. She did not allow herself to be addressed by her first name, that was a privilege reserved only for family.

"Agent I believe we have discussed this quite to death. Perhaps you'd like to borrow the satellite phone and call your cop girlfriend, so you can tell her exactly how upset you are and maybe just reveal all the secrets of the Bureau while you're at it. Won't matter much soon anyway, because apparently I've walked you all in front of a train, and a train by any other name would hit as hard." She threw her bag at him, strongly enough to knock him back a step.

"You ass," spat Max into loud rain and deafeningly awkward hummed notes.

Max took the phone, as directed, out of the bag and began to dial the Bureau, holding it up for Stone to see.

"Here," he said, "I think maybe you should have a one-way conversation with the big emotionless robot you love so much, and perhaps calm down a bit. It is, after all, the only thing in the world that means anything to you."

She stepped forward and slapped the phone out of his hands, sending it off into the black grass.

"Just because somebody decides that they have feelings for me, I am not obligated to reciprocate them. I don't need to be attached to anyone else that I don't specifically choose to be!"

"Oh, you're actually talking about feelings now, as if you have them? Is this the part where I'm supposed to misread the situation, recognizing the glimpse of some deeply buried passion and lean in for a kiss?" Max did lean in and closed his eyes, puckering up just to defy her.

A napkin-sized rough wet tongue scraped against his face and lips. Max opened his eyes, disgusted, to see Leslie standing up between them, picking at his claws, and looking reproachful – looking like a dog that wanted to apologize for the simple existence of conflict at all. Max pushed him away. Stone ignored them both. Leslie hummed.

"You, on the other hand, Max, if I told you that I

wanted you, wanted you *right now* in the way that Agent Fisher and Davison and all those sad people that need to feel so loved just to get through even a single day can't stop talking about. . . you would forget everything about 'Rose' and tell me you felt the same, just to please me." She unleashed everything she had ever thought about him all at once.

"I know who I am, and am constantly asked to change or explain it. You have *no idea* who you are, and everybody loves you. It is pathetic. You, Max, are pathetic," she jabbed him in the chest with her finger, delivering the final straw to his strained and creaking camel spine.

"IT WAS A FUCKING PLACEBO."

Stone backed off, confused.

"The pill that Wade, your god, gave you, it was a mother-effing cherry cough drop with nothing but intention in the gooey center," Max's voice peeled with acid tones.

"Yes, I know about it," he answered her look, "Gwen told me what he did, so I sent him a message and asked for a mental stimulant slash supplement friggin' thing to battle the magic better so maybe I wouldn't embarrass myself today and drag you down, like always."

Agent Stone was just watching his mouth move like a spider, something that needed to be crushed.

"You know what he said to me?

'Placebo.'

'Confidence.'

'Secret.'

And I promised not to tell anybody. Especially, not you! Because you know, for all your tough-shit talk and your holier-than-thou approach to basal animal ass-kicking that anyone can figure out. . . we all know how you work, and we care about you for some crazy reason, so we wanted you to feel like you weren't beaten, and that you couldn't be, so you wouldn't lose your edge."

Stone turned around, but not to walk away.

"Wade manipulated you. Like a test subject. Like a number. Like a—

She spun, trailing dark water and green light, connecting against his chest with a powerful roundhouse kick that sent him slamming into the tree trunk, where he sank into the muddy ground and didn't look up for a long time. He didn't need to see her to know where she stood.

Guinevere Quilway, the Aversion Bureau's resident Dream Journalist and annoying teenager had at this point dug through every ancient tome and backwoods internet forum that she had at her disposal. Even going so far as to glean message boards filled with that particular sect of humanity that, despite claiming uniquely significant supernatural appropriation that in no small way rang similarly with the popular fictional media of the day, still relied on a series of tubes to communicate effectively. She ate lunch, dinner and all three major snack breaks at the Bureau, but now it was getting rather late, with no new information to speak of. At least, nothing that could help the agents in the field. Without a very specific understanding of the nature and source of the magic they were facing, there was no magical solution – only one of pure ingenuity and MacGyver-like string and pencil problem solving. Natalie was the only one of these people Gwen knew before coming here, and she was more from the of the garrote-with-string and gouge-with-pencil school of thinking. Max seemed alright, if a little cowardly, and Dick Davison was the most strangely kind and honest douchebag she had ever met. Gwen had no idea what Agent Fisher was like, but all together she sincerely hoped that they would be able to figure it out. It wasn't their first time saving the metaphorical world at large from an extremely localized threat, she figured.

As Gwen made her way out of the exactly-as-described bean-bag chair room on one of the Bureau's middle floors and gave the hallway a cursory glance, she noticed that it, too, was devoid of either Director Bilge or Agent Andersen – as had been the thirty-seventh, forty-third and twenty-ninth floors. She hadn't seen either of them since waking up and having that call with the agents, wherein she had to tell the poor buggers she had nothing for them, and immediately afterward Bilge and Andersen had absconded for some reason known only to them.

So far, despite a wildly successful first edition of her dream journalism newsletter still desperately in need of a clever-er title, Gwen felt as though she hadn't quite proved her worth to the team. It was not a good feeling, being not only the youngest one in on the secret of the Bureau, but also not being able to contribute in any meaningful way. Well, that was a silly concern in truth, because the story of her involvement here had only just begun. There would surely be a time that they truly needed her, yet to come. *Hopefully.* She was probably the only one of them who actually read books, after all.

Her phone rang then, it was Bilge, and his ringtone had been specifically selected to sound like a walrus saying, well, anything – because that was what his mustache reminded her of.

"Guinevere! Are you still in the building?"

"No Uncle I've taken off to find a nice-looking young tradesman to impregnate me," she delivered with utmost seriousness.

There was no speaking on the other end of the line, only the expectant silence of bad news landing slowly, like syrup over pancakes, or syrup over a keyboard, or syrup in general.

A shuffling sound came through next, then the crashing, shattering boom of a workbench being chopped in half by a swift and brutal forearm. Gwen flinched a little.

"Uncle I was joking! *I was joking!*" she pleaded, having gone a little too far, "I was just looking for you two actually, I've been everywhere!"

And she had. Gwen had visited the Bureau's firing range, armoury, server area, laser gun firing range, interrogations room, barracks, infirmary, winery, LAN center, ice-cream truck parking stall and that secret bathroom that Bilge didn't believe anyone else could find, the one with the epic claw-footed bathtub and generally pinkish hues.

"Ah, yes, well, good show then. Floor forty-seven.

We've got something to show you, my dear," Bilge said, catching both his breath and sanity.

The forty-seventh floor, she hadn't even thought of trying that one yet. The problem with this entire place was that it was a much better idea on paper than in practice. It was impossibly large for its purposes and so nonsensical in design and execution that it was honestly really difficult to keep up with where everything was and wasn't. Going forward, her memory of each floor's specific contents was likely to never become anything better than inconsistent. Off to the top it was, then.

The weather had become so poorly over the course of the day that you could hear the wind and rain from inside the windowless walls of the building now. This was something she had been warned about before visiting, apparently it wasn't just the deathly frigid winters that were crazy around here, and even the mechanical whir of the climbing elevator didn't do much to mask nature's howls. Gwen listened to music for a little while and cleaned her glasses on her flowing blue paisley dress. She thought of the lunch room on the thirty-fifth floor, the one with the sign that read, in bold red letters: 'LUNCH WILL NOT BE PROVIDED', and chuckled to herself. This was such a strange place, and nobody seemed much to care. They had their simple tools and their complicated hideout and they had each other, whatever that may bring. Her first week here had already seen a potentially world-ending threat in the form of her favourite thing, which was magic. Perhaps post-secondary education could wait for a while, perhaps she would try and get herself one of those fancy badges some time.

She dropped her glasses on the floor.

"Pissing damn bloody damn," Gwen recited with the eloquence of one who had academically buried the other students in every class she had ever taken.

The elevator arrived.

There was a draft coming off of a large fan here, that was the first thing she noticed, immediately after that her peripherals registered the ceiling as absent. She looked up, then backwards, to see that this forty-seventh floor was actually *also* the forty-eighth floor and the forty-eighth floor elevator doors were presently still set up there in the wall, despite there being no actual forty-eighth *floor*. Gwen reacted not at all, slowly becoming immune to the folderol of her setting.

So the ceiling had been knocked out to make two floors into one, and both floors were wide open. To accommodate what though? First she wondered, and then she saw it, or rather, she saw a glimpse of it before a sweating, sweater-less Bilge walked up to her holding a comically oversized wrench and a blackened rag. He went to hug her but she had to step away to avoid ruining her nice clothing with his oil-stained belly. To prevent having to look directly at the face of a sad old man reacting to a denied hug from his niece, she deftly pointed right at him and went "ayyyy!" which made him smile. Crisis averted.

Gwen also spotted Wade Andersen over to his side, working with thick gloves and a welder's mask over a miniature forge, pouring a fiery red sauce of molten metal at the moment she noticed him and he looked towards her. Strangely enough, the mask almost made him look *more* human, as the reflective properties of the cycloptic pitch-black viewing window showed just a little more dancing light than his actual human eyes.

"Well?" asked Bilge, subtly referencing the situation as a whole.

Gwen looked upon the contents of the two-floor hangar, and was thoroughly impressed by the way it all played under the orange light of cooking wolfram.

"I was going to come find you two and speak about possible non-magical, non-research support we could provide the agents on such short notice," she said, "I see that you've kinged yourselves already. Should I go?"

"Heavens, no!" protested Bilge, "my good girl, how would you feel about helping us with some calibrations?"

Guinevere Quilway, daughter of Britain, semi-professional interpreter of night time mind-movies and sender of much needed assistance, straightened her spine and saluted her uncle right there on the spot – absent mindedly spilling the contents of her notebook floor-wise again. She beamed with pride, and got straight to work.

His dreams, for once, were not cold and brittle, they were not clanking or whirring nor hinged and unnatural, they were instead garishly metaphorical, and were constructed as such: In his dreams he was alone in the raining woods with a boulder, and something like a North Korean storm trooper he was purposelessly made to punch it bare-fisted thousands upon thousands of times until the event horizon of absurdity had been breached and the great big rock began to bleed. When his hands were finally painted brightly with the universal colour of regret, he began to weep uncontrollably into them. Suddenly he was aware that he had been crushed beneath the stone the entire time, like an escaping tube of toothpaste, and had only been trying to free himself. In time, the rain would wash them both clean and a lone bear would free them from their mutual struggle and disappear, like everything else, with the golden morning light.

Max Martin's first though upon waking up was that he should quickly write that nonsense down, as he knew a Dream Journalist that would lose her mind over it. His second thought, was that he needed to shave.

However it was not the baby-ass faced Agent Martin that needed to shave, it was the tremendous brown bear that was pressed bodily against him, snoring peacefully. Max momentarily forgot the last twenty-four hours and leapt to a conscious, standing, flight-ready position before realizing his midnight snuggler was only Leslie. Now everything came flooding back, some of it literally, as Agent Stone's adventuring pack – which was still in his care – began to float away from its old pillow-position on the ground in the gratuitous amount of water that was flowing through the grass. He grabbed it and put it on. It was disturbingly wet against his back, but his back was wet too, like everything else. The rain had not stopped, and perhaps had even gotten worse. The sun's light that had woken him up was very little to speak of. Instead of the purest black of a sea-trench the sky was now only a mean dark-grey. The kind of grey that plays too rough to be made into gym shirts.

Where the pair had been resting, exactly where Max had sat down after being kicked in the chest at the denouement of his argument with Stone, was a relatively dry spot beneath a tall leafy tree with dark hanging branches. They were both soaked, but compared to the rest of the forest – which appeared to be drowning – it wasn't so bad. Leslie slowly joined him in the land of the waking.

"I thought that we might both freeze if we didn't—

"No, don't apologize," Max allowed him, "you're probably right."

He offered a hand to the rising bear, who, as it turned out, was phenomenally cuddly in a way that Max just wouldn't ever be able to recreate with mortal beds. He rubbed his bruised ribs, victim so far to both a big-boned line-backing salmon and a lethally mechanized kicking machine disguised as a small blonde woman in a black coat – another hit like either of those and something was surely going to break. Now he thought of last night:

"Did. . . Stone come back?"

Leslie shook his great bear head, pink flower still tucked solidly behind his sleep-matted ear and unmoving.

Wind winded and rain rained. Max looked towards the faraway hill. The fires were still lit in the small huts that dotted it, and he could now see most of the so-called mountain, though much of it was lost to the mist of constant rainfall and blending with the exact colour of the sky. He wondered how alive it looked in person.

Suddenly Leslie froze, staring past his shoulder and into the trees. Max noticed this and froze too, then realized he should probably turn around and see why.

Something was staring at them. Something with four legs and a body type that was impossible to distinguish at this range, in the foggy air. It stood extremely still and simply watched them. Max's nerves tightened around his soft spots, and he reached to his waist for his sidearm.

"Spies from the mountain," thought Leslie.

"Squidwolves. . ." muttered Agent Martin, starting to shake a little.

They were both wrong.

"Liiiiiittle spoooooon" psychically hollered the deer who had obviously and disturbingly been observing their sleep, in the lilting tones of one who teases.

"God damn it leave us alone!" shouted Max, who unslung and drew his handgun, firing five times and hitting nothing but his own pride.

*Dick and Stone could break his bones, but words could never hurt him* – a mantra developed early on in his first year at the Bureau, one that had been entirely shattered on this adventure, much like that same year's expectations that this job might finally propel him to becoming cool. The deer pranced away.

"Stone would have hit him," said Max, feeling down.

"I know," comforted Leslie, placing a paw on him.

Somebody came walking from around the tree now, looking bright and alert, though similarly drenched, speaking:

"I could have killed that bully for you Max."

"We know," said Leslie.

Max jumped and covered his chest with both arms, trying to read her face, looking for signs of whether or not the fight was still happening. It did not appear to be. Stone was oiling her Katana with an orange cloth while she spoke:

"You're not supposed to get these things wet eh," she looked up, smirking, "whoops."

He relaxed, and Leslie, the eleven-foot tall sorcerous bear lord, started to hide behind him slightly less obviously. Max wasn't feeling angry anymore, not after finally resting, but a lot of harsh truths had been thrown back and forth last night, and he really didn't know if that sword was headed for him next or not.

"I was under the impression we were having a dramatic separation. Usually those last a little longer, I thought," offered Max.

She chuckled dryly.

"No. I wholly despise drama, and for that matter, we're on a tight schedule where our friend's lives are concerned. It would be selfish for us to squabble."

"I. . . agree," agreed Max, who did actually agree.

Yet he still tried to make it sound like his own opinion.

"This isn't a movie, or a television show, where the world stops turning to allow us our emotional faux-pas," she continued.

"Yeah, well you told me once that to become a great agent of the Aversion Bureau I would have to learn to embrace clichés."

She had.

"Yes. Clichés have power in their familiarity, they are a tool that should not be ignored. But the arbitrary separation of a party of heroes on the very eve of conflict is still not one that anyone enjoys. So I think we can skip it." Agent Stone sheathed her katana and held out her hand.

Max swallowed hard and shook it, finding it all refreshingly professional.

"You demonstrated strength when you tried to put me in my place, and that is really all that I have ever wanted to see come out of you. Good work getting mad," she said.

"If we should die below that bear's mountain, then we should do it as a team. If only because I have chosen, long ago, excellent last words, and I just *know* that most of humanity's very best ones have suffered from a lack of anyone luckier being nearby to hear them."

Stone let go of his hand and fixed her sleeves, ever too long for her short arms, as was the entire coat too long for her short self.

"Well alright, and you finally explained yourself to me, and kind of gave me an idea of why you are. . . who you are," Max swelled with pride at being complimented at all, "and that's all I need to follow you anywhere Stone. Even in front of a train—

"Let's retire the train metaphor now, please," Stone insisted.

"What is a train?" asked Leslie.

"Something that hits you when you ask for it,"

explained Max.

"I am not a train," decided Leslie the Bear, somewhat epiphanously.

Stone was pat-checking her gear now, looking pretty excited.

"Would you appreciate a high-five at this time, Agent Martin?" she asked.

"Wow, yeah, I think I might."

"Oh," she said, distractedly checking the rounds left in her Uzi's magazine, "I was hoping you would say that you were alright, as I don't really know how to initiate those things."

"I'm alright," said Max with a smile.

"Have you got your gun, the backpack, and your badge?"

"Yes to all three," said Max, who had put his rank-four Aversion Bureau signet on his wallet finally, yesterday morning, and showed her now.

Stone gave him, refreshingly, an only *partially* sarcastic thumbs-up:

"On your shirt is better, but this is appreciated," she told him, turning to the bear, "have you got your claws, your magic, and your mind?"

Leslie stared at himself for a very long moment, hands held palm-up, a confused aura around his blank bear face.

"Where would I have left them?" he mused, in an existential way, "and *how?*"

Wind winded, and rain rained. They all looked at each other in the light of a new day.

"Great. Let's go save the world."

Agent Stone cocked her weapon, beamed at them with the unnatural smile of a reluctant photography subject, turned, and marched down their hill towards the much greater one in the distance – splashing loudly in the sopping grass and soil that just couldn't hold it anymore. She was off like thunder, armed to the nines and charging headfirst to an unknowable fate like it was some kind of ridiculous comic adventure.

Max, for the first time across this whole mission, felt the warm trickle of morale going up his leg instead of the other kind going down it. He started to follow her, but Leslie caught him and turned him around quickly.

"Max," he thought.

Not once had the bear ever used their names. He assumed it just wasn't necessary when one is capable of projecting their thoughts. The people who are hearing those know that they're being addressed quite definitively.

"What's wrong?"
Leslie felt more serious than usual, in that he never did.

"Be not a storm, Agent Martin."

The bear's green eyes shone with their own light.

"Thunder is impressive, but fleeting, and lightning takes only the path of least resistance. Be the ocean, be the river that shapes stone."

Max simply listened.

"The presence of water defines the surface of the Earth."

# 12

## TEARS IN RAIN

Kayle climbed out from under her makeshift tent – constructed of a very thin sleeping bag and jacket that leaned against a tall boulder with a little overhang that kept the rain away. She dreamt of enveloping music and schizophrenic light displays, of bonfires and weekends. Her dreams were always something like this, guided by a specifically created playlist of dance music and trance rhythms. Although it was probably poor survival tactics to be listening to music whilst falling asleep in the woods surrounded by dark wizardry, one could only follow so many rules in a lifetime. Below the rock and near to the earth it was relatively warm somehow, and she managed to sleep soundly through the blackest part of the night until the faint and clouded sun made things easier again. She checked her watch and packed her gear.

Agent Kayle had been absolutely *sure* last night that she was going to make it to the mountain before nightfall, but the appearance of two gargling, wet-mouthed cephalo-cephalus dogs that tried to jump her in the crowded woods had delayed her some. It was not much of a fight, however, because the animals had a tendency towards a moist, heavy breathing pattern. Kayle heard them well before they reached her, even over the unrelenting rainfall. The first had come directly on at her, and she had put one of her knee-high hiking boots promptly under its chin, and pinned it to the ground with a readied arrow. A second had snuck up skillfully, however, and clamped onto her ankle from behind. She spun and shook free, smacking it away with her bow. It glowered at her through two bulbous, glistening black eyes that looked like they were preoccupied with their own escape, rather than sending visual signals to the brain.

This one had the same two tentacles around its mouth that she had seen on the others from up in the treehome, plus an additional eight that wormed their way out from under its ribs. All the tentacles dangled uselessly, unmoving but for the wind. The wretched creature bared its gums, wheezing through flaps of white flesh hanging from the bulbous mass that used to be its snout. Kayle felt uncomfortably reminded of the island of one Doctor Moreau, having seen the movie in childhood, and after being hunted by Beast Folk in her dreams for a solid week, she had almost considered giving up on her love of animals all together. Kayle also noticed that this creature in front of her rather obviously did not possess teeth, and after quickly spot-checking her ankle, realized the wretch had not successfully drawn blood at all, only leaving a nasty ink stain. So it was out of self-preservation, but mostly pity, that Fisher killed this one as well. With this pitiful animal, as with men, the quickest way to the heart was between the ribs at kissing distance.

When they were all dead she caught a glimpse of a third one off, into the trees, just staring. It darted away drooling black saliva and Kayle let it go. She would be surprised if it survived the night simply battling its own horrific physiology. They were awful as described, but even worse up close. She saw that it was as if the once-noble wolf had begun to melt, and then re-solidify into something paler and unrecognizable, as ice cream did when left out. She slit their throats to provide them quicker deaths, and even though she had always stuck to the bow and arrow as her weapon of choice for its relative humanity compared to blowing holes in things with hot lead coffin-nails, Kayle would be the first to admit that it didn't always seem kinder. She had a smoke immediately after – and swore off calamari indefinitely. There isn't a lot of difference between killing someone and having sex with them; after each of those things, the change in how you perceive them will last forever, but only after one of them will you still have to talk. She exhaled.

It was during this interruption that the sun had snuck away from her. She rationalized that if Davison hadn't been killed by nightfall then he wouldn't be any more dead first thing in the morning, and found somewhere to wait out the darkness. She found an outcropping of stone a short hike from her destination, and from there she could just make out the fires of the hill's small structures – something she didn't really expect to see. *They must all be as intelligent as Leslie*, she thought, *though dollars to doughnuts, not as kind.* Come morning, Kayle would be able to pack up and quickly make it across the loud river she could only hear for now and towards whatever waited, hopefully unexpected in the twilight of sleep. Ironically, considering how much time Kayle spent partying and looking for swarms of warm bodies to dance up against, her night-blindness was a problem, especially under a grey-roofed sky such as this. One too many bad angles with foggy laser lights had afflicted her with a case of moonblink that was more than temporary.

But now it was morning, now she could see clearly, and what she saw was not comforting. Away from her rock, and past the nearby edge of the trees after a short stretch of tangled open grass, was a stream that had forgotten to say "when" to the ocean. It was dotted with a very orderly line of boulders on this West approach, and they looked close enough to walk between. Following the water East, it wrapped around and returned North, cutting a large circular area away from the rest of the forest. That area was hairy – *seventies hairy* – with green life and climbed steadily to its modest peak, where a slightly less modest one began. It was a miniature-mountain that struck at the sky and curled away at the very peak, suddenly becoming self-conscious when it must have realized how much higher all the other mountains went, and vowing a future show of force. It was a witch's hat, or perhaps a sharp pile of whipping cream, yet either way it was quite impressive – so much more so than when Kayle had seen just the the tip of it from the wizard's home.

Along the base and middle of the hill's climb, there

were around a dozen small huts and lean-to's crudely constructed from nearby trees. One of them was simply a pile of ash and charcoal, which didn't seem too crazy considering how many of these flammable-looking little bungalows were lit with actual fire. Kayle could even make out the foggy, imposing forms of bears walking on all fours between the huts, and some lumbering in obvious patrols around the higher reaches of the hill. This was going to prove an impossible one-woman charge and Agent Fisher was experiencing a moderate amount of regret to have broken away from her fellow agents. The strong woman found a wide nearby pine and hid behind it on a log, wringing her toque from a state of 'fallen down a well' to 'washing machine with a crappy spin-cycle' and lighting her last rolled cigarette – savoring the organic tobacco flavour – and receiving only slightly less carcinogens than the plebian, brand-puffing masses. Kayle loved the natural world, but she also loved to party. She loved the silence of a craftsman's stilt-legged shack in the woods, as much as she loved the feel of five-hundred pumping hearts moving as one on a sweat-stained concrete floor. She took a long drag on the bone-white dart and coughed a little, rubbing the gnawed-at back of her ankle. There were only so many rules worth following anyway. Everything in moderation.

Roughly four years ago, when Fisher first left the full-time Bureau business in order to find herself – a mission that, to this date, had only gone to prove that 'herself' was at home in company – Agent Stone had been much younger, and probably too young to be doing what she had been doing there. In the same way that a famous concert pianist on the eve of his life can have his greatest works utterly incinerated by the machine-like precision and dedication un-impeded by obligation that prodigal seventeen year-olds seem to possess – a young Agent Stone could show you how it was done. Even then she possessed the tactical planning needed to out-maneuver a necromantic godking wannabe channeling Sun Tzu's puppet soul and leading terracotta ghost soldiers, and the disciplined form required to sunder important joints on a lupine moonknight and bring it low where all the good neck-chopping action was at. But she never really seemed like much of a teenager, like she doesn't seem like much of a person at all, even now. Time doesn't appear to have changed any of that – not any of the time that's passed already, at any rate. There was still a lot left to go.

To Kayle, the kid had always come across quite obviously as an only child, even though she never spoke about her family – not that she spoke about anything else much. . . so whatever had caused her to grow up chewing iron for breakfast and acting like a completely unrepentant try-hard was information that almost nobody possessed. Kayle was quite the opposite, growing up with two younger sisters and no boys around to do the protecting from neighbourhood punks, she had to learn to pinpoint weaknesses – testicles – and deliver noogies with extreme prejudice. She lived her life to her own design, above all else, discovering her own values along the way and filling the time in-between with fun, something almost nobody ever remembers to do anymore. She exhaled, halfway done, feeling buzzed and calm.

Kayle had been thinking about returning to work, even just because of how excited she felt when the prospect of an adventure had come back to find her, but things were obviously going to be the same as before, and had degraded to that state quicker than a Styrofoam boat fording waves in a sea of nail polish remover. Kayle felt different, but she couldn't be sure that certain other agents did. And it was Stone's reaction to her very best stories that still belied her twenty-something age. She always, sometimes overtly and sometimes not, had a disgusted reflex to whisperings of sex, or physical closeness. Despite the girl's wildly accomplished and self-driven nature, this was how Kayle knew she was stunted.

Sex is the most natural thing that has ever blinked in the eye of the Earth. Every human interaction on its basest level, comes down to the primordial, cellular, fully sub-conscious debate of whether an opponent can be humped or eaten, in either order, and that is where the often physically superior males of a species derive all of their intrinsic confidence – and why they are so threatened when one of those two routes are closed to them. They don't even know why they're uncomfortable when they meet a woman like her, they just know – way deep down – that they probably couldn't eat her, if they had to, to survive. There is no way to describe or rationalize that kind of fear, because it is *mitochondrial*.

But due to those aggressive undertones, people often see the act of allowing sex as a weakness, as submission, but such a notion could not be further from design. A strong person knows the difference between decision and compliance, and a strong person learns how to wield themselves as they would anything else. Kayle closed her eyes.

In her many years of "gettin' some" and doing so on her own terms, often in the shaking arms of smaller, confused, and yet entirely willing men – she had heard, directed at her repeatedly, the worst metaphor of all time. Roughly: when a key opens many locks, it is a skeleton key, and when a lock is opened by many keys, it is a shitty lock. Yes, even in the way that profoundly specific examples of two entirely man-made physical objects so often accurately represent the intricacies of emotional love, this phrase fell on her reluctant ears like an egg on the kitchen floor: utterly apart. You see, there is no key without there first being a lock to open. The key was invented to serve the purpose of the lock, and the lock accommodates the very existence of the key. The key worships the lock in its very design, for without the lock it is nothing but a fanged stick suited for no other task. Neither should be counted above the other, for they work only in tandem, yet sometimes the key forgets itself, and sometimes two locks just say screw it, smashing up against each other and rattling like. . .

Kayle shuddered on the smoke between her teeth, suddenly remembering herself. She sniffed at the smoldering stub between her fingers. Definitely tobacco. Odd, considering how philosophical she had just waxed. She stuffed it into a little pouch of dog-ends inside her coat, rubbed white ash from her brown skin and pulled the soggy toque back over tightly-pulled midnight hair, slinging the braid over one shoulder as always. Kayle peeked around the tree and took another look at the huts. There was one on the far West side, her side, that had a broken pinewood cage out front. If Davison was still being held, it would be in one of those things, and if none of them yet had a wall punched out, he was still here. Probably – she deduced, wringing every ounce of value out of her half-finished college degree – in the one that had the closest association with cages. She got into position.

He gripped the barrel of his shotgun, holding it like a bat meant for an unfaithful husband, but because of the low roof his cage provided, he was hunched in a rather caveman kind of way. Despite their kind's renowned familiarity with clubbing, adopting such a pose didn't do terribly much to improve his situation.

*SMASH*, nothing.

*SMASH*, again nothing.

*SMASH*, a complete absence of change.

Dick Davison was starting to become a little stir-crazy. Despite being very sure that his remaining shells were best saved for the obvious leader of the coven, and not the small, dopey looking black bear across the hut from him currently trying to chomp a mosquito from the air, he was nearly at the point where he would shoot the bastard purely out of frustration. It might not even have an effect, however, as hours earlier, in the dead of night after a fitful sleep nursing a bruised back, Davison had called softly to the sleeping guard and convinced him to come close to the cage in order to inspect a neat-looking bug – and it had succeeded. When the sleepy bear got close enough, Dick began to strangle it with hands big enough to actually do so, using enough force to shatter an insistent clock radio. However, the bear only considered the act to be a pleasant massage and drifted back into the world of dreams, now leaning up against the cage, thinking a faint:

"Thanks. . . man."

Dick wasted no opportunity and searched every crevice of that bear, treating it like a shifty airplane passenger, and even looked in the pockets of the ridiculous, likely-stolen wizard's robes it wore, hoping to find some kind of arcane key that would allow him to shatter the otherwise flimsy-looking bars of his cage. He pushed the rotund little animal away in anger after finding nothing but grass and clumps of mud – it caught itself right before falling face first into the low-burning warming fire in the center of the hut, unfortunately.

Now it was morning again, and Davison had not yet been rescued, this optimism slowly fading, he began to wind up for another round of cricket – so far as he understood it. It has been said that insanity is defined by doing the same thing over and over again and expecting different results, except that on this day, at this exact moment, that is precisely how it went down. In a world fraught with insanity and things unexplainable, perhaps it pays off to occasionally play along.

Out of nowhere, an arrow nearly struck the guard bear who was sitting up against the far wall. It skewered his thick velvet wizard's hat instead, carrying it off of the bear's head and onto the floor. The bear only retrieved it, patted off the dust, and returned to catching insects with his teeth. This shot was a little too high.

Dick Davison was immediately excited, because in his personal experience, arrows didn't normally do that kind of thing. Almost always, someone was at the other end of them – well, except for that one wind tunnel incident at the Bureau a few years back, but his psyche had mostly healed from that.

A second arrow whistled into the jail and stuck solidly into the bear's leg, causing no reaction. It was a little low.

Davison's mind was wheeling, he expected this to be Stone and Max come to save him but neither of them used a bow and arrow. Stone loved the precision of her rifles too much and Max was barely coordinated enough to fire a rubber band. Who could it be then? Then suddenly he remembered, with a smile.

A third arrow, now compensated correctly, found purchase in the exposed neck of the distracted bear. It was *just right*. Davison pumped a fist, expecting this to be it, but it didn't appear to effect the bear any more than the arrows currently sticking out of its hat and leg. It still clacked its teeth happily at the flies and other insects taking refuge from the rain with them.

"*Are you friggin' serious?*" wailed Dick Davison, who grabbed two bars and smashed his head frustratedly against a third, wondering if God was actually a bear, or just anything else other than what he pretended to be.

Davison looked up and to his right, at the endlessly pissing sky and the cold grey clouds and the curiosity-riddled face of his long-ago friend and closest physical competitor, Kayle Fisher, peeking low from around the corner. She looked at him, and at the bear-becoming-porcupine hybrid, mouthing Davison a silent but distinctly three-syllable question. He shrugged, and so did she. Dick was desperate now:

"Alright listen bro, is there *anything* I can do to just get you to leave for a minute?" He was willing to try anything, especially a blunt approach.

Blunt was his favourite flavour of approach.

"Lunch," thought the bear, surprisingly succinctly.

"Lunch? Uh, yeah! I guess I can do that," said Davison, who motioned for Kayle to stop and, well, *not* come in and try to kill the bear again from closer up.

He wanted this to go as smoothly as possible, and yet the situation already felt like wiping with sandpaper. Dick dug around his never not-trusty fanny pack, between mint wrappers and crumpled receipts and the remnants of some healthy snacks eaten last night simply to stay alive – there was nothing to offer the bear. That was, until he got his fingers around a freezing cold, condensed soup can sized object. This very object turned out to be a rough-hewed pewter statue of a bear, and while it possessed no known magical properties to speak of, if it was going to be significant to anyone at all, it would probably be a bear. Davison tossed him the idol. The bear immediately fumbled it to his mouth and attempted to bite it, making a cringe-inducing cracking noise that did not appear to harm the statue. It didn't look like it was working, until the bear pulled the statue from its lips and had a good look. His expression did not change, but his energy did.

"This. . . food reminds. . . me. . . of someone," he managed, wincing through the effort of thought.

The black bear stroked the tiny statue with one claw, and put it back in its mouth, getting up on all fours.

"I will bury. . . this. . . with my. . . things."

Davison waved Kayle over frantically while the bear walked heavily out of the room, and she snuck inside behind him, tracking water all over the nice rug they had in there, the one that appeared to be a blazer taken from a watch salesman or something.

"Please. . . stay there. . . Bill will be. . . back soon," thought the bear, from outside.

The fletching from the arrow in the bear's neck snapped off as it hit the doorway. The bear continued on, unfazed.

"Screw that," muttered Dick, who pounded Fisher's knuckles through the wooden bars.

"I am so glad you're here bro, you gotta help me with this friggin' cage! It's magic or some crap and I can't break it no matter what I—

Agent Fisher reached out and pried one of the thin, splintery pine bars away with her impressive upper-body strength and kicked out two more. Dick just knelt there, questioning his own sanity.

"No, you don't understand, it was enchanted I swear!" he pleaded.

"Sure, yeah, no I know," chuckled Kayle.

Dick climbed out of the cage and sorely stretched his muscles, which took a while – as he would tell you –

due to his large number of muscles.

"I swear it was magic, bro, that guard must have been the source or the channel or the spell-caster or *somethin'*. And I don't even think he knew!" Davison said to her, desperation in his eyes and voice, his utter manliness on the line.

"Trust me man, I believe you." She did.

They hugged briefly, it was one of those chest-slamming, back-slapping hugs between close-but-not-too-close friends or guys that have trouble accepting how they feel about the men that they have, for all intellectual intents and purposes, fallen in love with. Agent Davison thought of Agent Fisher as totally exquisite, and enjoyed her companionship immensely, but felt like doing anything beyond that with her would be like making out with a mirror – which he totally had no frame of reference for – and for all of her bravado she had never asked him anyway. She felt the same as he did about the two of them. At least, he hoped that she did. He smelt her hair a little – accidentally.

"Thank God you're here, bro, the leader of these dudes is pretty gnarly and I don't think I had much time. Where's the other two?"

Fisher's eyes went wide, she looked around the room and at her watch, then back at Dick, slapping her own forehead.

"Damn it! I *totally* forgot to get back to those guys!"

"Were you the recon?" asked Davison.

". . . Yeah. . . I guess I was. Oh well, Stone was being a child anyway, I'm sure they're gonna wait for me," she explained.

"Sorry to hear you two are still having problems, bro. Hope it's nothing major."

"It's fine. It's fine, I'm just glad to see you again man! You're looking big as hell!"

Davison smiled at that.

"Is everyone else okay?" he asked.

"For now, but we should go get back to them."

"Agreed," nodded Dick.

They snuck a look out of the door the bear had taken, and again out of the door that Kayle had entered through, which was easy because the whole structure was only as large as your average bedroom. The pair opted to leave through the back and attempt regrouping with their comrades. They left the hut and began to walk quietly through the tangling grass that was so long and soaking that it felt like the plants that catch your foot at the bottom of a lake and put your imagination into a state of frenzy. Like seaweed but. . . not quite.

With the prison hut behind them, they considered their escape route covered to anything back and further up the hill where most of the huts were anyway, not expecting to suddenly see three new bears coming out of the woods, down by the river, moving towards the crossing-stones. They were medium-sized, as bears went, and a scale of brown colourations. Dick and Kayle dropped silently to the ground and began to crawl commando-style through the choking, soaking plant matter.

"We have to cross somewhere else, bro," whispered Davison.

"What do you mean? The river's totally overflowing from the rain, we can't cross that! We need to use those rocks," she whispered back.

"No way, it totally isn't," he gestured subtly with his eyes and she turned her head on its side to look back at him, "when I first escaped I ran friggin' *so fast* right over the middle of that thing, the water was only up to my knees and the stones were all crunchy and small underneath, like pebbles or whatever, I felt them."

Kayle looked a little disbelieving of his account, but believed very much in the approaching bears.

"I guess we can try it, it just, it looks like it's a lot deeper than that. Can you see how tall the little waves are that the wind is making? The shore is just grass, too, no sand or mud, it has to have come up a lot," she explained, in hushed tones.

"I thought so too but bro, I booked across that thing yesterday and went through fine. My mom was pretty Catholic too, so, if I was actually Jesus she would've noticed."

"Fair enough," agreed Kayle.

"Probably would have gotten better Christmas gifts too," he muttered.

The two of them diverted left and kept extremely low in the sea of grass around them. It was slippery and miserable and cold from the rain, but thanks to the gathering fog and torrential downpour, they were nearly invisible. It was impossible to hear the approaching convoy of bears until they were very close, close enough that their weakly projected, brutish thoughts became audible, and the agents waited for that sound to guide their next movement. Although an overheard thought is very difficult to discern the distance and direction of, your mind has ways of guessing the location anyway, at least roughly, and the two sneaking agents were probably within twenty feet of them now, about to stealthily slip right by. Davison was wholly silent in his slithering, but soon heard something that caught his attention, and made silence very difficult.

"The two little ones. . . they are gone," thought one of the bears, "Bill. . . won't find them. . . now."

*Little ones?* thought Dick, *my bro and ladybro!?*

"Must have. . . been eaten. . . by Leslie," thought another.

*Eaten?* thought Dick, frantically.

"Maybe he is more like. . . his brother. . . than we thought!" said the last bear, through his mind, with an energy of slow, mocking laughter.

This was too much for Davison to contain himself over, they were laughing about his dead friends and he would break them for it. Worse still, for some reason, Kayle wasn't even reacting to this. She was hearing everything that he was, after all, about how this Leslie the Bear that he had been mistaken for was out there eating people that sounded quite a bit like his friends. She was ahead, and couldn't see him stirring, but as the first bear began to loudly wonder over their taste, Dick Davison *shot* out of the grass with a powerful push-up. The bears did not immediately react, and as he drew to his full height he addressed them. Kayle flinched as she saw this in her peripheral.

"My friends are not porridge you damn, dirty bears!" he bellowed, pointing at the first and largest, who was actually only at arm's reach but had sounded so much further in Dick's mind.

The bear had hardly squeezed a reaction out of its boulder brain before Dick delivered a quick and devastating left-handed uppercut to the beast, carrying it forcefully off of its two front legs, up and away from the point of impact – which was just under its rain-drenched chin. Like a once-great nation the bear experienced a theatrical rise and fall, back legs rooted in place, front ones flailing around as an interpretive-dancing art school fish attempts to demonstrate the folly of consumerism in a powerful and satisfactory manner to an audience seventy-percent comprised of its mother. The bear's thoughts were incomprehensible hoots of dismay as it tumbled backwards, landed bodily and slid down the wet hill a few metres, splay-legged like someone pushed into a waterslide before they're ready. Kayle leapt out of the grass and cuffed him wetly on the shoulder.

"What the hell are you doing? If anybody gets to hit one of 'em it's gonna be me! That jailor stole Levi's laundry, damn it!" Agent Fisher seemed more concerned about the punching order than the other two bears.

"But they said that Leslie *ate* Max and Stone!" protested Dick.

"Ate them!" he repeated.

"No it can't be them, you just haven't met—

"Halt!" spoke the medium-sized bear with a forceful will behind her, holding a single massive paw straight up at them.

Dick and Kayle both froze in combat stance, fearlessly competing to see who would be doing the first clobbering, but waiting to see if some actual magic was going to try and come out of that thing. They two, who were of similar mind and body, figured that even when faced with an opponent that was possibly immune to pain, a bear certainly was still no creature of grace and was therefore fully capable of being smacked around until it up-ended like a turtle. Such an event would be hilarious to both of them and they each wanted to see it happen again. They would get their wish.

The bear's paw lit up with green sparks of impossible physical origin. They sputtered mutely for a moment, then disappeared, and immediately what followed was a torrent of magical water which burst forth from some non-Euclidian space between the bear's palm and nowhere at all. This magical fire hose fruitlessly drenched and stunned the agents only momentarily as the propulsive force of the rushing water soon manifested on the consistently fun-ruining ledger pages of the Real World, and pushed the bear backwards, slowly at first, until it lifted her off of the ground entirely and – not at all unlike a deflating balloon – tossed her backwards in an uncontrollable wavering serpentine. As her unstable arm repeatedly failed to cease casting its hydraulic cannon, her pattern of flight spun her in the way that inflatable men excitedly try to sell cars by the highway. The third and smallest bear watched wide-eyed and with a worrisome aura as his friend's frankly hilarious ragdoll bashed into the ground, flew into the air, spun sideways through the sky and sputtered out hard, dozens of metres away over the wide and roiling river. She fell from the air and crashed limply in the center of the water, yet she stopped, as Dick might have told you she would, right below the surface.

The final bear looked at them, both agents currently trying to hold back the kind of gut-rumbling laughter that just brings itself out unbidden when witnessing quality slapstick unfold, then it looked to the river and chose the latter. It ran on all fours, hopping the flailing form of its largest friend in favour of the one who was flat on her back – snout and belly and toe-tips peeking out – just below the surface of the murky, muddy water.

"Not allowed," thought the bear, as it took off.

The agents took off too, sprinting for the safety of the crossing stones that were now wonderfully bear free, even if Davison had been right about the water level the whole time. As they reached them, Dick was distracted by an odd, unfamiliar, and yet still halting sound – a bear's mournful wail. He looked over to see the third bear, standing at the edge of the river and struggling to find the courage to go in, pawing at the surface, and speaking in the physical, bestial tones that were natural to it – not the crude telepathic projection that they all seemed to use instead. Purely as an animal, it looked worried.

The bear lain out cold on its back started to sink now, slowly, halfway disappearing in only a few long seconds. The bear on the river bank barked and huffed its reluctance and, after looking at them again, hoping perhaps for aid, began to finally enter the river. If it was possible, the beast looked honestly afraid. Davison had stopped to watch, along with Kayle, as the floor of the river slowly lowered and swallowed the animal that had landed in it – seemingly just to prove a point about depth. There was an uncomfortable silence in the air, one that had a very distinct emptiness that was only broken by quiet, dismayed sounds from the hesitant bear and would-be rescuer, silence as would not be heard again for a long while.

"ENOUGH," a new voice barged its way into their minds with an unnerving power.

The third bear stopped, and slowly backed away from the licking edges of the stream. The agents found themselves compelled to be still. Dick unfortunately recognized this voice.

"The sacred waters are never to be entered, and you will forget what you saw."

It nodded sloppily, and animal-like, yet obediently, still animal-like. On the hill, back up and towards the so-called jail house, stood Bill the Bear, but as Davison knew him, only a thirteen-foot goliath of fur and muscle and strange energy that drew the eye, as well as the mind. Beside him was a small black bear in absurdly poorly-fitting human wizard's robes, sporting three protruding arrows that actually suited the colour of his fur quite flatteringly.

"I believe that these are yours," spoke the one true king of bears, with a mind that directed your focus more specifically than any hand could.

The black bear merely perked up and looked at

them as though it recognized someone.

"It makes me glad that you brought a friend today. Today is an important day. I will enjoy it more in company." His tones were heatless and commanding, they were the echoing words of a god.

Two nearby bears approached the agents from their sides, providing an impetus to move again, only, to move towards the mountain, which hadn't exactly been the plan.

The wind bent them, the rain lowered them, and the river raged against its boundaries, severing them from the rest of the world. They were under the shadow of the mountain now, on a day when no shadow could be seen.

Max looked up at the sky for just a moment and promptly caught a fat raindrop straight in the cornea. It stung, and made him wish that he owned something to prevent this exact scenario, something like a small set of umbrellas for his eyes – glasses, perhaps. A realization also hit him, drop-like and rain-like as well.

"You guys notice that there isn't any thunder?" he asked Stone and the bear.

They continued their march towards the edge of the tree line.

"There doesn't always have to be," responded Stone.

"Alright," agreed Max, "but this storm has been raging for two days and the rain is practically biblical, the sky's so grey it's almost black! The wind has been non-stop! Don't you think that this would classify as a storm? Why is lightning the only thing missing?"

"I do not believe it is a storm," admitted Leslie.

"So it's your brother?" offered Max.

Leslie shook his head.

"I feel as though I don't know anything I once did."

Max patted him with a small pink palm. Leslie seemed to enjoy patting, as a practice. The weather itself felt malevolent somehow, and it was occurring to Max now, for the first time, that it probably never had anything to do with nature.

Then they saw it, peeking through to the edge of the forest, it could be seen. The hill with the crude houses, the tall dark trees that bordered it where the spilling stream did not, and the mountain itself, tall and beckoning.

"Looks a little like a giant shiv," said Stone.

"A bear's tooth," corrected Leslie.

Max wasn't sure what it looked like. Whatever it was, it was pinching the tip of his tongue – he would think of a word later, for now there were more pressing matters.

"Alright so how are we getting up there? And where are we getting up *to*?" asked Max, checking that his sidearm was loaded.

Leslie pointed to the crest of the hill, at the base of the tremendous stone castle. There were many huts, some with orange eyes, but there didn't appear to be any movement on the lower reaches where the mist was lightest.

"Past the homes, above the hill but below the mountain, there is a cave that my brother and I once dug. Inside we keep the scroll. We must go there first to commune with Bill, then I will know how to stop this."

"But what, you just want us to walk up there with you? What if he isn't interested in stopping it? Because it sounds like he probably wouldn't be!" argued Max.

"Perhaps. Yet all your stealth will count for nothing when you see his strength."

"And what is your plan for the other bears? Surely there will be guards," suggested Stone.

"I can keep them away."

Leslie motioned for the party to continue, his brown fur dark from moisture, his movement awkward as always. He took them to a series of boulders that struck out from the rushing water on the Western reach of the island hill.

"We will cross here," he informed them.

Leslie's thoughts were uncharacteristically serious again and it made Max uneasy. Stone probably noticed, but wouldn't likely care. She climbed up on to the first large rock and stepped carefully to the other one, making her way across, trying not to slip.

"We will confront my brother and force him to stop, if we must." Leslie hummed slightly below his thoughts, as he went to cross the water.

The great big bear waddled up to the first stone, placed two paws upon its relative flatness and hauled up the rest of his bottom-heavy self, short back legs scrambling for purchase. He was a toddler climbing a kitchen chair to retrieve the golden nectar of apples at a time when his allotment had already been fulfilled. Leslie successfully climbed the first stone, and turned back to look at Max with a faintly smiling mind. Max gave him a thumbs up, which briefly caused the balancing bear to look confusedly towards the sky. He waved it away, and the four-legged perching owl impersonator strode between the next four or five boulders using its exceptional reach to make short work of it. Now it was Max's turn.

"Try not to enter the water, it is sacred to our god," explained Leslie, to them.

"Well I don't really know that I care about that," boasted the blonde one, who had already made it across the preferred way simply because the stones looked more difficult.

"He's right Stone, you use the doormat when you visit someone's house," said Max, "especially when they're a god or whatever."

Agent Martin walked up to the boulder, looking left and right to see that no, not even as far as the river's ends curled away beyond the trees, were there any jet-skiing bear henchmen or – god forbid – *sharks* waiting to ride him down half-way. Max had always been afraid of deep, unclear water, and this river was at least fifty feet across, murky and restless. Looked easy enough though, now Leslie was almost there, as he certainly was no gymnast.

"Come on, Max! It isn't that hard!" shouted Agent Stone, never straying too far from herself.

Max steadied his hands on the first rock and went to take a step when he began to hear a very distinct, if faint, gargling sound from behind that chilled his blood. He then heard Stone again:

"Max, we got a wolf! Hurry up!"

Agent Martin leapt to the top of the rock faster than any living human has ever left a basement after turning off the lights, such was his surprised fear. He turned to look back and put a hand on his holster, expecting to need it.

What the agent saw instead of a pack of lean, mutant killers pouring from the trees, was instead a lone squidwolf, loping unmistakably towards him but sputtering like an old car, and trailing a black ink from its open, fangless jaws. As it neared him it slowed, and Max prepared to shoot it. . . during which time it glanced up at him, lifting its heavy, fleshy face and immediately having to lower it again. He was horrified to see that the beast's eyes were no longer bulging and squid-like but absent, and more akin to craters leaking black jelly – its paws were also shorter now and deformed. It displayed an obviously pained gait as it lessened its run to a jog, approaching the river. Max was transfixed on the miserable creature and did not fire.

"Kill it, Max!" hollered Stone, never one to mince words.

The dying squidwolf stood on two gnarled hind legs and leaned against the crossing stone, it lay its finned and fleshy head at Agent Martin's feet, looking up at him with nothing. It slid sideways from the rock and splashed heavily into the stream, half in and half out. Max turned away, shuddering, and continued to cross the stones to join his team.

"It's dead. It's just dead, don't. . . worry," explained Max, continuing to cross.

"I wasn't," said Stone.

Just then Leslie let out a mental gasp, sharp and sudden it caught Max by surprise and he slipped off of the final boulder, landing one foot into the stream ten feet from the far side, sunk up to his knee. The stream bed crunched a little under the weight of him, and his arms both clung for dear life to the boulder. Leslie was pointing towards the squidwolf corpse. Something was happening. The corpse was moving.

Small red crabs, large white ones, medium brown ones and a host of other wet things had latched themselves to different parts of the wolf's confused physiology and were dragging it below the river's small waves. A blue and purple octopus sat on the wretched creature's neck, its probing tentacles extracting matter from what remained of the wolf's deflated skull. The little monsters worked in the dead way that ants do, towards their utterly emotionless machinations, pulling skin from a face that once was capable of recognizing others – without so much as thought.

Now Max felt the thing that once pinched his tongue, pinching his ankle, he looked down and saw something below the surface of the river.

"Shit! Oh holy shit!" yelped Max.

Vaguely, he saw *many* somethings that composed a surface that was not the true bottom of the river at all, and they were moving. Max *tore* himself from the water and stomped frantically to the shore with the power of a two-shoed planet-smashing hammer, collapsing into Leslie, who held onto him tightly.

"I always believed the Call was only for greater

beasts and those with warm blood and minds to hear Him. It appears that many more were called. Ones that. . . I could never call brothers," Leslie thought out loud, staring at the now-innocent waters.

Stone just looked concerned, and adjusted her sleeves:

"Well they're technically part of nature, aren't they?"

"I suppose so, yes," agreed Leslie, who felt unconvinced to them.

"It was warm," said Max, finally, standing on his own legs again, "the rain is cold and the wind is colder but that river. . . was *warm*."

"Are you sure you didn't just experience your fear in a very specific way, Agent?" Stone was teasing him, but lazily, because she too, was staring.

"No, shut up, that was real. The water was warm."

"We have to see my brother immediately," warned Leslie, as he began to waddle up the hill towards the tiny village. The two agents followed suit, Max unclipped his holster, Stone cracked her knuckles.

As they passed between the pinewood huts and lean-to's and bark-roofed three-quarter cages it became clear that these were the structures that had been made by the beavers, the same two who had absconded from the mountain, probably after seeing something like what the agents had just seen.

Inside each small home there burned a fire, and yet none of them were occupied, one hut had even burned down some time ago, and still had a fire going in the husk of it. The grass was thick and choking, it grasped your ankles as you waded through it. The bushes looked frozen and hard, the flowers had long petals and odd shapes to them. Oddest of all were the pines that defined the borders of the settlement – they were so dark green as to appear nearly black, they leaned towards the mountain and their branches drooped in the rain, what few needles remained on them seemingly blurred together.

"Everything feels wrong here," spoke Agent Stone.

"How did you not see how unnatural it was all becoming?" asked Max, "was it always like this?"

"Until now I had never seen it through anyone else's eyes. My brother and I, I always thought of us as one, yet it appears—

". . . What?" asked Max, they were coming nearer to the edge of a sort of plateau at the top of the hill, still no bears in sight – none in the houses, none at the fire pits outdoors.

Stone silently regarded the mountain as it loomed above them. She was lost in her private thoughts. Leslie looked at Max and spoke to him specifically:

"Is it possible for a soul to be both evil and. . . not evil, at the same time? This is something that I wonder over."

Max thought about it. He wasn't really sure how he had become such good friends in such a short amount of time with this person that wasn't even a person, really. The question itself was even a little beyond his own occasional existential musings, and there were some much more corporeal concerns on the front of his mind right now. He still wanted to give a good answer though, for what it was worth.

"There are two sides to everything, Leslie. I think that all you can do is just protect the people you care about." He looked towards his partner, who seemed to be practising her latent psychic mountain-sundering abilities.

Hopefully she'd be ready to share with the rest of the class soon.

"Everyone makes mistakes. The thing is admitting them, and doing your best to try and fix things after," Max explained.

Leslie put an arm around him, his energy smiled as bright as his flower:

"Then I will hold out hope for my brother."

Max nodded, but really just wanted to say "No, that guy's probably just an asshole."

They could see the end of the climb now, where the hill flattened out before the mountain. They could hear an assembly of bodies breathing and chattering up there.

"Should something tragic befall us, I would have you know that I have always enjoyed the scent of you, Max. Scent is a powerful thing, and it was how I felt that I could trust you, when first you found me."

Max was not entirely sure how to respond to that.

"My. . . scent? What is my scent like?"

"Oh," the bear recalled, "faintly like lavender."

The party reached the crest of the hill and climbed over it, standing now on a flat, wide area where everything they had searched for all at once gathered together out of convenience. Lucky them.

They took in the scene. There were almost two-dozen bears assembled of all different species, black and brown and short and tall, there was even a solitary, sweaty-looking polar bear who probably escaped from the zoo from the looks of the city-bear way he fanned himself. Some of them sat on stumps and some of them simply stood on all fours. In the very center of the makeshift amphitheater, both Agent Fisher and Agent Davison were tied – weapons still with them, in a show of both power and arrogance – to either side of a low, wide tree trunk by means of a rope of roughly hand-woven grass that some bear in the crowd was feeling very proud over indeed. It was like a giant wooden candle with human wicks on both ends. Behind them all was the base of the mountain, in front of that was a hill of piled earth that opened to blackness and perhaps most importantly, a thirteen-foot tall brown bear towered above the agents on two legs. A great-horned owl flapped to his shoulder and perched wearily. Bill spoke across all their minds with a voice like mountains moving:

"Greetings humans. . . greetings. . . *brother*. I heard of your approach, and I have waited just for you, just for a little while. . . "

A bear in the audience yawned, proving his statement, showing that it might have been a long little while too. The trio made their way towards him, with Leslie in the middle, they walked amongst the watching bears and stood across from Bill – Davison and Kayle both saw them approaching. Dick jumped in his seat and looked confusedly from Leslie to Bill, noticing, as

Max was at this very moment, that they were shockingly similar, even for bears. Must have been twins, although one was much larger.

"I know your names," thought Bill, trying to intimidate the agents in the rumbling tones of an ancient castle shifting.

"I am Leslie," confirmed Leslie.

Bill seemed annoyed by that, he shook his great head, pointing to the two humans that flanked his brother.

"Snacks and Boulder!" declared Bill with a grand flourish.

Davison's laughter broke the silence first, as Bill looked around and saw no recognition, he spoke again:

"Was that. . . not correct?" he said, with a similar sweeping gesture for some reason or another.

"Max," said Max.

"Stone," said Stone.

"Dick Davison, bro!" said Dick Davison.

"Yeah, I'm Kayle," added the other tied-up agent.

"Leslie," repeated Leslie, with dead seriousness.

"Alright, alright, I don't care!" bellowed Bill in his bowl-rumbling mental voice, swatting the messenger-owl from his shoulder, she who had clearly heard their names wrong and had just made a total ass out of her glorious leader.

The haggard looking bird flew over and perched with the congregation, bag-eyed from being made to stay up all day, just for this crap.

"Carrying on then. . . today is an important day, because today we summon our god! He has called to me and I have heard Him. Today is our day of ascendance!"

Bears in the stands erupted into roars and growls of approval with slow, scattered sentiments of "I am excited" and "yes good" emanating from their minds. Some of them, however, were more silent, and some of them shifted uncomfortably. Bill ignored these ones, Leslie did not.

The Once And Future King of Bears slammed his mightily clawed hand onto the center of the log that held the agents, drawing up with him as he raised his paw again, a tall green flame that flickered and grew, beginning to ignite the wood in defiance of the rain. Bill himself stood over them improbably, likely magically, almost bone-dry in the torrential downpour – as though he were in cahoots with the weather itself – as though he and the rain had come to an understanding. Leslie stepped forward and held his own paw out ahead of himself flatly, then lowering it and bringing the flames down too, until they ceased to burn. This was a spot of sibling rivalry that was sure to reach the high court of the front seat.

"What are you doing, brother? Why would you defy me?"

"Because this is not what we wanted!" pleaded Leslie.

"Not what. . . *you*. . . wanted. That is why we are two and not one."

"I. . . I don't understand," thought Leslie, unhappily.

Max looked nervously to his partner, and drew his gun as she drew her sword. He could see she was communicating something subtle, yet complex to the two other agents with an intricate series of nods and head                                                    tilts.

"Rise, warriors! Rise, clan of Twobears! Rise and fight for your king!" Bill commanded.

The assembled bears, all at once, though some slower than others, got to all fours and took steps forward.

"Sit! Do not listen to him!" argued Leslie, who swept the crowd with a motion from his hands, and they sat again quietly. One of them coughed.

"Rise! *Destroy them!*"

They rose.

"*Be calm!* We have not come to harm you!"

They all sat down again, beginning to groan with the effort, one of them at least now thinking rude things. It couldn't be told whether they were all of one mind to destroy the invaders, or simply wishing to be left alone to do their bear business. Kayle looked towards the small one still wearing her arrows and hoped nobody else would. Bill stepped on top of the log, which was wide and flat enough not to roll, roaring in frustration at his indecisive soldiers. Max noticed still more nodding amongst his comrades and wondered why he wasn't in the know.

"Why must you *always* deny me what I wish for?"

"Because what you wish for is destroying our home! Have you seen what has happened to all the creatures not brought under our power? Our magic is dark, not like we thought."

Bill chuckled the evil laugh of a being that knew all,

and shared little. From the top of his pedestal he addressed the small party of heroes:

"If you would see me undone, if against all odds and favours you would oppose me. . . then I should wish to see you try. Come then, for I am woven of the Earth! Send your strongest man to *break* against me."

Bill was distracted slightly now by his sweeping commencement address, gesturing towards the heavens, backed by the scattered hollers of his brethren – by the 'woof' and 'sheesh' of an over-heating polar bear.

While he peacocked, the agents acted quickly: Stone dashed forward and cleanly sliced the grass rope tied messily around the log and holding the others in place – Kayle Fisher, now freed, stood up fast and drew an arrow from her hip-belted quiver, nocking it on her bow and training it on Bill, waiting only a millisecond for the last step.

"I, who could stand against the fist of the sea and be unharmed—

Dick Davison rose, dusted his lapels theatrically, wasting a little time, but not too much – a well-honed skill of his – and stepped towards Bill, dropping down to one knee and delivering a haymaker of tectonic force to the beast's exposed ankle all in one liquid-smooth dance. Bill the Bear buckled under his own weight and *slammed* backwards into the wet ground. Max Martin felt left out.

"OH, MOTHER. . . *NATURE!*" hollered Bill as he grasped at his shattered foot-wrist.

It was definitive now, the two smartest bears were intelligent to the point where they devoted some mental capacity to the understanding of pain, and apparently, self-censorship – a tell-tale sign of sentience.

"You will all pay dearly for this, you *worms*, I am a mighty warlock!" threatened Bill from the ground, where it meant slightly less, "*I am more than you!*"

"The only payment you'll be accepting soon is Hell-dollars, you know, so you can purchase goods and services where you're going!" shouted Kayle, who stood over him with a loaded arrow aimed between his eyes.

She looked up and over at Dick Davison hopefully, for guidance on the delivery of that finishing line. He only shrugged, because as far he was concerned, that was actually pretty good.

"Yeah, that!"

Agent Fisher loosed the arrow from nigh on point blank range, it soared like Helios' own javelin a full two feet until it merely powdered itself against Bill's shimmering green energy field. Kayle jumped back to avoid shrapnel, and stood in awe of his imperviousness.

"Ooh, yeah, I forgot to tell you guys he can do that when he's paying attention," Dick informed them, sucking on his teeth reproachfully.

Bill climbed to his feet again, standing un-easily on his left leg. He looked around at the small army of bears that surrounded them, and the one who defied him most directly.

"They won't help you, I will make sure of that," Leslie told him.

"They won't be necessary."

The four agents surrounded Bill and readied their weapons for another strike, they gambled on the idea that he couldn't deflect them all at once.

"But why are we fighting again, Brother? You need not spend your final breath in battle. It appears you have forgotten the way of our god, it appears you have forgotten much."

Leslie stood stock still, focusing. His fur tossed in the wind and ran with water, but his small pink flower remained unmoved.

"Would you like. . . to hear Him, again?"

Max looked at Leslie, and Leslie looked at Max, as well as the two brave warrior women he had come to respect as highly as fellow bears. Leslie looked last towards Dick Davison, who was the one he had sent to potentially die, due only to his own cowardice and a misunderstanding that did not excuse it. The stoic bear turned its green eyes on Max and closed them.

"No, thank you," spoke Leslie.

Bill leaned forward and slammed his paw into the fallen log, shattering it like brittle chocolate. He brought his second paw down and assumed the feral position that only four legs can properly represent.

"Very. . . well."

They all heard it, his volcanic voice coming from the sky itself, perhaps. The massive, muscled back of the bear who once was merely Bill *split open* following the fault of his spine and peeling away as an old shell would, while something glowing bright like liquid emerald burst out from inside with the sound of a perfectly good rug being ruined. All that was bear flesh curled away and made room for the fresh form below, whatever it was. The new creature looked awfully similar to a bear as they remembered it, only so much larger, with fur that did not blow in the wind – fur that was hard like carapace and alive with swimming, insidious ichor.

The agents wasted no time closing in on the demon bear with everything they had, and it wasted no time in laying waste to their efforts. Davison immediately fired two shotgun blasts into its side, both glanced away or dissolved so quickly he couldn't tell they were ever fired. Kayle shot her arrows, and ran to stab at the bear with her knife when they, too, became dust against his jade armour. Max emptied his magazine uselessly at its hulking joints and Stone charged confidently forward, leaping into the air, swinging her katana for its monstrous hollow eyes that glowed with the light of an other-worldly sun.

As they came at him ineffectually, Bill pounded the mud with one great paw and shuddered the hill itself below them, knocking all but Stone straight into the slippery ground. She threw her sword blade-first into the grass and drew her fully-automatic, bracing the weapon with both hands she unleashed her fury in the form of thirty-five boiling metal slugs erupting from the short barrel in only a few forgotten seconds. They tore at the bear's face as it opened its jaws to answer her, and ricocheted around its cavernous mouth until they ran out of energy and clattered together on the ground. Stone drew her breath heavily, not even aware that she had been screaming obscenities under the cover of gunfire. Max witnessed all the nothing that they had accomplished with their assault, and, looked to Leslie, who was now working his hands in a complicated pattern – eyes closed, humming coolly. What shocked

Max more than anything he had seen or heard today, was that the humming sound that often came from this bear, for once, he noticed, was. . . *harmonic.*

The telepathic crowing of the assembled bears grew muddled and suppressed. They didn't move, in fact they were curiously still. They were silent pewter statues in the screaming wind and rain.

Suddenly the sky fell. Not literally, but that is the only possible way that the sensation could be described. As Leslie lowered his high-held paws slowly and deliberately, Bill became hunched and compressed, like the roof of the world closed in on him with every second. His spectral growls gained volume as the agents picked themselves up, and advanced again. Dick Davison grappled the demon bear by its shovel-sized ears, pushing it down and hammering it with elbow, fist and forearm. Kayle single-handedly ripped away one of the bear's hind legs as it dug into the ground, and began to pull it from the body with all of her considerable strength so that it couldn't stand against the beating it received. Agent Stone calmly retrieved her sword with a smile and moved to don her executioner's hood. They appeared to have the upper hand now, with Leslie's assistance, but Max was worried, because even over all the wailing madness that invaded their minds from the losing mountain, he could still make out his friend's quiet thoughts.

Agent Martin got up against the pushing wind and went to Leslie's side, he looked at the bear's face. Its eyes were close tightly, and until Max placed his small hand on the bear's large shoulders, they didn't open. When they did, Max met them with his own, and he didn't even have time to ask. Leslie shook his head slowly, thin streams of bright green energy leaking from his eyes, washing away in the wrath of the ocean that fell around them.

Davison delivered a crushing full-bodied elbow to the beast's brow and a piercing shatter could be heard over the hill as one of Bill's great solar eyes burst and shone hot emerald rays into the dim woods. Dick was about to yell something victorious, but at the moment Max finally understood Leslie's silent thoughts, he whipped around:

"THIS ISN'T GONNA DO IT, *MOVE!*"

*CRACK*, went the roof the world, as Leslie lost control.

Bill shook off Agent Kayle and pushed up against the ground to defy the impossible weight that pressed him down, lifting the entire three-hundred pounds of muscled human punching-machine that hung off of his snout –opening his canyon jaws and with the sound of the very air around them *bursting*, fired the agent into the sky with a blink of bright light. Davison flew thirty feet and crashed into a hard-looking bush that shattered upon impact with the man. Bill emitted a mental laughter, the sound of which invoked a voice belonging to the space between stars. With another *CRACK* and then another, Bill fired two more bursts of starlight at Agent Stone, who deflected some of it with her blade, and Fisher, who tried booting it away like a deathly soccer ball and ended up flat on her back again. Leslie collapsed and Max tried to catch him, instead going down *with* him, because Leslie weighed more than all four agents combined.

"You will never. . . be stronger than me," Bill spoke to all of them, but specifically to his brother.

The green-eyed monster lifted itself slowly to its imposing full height in standing and pounded forward to the defeated bear. Leslie managed to stand, eyes-closed, with well-meaning but utterly useless help from the doting Agent Martin. Max tried to alert him:

"Leslie, are you hearing me?" he snapped wet fingers.

Leslie stirred, and opened his two dimming suns. Max tried to make him smile one more time.

"Did you hear yourself? Man, I heard you, you finally did it! Your humming was finally beautiful. What a time to master something, eh?"

The waking bear gave him a curious thought:

"What is. . . *humming?*"

Max was surprised. All this time, all these different moments, was he *never* aware of the sound he made when things became tense? They were interrupted.

"Will you return to me now? You must join me under the mountain, or He will never rise," Bill explained, in a voice that filled your entire mind as it came, leaving only room for fear, "can you hear Him now? He is calling us again, just as promised."

Max watched Leslie, who was clearly distracted. Perhaps he *was* hearing something again. Although he trusted the bear, there was nothing they could do if the Call proved too strong.

"I cannot believe what you have done here,"

thought Leslie, defiantly.

". . . What *we* have done," corrected Bill.

"I have imparted *none* of this madness!"

"Yet you. . . are a part of me," said Bill, "and that is your greatest sin. Do you remember?"

"No! No, I don't remember anything" fought Leslie.

Max looked to his allies, all stunned on the ground, Davison still unmoving. He was afraid he would be shot down if he rushed to help them, so he had to stand with the bear for now.

"When He found me, you and I were of one body, and when He took us, all the parts of me that would not acquiesce. . . became *you*."

*Holy crap*, thought Max. He felt Leslie tense:

"Impossible, we were brothers and thus are wholly separate, this monstrosity you have become is never something that I could ever be."

"Exactly," chuckled Bill, "and that is why the voice of our God has never left me. Only you."

"But you told me—

"I have told you many things, and you have believed many more, for it is your nature to perceive only what is good."

"But the family we created! All of these fellow bears and creatures we raised to join us, what are they to you?"

"Soldiers. Albeit in need of training. My pact with Him was to protect His scroll, and His river, and His mountain. In return I, or rather, *we*. . . will be granted *immeasurable* power! And when this power comes I will require an army to lead." Bill explained the situation calmly, feeling, as villains often do, that there was no possible way it could all go wrong now.

The tremendous, eminent, emanating bear king currently lighting the grey world with the colour of life held out one terrible hand to its smaller self.

"He is asking us to return to him. Will you join me in becoming eternal?"

Leslie glanced at his home, perhaps for the last time, seeing roughly two-dozen bears, an owl and the ghosts of others long-lost, watching him from around the mouth of their cave still frozen, though frozen now in awe. He looked back upon their modest, fire-lit shelters and the verdant rolling hill they had always called home. He looked South, under the stone-grey dome of the sky towards the human mountain where the strong girl had sat to see him. Leslie looked at each and every human that had come to know him as a friend – as they struggled to merely stand – then finally he looked at Max. Max stared up at him, wiping rain from his small brown eyes.

Leslie removed the pink flower from behind his big ear, the one with the wide floppy petals and the happy yellow face, and placed it in the chest-pocket of Agent Martin's brown jacket. It stayed there, standing out brightly, defying the weather.

"Max. If a demon from your past should ever come to take you. . . just make sure, that it takes only you."

Leslie the Bear stepped away and touched his own hand, the image of Bill drained from sight until it had filled their singular body with all the magic that it would take. Leslie was no longer Leslie, he was now, as he had always been: Twobears. Two very different souls had been combined to create a single form once again, and after a flash of light it could be seen that what now stood in the shadow of the mountain was neither of them.

Natalie sheathed her sword in a piece of splintered log and helped Agent Fisher to her feet. She had heard the exchange, she had seen the flash, but she was still surprised by what was ahead. Getting down on all fours across the grassy plateau stirred and whipped into a muddy froth by combat, was a simple brown bear of no particularly exceptional size. There was nothing special about it at all – except no, it did have something, it was veined with a green ether that flowed and glowed beneath its fur – and as soon as she saw it, it was gone, and then back.

Max had moved to Agent Davison's side and the bear, currently fully aglow with energy, was only a dozen metres from the cave and running full tilt. This couldn't be good, as this was exactly what Bill had wanted. Natalie moved to chase and intercept, but then something changed, and it stopped so suddenly it fell over, shaking its head madly and spinning around. The bear smashed its paws against the hill and roared at no-one in particular. The other bears were crowding around it now, trying to help, as it would seem. Flickering again with the energy that spidered its body, the bear set glowing green eyes on Agent Stone and charged. From where it was, she had ten seconds to react and started by retrieving her sword. The bear was violently shaking its head the entire time and growling to itself. It occurred to Natalie now that two bears were charging at her, but only one of them was in control. When she saw the eyes up close, she knew which one.

The rampaging ursine royalty came within striking distance, and swung a claw at her, in the last seconds before impact, all the bright energy swimming inside of the bear went dark, and what came upon her was momentarily – nothing more than an animal, or a friend. With a move so perfect it almost appeared to be specifically practiced for, Natalie dodged low, hopping back, and coiled to strike. The already-dripping silver katana held by the small warrior plunged under the bear's chin and through its neck, mouth and skull, presenting itself neatly between the massive ears on top. An expertly timed riposte, and when she saw Leslie's eyes in the muscled face, lightless but still recognizable, she allowed herself a smile. Two bears died on her sword in that moment, one gratefully, to the lamenting chorus of twenty others who watched nearby – or so she thought.

Just as the spoon-sized lids began to close, they burst open again suddenly, green fire pouring from behind the wild solar orbs inside, and running through the skin like magma under a mountain. One of the two bears, and two guesses as to which one, opened their mouth wide and *jerked* hard to the side, snapping the katana blade in half with only a short and brittle lean. Bill tore them away and pounded back along the grass with the mighty second wind of a dying animal. Natalie stared blankly at the jagged edge of her broken third arm.

"That wasn't how that was supposed to go," she

said flatly.

Max Martin, satisfied with his partner's expectedly quick sword work, had turned away, only to be immediately alerted by the twang of snapping steel. He looked from the slowly rising Dick to see Bill, one of two bears, again leading their shared body to the cave mouth below the mountain – twelve inches of sharpened sword blade still stuck firmly in their skull, skin glowing with a river-map of bright energy. The one package stuffed via factory error with two bears flung itself wildly towards the mouth of the cave, internally conflicted on a scale that even the most highly over-paid psychiatrist could not begin to fathom – the entirely literal magical situation of unsuccessfully sharing one body together and two minds apart. Max felt his heart sink into his stomach and begin to dissolve, as the two sorcerous bears that had, only a short time ago, seemed very much like the be-all and end-all, went flailing into the maw of the black cave like a massive red herring.

A few silent moments passed where the agents assembled under the mountain, and the bears crudely, mentally, argued amongst themselves in the absence of a leader – or at least they did for a little while, as a pale green smoke began to rise from them. Those bears who had been standing up now reverted to four legs and the messily projected thoughts that could be heard from where they all gathered degraded into gibberish before fading entirely. Soon the animals were simply that, all standing around, pawing at each other with massively confused expressions on their hairy faces – exactly like a rugby team transported suddenly to a basketball court. A small black one wearing burgundy wizarding robes stolen from a strange forest-man even less deserving of them, fell forward into the mud, dead from arrow wounds.

The pale ether that *was* them, all that they were, rose and danced away, heading inside the earth and following the two bears. Their magic was gone now, it disappeared within the cave that, in honestly, was really more of a pit – a pit dug by the bears themselves to hold the artifact that spawned their whole confused religion – the religion that had given them purpose and sentience. All of this begun and ended below a glooming mountain – as they kept referring to it – though it really was far too small to be a true mountain, and was something else, something that didn't have a name yet – or didn't want one.

Whatever it was, Leslie had called it a bear's tooth. Whatever it was, Stone had called it a weapon. Whatever it was, its true shape pinched at the tip of Max's tongue just as the river had pinched at his ankle, and now, seeing it up close, he knew what it looked like. . . *a claw*.

It was at that moment – one of brutishly overt poetic significance – that an inexplicably present passing dove chose to die in front of them. It fell from the sky, its corpse squelching into the mud and seaweed-fingered grass at Max's feet – so he inspected it. Its neck was grotesquely elongated by the forced arrival of gills. He showed it to his team.

Agent Natalie Stone had nothing left to do now but agree with a long-dead conversation she had held with somebody who would have really been worth listening to:

"This is not bear magic," she admitted.

# 13

## LITTERA SCRIPTA MANET

In the relatively short time it takes to button your shirt, or put on a hat, or end a long-term relationship over text message, turn around and begin another one, everything changed – but not quite as drastically as the kind of change that putting on a new shirt would have been, because that kind of thing can really turn a day around – and this kind of change really just made everything worse.

The rain that had battered them relentlessly for two miserable days stopped suddenly and evaporated into the wind as quickly as you could notice it changing – having apparently served its purpose. The sun was out now, a welcome sight in any other circumstance but oddly disquieting in this one. It sat directly above the great stone claw, swollen but cold, at what was likely exactly noon. Eldritch evils seemed oddly specific about time, it always seemed.

The Earth itself began to rumble and shift, so much like an earthquake but so much more specific than that. They heard a creeping, multifaceted, deafening crack – one that could have been the sound of an iceberg splitting, only, it would have to have been an iceberg the size of the moon. House-sized sheets of rock fell from the mountain, sliding into the woods ahead and to the sides of them, crushing countless unlucky trees that, should they have been alone in the forest when the mountain fell, would still have been clearly audible as cursing their legless forms to the high courts of heaven. More stone fell, and more things were crushed, though nothing on the grassy hill – nothing from the claw to the stream – was so much as dusted with pebbles. The boulders only fell away, and elsewhere. The agents struggled to keep their footing as the ground shook, but remained on guard.

Finally the thin remainder, the two hollow halves of the so-called mountain's whole form, fell apart like a lazy walnut, East and West, everywhere except on the hill or the stream. The assembled bears and singular owl began to scatter, heading towards the water, or wherever the sky was not currently falling. Dick Davison himself possessing of a powerful survival instinct eventually turned to run from the avalanche until Agents Fisher and Stone pointed out to him that it was safest to stay put.

As the tremendous stone shell molted away, a bright red claw – exactly as Max had called it in his head and would surely brag about later – was left standing in its place. Only the bottom third remained encased in the mustache-and-glasses disguise of rock that it once wore. The claw was greatly jagged and gnarled around the edges and ended in a sharp, hooked point near the top. It looked exactly like a lobster's claw, only more *evil*, if that wasn't too plain a way to put it. It looked to be pockmarked in a planetary way with. . . craters? It seemed impossible, but hey, who's really the judge of that?

"Huh," said Dick Davison, in the tones of one who is glad to finally know something for sure:

"God is a lobster."

"What the *hell* are we going to do now?" asked Kayle.

"Fight," said Stone, cleaning her half-katana.

Kayle scoffed:

"Fight? Christ' sake, you little over-achiever. Fight what?"

Stone was on her way to answering when Max noticed she was turning green, and she probably wasn't sea-sick, although that would have been ironic. It wasn't her, instead, it was the sun.

They heard it before they saw it – a low, revoltingly unmusical, and epiphanously familiar hum invaded the brains of every living thing for miles – and they could all tell where it was coming from, and where they had heard it before. Max felt deep pity for Leslie, who he now sincerely hoped had died in that cave, such would be the only sure route to peace from this. Looking towards the gargantuan lobster hand, you would have also seen the sky slowly becoming a sickly shade of lime green – something like pond scum, tinted by the celestial magic of the Great Claw. The hum was not obnoxious, like an uncomfortable bear's would have been, it was instead maddening and invasive. Coming from its true source now, the hum was devilishly focused and not at all whimsical. You could block your ears to it with plates of lead and it wouldn't become any quieter.

As the baleful sound began and the once golden sunlight, as though filtered through the blue ocean itself, turned the colour of greed – there were rumblings down by the river. The long row of large stones that had once provided the only crossing to those who wished to pass the 'sacred' stream now cracked and burst as well, the five grey points becoming five red points on a spiked and ragged lobster tail rising from the stream, creating a wide, flat wall that dammed the river and slowed the flow of its bursting banks – as well as tossing an unlucky bear that had been the first to try to cross it and flee to the relative safety of the woods. There were other bears charging towards the stream now as well, at this moment caring very little for what was once sacred. The first two were dragged below as soon as their front paws hit the water, roaring uselessly as a hundred tiny hand-beaks pulled them under slowly. This caused the other twenty-or-so to back off and pace the tasting edge of the water unsurely.

"Shit, dude," appraised Dick Davison, feeling as sick to his stomach as everyone else.

As the green light soaked in and the mad, million-voiced mumble of the Great Claw picked up gradually, *things* began to finally emerge from the river, things that nobody had ever seen before, or had ever wanted to. The bears retreated as the surface broke in a dozen places at once, back up the hill and towards the agents.

The first things out of the water were the crabs. Some stood tall as a man now, walking on stick-legs that invoked all the racking fear of a spider in armour, some were still low – but wide, and cruelly mutated with huge spines that they struggled under the weight of. Others came from the water mostly unchanged, but with new arms and legs and more and bigger claws bursting from their old ones like Robin Hood splitting arrows in reverse. They shambled out of the river and up the wet bank in droves, utterly horrifying to the one of them.

Next came the fish, some had grown extra heads and vaguely hominid-styled tentacles to propel them out of water, and a few had even been bred with crab kind in very spur-of-moment ways. One extremely large, now shark-sized salmon, emerged sporting only two thickly-muscled man legs. It looked directly at Max, and broke into a loping sprint that chilled him to his core. It fell down almost immediately though, because it was a fish with legs.

Although most of the coming monstrosities were born of fish and crabs in the nursery of nightmares that the mountain's ring-river had apparently always been, some were crayfish turned large as wolves – and there were of course the occasional once-octopi sporting upturned nests of nine or more legs and the amorphous cranial dome to climb them gradually towards prey. The ranks of unknowable horrors moved silently, powered by the green drone. All the other noise in the world came from the mammals on that hill, and perhaps the *last* noise of the world too, looking at how things were going. Max noticed that amongst the sea's army were creatures that were not even capable of surviving in this biome under any other circumstances, and he could not

fathom where they had come from or from how far –
perhaps the world had only the irresponsible hubris of
nearby specialty restaurants to blame for that. However
they got here, they had enjoyed the safety of months to
gather under the protection of a thoroughly foolish bear
clan, and an unnaturally warm, 'sacred' river to wait in.

More came, mutating straight from the river and
onto the shore, more and more until there were too
many to count. Bears were running past them now, back
to the oddly consistently assumed safety of high ground
in situations of potential murder – as discussed earlier.

Dick Davison sighed, and simply began to stretch,
limbering up for what would surely be something to
drink over later. Stone grabbed for the satellite phone in
her bag on Max's back and dialed the Bureau for
backup. Kayle nudged the nervous agent with the
soaking black helmet of hair, saying:

"I've got an idea, man, follow along."

She stepped ahead as the bears came stampeding
back up the hill.

"Builders, scholars, men and mothers, proud
warriors of the Twobears clan! I know you can no longer
speak back to me, but I am sure that you can still *hear
me!*" Kayle addressed them as loudly as she could.

Some of the bears looked up at her and stopped
running.

"*He* bears the favour of your leader, fight with him
and you fight with the memory of your king!"

Max caught on and started pointing out the flower
in his chest pocket, the one that Leslie had given him.
Some of the braver looking bears ceased their

'regrouping' and wandered over, sniffing at him. Max was shaking a little, as even a calm grizzly bear was still a very huge thing to stand so close to.

"These are your homes, and even without your magic, you must try to defend them. Are you not *all* kings of the forest?" Kayle continued, quite convincingly.

She really had a knack for this. Max added to it, feeling immediately silly:

"For the forest!" he yelped.

"Break them with your bear-hands!" shouted Dick Davison, who snapped a branch over his leg as he did so.

The tell-tale blackened fur of the previously self-immolating grizzly bear – actually *glad* to be magic-less now as he never quite got the hang of it – was still an impressive beast, spells or no, if a little over-cooked, and he roared his smaller compatriots into position. It was working, and a battle line was formed on the plateau of the hill under the mountain. Twenty-one angry bears, four brave agents of the Aversion Bureau, and one groggy, grumpy, yet determined-looking owl stood stoically in the green glow of the alien sun. Below them, hundreds of yards away, an army of sea-themed waking nightmares of all sizes and descriptions floundered towards the forces of good with their various propulsive limbs as slowly as the tide. They would make their stand now, or be washed away.

"Damn it! The connection won't go out! We're on our own, agents!" yelled Stone from the back of their ranks, she ran up and *lobbed* the satellite phone down the hill where it found a recently-upright, sprinting again, man-legged salmon and knocked him off-balance so he stumbled and ploughed through a burnt-out domicile.

The huge blackened grizzly barked his anger at losing his home and began to charge, so they all began to charge. Fur and fury rolled down the hill in an earthen wave of rage, screaming their vengeance at the silent, soaking enemy. Somewhere along the charge, two very familiar deer leapt suddenly out of the hill's dense trees and joined them, volleying insults as they ran, something about 'gross bug faces' and 'polio legs' – which finally was going too far in right direction. The burnt grizzly bear, Dick Davison a la shotgun and the crazed pony-tailed samurai lead the van, while the formidable Kayle Fisher rode a willing mother bear into battle on the far end of the line, firing her bow from atop its muscular hunch. Max tried desperately just to keep up and not shoot himself in the foot whilst running.

The two armies smashed into each other halfway up the hill under the green sun, and for all the eyes between them nobody could remember what specifically had happened to each of them next. It was complete chaos. The largest of the bears broke the brittle limbs of the crab folk with no effort, and crushed the smaller ones underfoot absent-mindedly. The great-horned owl flew from mutant to mutant, plucking the eyes from their stalks and screeching with joy while she did it. Davison ran out of shotgun shells quickly and begun cracking claws with his new silver club instead, whilst Agent Fisher was fighting deftly with a severed crustacean leg at some point, one that she couldn't even remember picking up. And lastly, for being only half a sword, Stone's blade was razor sharp, as well, she knew how to gut a fish – which put the bear warriors into a feeding frenzy that only helped their cause.

The battle was not without casualty, however, as Kayle's riding bear was pulled from underneath her by grabbing tentacles and bludgeoned to death by hammer claws. Some of the smaller bears were simply overrun by many-limbed cat-sized shrimp and picked to pieces. Eventually, both of the jeering deer grew silent, their creative insults no longer audible over the screams of combat.

As Max was finally running out of bullets, and down to less than half of a full clip, someone familiar approached him. His appearance was foreshadowed by the distinct rumble of a diesel truck engine, and the obnoxiously loud footsteps that only mankind makes, splashing and spluttering through the river towards it all. At this point Max was prepared to see anything, anything except for what he actually saw. Come dripping wet and stomping through the press of war, impatiently pushing aside a stilt-legged sardine with fangs and tentacles, was the plaster-haired, popped-collar Duke of Brodom from two nights ago at 'Da Club' – the very same bro from the first time that Max had ever started or won a fight. The man looked sweaty and uncomfortable, his chest seemed to throb noticeably under his tight, deep-necked shirt.

"Whoa! Dude! I didn't expect to see another bro out here. Are you like, here to offer your vessel to the dark god too? *That's cray!*"

Max didn't even know what to say to the man, he simply pointed his gun, finger on the trigger.

"Hey. . . wait, don't I know you? Yeah you're that little prick who broke my tooth! Man you're gonna get it now 'cause your girlfriend ain't here to—

What passed for human speech in some circles suddenly changed to choking and suffocating noises as he tore off his douchey branded clothing to reveal the sprawling octopus tattoo he still sported over his spray-tanned dime-bouncing breasts. His arms and legs elongated and warped with sickening sound effects, the flesh of his neck extended to join his quickly accumulating number of limbs – and so the octobro was born, born of flesh and madness, born of a fatally specific animal tattoo choice made six years ago at five am on a Tuesday morning whilst high on raging testosterone, amongst other things.

Much and more happened after that, but most of it Max would never be able to recall, all thanks to a specific event yet to occur that would make it difficult. Dick Davison may have shown up at that exact moment – he wasn't quite sure – and side by side, they may have matched each fist-tipped tentacle of the octobro pound for pound as they beat it back down the hill, where a timely appearance by Agent Stone had rendered its primary neck both broken and severed – its corpse still reeking of cologne well into the remainder of the battle. Hell, there may have even been a time when two forgotten beavers had ridden a gargantuan oak downstream coming from the West and *cracked* the great tail of the mountain, allowing a torrent of pent-up water to wash all but the largest sea-demons far away to their distant fates on the covers of schlock maritime newspapers. There could even have been a later time when Kayle's warrior braid was cut a few inches short by clacking mutant crab claws – and in her entirely possible fury, she may have struck the offending horror so strongly with her elbow that its spraying innards had blinded a nearby ten-legged eighty-eyed trout monster so severely that it picked its next fight with a hungry grizzly and was promptly mutilated. Many things may have happened. Many things were likely forgotten, because eventually, the big salmon with the long legs found its old enemy with the short ones.

At some point when the battle was nearly balanced in their favour – the half-dozen bodies of pulled-apart Kodiaks and black and brown bears far underweighting the all-you-could-kill forces of the enemy – Max was alone, catching a breather and scrounging his bag for extra nine-millimeter ammunition on the far side of a yet-undestroyed bear shack. That was when it found him – the same man-legged, six-foot tall few-hundred pound salmon from before, well, it didn't have legs back then – yet somehow max just knew that this was the one that had tackled him on the bridge, as it had the same humongous pink belly, now partially shredded and spilling golf ball caviar. The fish came on, leaning into its macabre locomotion. He remembered the pitiless look this thing gave him on the bridge whilst he had sat there unbreathing, and gathered a similar amount of empathy to return to it. Max swung the bag back on and aimed his last three bullets.

"You smug son of a bitch, *how are you still alive?!*"
*POW – POW – POW*

Three bullets were nothing to the huge flat head lowered at him by this stubborn fish, and it bore right through them, though it tripped unsurprisingly at the last possible moment and *smashed* into his chest again – sending him flying into the mud to lose a little consciousness. His last thoughts were of an article that once told him getting beaten up by fish imbued good levels of omega 3 or something. . . maybe that was wrong. . . *maybe. . .*

When Max was roused the sky was still green, and the smell of dead seafood still permeated. It couldn't have been more than a minute that he was out and perhaps he was a little upset that he hadn't simply missed the whole thing – Hobbits had always made it look so easy, and brain-damageless. Max checked Leslie's flower – it was still there.

Stone was standing above him. The talented agent unsheathed her sword from the nearby brain of a scythe-wielding crayfish that had one eye bulbously malformed around a rock lodged within it, one that must *really* have had it out for her to see the state of its limbs upon death. She spoke to him:

"You should really stick with me, Max," she said, helping him up, "you're just lucky Smokey was here and likes salmon so much."

Agent Martin looked over and saw the hulking, sweaty polar bear from earlier gleefully submerged in the biggest, most man-legged salmon that ever there was

– having himself a little picnic. Max had expected to see the de-facto leader of the bear army, the hulking grizzly with the old burnt fur, not the exact opposite of that, which was the exquisitely non-smoke coloured one.

"Smokey?" he asked.

"Just a default bear name, I like to think," offered Stone, shrugging.

The battle was winding down, and the river was no longer acting as a nightmare factory. Only a dozen assorted creatures did battle with their army now, and most of the bears were preoccupied feasting on their kills. The rumble of the Great Claw remained, however, and that made them both nervous.

"It was a battle, sure, but it was almost like they were just *feeding* themselves to us, they did not fight any harder than I imagine nature has programmed them to. Now that I think about it, they just kind of. . . walked up the hill," Stone mused, not pleased, looking towards the claw.

"I thought the power might leave if we killed them all. It's never that easy, is it?" asked Max.

"Almost never," agreed Stone, "we should grab the others and check out the bear's cave *right now*, see if there's somebody we have to kill in there and—

She stopped talking suddenly, her face frozen in green.

"They *were* feeding themselves, only, not to us."

"That's a bit of a leap, don't you—

Then he saw it too. Far behind them, way up at the tip of the claw – there was a change. The kind of change that is so subtle and distant that you could not see it until it was pointed out – a detail in the back of a painting that suddenly moves when your head is turned. The Great Claw was now slightly open, and dispersing from the depths of its wicked hinge were many small shapes, small only by virtue of their distance, and as they got closer their size was clear. As large as cars at the smallest, and good cars too, like, sweet cars that went fast – not like your first car, the one you pretend you're okay with when you only have six hundred dollars and your own blood to offer.

They were lobsters, unmistakable but for their tremendous size, eldritch patterning, and honest-to-goodness *bat wings*. A cloud of six or more were coming, the true servants of this dark god, not like the pick-and-mix seafood buffet that had stumbled out of the river. It seemed now, that those were probably only feeder fish, and that these flapping calamities could get even larger if you let them. Not a fun thought. Agent Stone spun him around and held him on both sides.

"Agent. I'm heading up to that cave, and I'm going to see what I can do about shutting this bastard down," she said.

"Wait, *you* go up there, and leave *me* on defence?"

She thought about it, her cognizance grinding against her one-way determination. Somewhere inside, a lightbulb was thrown against a wall.

"Yes. You're right. *I* will stay here, *you* will go up there."

Max nodded. She let go of him.

"Look I'm glad to go, but what do you need me to do? What can I even try?" he asked.

"Max, you were right. Guinevere was right. This is a train, a magical train, and a train is a train no matter how I feel about it. Go in there and find the engine, then piss on the coals, or whatever stops trains," she said to him, keeping an eye on the slow approach of the monsters.

"I thought we were done with that metaphor."

"Shut up. I'm admitting I was wrong, and that we need to play along, because whatever those are up there, they don't listen to reason, they aren't born of reason, and it's a fair shake they don't die reasonably easy either," she was using her commander's voice.

Max shook her hand. It was all refreshingly professional.

"Gwen told me that there is no cure-all for magic. You have to figure out how it works and change it. Is that clear?"

Max looked towards the claw and shuddered, but felt resolute. It was nice to finally be trusted with something.

"Remember our deal? You can't die until you've heard my last words. They're pretty good," she smiled honestly at him, for perhaps the first time ever, and hopefully not the last.

Stone turned to their army, thrusting her shattered sword at the sickly sky while she ordered them in a rare display of infectious charisma:

"Davison, gather the weapons! Fisher, rally the bears! The cavalry has arrived, and it *ain't ours!*"

Max took his first step towards the top of the hill and immediately realized that one or more of his ribs had indeed been broken by that bloody fish. He held his side and sucked it up, it was the least he could do after being trusted with a vitally important mission – not to complain for once. He gritted his teeth and ran up the rain-soaked slope doing his very best impersonation of the kind of guy who would never trip on his face.

Max was halfway there when he heard first contact. Each lobster demigod shook the ground when it landed, and their wingbeats were like heavy bass in his ears. There were shouts, the sounds of death and gunfire, the roars of bears and catastrophic crustaceans alike. At one point Max allowed himself a quick glance, and wished he hadn't. Three had landed, even larger than the cars he had first imagined. They each had all the requisite lobster parts – no formless mutants here – except that their lowest two legs were unnaturally long and thick so they could walk upright, supported by wide, terrible tails that raked the gore they left in their wake. They swung their serrated claw hands slowly and powerfully. Max saw Smokey pounded messily into the ground, and Smokey 2 cut clean in half. He saw Davison and Kayle run a sharpened log through the throat of a tall, spiral-patterned green one and bring it low to the angry swarm of bears. Max returned to his mission, rather macabrely counting his remaining time in bear lives. There were about eleven left, still counting the biggest and baddest. Maybe that would be enough to find the mountain's coals, and relieve himself on them, of them, and by them.

Agent Martin was stepping high out of the deep land-borne seaweed, and moving around low bushes that had, now obviously, been turned to coral. The pines that bordered the hill, he could also suddenly see, were clearly in the final stages of being converted to kelp. All of this was so clear now, even under the maddening green sun, but none of these connections to the ocean had ever occurred to them before, somehow. Max thought it might be high time that the Bureau hired an actual detective. . . or rather just one who wasn't a cat, and above that, one who, unlike Agent Whiskers, would actually show up for work. The mountain shook slightly. He looked up from his distracted thoughts.

Wonderfully, one of the largest cosmic lobster knights had landed right before him, steadied on its tail and lower legs, with six others clacking rhythmically against its armoured chest and its evil leathery wings folding up behind it. The nameless horror had positioned itself in-between Max and the cave – by no manner of coincidence – and was standing right on top of old bits of Bill, most likely. It looked down at him, muttering psychic nothings and clattering its multifaceted bug mouth, gesturing towards him with its pike-long antennae, wanting to taste him. The hum of the Great Claw was louder now, battering his ear drums violently.

*Why do people eat these things?* Max wondered, in the defense-mechanism sort of way that he ignored nagging problems like imminent supernatural death.

The hum was deafening, but also, no longer a hum – it was an engine. Very specific parts of the lobster began to explode one by one, parallel to each other in a left, right – left, right – left, right pattern all the way up to its face which came apart in three pieces, all equally gory. A distinctly friendly biplane turned up and zipped over them as the creature collapsed backward and a faint "Tally-ho!" could be heard on the wind.

"Bilge," yelled Max out loud, "you beautiful, insane old bastard!"

His biplane rode the face of the claw back to the sky, then performed a flawless Immelmann and brought death to the death bringers once more. The boiling barrel of the plane's mounted machine rifle coughed up dragon fire – specifically, the fire of a dragon who'd just been choking on a bit of metal.

Max wasted no time and bolted for the cave. A still-living antennae tried to grab him by the leg, but he simply reached down with his left arm and *tore* it from the chair-sized fragment of skull that it clung to. *Damn, I really need to keep up my physio when I get home*, he thought proudly. Before entering, Max quickly looked to the sky to gaze proudly at his boss, seeing only that the biplane had already attracted its expected attention, and that three of them – black, red and yellow – were firmly on his tail and keeping pace. Max remembered his mission and hurried inside.

Entering the bear's cave was like being transported to another world entirely. Somehow all the sounds of battle were deadened at the threshold, as was any outside light, or sense of hope. Max felt around for his path, noticing the claw-marks that defined the surface of the walls and ceiling here. Hand-dug, Leslie had told him, and for the purposes of protecting the scroll, Bill had admitted. Now that the mountain had revealed itself to actually be a filthy, duplicitous, possibly extra-terrestrial sea god, it only made sense that this hidden cave was meant instead as a crude shrine, to make sure the scroll stayed as close to its author as possible – Old Magick was big into self-publication.

Darkness didn't last long as the tunnel came to a head and Max could make out the luminous form of curled paper hovering over a slab of driftwood, with an unfortunately familiar corpse silhouetted on the ground in front. He had no time to mourn it, or even to confirm it, he only had time to focus on the magic. Max took a few more steps, and a mole appeared – it possessed a small dorsal fin in what was perhaps the most useless display of physical adaptation a terrestrial being has ever exhibited, next to out-of-water ink clouds, of course. This mole was burrowing out of the wall between Max and the scroll when it sensed him – it looked over and tried to dart away, deciding that it probably *couldn't* get by him and his perhaps cat-like predatory reflexes – so it headed the other way, and after coming within just two metres of the scroll was immediately incinerated in a sorcerous conflagration.

"Ah," said Max, "thank you, Mother Nature."

Max made his way towards the pedestal slowly, carefully, bending his intellect against the might of an unknowable evil that may have existed before time itself. He—

He tripped. Max caught his foot on the outstretched paw of the dead bear and fell face-first against the force field that surrounded the magical artifact. *Bill,* he thought bitterly, gathering his balance. But upon realizing that he did *not* suffer the same fate as his fleeing friend the mole, he looked at this jacket pocket where the goofy-looking pink flower still stuck out. *Leslie,* he thought warmly.

"So close, God-damn it," he swore, looking around the small cave for anything that would help.

The scroll itself was a roll of dark yellow, old, old parchment with an ancient, pictorial kind of writing that Max had never seen before. It floated above an amethyst coloured protective tube that looked to be made out of oyster shells or something else. . . oceany. *I can see why somebody would pick that up,* Max imagined.

The fate of the world now rested squarely on his round shoulders, and this was a lot of pressure, so Max 's first action as planetary saviour was to promptly kick the force field uselessly and spit on the scroll. It landed with tiny splatter. He spat. . . *on* the scroll. Max took a moment to consider that. He spat, and it *reached* the scroll, despite the rest of his body being pressed up against this force field like a naked butt on a window. *Typical,* he thought.

"This is one of those moments nobody's ever around to see," Max shared with the two dead bears.

Agent Stone climbed from segment to cursed segment up the back of an apocalyptic yellow lobster – and it did not deign to notice her – alternately ripping chunks of flesh from a meaty, still-living black bear and a horse-sized crab with two torsos and only half of one head, each held in one gargantuan claw. Moments later, the crab possessed an equivalent torso-to-head ratio.

Stone stood on the topmost ridge of its tail and looked over its shoulder, ignoring the obnoxious open-mouth chewing that demigods wrongly believe they can get away with. Down by the river, the exhausted-looking agents Davison and Kayle were working with a team of bears to dismember a fallen red lobster knight. They used small tree trunks from the hill's crushed huts to pry its limbs apart at the joints, whilst the bears chewed its wicked face clean of features. They had learned their lesson already with another one that proved that limb regeneration is not only real, but horribly exaggerated in crustaceans of the Deep Dark and Very Evil variety. The lesson being that it was best to take all the parts at once, or none at all. Almost three-quarters of the bears were now dead and scattered across the grass, but still the remainder fought valiantly. They knew that there was nowhere these monsters wouldn't find them if they ran, and so they battled on side-by-side with the agents. Davison himself was working with a torn-open back, still quite red and noticeable, even in the eye of the green star.

All of this sudden and effective counter-offensive had been made possible by the timely appearance of Bilge piloting Lady Mayhem, his prized biplane. Stone knew, even as the useless satellite phone had soared down the hill towards the ocean's legions, that he would come. Across her entire life he had never let her down once when it truly mattered. Bilge's strafing runs had obliterated a half-dozen of the demons already, and perhaps more importantly, had taken focus off the ground forces for a while, allowing them to defend themselves on just one front at a time. He had brought some truly mean armour-piercing ammunition – which she could almost certainly thank the brilliant Agent Andersen for – but a flock of the bastards were on him now, and one had even grabbed the wing of his plane, tearing some paneling loose.

Black smoke was trailing from Lady Mayhem, and Stone was sick of watching now, even for the mere moment she did. She was also *very* sick of listening to the lobster's giant motor-mouth grind dead flesh. Natalie dropped down to one of its folded, leathery wings and she used that position to lean over and plow her hilt-shard into the connecting joint of the other. She then went leaping from the creature's back and *wrenched* her weapon to her as she fell. Stone landed softy on the deep wet grass and sidestepped the falling tent flap. She gazed towards the Great Claw and the cave below it. Reinforcements were coming, and over the pained screeching of the gluttonous hell spawn towering behind her, she bid Max hurry.

*CLACK* went the fourth rock, also uselessly, this time bouncing off of the scroll's discarded shell. He had hit the scroll itself a few times too, and it appeared impervious. Max wasn't sure how to interact with this thing in any meaningful way without being able to move organic matter past the barrier – so he threw more rocks.

With every missed throw or wildly inaccurate toss from only about six feet away, he angrily thought about the distinct possibilities of Bilge getting pulled out of the sky, and about Stone and her broken sword being crushed into jelly. Davison could be torn in half by now and Kayle could be pulled off of one of her wicked-cool bear mounts and dropped from cloud-height for all he knew. All this because he couldn't figure out a puzzle, couldn't even do the *one* job he had. Max couldn't even throw these stupid rocks very well because of the dumb backpack he was wearing. He shrugged the bag off and threw it hard to the ground, suddenly remembering that it was actually Agent Stone's backpack he wore – this meant the contents had a slim chance of actually being significantly useful. He searched inside for something that might help.

"There's *gotta* be a gadget or a tool in here," he said to himself, or perhaps to the hulking corpse that was becoming his confidant for lack of any others.

Max stopped digging for a second and looked quickly at the still familiar, now-orange eyes of the brown bear corpse that shared this cave. There was one on either side of Stone's embedded katana blade – he choked – but there wasn't any time to think about it right now. The worst part was, however, that he couldn't even tell which one had been in control when they died. He hoped it was Bill, but that was a selfish thought – they were the same soul after all, and neither one deserved this.

Stone's bag had been emptied of her weapons and ammunition before the fight, now there was only her cellphone and a Swiss army knife and some rope, probably the rope that Wade had given them before leaving. Rope wasn't going to be helpful right now, and neither was this stupid binder clip that – *hey*, he thought, *this was in my pocket yesterday*. Max ignored those, but found a marker and pulled that out instead, mistaking its metal body for a canister of secret agent anti-force field spray, or perhaps something that actually existed. The marker was held tight by the binder clip, which was tied to one end of the rope – it was a package deal, apparently.

"Did the wizard make this?" Max asked nobody.

He looked more closely and saw Long-Writer™ carved into both the pen and clip components, and written directly onto the rope part quite conveniently in thick black lines. He thought about what Stone had told him, back when she was admitting that her patented brute force approach would be useless here. Something about discovering how the magic worked, and changing it. He rotated the marker in his hands, staining them black, black like the lines of the symbology present on the sea scroll. . . *changing it*, he thought. 'Permanent' it read. He removed the cap.

Suddenly Max had a stroke – of genius, not blood clots. He stood up and walked back to the pedestal, swinging the clever craft like a lasso and smirking to himself. He would use the rope to get the marker through the force field and alter the symbols on the scroll, changing the way they manifested their magic, or ruining them entirely – whatever worked faster – then everything would go end-over-end for the Lobster god. Max wasn't exactly sure how if it would work, but that's what seemed most fair.

"Get ready to meet your marker," said Max, knowing that nobody would ever be witness to how lame that sounded, and he really just wanted to hear it out loud.

Agent Martin approached the pedestal, once again very carefully, he just had to be *extremely precise* with the first toss. . . he just had to—

*Clap* went the blinder clip as inevitability plucked her putrid harp and the little metal mouth lost grip of the smooth marker that was its charge. It went shooting straight ahead, carrying with it the future hopes of all mankind, being ferociously sworn at, by but one man.

Well this was it – he thought – as soon as that pen was behind the barrier, Max could the kiss the world goodbye. Worse still – he couldn't *actually* kiss the world goodbye because it would surely be long gone by the time he crawled out of this dirty cave to gaze upon the mutant Earth in all of its new, under-the-sea styled glory.

*FFFFF*, went Max.

*Sqqqueeeeeeeaaaakkk*, went the marker.

A midnight-loaded chisel tipped dart hit the surface of the scroll at the perfect angle, sliding smoothly across the length of it and creating a glaring black line. Max could not believe his luck. He ran forward still holding the rope and found the barrier was pushing no harder now than someone's angry grandmother in line for lottery. Slowly, the endless doomsday hum of the world-claw began to warble and change in pitch.

Max was never one to taste an opportunity for overkill and say "no thank you," so he scrambled to find the marker on the floor of the cave and draw as many stupid things as he could think of, all over the wide, metre-long parchment. It steamed against the touch of his writing hand but couldn't harm him, it tried to curl around his limbs like a boa constrictor but he simply untied the binder clip from the rope and clamped its futile corners to the driftwood stand, holding the other end down with his strong left arm.

Where there might once have been a darkly rendered symbol of a sitting king with tentacles for hair, there was now a sitting king with testicles for hair, and a rather impressive erection. Max drew top hats for the fish shapes and mustaches for the demon faces. He altered whole passages that had once been spoken in hushed tones at the birth of the world, he crossed out entire lines that countries had been burned for simply knowing, and generally, he made a mess of such full-spectrum magnitude as had never before been seen neath a finger of ink – toddlers with crayons let loose in expensive homes could only aspire to a dull facsimile of such planet-rending greatness.

As his god-altering vandalism continued, the dead hum could be heard flitting above and below the range of human hearing before it disappeared completely. And as it did so, the coloured light that emanated from inside the scroll itself changed, tasting the entire rainbow and beyond – to the real fun stuff that humans can only witness with chemical assistance. The power that lived within this ancient paper was transmitting on a different frequency now. The symbols that translated its influence to the reader had been made so gruesomely non-magical that if anything out there could ever feel the call of this artifact again, it would have to be a pretty ridiculous creature indeed.

"Geez, I really hope this is actually working like I think it is," said Max, in the eerie silence of the cave.

As a final act of defiance he signed his name to the bottom right corner of the scroll, even going so far as to turn the lowercase 'A' into a heart – and when he moved his hands the scroll trembled into a loose curl against its clipped side, like a dead spider that really wanted to be left alone. The Earth was moving again, and not in a way that boded well for people currently standing inside of it. Max grabbed his bag and ran, but turned around before he got too far, remembering something else, and went back quickly. With clumps of soil still landing around him, Max reached to the chest pocket of his jacket and removed the childishly happy pink flower that rested there. He slid it behind the left ear of the two bears that lay dead in the cave, and brushed some fur over to hold it.

Then Max Martin, proud soldier of the Aversion Bureau, technically qualifying secret agent, cop-dater and god-confuser – shipped ass out of that swallowing cave like a professional ass freighter, diving out of its closing mouth and into the hot afternoon rays of a yellow sun.

# 14

## SUNS AND DAUGHTERS

Max picked himself up off of the ground, untangling his hands from some of the now-crunchy seaweed grass and brushing his ridiculous towering hairdo out of his eyes; life was coming out of the spin cycle and into the dryer, and as long as somebody had remembered to empty the lint trap, they might yet make it home without bursting into flames.

*KRAKOOM*

It was the sound of planetary billiard balls clacking together as the Great Claw's longer half sundered under its own weight and came crumbling to the Earth. Max watched it fall against the beaming yellow sun, knowing definitively that he had done it – whatever it was he had done. This time, however, no magic at all was in place to prevent the sky falling on the hill and stream – so Max began to run, awkwardly and holding his ribs, adrenaline masking most of his discomfort. The immense carapace tumbled towards him, striking the plateau of the hill as he left it – flattening the cave and burying the king of bears neatly in a tomb made of, by, and for royalty. If the scroll yet lived, in whatever form it now took, it would be pretty hard to get to, he liked to think.

Thanks in no small way to nearly two full days of torrential rainfall now obviously, in hindsight, meant to swell the rivers and incubate the lesser nightmares – the hill was still fairly thoroughly soaked, so Max slid where he could, and sometimes where he didn't meant to, as huge boulders of red god crashed along beside him. He dodged corpses left and right – huge crabs, mutated fish and octopi, impossible lobster knights from beyond comprehension's veil, and the occasional deserving deer. A piece of the mountain that was at least the size of two Dick Davisons or one and a half Leslies tumbled past Max end over end with gravity's special kind of help – it was turning grey as it rolled, losing its sheen and colour. The claw-chunk boulder soon collided with the remains of what, at fleeting glance, could have been a one-day thriving bear community center, and powdered amongst the logs, sending tiny grey meteors in all directions.

Agent Martin reached the bottom of the hill honestly shocked at his own continued existence, and dove down in front of the river's shore, covering his head as a stampede of small and medium rocks passed him to settle in the water. He was safe, and this is usually where the credits might roll – but unfortunately, despite everything described and witnessed, this was Real Life, and she was a cruel mistress never content to let things lie.

"*Max!* Holy crap bro, you're alive! You did it man, the big-ass claw is falling apart!" Dick Davison's voice could be heard.

No other voice was more immediately knowable, thanks to its uniquely frequent use of the non-word 'bro'. Max uncovered his head and looked as his friend Dick stood tall and proud as always, his feet on the edge of the stream. He held a gaping wound in his chest closed, poorly, and was bleeding quite a lot. Max was really just pleased to see he was still alive.

"Dick you don't look as excited as you sound," hazarded Max, hoping the dejected look on his face wasn't in reference to anything even as huge as his chin.

Dick just nodded his head backwards, unsmiling, towards the West bend of the river where the lobster god's titanic tail had attempted to slow the flow of the water, and eventually been broken – it was mountain rock now, just like the rest of the once-mighty crustacean godking. Davison helped Max to his feet with a bloody hand and the pair ran upstream, past the tail, to see what had happened. In the once again clean-looking light and clear blue skies of a normal afternoon, Max could see bears returning from the cover of trees to their wounded on the hill. He saw a brief glimpse of two beavers and an owl helping out as well, much kinder a sight than what the big agent showed him next.

Still abnormally high here, the waters of the river were lapping against the battered frame of Bilge's biplane Lady Mayhem, which had crash-landed short of the bank. A frantic-looking Agent Stone was pulling the director over the shore's green grass, trailing some red stuff. Kayle had torn her shirt to shreds for bandages and was wearing her jacket only, her bag of supplies long lost to combat. Max walked up.

"Hold on, Thomas. . . you old goat" Stone said to him, removing his flight cap and wiping his brow.

"*Shh. . . shh. . .* Natalie my girl, how *dare* you call me Thomas," the old man smiled from under his mountainous white mustache, "you worry. . . too bloody much—

Bilge coughed through a laugh.

"What happened?" asked Max.

"Lobsters hit the engine and a piece of shrapnel got 'im in the chest looks like. He landed it but if they didn't peel off right then. . . who knows," Kayle described.

Stone was still whispering to him and shaking him.

"Bro, we've got another problem," Davison pointed to the sky, South, towards the rest of the forest – and eventually, the Bureau.

Three final bus-sized sea horrors lurched through the air on their demon wings, fleeing the mountain, heading straight for everything else. They were a green one, a white one and a brown one. Max's heart began drumming again.

"What? Why didn't they just *poof* when the mountain fell?" he was legitimately confused.

"Maximillian," began the delirious director in the deep blue sweater with the orange fox and walrus locked in a swirl of yin and yang, "nothing ever just. . . goes away," he spluttered again, like a failing engine.

Just as the bears retained their variably increased mental capacity even when the magic left them, the monstrous lobster minions were still what they were, and they still needed to be stopped.

"Use the Vickers. . ." suggested Bilge, pointing

weakly to Lady Mayhem who faced East, just above the water.

He was referring to the machine gun mounted to the hood of the plane, and Max looked at it unsurely. Davison dove into the stream and set to work removing the weapon immediately.

"I know how to handle a lady," he boasted.

Max didn't feel confident about this. Shooting was not his specialty and there wasn't a wide margin for error here – he really didn't want to push his luck. Max looked toward Agent Fisher, who was helping tend to Bilge. She noticed him staring.

"Don't look at me, kiddo," she warned.

"But you were in the army!" Max protested.

"Not for long. That job doesn't last a real long time when you don't know how to handle guns," she explained, "it's just a principle thing, and I can't figure 'em out."

He looked at Agent Stone, she was the best with guns, everyone knew that, but she wasn't jumping.

"Max would you just get on the damn machine gun?!" she snapped at him, looking up when he came over to her.

Her eyes were thinly outlined in red. Max had never seen that.

"Come on, bro, *somebody's* gotta fire this thing!" barked Dick Davison from the other side of the river.

Max jumped into the water and swam across as fast as he could – which was medium. When he climbed out, Dick offered him the trigger and turned his back to the sky, resting the long, wide barrel of the Vickers machine gun over his left shoulder – then going to one knee, and grasping the two mangled and unusable legs of the bipod with all of his might against his thick chest.

"Why are you *holding* the gun? Max asked him with an air of psychiatric evaluation.

"Because the plane is in the river dipshit!"

Max couldn't argue with that, and was quite impressed with his friend for finally delivering a succinct one-liner.

"Alright, *do it!*"

The Dick-steadied, Davison-elevated firing arc was perfect, but the three targets were slowly becoming smaller and smaller, so Max took the two handles of this big, tube-like weapon and squinted one eye down the—

"Wait!"

Agent Davison reached one final time into his trusty, incredibly still undamaged fanny pack and removed two travel-pack tissues, stuffing them into his ears and putting Bilge's soggy pilot earmuffs over them. He nodded. Max really couldn't deny that kind of utility, and decided then and there to invent a time machine so he could go back to the nineties and buy one too. Now, Agent Martin was a veteran gamer, but the games he mostly preferred put you behind the optics of something invented in the current century or beyond – whatever was up with *these* sights, this stupid box-suspended-within-a-box thing, he didn't much care for it. Max adjusted the interior box over the distant, flapping behemoths, hoped it was the right thing to do, and pulled the trigger – a bit too hard.

*BRAPAPAPAPAPAPAP* went the sound of a

thousand sheets of folded air being ripped all at once. The handles of the big gun pounded backwards with unexpected force and *slammed* Agent Martin's own wrists into his chest, sending fresh spikes of pain through his compromised ribs. He stumbled back and hit the ground hard, entirely and utterly winded. His exhalations were the end of can of compressed air. He was trying not to breathe so hard as to hurt himself, which proved impossible. Davison looked over his right shoulder, dumbly excited.

"YOU KIND OF CLIPPED ONE," he yelled deafly.

Max gave the human bipod a shaky thumbs-up.

"Guys they gotta be a kilometre out by now, you're losing your window!" Kayle watched the sky with hand-shaded eyes.

"Kid I can take care of him just fine, get over there and do what you do," Max heard her say.

"LADYBRO WE NEED YOUR EYES," spoke Dick Davison, in his outside voice.

"Go!" insisted Agent Fisher.

Max wheezed in agreement, sitting up slowly. He could only take tiny breaths against the pain now worsened by a machine gun having boxed both his nipples inside-out simultaneously six times in under two seconds. He leaned on his wrists, filling his lungs with a thimble.

There was a splash, and she was already there, crouching low in front of her gargantuan partner and above the other one on the ground. Stone adjusted her sleeves and closed one eye, finessing the two dumb boxes that claimed to gauge distance.

"Davison you have to hold this steadier," she told him weakly.

"WHAT?" responded the manpod.

Suddenly, Max had another stroke – at this point, however, he couldn't be sure it was merely genius that clogged up his brain.

"Dickson Peterwilly Davison," addressed Max in a small voice that didn't need to be loud.

"WHAT." Dick cocked his head, but Max was fairly sure he heard, as this was not a question.

Max said it again, pronouncing each ludicrously unfortunate syllable of Agent Davison's full name in an obvious way, staring him in the eye.

"Dickson."

"*Peterwilly.*"

"Davison."

Comprehension reared behind the large man's eyes with all the heat-bearing light of a Mercurial dawn. He squeezed the machine gun's stick legs inches into his flesh, flexing so hard his short neck bulged with roots, and his wounds began to bleed further.

"Perfect," whispered the Valkyrie.

In the very precise, no-nonsense way that a Morse code communicates your imminent beheading to waiting friendlies, Natalie Stone tapped out a message to the deep corners of the cosmos whose specific job it was to give form to blackness and loose it upon the various domains that life endured within. The message went as follows, written across the blue sky with lilting trails of warped air:

*Yours is the eclipse of old, finding power in the*

*vacuum of understanding. The sands that fall around you now do not all wonder who you are, and are not maddened by the feel of you. Come now, break upon the minds that know their shape apart from whispers, our fields will grow lush on the pulp of your hearts. We shall shred your terrible wings, and bring you low to where you must raise your many dark eyes to meet us. Test our unknowing, and be so ended.*

As the storm of chitin and flesh gave its final patters to the ground, the end finally came.

"NICE SHOOTING," whispered Dickson Peterwilly Davison.

Now they had to get Bilge home, and they had to do so *immediately*. A coordinated effort of frantic corpse-defiling found the keys to a miraculously undamaged four-door highly suspended pickup truck that the infamous octobro had used to come and meet his foul maker. It was parked South of the river, and its sturdy-looking grill had been bashed to ripples by sapling trees and other things that had tried to interfere with the dead man's desperate self-offering. Max had left the beasts of the hill alone to their healing work, confident in the knowledge that their crudely elevated minds would eventually lead to a golden age of bear society in this particular forest, or perhaps just become a thriving tourist trap – in the entirely literal meaning of the phrase.

Davison drove the truck, wrapped safely in bandaging from the bag Max returned to them, the little agent himself rode shotgun and somehow, all stuffed in the back, Agents Fisher and Stone provided emergency medical attention to the fading director whose bushy white mustache was stained with the blood of gods – he was kept as still as possible on a pile of dirty tents and sleeping bags across the backseat. They headed East, retracing the original tire tracks by the river for half an hour and finding, through a flattened thicket of foliage, the muddy climb to a secret off-road, probably used exclusively by park rangers and highly-murderable teenaged campers. Agent Davison took them carefully across the path and back to the highway when they found it, then illegally fast down the road to the Bureau. The entire trip took only four hours, during which time each and every agent remained politely silent about the fact that they could have probably just driven to the mountain two days ago, saving all of them a monumental amount of hassle and pain. But as a recovering Director Thomas Bilge would later remark:

"If the eagles had simply flown the ring to Mordor, you wouldn't have watched three movies."

The lobby of RGI Insurance was dead on a Saturday. Not a soul in sight save for Max, Kayle, Dick – and a rather garish octopus statue replacing the old lobby fish tank – otherwise, no one else was around. Stone had dialed ahead in the truck so that a silent Wade, fretting Guinevere and sturdy gurney had greeted them at the door to the building – the door that Davison almost drove directly through in his hurry. Agent Andersen took it from there, with only Bilge's niece and highest-ranking agent accompanying him. Wade was a master surgeon, in that he essentially was a master of anything that involved miniscule movements and utter silence.

Max could breathe easily again, and not just for lack of nearby monsters. Although he had been *sure* his ribs were broken, and thought he had felt them shifting, they were suddenly no longer bothering him. Even by the time they reached the Bureau, he hadn't even thought of bothering Wade for an X-ray. The pain was faint, and the bones felt totally solid, so perhaps they were never broken, only brutally bruised. Just something else imagined, he figured.

The three remaining agents sprawled on waiting-room couches each designed to fit three or more lesser humans. They spoke to pass the time and dull the worry that stung at their bellies.

"I think I'm gonna stick around. . . I've been thinking about it, and I kind of miss having an important job," mused Kayle, to the room.

"I guess you can only party so much," she added, chewing her nails in lieu of smoking, which was not allowed indoors.

"I do not understand that sentence," Dick said to the ceiling.

"The adventure's what I miss most, man, I missed the feeling of saving the world," she said.

"Eh, it gets old sometimes," admitted Max, ". . . I like the people you get to meet, though," he thought of flowers for a moment.

"Guess I'm going to be looking for an apartment pretty soon," Kayle continued.

"Bro, I've got a bit of extra room at my—

"You know, or maybe like a shared home thing."

Dick silently experienced embarrassment, changing the topic immediately:

"Well I know that when *I* get out of here, bros," Davison was speaking in an unsettlingly lascivious tone, "I can't *wait* for the first moment I get to lay my hands on—

"DON'T TOUCH MY MOM," blurted out Max, covering his mouth too late to save himself.

". . . My *car*," finished Dick, making a ten-and-two in the air with his hands.

Fisher was on the floor laughing, trying not to wet it. Even *she* had been emailed a copy of the Dream Journal's first publication, and had read it on the way back with her phone.

Max Martin momentarily revealed his true form as shame incarnate.

"No, no Max, I wasn't laughing at you," she lied, "it was uh. . . this email I got from Levi that is *super* funny."

Agent Fisher rolled to the adjoined benches the guys were stationed on, she sat up against the seats and shared her phone screen with them. On it, there was an unread email she tapped to open.

The message simply contained a picture of the treehome standing proud on its four stick legs over the horizontally piled form of its namesake downstairs neighbour, 'tree'. This tree, like so many others on the eve of the rising tide, had deepened its hue to that of a dark green-black and begun to paw at the ground with its boughs of heavy, mutated kelp leaves. The brilliance of the treehome's designed disassociation with trees in general had finally won its medal in the field. A smug-looking craftsman covered sixty percent of the picture with his face, in true selfie fashion.

"Clever bastard," remarked Agent Davison.

*Bleep*, blooped the phone. Another email, another picture.

*This* picture was extremely similar to the last, except that this time, piled on top of the rotting tree, there was also a splintered and familiar looking tree*home*. And on top of those two sad shapes was the bullet-riddled corpse of a brown-shelled eldritch monstrosity as large as coincidence. Most of the scene was still blocked, this time by a sad, pouty-lipped man in a wilting hat. The subject line merely a colon and left bracket brought together in sorrowful union.

"Oh. Well I guess he'll be moving back to the city too. Heh, and he *ain't* staying with me," said Kayle, shaking her head, "Dick, you mentioned some extra room at your place, eh?"

He just looked at her and nodded excruciatingly slowly.

"Yup," he said.

Max attempted to reassemble the crushed remains of his big buddy with a friendly shoulder punch. Guinevere Quilway appeared in the lobby.

"You can see him now," she said quietly.

They got up together.

Max saw her standing by the doorway to the infirmary with her arms folded behind her back as usual, illuminated by the faint blue glow of the machines that beeped along with Bilge. Still as stone, she was.

"Shrapnel. Punctured lung," explained Doctor Wade Andersen, who *was* an actual medical doctor when he needed to be.

"How bad?" asked Max.

"Survivable," Wade told him.

"No more front line," he added.

"Long recovery," he finished.

Max peeked into the room. Bilge was there, pale-white as always under the baby blue covers, breathing through a tube and receiving blood from a machine. He hoped he'd never have to see the poor old man's life held in robot arms ever again. Bilge was *way* too old for this kind of bounce-back, but he was, at the same time, inhumanly accomplished – so Max didn't worry too much more, unlike the woman who watched him.

"At least Wade sent him in with exactly the right swinging arms," remarked Gwen, "it sounds like he made a big difference."

"Always does," said Dick, smilingly sadly.

"Specifically designed," Wade told them.

"*Pfft*, alright. How is that possible? We didn't know what was going to be there when he arrived!" Gwen had already found her niche at the Bureau in combating Wade's arrogance, as it so often went unchallenged.

"I did."

"Uh. . . what? WHAT? *How* did you know?" Guinevere marched on him and grabbed the black vest he wore over his long sleeved grey-green shirt with both hands, pulling on it.

"Deduction," answered Wade uselessly.

"Why didn't you tell anybody?!" Gwen was furious.

"Would not alter the approach, would only instill worry. Bilge was armed appropriately. That was enough."

Guinevere's response was not comprised of a single English word, just a frothing peal of madness came forth as she shook him, or at least tried to. He was quite a large man.

"How did you figure it out before anyone else?" asked Max, not entirely shocked by his behaviour, and totally without the energy to feel feelings any more.

"Cuttlefish."

"What?"

"Cuttlefish from lab. Mutated and escaped three nights past. Was not sure if I was cause, or another force," said Wade, impossibly calmly.

Gwen had buried her head into his chest and stomach now, screaming with the muffled rage that only pillows could ever understand.

"Overheard phone report with Agent Stone confirmed suspicions. Knew then."

"What's a cuttlefish look like? I don't think I killed one of those," Kayle interjected, rubbing her chin instead of biting her nails.

"Masters of disguise. Though mostly like an octopus," Wade explained.

"Probably a little like that statue in the lobby," suggested Agent Davison.

"Statue," said Wade, a question with no supporting inflection.

The platinum-blonde goliath stared internally for a

moment, then produced a comically-oversized syringe from his chest pocket, filled with purple liquid, and made for the elevator leaving young Guinevere to pull her hair out on the floor.

"Excuse me."

Machines beeped and doors closed. Time tripped ever forward.

"I'm glad you're all back safe," managed Gwen, eventually, with a reluctant tone.

She stood up and reassembled her various bracelets and rings into their usual cluster points, the bright golds and silvers standing out on her smooth, dark skin. Gwen walked over to an unresponsive Agent Stone and took her by the arm, leaning into her shoulder with a bushel of curls.

"And I'm especially glad *you're* safe, Stone, 'cause I could not-bloody-likely handle almost losing my uncle *and* my cousin."

Everyone froze. Guinevere froze the hardest, and Agent Stone, who was already frozen, froze a little more. It was the subtle feel of already-formed ice becoming slightly harder.

"That was a mistake!" corrected Gwen immediately, turning to face the others, finger in the air – she was shaking noticeably.

Guinevere's practiced look of righteous indignation in the face of lies being cast about was crumbling fast. A few moments dragged.

"It wasn't," admitted Stone with exhaustion on her breath.

"Wait," went Max.

"Whoa," went Dick.

Kayle just watched, wide-eyed.

"Oops. . ." went Gwen, her voice wavering.

"B-Bilge is my uncle. . . *and I*. . . I call Stone my cousin because. . . *she*," the little girl's huge dark eyes were welling up, magnified by her owl's glasses, "I'm *so* sorry, Nat."

Agent Stone stayed her cousin's shaking with a gentle hand, and sighed deeply as something invisible slid from her shoulders.

"She calls me that, because Director Bilge. . . is my father."

The sound of the 'F' in 'father' came out of her round mouth like a square block, and while she spoke of it, something cold swam behind her eyes. She tensed, ever so slightly. This was an old secret; it was never, ever meant for them.

"Eight years, bro. Eight damn years and I never knew that," Davison remarked, shaking his giant chin, and by close association, his head.

"Natalie, what—

Stone held up her hand at Max, not in the commanding way she normally did, with much more of a 'please' this time.

"You have each done this institution proud today, and countless lives, human or otherwise, have you to thank for their continued existence," she adjusted the too-long sleeves of her old black coat again, "please enjoy your respective weekends."

Agent Natalie Stone, highest-ranking agent of the Aversion Bureau, decorated athlete, swordswoman and tactical commander – made her way quietly down the hall, and disappeared.

"S-See you guys, M-Monday," Gwen managed, and hugged them each very briefly, sniffling all the while.

She too disappeared, down the hall after her cousin. Max, Kayle and Davison all looked to each other totally unsure how to feel about what they had learned, so they just stood, and reflected on it.

"See you Monday, bros" Dick eventually smiled and pointed to them, then headed over to the elevator.

"It was nice to meet you, man," said Kayle, shaking Max's hand hard and heading over to catch a ride.

Soon Max was the only one left, and before leaving he said goodbye to the walrus that lay resting. An old man with more stories than time, and more secrets than both of those. A good man – a man who would fly straight into the sun if it meant protecting you.

Max Martin drove home in the evening orange enjoying silence, for a change. He was too busy slowly, mentally sifting through the last forty-eight hours to get distracted by music now, and any song that had a tone in it that came even *remotely* close to humming was getting a call in to the radio station about.

Perhaps more surprising than even the appearance, and subsequent slaying, of an ancient god, had been the sudden revelation of his long-time partner's under-their-noses parentage. It was a secret that had been kept from everyone, for an impossible amount of time. He had seen them act closely, and he had seemed them fight – literally he had seen them fight nearly to the death with swords once before – yet he had never gathered the intention that they might have been father and daughter. They looked nothing alike, even as a small, fit, sun blonde twenty-something woman *usually* looks dissimilar to a tall, fat and mustachioed ex-special forces operative in his comfortable eighties.

Max wondered why they had kept this information so desperately secretive for so very long, having it only now come to light when a close relative slipped up – could it really have been *purely* for professional reasons? That seemed like a Stone thing to do, but perhaps it was something more. He still didn't quite understand it, and he had a lot of questions. Questions were for later, however, because it was finally time for some well-earned rest.

He pulled up to the parking stall, got out, then checked his empty weekend mail pointlessly, reflexively, and opened his apartment building's front door. Everything about the building was the same as he'd left it, a bold and exploratory cacophony of cooking smells assaulted his senses on every floor, all backed by the faint, ever-present stench of cigarettes left over from the sixties. Max went to unlock the door of apartment four-hundred and four, and found it *already* unlocked. He was almost seventy-one percent sure that he had indeed remembered to lock it before the big mission. It made him a little nervous. Inside there was a draft, and the window in the living room was wide-open – this smell of fresh air? That had definitely not been him. Agent Martin kept his shoes on, and his coat, drawing his spent handgun and leading it ahead of him on his way to the empty bedroom that used to contain his roommate Jackie. Max heard nightmare sounds – he heard the scraping of metal, the clicking of bolts and screws. . . the creak of. . . *hinges*.

"Don't shoot!" yelped Agent Whiskers, the orange tomcat who possessed the incredible and yet unquestioned capacity for speech.

Max was standing in the doorway of the totally empty room now, whist the small animal worried at a bag of washers, sitting directly on top of some folded paper instructions under the shadow of a half-assembled alien structure of hoops, barrels and plateaus with zero semblance of any architectural know-how involved in its inception whatsoever. Such a structure as would be dropped from the cliffs of Sparta at birth, in human form. A cat tree, Max deduced.

"Jesus Christ, kid," Whiskers let his breath out and put his paws down, removing the bag of parts from his mouth.

"Sorry," said Max, "you would not believe my day."

"Bureau stuff, say no more, say no more," spoke the oddly accented cat with the light beige spots around his left eye and right cheek.

Whiskers stood up and stretched in a contorting arc, licked his front paw once, and sauntered over to Max's legs to brush against them in greeting, wholly unable to control certain impulses.

"So you're all moved in, then?" Max motioned to a rack of fine liquors and a feeding bowl that had 'Me' on it, the only other objects currently in the room.

"More or less," answered the cat.

"Can I ask you something?" Max wondered.

"Shoot."

"Did you notice if the sun was *green* today? Like, did it look green to you at all?"

The animal agent turned its head at him, in a questioning way.

"No. . . but I ain't got the best ability to distinguish colours, you might remember. Did it look green to you? Where were you?"

"Somewhere else."

In the awkward silence that followed: Max holstered his gun and removed his holster, hoping not to need it for a while. He moved to the nearby door with the often tragically misinterpreted 'NO GIRLS ALLOWED' sign, and turned the handle below it, changing the subject as well.

"Hey, did you know that Stone is Bilge's daughter? We all just found out today, and that's like, a huge deal right?"

"You don't say," remarked Whiskers, in the smug tone of someone who already knows something.

It was his business to know somethings. He was, after all, their master spy. Well, he was a spy anyway.

"You're kidding?" Max had detected his sly sarcasm, "Who *else* knows?"

"Less than you'd think, kid," he stretched again, accompanying Max to his room, "it ain't exactly news."

"You don't think so? I think it's a pretty big deal. And there was something weird about her when she told us. . . you should have seen it," said Max.

"Maybe I will," offered the cat.

The man sat down on his bed and Whiskers leapt up to join him, beginning the ritualistic circular walk prerequisite to all animal rest.

"Whenever Bilge would get drunk, now and then, and tell us stories, he would often tell this one about how he founded the Bureau. But Stone would *always* cut him off before he ever told the parts where he was actually over here, and actually *in* the building."

"Certainly odd," agreed Whiskers.

"Maybe his wife, and I guess. . . Stone's mom, was just a real piece of work," ventured Max, "I've never heard a word about her, and Bilge doesn't wear a ring."

"Look who's the detective now!" mocked the orange tom with the beige strips across his back and chest, now tightly curled on the messy covers, leaving his short bright hair everywhere.

"You don't wash these much, do you?" he grimaced.

"Don't pretend like you care," said Max.

The cat shrugged. A cat shrug is imperceptible amongst their behaviour as always presented. Cats are constantly in a state of shrugging.

"One day," Max started, staring at the ceiling of his calamitously messy room, "you and me are gonna get Bilge drunk, and we're going to finally hear the full story. No more secrets."

He brushed hair out of his eyes, and rubbed them.

"Secrets are just. . . bad for teamwork," Max justified his suggestion to a character who needed no such sugar coating.

"Careful now. Secrets are the dirtiest money there

is, and the exchange rate can really kill ya," warned the spy.

Max got defensive:

"I just need to understand those two better. It would honestly help me. Help me do my job," he rationalized to himself, "I want to respect their privacy but there's obviously just something *deeper* there, and I don't want it to come back to bite either of them in the ass simply because they won't address it. You know how they are."

The cat watched his friend from a comfortable position, blue-eyed over his long orange tail dipped in yellow cream.

"Alright man, I'll help you, but you're going to help me at the same time. You remember that time when I got Bilge *really* drunk and took that money? Well I mean, did something that implied I might have. . . borrowed some."

There was a sound that might have been a cat's cough, if such a thing existed.

"Yes, it was like two months ago. You remember when I found out it was you and promised not to tell anybody so you would move in and help me out on the rent? How I kept huge secrets from the Bureau all this time just because we're friends? They've noticed you haven't been around, you know."

"Somethin' like that. And yeah I do."

"Well, what is it then?" asked Max, laying horizontally on his bed sheets and giving no damns to the almost guaranteed transference of mud and rain his clothes were caked in.

"It's big, too big to go to the Bureau about," Whiskers looked around the room, "there's eyes in that building, man. I can't risk it."

Ominous thunder announced the arrival of a text message on somebody's cell phone through the thin wall of the apartments. The cat's ears perked, then settled.

"But yeah you're innocuous enough a human to find out and not blow it for me, I figure."

Max was intrigued, and flattered due to his inability to remember what "innocuous" meant.

"I promise it's not some evil crap, it just ain't safe to let Bilge or the others know. You and I are going to pull the end off of a long, *long* con I've been working on. It's gonna be a big deal. You in?"

"Hey, what did I just say about keeping secrets from the team? I'm pretty sure I'm against that."

"What, you can keep my secrets, but the Bilges can't keep their own? Or the Bilges and Stones, or whatever."

"Touché." Max rescinded his opposition.

"Anyway this is my one, so you're just an accessory. Accessories always get at least a modest amount of credit for the plan if it all goes right.

"Deal," dealt Max.

"I'll explain over dinner, which we should totally order in to celebrate our renewed partnership. How do you feel about. . . *fish?*"

Max Martin nearly vomited right there. Agent Whiskers hopped down from the bed in a huff, and slinked off presenting the underside of his tail to show his mood. Max shook away images of seafood, and butts, grabbing his cellphone. He found Rose, and dialed, she picked up after only two rings.

"Hey, it's Max. . . yeah, I know I sound tired, look. . . no I haven't been back to Da Club. But hey, I have to talk to you for a little while, and you're going to be hearing a lot of euphemisms. . . what? No, not like sex stuff. . . no just stuff I can't really talk about. Trust me, it's important. I just need you to listen if you have time. . . you do? Great! Thank you. . . "

The fat golden sun sank low in a purple sky, throwing fire into a small apartment of no particular importance. The whiskered one buried his head into a bag of goldfish crackers, chewing noisily in the very center of the living room in protest of his new roommate's needless pickiness. The one with the absurd black hairdo, loosened red tie and haggard expression whiled away the night talking to a friend who listened intently, taking notes. Somewhere else, a tall woman danced and sang under colourful lights, and a tall man fell asleep on his couch catching up with prerecorded daytime television. Young people stared at their computer screens through teacup spectacles, and older ones simply through quiet, tired eyes. A woman finally undid her ponytail and fell asleep in a white chair, watching an old man breathe under ghostly blue light and metronomic beeping. Time passed, and things changed, though you wouldn't have known that for watching.

In a man-made mountain far away from the sleeping city, an anything-but simple mouse was being put to trial for crimes of war. He watched as his crimson banners were struck around him, burying the once grand empire that had churned within these walls – burying it in the graveyard of a nearby trash bin. In his final moments a voice came upon him, to him, and also to the blue-cloaked assembly that would see him hung from the kitchen tap like a mere commoner. It was slithering into the back of their minds, turning handles and asking for room to be spared. The blue mice looked amongst each other, and to the sapphire paw that was their standard as it waved, looking mighty in the wind of the air conditioning vent above them. They had no time for gods. The red mouse went diving on a stiff rope.

Come Monday morning, the janitor would find him.

# ABOUT THE AUTHOR

S.R. Ringuette is a British/French-Canadian crossbreed that successfully reached maturity in the harsh (although friendly) climate of Western Canada. His mission has always been to create as much entertaining content as possible, across as many different mediums, and has been publishing his cartooning work online since 2007. He is the creator of multiple online webcomics: Exploding Wumpus, The Aversion Bureau and Gamer Roommates. In the ephemeral free time he has between meeting cartooning deadlines and preparing for conventions, he has begun to write novels as well. He believes free time is a luxury afforded only to the sane.

www.ingramcontent.com/pod-product-compliance
Lightning Source LLC
Chambersburg PA
CBHW030547180626
46816CB00005B/1443